SHE'S
A
LAMB!

MEREDITH HAMBROCK

SHE'S A LAMB!

A NOVEL

Published by ECW Press
665 Gerrard Street East
Toronto, Ontario, Canada M4M 1Y2
416-694-3348 / info@ecwpress.com

Editor for the Press: Pia Singhal
Copy-editor: A.G.A. Wilmot
Cover design: Lisa Pompillo
Cover artwork: © CSA Images

This is a work of fiction. Names, characters,
places, and incidents either are the product of the
author's imagination or are used fictitiously, and
any resemblance to actual persons, living or dead,
business establishments, events, or locales is entirely
coincidental.

LIBRARY AND ARCHIVES CANADA CATALOGUING
IN PUBLICATION

Title: She's a lamb! : a novel / Meredith Hambrock.

Names: Hambrock, Meredith, author.

Identifiers: Canadiana (print) 20240496760 |
Canadiana (ebook) 20240496779

ISBN 978-1-77041-789-2 (softcover)
ISBN 978-1-77852-375-5 (ePub)
ISBN 978-1-77852-376-2 (PDF)

Subjects: LCGFT: Novels.

Classification: LCC PS8615.A412 S54 2025 | DDC
C813/.6—dc23

This book is funded in part by the Government of Canada. *Ce livre est financé en partie par le gouvernement du Canada.* We
acknowledge the support of the Canada Council for the Arts. *Nous remercions le Conseil des arts du Canada de son soutien.*
We would like to acknowledge the funding support of the Ontario Arts Council (OAC) and the Government of Ontario
for their support. We also acknowledge the support of the Government of Ontario through the Ontario Book
Publishing Tax Credit, and through Ontario Creates.

PRINTED AND BOUND IN CANADA

PRINTING: MARQUIS   5 4 3 2 1

*"You do have a choice though. You can see it for what it is,
or you can imagine what it could be."*
— DEREK DELGAUDIO, *IN & OF ITSELF*

*"One must know how to bear one's cross,
and one must have faith."*
— ANTON CHEKHOV, *THE SEAGULL*

I

For a while I've had this very incredible and powerful fantasy that goes like this: my career blossoming, of course; my skin, glowing; my dress, gorgeous — something timeless, sleek, mature, forward-thinking, couture maybe — me, sitting in the crowd at the Tony Awards, waiting for them to announce Best Performance by a Leading Actress, Musical. I smile, close lipped, a serene expression slapped on my face to disguise the anxiety within.

Drumroll. A sharp inhale. A bead of sweat trickles down my spine. And then of course, they call my name. I throw my head back in delight, smile at my father, who I brought as my date — you know, for the photo op, for the tabloids to call "so sweet" — and walk toward the stage, hand pressed to my chest in apparent shock.

They hand me the statue. Everyone is looking at me. Everyone. I put the small dime-shaped thing on the ground and stare out at the audience, at the other actresses from my category literally salivating at the prospect of me freezing or fainting or both.

Instead, I make a joke. Then, with the class of someone twice my age, I reject the award, making a timely political statement that resonates with the hearts and minds of the crowd. We're doing important work here, but out there? Out in the world? Real life is happening. And I am so aware of it. My ego? Dead. My career? On fire.

Everyone leaps to their feet, applauding my bravery. The metaphorical phone is already ringing. I stride off the stage and into a flood of media attention — people shouting, thousands of cameras flashing. Someone captures video of my speech, puts it online. I get hundreds of thousands of followers. My manager sets up talk show interview after talk show interview. I'm immortalized forever, beloved by everyone —

"Jessamyn?"

I jump. It's my manager. Marge. Yanking me out of my manifestation and back to the 650-seat theater I'm supposed to be working in. It's a half hour before curtain, and I'm meant to be showing people to their seats, which is what they're paying me for, but like, c'mon, these people come here all the time. Seriously. Do any of these rubes really *need* help? Or do they just *want* help? I'd much rather be using the power of positive thinking to transport myself away from the humiliation of customer service and into the version of my reality where I've already become a star.

"Go hand out some programs. And make sure the aisles are clear. There's a house left exit during act one."

I grab a stack and go. Marge really is a troll.

The nightly monologues she's been giving lately, about taking initiative and personal growth, are getting really annoying. Get real. Who takes a minimum wage job for personal growth? Like, how paternalistic is that? Besides, these lectures, which she forces us to sit through once all the patrons have gone home, interfere with my personal debrief. The show we have on right now is terrible. And if I'm going to be forced to watch such substandard performances each night, I should at least get to deconstruct the choices of each actor, to take into account what if anything has changed from the night before. To see if any of these so-called professionals suddenly gain artistic awareness and address any of the notes I silently make in my head.

Of course, they never do, and I'm not sure it's entirely their fault. The director seems like a gutless moron. Every single night, for the entire stretch of previews, he's been in the lobby, puking, his glasses in his hand. Just spewing. And not being quiet about it. He'll let one rip, scream as if the devil's attempting to escape his guts, then stand up immediately after, straighten his stupid button-down shirt, put his glasses back on, and walk back into the theater. Only a man would do this. Women know how to keep this kind of agony private. Men always make their feelings other people's problems.

And he's misread the text majorly, sending all of his actors into melodrama. Every night is a train wreck that I'm forced to watch over and over again for meager pay. God forbid I doze off and one of the aging patrons gets up to use the bathroom and without the guidance of my flashlight, breaks a hip.

"Did you read the review?" Two men I'm pretty sure are a couple stand near the door to the theater, drinking cocktails.

"Of course, I did, I've got it here. Listen to this: *'I felt as if I was stuck in some sort of purgatory where reciting poetry while bombs go off in Afghanistan is supposed to be a real human response, instead of screaming, oh fuck, oh no, those fucking Americans blew my leg off.'"*

"Incredible. I cannot wait."

"I love bad theater."

"Right?"

I look around. Marge is now up in the balcony, thank God, helping a man down the concrete steps to his seat. We're understaffed, as usual. And they're not hiring, which is strange. Marge glares at me. Better go do something. I take a lap.

As I walk around, this woman flags me over. "Excuse me! Excuse me! My seat is wet."

Usually, this kind of complaint is made up, a way to move from a cheap seat to an expensive one, but this woman isn't joking. When I arrive, I'm greeted by a gigantic blotch in the velour.

"Oh," I say, rummaging around in my brain for a lie. "Well, they're repairing the ceiling. Must just be a drip or something. Do you want a cushion?"

"One of those?" She gestures to the corner where we dropkick the velvet pillows we give to kids at Christmas time to sit on so they can see the stage. More than one dirty diaper has sprung a leak on those, and I'll tell you, they never get cleaned.

"One of those," I say.

"Fine." The woman sniffs.

I deliver her the cushion. "I'll have a program as well," she says. I hand her one, then hurry off because really, what's next? A massage?

The final seating call rings out through the doors, the lobby lights flicker, and people start to stream in from the bar. I arm myself with another stack of programs and do a lap, passing them out, kicking umbrellas and jackets out of the aisle, ignoring the scoffs and glares as I do. Well, if these unwashed hounds didn't want me to kick their belongings, then they shouldn't have flung them to the ground in a public space.

As the house doors close, I realize I'm standing in front of the crowd. I take a moment to look up at their faces. So many faces. It's stupid, because I'm at work — I'm the staff, not talent — but it's still a crowd of people, all of them sitting there in front of me. And, well, they should be looking at me, but they're not. They're not seeing me at all. I'm blending into the background of the set, the stage, the pre-show hum. But they will see me. One day.

A hands waggles at me from the sixth row. "Miss! Miss!"

It's an old man with an oxygen line snaking out of his jacket, the tank snugged under his seat, sitting on the aisle in one of the most expensive seats in the theater. Can mean only one thing — he's got one foot in the grave. A bored woman in her forties, likely his daughter, maybe his much younger wife, sits next to him, typing something on her phone with a speed and focus that tells me she has other places to be. Marge pokes her head in. We're but minutes away. I walk up to him and crouch.

"Would you like a program sir?" I ask. "We're just about to get started."

This man, though, there's something off about him. Or maybe it's his flesh-toned jacket. I don't trust flesh tones. Why are you trying to blend in? What are you hiding?

"You've got a hair —" he says, then gasps for air, and before I can stand up or jump away, he's pinching my boob, the left one, between his thumb and forefinger.

"What are —"

"There," he says, holding up the culprit. Blonde and long. "That was bothering me."

The woman next to him doesn't bother looking up from her phone, doesn't care to notice what's unfolding under her nose.

Marge is at my side, hand on my shoulder. I stand up, raging, shocked, my cheeks burning, my left tit aching where his fingers grabbed at me.

Some things, Marge won't tolerate. I know it. She says so all the time: *If anyone ever makes you uncomfortable, anyone at all, you tell me. You tell me right away.*

Instead, Marge hisses into my shoulder. "What the hell are you doing? I've closed the doors."

"I can't . . ." I trail off, my cheeks hot. The hair the man pulled off my sweater is on my pant leg now. He's faced determinedly forward, a small smile on his lips. Celebrating.

"Get up there," Marge says. "We're already late."

"Oh, miss?" He gasps for air again. I turn, expecting an apology, or at the very least an acknowledgment of me, here. Instead, "the program?"

I clutch the stack in my hand but I can't move, am frozen in place, my entire body throbbing with humiliation. Marge nudges me with her elbow and when I don't immediately melt into a smile, a laugh, a customer-friendly apology, she reaches around my body and plucks a program from the stack and hands it to him, gives me a harder nudge toward the house doors with her elbow.

So I go, hurry away up the aisle, biting the inside of my cheek to distract myself from the rage, which usually brings tears, which is even more frustrating because when you're enraged and sobbing, no one is afraid. No one really regrets their treatment of you. They simply feel bad because you've revealed weakness. Rolled over and showed your belly. Like a dog.

But I am not weak. I am not.

And don't get me wrong, as a performer, it's easy for me to cry on command. I do it all the time. When it serves me.

It's *not* crying that's difficult. Holding it back. Especially when you need to just let it out. But no. Not now.

I pause in the light lock, the liminal space between the theater and the lobby, to take a deep breath and try to calm down. Inside the theater, Marge is starting the performance. Telling people to turn off their cellphones, listing the sponsors.

When these moments of indescribable humiliation take place, usually at the hands of men (as a hot person, I get groped constantly), there is only one thing to do.

And so, I take a breath and picture that man. His sagging jowls and the central line of his gut pressing against his sweaty khaki shorts, making it look like a single, bulging testicle, the dying gasp of his inhale. And I imagine that instead of letting him pinch my breast, I caught his hand in the air and pulled out a razor. Not a straight razor, no, a pink razorblade, the kind I have in my purse, just in case I need a touch up before an audition. If I really wanted to, I could go grab it right now, hold his wrist down against the armrest and slice open an artery, watch him bleed out in seconds. I smile a little, picturing it, and feel so much better.

I suppose it's a privilege I just gave him. Yes, that's it. Not only is mine likely the best tit he's ever touched, but judging by what he shelled out for that seat, the gasping of his breath, the oxygen line I could've ground my heel into, it's probably the last tit he'll ever touch.

Lucky him.

In the lobby, Sudi is waiting for me. "Oh my God. Oh my God, Oswald is here. Oh my God, he's such a creep."

"Sure," I say. Oswald is a regular who likes to pick a girl usher to corner for the fifteen minutes he's in the building before showtime.

"One time, he asked me where I live. What the fuck?"

"Gross." I sit down on one of the benches in the lobby. "An old man just pinched my tit."

It's not a good idea to tell Sudi anything, because the only thing she loves more than this job is pretending she hates this job and all the middling abuse that comes with it. One time, an old man slapped her, right across the face. Turns out he had mild dementia, and his sons were just dropping him off before the show and picking him up after, thinking we would just deal with it.

"What?" Sudi says, losing her mind. "He pinched your boob? Oh my God, the patrons are disgusting. The Company does not give a shit about us. You have to tell Marge."

"I don't know." I think about the man and how casually he did it. "I have an audition here tomorrow — I don't want this going out in a house report with my name attached. Michelle's going to see it and then that'll be how she knows me."

"Oh my God, you have an audition? That's amazing. For what?"

"*The Sound of Music*," I say. "It's in the bag, I played Maria in high school." This is a lie, of course, but I put it on my resumé. No one ever checks that stuff anyway. Plus, the part should be mine. It has to be mine.

"That's crazy, congrats. Finally," Sudi says. "How long have you worked here? Like, three years?"

Sudi. She always likes to remind me. It's not like I haven't worked as an actor in the past three years. I work. Just the other day, I did a commercial for life insurance. A part is a part. But this would be a big step up. Not going to lie, things haven't been going well, necessarily. But it's, like, ninety percent luck anyway. That's what everyone says. Like, ninety percent luck. And musical theater is really my thing, you know? So when I say it's in the bag, I mean it. It's in the bag.

II

The holding room at the audition is packed. It doesn't matter what time they tell you to arrive, this room is always full. Could be a scheduling error, could be something the Company does to torture us — I don't know. I'm basically already aware of almost everyone here; it's wall to wall wannabes. Most of them are aging women I recognize from years past, from the chorus line in shows at the Franklin, whose careers are a cautionary tale; makeup caked over discount Botox, inventory from whatever small side businesses they own — a tea shop maybe, or handmade soaps — stuffed inside their bags. It's poisonous being around them — their sadness at never really making it seeps into the air. I cannot imagine being their age and still doing this. Open calls for Christmas musicals at regional theaters? At forty-five? Come on.

I'm pretty sure I saw one of them getting off a public bus.

And of course, as I try to distance myself from them, I spot her staring right at me, a wicked smile on her lips. The king bitch herself, Samantha Nguyen.

"Oh, hello you," she says, stepping over a woman in a leotard stretching out her groin on the floor, which makes no sense because there's no dance call today.

"Sam," I say. "Hey."

We make a little small talk. Five years ago, we both were part of a summer festival in the Okanagan. A musical rendition of some Shakespeare shit. Sam had the lead; I was briefly in the chorus before leaving due to circumstances beyond my control. Now we see each other occasionally at auditions, but it's been probably a year since we've spoken. Maybe two. Who can keep track?

"I saw you at the Franklin the other day," Samantha says. "Sorry I didn't say hi, the cast invited me backstage after the show. How's the coat check?"

I shrug and smile. It's humiliating, of course. But I say nothing, force her to stand in the silence for long enough that she'll get uncomfortable and fill it herself. And she does.

"So, you're still going out for this stuff?" she says, leaning next to me. It's a tactic. My rep, Adam, prepared me for this, said it was important to know that everyone in this industry is out for themselves. It makes sense. There are so few parts it's important to protect yourself from people who want the same things you do. Give what you get and don't look back. He's really smart, Adam, and I absolutely trust him. I mean, his judgment is impeccable. He signed me.

"Of course," I say, not giving her the satisfaction of having gotten to me. "I'm going out for Maria. But what are you doing here? Aren't all the roles in this show a little . . . blonde?"

She winces a little. It's a low blow, but, I mean, come on. She started it.

"They asked me to come in," Samantha says. "For Maria."

16

There's a smile I've been practicing for years in the mirror. The perfect smile for a situation like this — a smile that says, *I don't believe you*. A smile that says, *Nice try*. A smile that says, *Oh, sweetie. Oh. No.*

"Oh, they did? For an open call?" My delivery is excellent. So surprised. Her eyes narrow.

"Well, I was supposed to have an individual appointment this morning, but I had a callback at the opera, so they're slotting me in this afternoon."

"That's so great," I say. "Opera. Wow." It's difficult not to roll my eyes. Opera. Who even goes to the opera anymore? If you stopped any person on the street, could they even name an opera? Probably not. But everyone, literally everyone, unless they're some illiterate living under a rock without a soul, has heard of *The Sound of Music*.

"Yes, well, it's great to be working," she says. "Steadily. You know? It's such a relief for my parents."

"Sure. I mean, if you're willing to take any part . . ."

She ignores my slight, the tiniest wrinkle appearing on her forehead. "I'm surprised to see you here."

"Why?" I ask. "It's an open call."

"I just mean —"

"And I have a resumé, so I don't know why you'd say that."

"I thought you were going to focus on other things. After what happened at Shakespeare on the Lake."

Of course, she'd bring that up. What was to be my biggest step forward crushed by, well. Whatever. If you don't think about these things, if you don't let them in, they don't matter. Better to just flick them away, because in the grand scheme of things, they mean nothing. Just like Samantha.

"Sorry," she says, her voice quiet, gentle, as if she thinks I need it. As if she thinks I'm upset. I'm not upset. I am absolutely not upset. "I'm sorry, Jess. I still get nervous at these things. What song are you doing?"

"'Something Good,'" I say.

"Oh, me too," Samantha says. "Isn't it so beautiful?"

My cheeks burn. I can't believe it. "Gorgeous," I mutter. It is the best song, but I didn't think, in a million years, that any of these vapid assholes would choose it. It's so understated. A brave choice. Any jerk-off who just waltzed off stage at theater school could belt out "Climb Every Mountain," or skip around onstage to "The Lonely Goatherd" or, you know, the big money choice, "The Sound of Music" — the hills are alive, baby, and I'm bringing them to you right here.

But "Something Good" is the best song in the entire show — simple, loving, the Captain and Maria marveling at their own good luck having found one another. Undeniably powerful, so quiet, so much required, so much honesty.

"I thought you would've wanted a belter," I say to her. She smiles knowingly.

"They know my range," she says. "I've been in front of Michelle a few times. This time I want to show something more emotional."

"Exactly," I say, hating that these are all the same reasons I decided to do it. I look around the room, paranoid. What if everyone picked the same song? What if this is the choice that loses me the role?

"Well, good luck," Samantha says, squeezing my shoulder. "I'm sure you'll kill it. Oh, and hey, did you subscribe to my channel?" She reaches into her pocket and hands me a card with her face on it. A business card.

"No," I say. "I didn't know you had one." A bald-faced lie. She shills for the channel all over her social media, and of course I've watched every single video. Constantly posting about her auditions, her experiences in productions, backstage tours, interviews with her co-stars. Sometimes she does covers. Pop music, whatever.

"Make sure to like and subscribe," she says. "We've got to help each other out, you know?"

"Of course." I tuck the card in my fist. I might consider subscribing if she had me on as a guest. I don't say it, but the content itself is pretty boring. The videos are all just her sitting at a dressing table in her pink bedroom — she still lives at her parents' house. Sometimes her dog comes in and noses at her while she's singing. His name is Treble. Like the clef. Just terrible.

Once in a while she'll post a video of her grandfather reacting to her singing some kind of '80s hair metal song. "Cherry Pie" or whatever. He always seems shocked at the salaciousness in the beginning, but by the end, he's smiling wide, and if he isn't crying, his big eyes are at least watering. In every single one, he gives her a gentle kiss on the head and calls her the most talented girl in the world. I always tear up at that part because it's totally manipulative. Basically elder abuse, if you really think about it. Can he even consent to being in the video? He seems medicated.

The channel is such a bad career strategy. It's as if she has no appreciation for mystery, for mystique. No, instead she just surrounds herself with children on the internet, as if their attention means anything. See, I want to be discovered by the industry. By people who know something. Not drooling, sugar-soaked midwestern teenagers. Professionals. I want to make it on craft, on the purity of my talent. I don't want to make it because some twelve-year-old girls in Iowa liked my crappy Rihanna covers they found online, you know? I want to *be* Rihanna. Obviously. Why is this so hard for people to understand?

I want to be discovered. And I'm about to be. Today.

A stagehand, some nobody pokes his head out into the hallway. He doesn't even have a clipboard, just a spiral notebook with a sheet of paper on top of it. "Samantha?" he calls.

"Here!" she says, her hand shooting up. My stomach clenches. Of course, she gets to go in first. Of course, she gets to sing this song first, to create the standard against which the rest of us are going to be measured.

"Good luck." It comes out pathetically fawning, though, and too late — she's already darted down the hallway, swishing in her jeans. It doesn't matter. She can't act. Maria is warm and tender and kind. Samantha Nguyen is a stone-cold bitch.

She was the lead at the Shakespeare festival, and well, I suppose I've been seeing her on a few posters around town. In my expert opinion, her voice is just so boring. The tone is dull. Lifeless. Yet she still keeps getting all of these parts. Who can say why? Probably some combination of her sucking up to company directors, her undignified hustling on social media, and well, I don't want this to sound awful, but diversity certainly comes into play. But it is so important. Like, representation is everything. It just means that for once, being a deeply attractive blonde woman is counting against me. The world has really changed. For the better. Obviously.

I sit down against a wall and close my eyes. I don't want to see Samantha Nguyen when she exits the audition. I don't want to hear about how it went, don't want to see the expression on her face, so I scoot into an alcove and focus.

My last vocal audition was terrible. The snarky little twink sitting behind the table in a crushed velvet magenta T-shirt, a representative from a cruise line, no less, cut me off not sixteen bars into the Whitney Houston song I'd been assigned and shouted, "Next."

"What?" I'd said. "I barely started."

"Honey, you can't sing," he said. "Not professionally. Now I've got sixty-three girls to see before lunch, so you know, move along. Go have fun at karaoke, okay?"

Of course, I booked an emergency session with my vocal coach, Renée, right after. She charges double for last-minute sessions, and I always have to pay cash, but it was worth it to spend time with someone who understood what was going on. She turned on the diffuser and massaged some peppermint oil into my temples and we spent half an hour inhaling, then puffing out of our diaphragms, centering ourselves, grounding our feet. It was everything. It was beautiful. At the end, I cried into her shoulder. She rubbed circles on my back and didn't get weird about snot.

"A cruise ship audition? Is that really what we care about?" she whispered to me. "Come on now."

And really, if you think about it, she's right. Of course some bitter old cruise ship musical assistant director is going to say stuff like that. He works for a cruise ship. And he was like, probably fifty? Like imagine if that was your job. At fifty. Obviously your judgment is poor. Obviously you have no taste. And it wasn't even, like, a good cruise line; it was some dinky one I'd never heard of. He was obviously a talentless hack. Couldn't recognize greatness if it spat in his mouth, which I'm sure he'd enjoy.

I'm so grateful I have Renée. She always brings me back to the truth. When I pay her, it doesn't feel like I'm losing anything. It feels like I'm gaining an entire new block of energy that'll carry me through the month. It's like I'm buying a hand that can reach into my heart and remind it to keep beating. She's like therapy, but better because there's no talk of parents or childhood or whatever. Just the simplicity of a note sustained, both of us lost in the act of creation. In there, next to her, I am a god.

A pair of shoes appear next to me. They belong to some stage-hand and they're old, orthopedic. They suit his skinny and tired body. "Are you Jessamyn?"

"That's me," I say.

"They're ready for you."

I reach up instinctively — I don't know why I expect this guy to help me off the ground — but he's already walked off. I clamber to my feet, dust myself off, and hurry after him.

The pack of women has dwindled down to four. And as I examine the faces of those remaining, one of them (how embarrassing) wearing a nun's habit, I start to spiral. All of them are old. Panic grips me. I'm not old. I'm barely twenty-four. Well, twenty-five. And a half. But still. It's an outrage. There's at least two decades between me and the youngest one left in the waiting room, and she's the one dressed like she's about to audition for *Sister Act 3*.

"How did they call us in?" I blurt out as he leads me down a long concrete hallway. "What was the order?"

"Oh, I don't know. It's after five. Maybe everyone here has a day job."

They cannot think I have a day job. No. A day job is the real career ender. And I'm not talking about, like, waitressing or scanning tickets or temping. It's the second career. The nine-to-five grind that sucks your soul out through a straw with every Tupperware lunch snapped open in the windowless breakroom while some wenis named Brandon asks you if you still send nudes to your boyfriend. No, I can't be lumped in with people who have day jobs.

But it's an open audition, I remind myself. This stagehand doesn't know anything. The order they've called us in is probably random.

"Got your sheet music?" The stagehand and I are at the door. He presses an ear to it while I dig through my bag for the folder Renée gives me when we prep for all my majors.

He opens the door a crack and peeks in, then throws it open wide. "I've got Jessamyn for you."

It's raining. I'm waiting under an awning, my peppermint roll-on practically stuffed up my nose. The one thing I love about crying in the rain is that at least you're not weeping alone. Ha! God, I should write that down for my one-woman show. It's called *I Have a Dream*. All I have is the title so far, but it feels right.

There are two texts on my phone, both from different boyfriends. One is a real estate mogul-slash-entrepreneur who gives me money and always sends an Uber to pick me up. The other is (partially) unhinged. And I say unhinged because he used to stalk me. Literally.

See, I was doing this independent musical, very edgy, very important, as part of the Fringe Festival. He came to all my shows and would wait outside of the theater, chain-smoking until I exited. Then he would try to talk to me. When I ignored him, he threw lit cigarettes at me, then would catch up with me blocks later and apologize while crying. It was incredible! Like I was in a movie.

And okay, sure, the first few times it happened were scary. Because it's, like, a man, following me, basically saying he wants to drag me back to his apartment and do perverted things to me. But because he never actually did anything violent, the police said there wasn't anything they could do.

Because the cigarettes never actually hit me. Because I never got burned.

Which if you think about it? Pretty messed up. Some man is saying he's going to kill me, and the cops are like . . . well, we have to wait until he *actually* kills you to try and stop him.

They offered to ask him to leave me alone. Which, you know. Cute.

Come on, can you even imagine? As if that wouldn't piss him off at all, to find out I called the cops on him. As if that wouldn't be the thing to push him over the edge.

So, as a living, breathing woman with hopes and dreams who was sick of living in fear, I was forced to pivot and decided I would make him my first fan.

And when you think about it, the lit cigarette thing — the police were right. The cigarettes never actually hit me. Like, if he really wanted to hit me, he would.

Every woman has heard that advice before, right? When they're complaining about a guy not calling them back. It's the ugly truth with men. They are simple creatures. If he wanted to call you back, he would. If he wanted to kill you, he would.

And so, when he was chasing me home, I shifted my mindset and focused not on the abuse he hurled at me but instead on the attention. And I love attention. I figured he was just a lost soul, much like me, who wanted his life to be bigger and more exciting than it was.

His name is Anton. And what I realized while he was running after me and howling was, if you're going to consistently be harassed and abused, and if no one is going to do anything about it, you may as well find a way to enjoy it. To make it work for you.

And so, I decided to accept Anton's adoration. Now he's one of my boyfriends.

See, when I'm with Anton, we both get to play pretend. He gets to pretend he actually means something to me, and I get to be worshipped. As I should be. It's like a little preview for what's to come.

A few sample text messages:

Break a leg my darling not that you need it I hope you know you are the most incredible performer this world has ever seen and soon everyone will know it.

Your so sexy

*You're

Was thinking about you last night come over come over right now

Your voice is so beautiful I was listening to a recording I made of u it was beautiful and got me through the day

So gorgeous, come over

Are u awake lol

I'll come get u where are you

I was thinking about when you did the show at the fringe and how amazing you were today stay amazing have an amazing day

Thirsty, but more importantly devoted.

Anyway, obviously my *Sound of Music* audition sucked, because the universe is just not on my side as of late. Now I'm standing in this alcove, weeping, hoping someone will come by and say, "Why, girl . . . why are you crying?" and maybe cast me in something. This is a very creative part of town. And I know I'm good at crying beautifully. It's something I perfected at the age of twelve — it was how I was able to get my dad to pay for theater school, and then my rent for a few years. He cut me off eventually, once he figured out that I'd dropped out of theater school and didn't actually get a degree. He said poverty would be character building. Which, I don't know, hard disagree? I guess?

The audition, it's like, I don't know. It was weird. I walked in and said hello. Michelle, the director of this show and the artistic director of the Company, was there, grinning, sitting next to the associate producers, Stefan and Georgia. Both of them painfully bored.

"Hi, Jessamyn," Michelle said when I handed her my head shot, trying to smile past the sinking dread in my stomach. One big fat juicy beef I have with the universe is that this feeling, this nervous, empty feeling, has been pigeonholed by popular culture as "butterflies."

Renée corrected this for me. She said calling them butterflies was a form of self-sabotage. That dread is your friend, she said. It's your passion, it's your love in bodily form. It's your heart reminding you what makes it sing. And to try to explain it away as some fragile, delicate insect is to constantly devalue that love. Best to own it. Climb inside inspiration's mighty womb and stake one's claim. It's hard to live that energy, though, when your entire future is hanging in the balance.

Michelle took a long sip of water from a disposable bottle. The plastic crinkled as she sucked hard on that thing, as if she'd been sitting in the desert all day. And I don't know, maybe she had. A talent desert. And there I was, a beautiful oasis. "What have you been up to since we last had you in here?" she asked.

"Lots of training," I began. "With my vocal coach. And I did a musical."

Michelle eyed my resumé, an unreadable expression on her face. "Is this the *Alien XXX*? The Fringe one?"

"Yeah, it was kind of out there. But I think I was able to give a great performance with what I was given."

"Hmm." Michelle stared at the sheet, nodding.

"And the XXX thing wasn't, like, it wasn't naked. I mean, the reference wasn't —"

"It's all right, I understand," Michelle said, smiling. "I know the director."

"Really?"

"For a long time. Since theater school. But I do have a question for you before we begin."

My heart was pounding. She was going to ask about my schedule, my availability, if I mind missing Christmas with my family to dedicate myself to this part. What am I willing to do? The answer is obviously anything.

"Why no plays?"

"Hmm?"

"You know, plays. Without music."

"Oh." I laughed. What a strange question. "It's just not what I'm passionate about."

"Hmm," Michelle said again, her big glasses sliding down her nose. She pushed them up again with a knuckle. "You're such a great actress."

"Thank you," I said. "Acting skills are important in musicals, too."

"Yes of course. And what are you performing for us today?"

"'Something Good.'"

"Oh." She scribbled another note on the yellow legal pad in front of her. "I think only two of you picked that song."

"Yeah, her and Sam," Georgia said. Sam. It was difficult not to bristle at the familiarity, the nickname. Sam. As if they work together all the time. Maybe they do, I don't know what these fools do outside of their administrative work. Maybe they direct low-rent operas for rich assholes. Me, I'm for the people.

"Just out of curiosity, why did you pick it?" Michelle asked, looking up from her notes.

"I think it's a really powerful scene," I said. "And it's really romantic in, like, a really stark way. I don't think anything modern touches it, for just being so incredibly earnest. You know?"

"Earnest is a great word," Michelle said. And if I'm being honest, she's sort of the definition of earnest, with her big glasses, and with the crying all the time at the back of the theater when she thinks no one is looking. I see her, and I know what she's doing because I'm always crying, too. It's usually at that soaring moment in a show where everything is coming together in a beautiful and powerful way. We are the same, her and I. I just need to show her.

"Whenever you're ready, Jessamyn."

The accompanist was seated on the other side of the room, waiting, casual. I signaled him and began.

And I thought it went well. My dynamics were quiet and sure, and I performed it exactly as I rehearsed with Renée. I didn't bother singing the male part of the duet; I waited, trusting that these three knew the song well enough to understand what I was doing.

When I finished, I smiled and said thank you to Michelle, who was watching me with this perplexed expression on her face. "No, thank you, Jessamyn." And I walked out of there. As the door was closing behind me, I heard Georgia turn to Stefan and say, "What was with all the gaps? Why did she just stand there? So awkward."

"Be nice," Michelle says. "She's one of the Shakespeare girls that never —"

And then the door slammed behind me before I could hear the end of her sentence. I hope she wasn't burdening my audition with some tawdry gossip. That would be the height of unprofessionalism. Though I suppose I shouldn't expect much more from this place.

And now I'm stuck in purgatory, trying to decide which boyfriend I'm going to let cheer me up. My phone glows — a text from Anton.

I'm sure you were amazing.

Let me come get you.

I'm leaving right now, don't move.

It's raining though, and he only has a stupid bike. It's got this Dutch box on the front of it he uses for grocery shopping, and very, very occasionally, I allow him to pick me up in it.

But it's not exactly what I'm looking for in this moment of emotional pain. Plus, it's raining. So, um no. Not tonight. Instead, I text Mr. Real Estate and give him the address of this alcove. He replies immediately and tells me he's sending a car.

And I stop crying, because at least I get to make a choice tonight. At least I get to decide where I'm going.

Laughter on the street. I swipe at my tears quickly.

"Well, that was a long one. Thanks for sitting through it with me. These open calls really keep the union off my ass." It's Michelle.

"At least we found her," Georgia says.

"No question," Stefan replies.

My heart swoops. If they wanted Samantha, they'd just give her an offer, right? This means they found someone today, in the pile. Someone they weren't expecting.

"I'll give her a call tomorrow. Have you got her number? Her resumé just has reps and I want to talk to her."

"Oh yeah, we were just texting — don't worry, I didn't reveal anything. We're going to the movies later."

Fuck. I check my phone, dumbly, even though I know it's not me. I don't know Stefan, and I don't know Georgia either, outside of all the times she's drunkenly yelled at me at the doors to the Franklin at opening night after-parties, angry because it's my job to stop her from taking her glass of wine outside. I don't know these selfish jerks at all. But the fact that they're choosing to cast their friend over someone who truly embodies the spirit of the role (me) speaks volumes about their professionalism.

They talk about a meeting tomorrow morning where they'll finalize the chorus, the nuns, the children. Offers out by Friday. Way behind schedule. A car pulls up out front, an Uber. The guy leans out the window. "Vishal?" he shouts. I really don't want to step out of the alcove and be seen by these unethical tyrants.

"I think my Uber is here," says Michelle.

It's actually mine.

I dart out and dive into the car before they can see me. Slam the sedan's door behind me. "Hi," I say, breathless.

"Vishal?" he asks, confused.

"My boyfriend."

"Lucky guy." The Uber driver pulls out onto the road. I slump down in the seat.

We drive in silence for a while. I notice the driver's eyes flicking up in the rearview mirror, looking at me. I rest my bitch face.

"So, how's your night going?"

"Fine," I say.

"You want to get a drink?"

"No."

"You don't have to tell your boyfriend," he says. As if that's the problem.

The clicking of his turn signal throbs in the silence. I really do hate these sexed-up losers. And I'm always surrounded by them. It's exhausting.

"Can I have your number? I want to take you out." His fists tighten on the steering wheel.

Lights blur through the rain on the windshield, and the ticking of his turn signal really highlights the fact that I'm alone in the car with this weirdly horny Uber driver.

Sometimes I dream about a version of my life where I don't have to deal with men and their panting, bottomless desire all the time. Is it my fault I was born with gorgeous almond-shaped eyes, beautiful blonde hair, perfect breasts, and an eyeball-melting hip-to-waist ratio? I am everything most men have ever wanted, and they never let me forget it. It's absolutely exhausting.

I don't say anything, just let the silence dig in. My nails are long, at least, and kind of pointy, so I have that going for me.

He keeps driving at least. I wish I had a roster of one-liners to devastate him with, but he's caught me at my most vulnerable, and my mind is drawing a blank. And sometimes in these situations it's best just to stay quiet. You don't want to make them angry. Men.

I think about my necklace. It's thick, silver. I could shift so I'm sitting behind him, wait until he stops at a red light and slip it off. Jump forward, pull it tight across his neck, and lean back. What a thrill it would be to listen to him try to draw breath, to flail against the pressure. Put my feet up on the seat and really yank until the metal links break skin. Until he stops flailing. Until his body stills and he is quiet and can't bother me anymore.

Instead, I sit quietly. Eventually he puts on some thrash metal and starts blasting it, which is fine by me, because it means I can cry as loud as I want. And I do.

A few blocks go by. He looks at me again in the rearview, notices me sobbing in the backseat and pulls over.

"You'd better not be crying because I asked you out. Snobby bitch."

"No, I'm crying because I didn't get the part I auditioned for. Even though I deserve it. You're just some loser. You're the bitch."

He sits with this insult, considering what to do. I can feel it. Fear arrives, fear that he's going to drag me out of the car by my hair and beat me to death. Or that he could be taking me to some rape den. It's totally possible, I've read all kinds of articles about it.

"If you report me to Uber, I'll tell them you tried to punch me in the head," he says.

"And I'll tell them you were trying to sex traffic me." He pauses, seemingly weighing both threats. I almost regret giving him the idea. "Or you can face forward and drive me to my rich boyfriend's house, and I won't tell him you spoke to me. He'll tip you eighteen percent because he's a sucker. And we'll both forget this ever happened. Deal?"

He pulls out onto the road again and follows his little route, as outlined on the app. Tacit agreement. Good. I don't need anyone to protect me. I'm fine. I finger the clasp on my necklace. Consider sliding it off just in case he pulls over again.

"Can you put that music back on?"

He concedes, just blasts it and doesn't look in the rearview mirror for the rest of the ride, which, frankly, is perfect. I get the tears out. I even scream a little. Vishal has said at least ninety times that I can't cry in front of him because it bums him out, but Anton loves it, so you know. There's some real logic to having two boyfriends. I honestly recommend it to anyone whose life is as complicated as mine.

IV

"You have to come!" Sudi's practically on her knees in the coat check. Show's over. A few patrons dawdle in the lobby waiting for rides and Marge is upstairs, probably untying her neck scarf, eating a ham sandwich and fucking up payroll. Only three of us ushers are left down here packing up our stuff.

"I've got an audition tomorrow."

"Just one drink," Sudi says. "We have to celebrate this stuff or else it just flies by. Come on!"

Sudi wants everyone to come out and celebrate her making the top three in some stand-up comedy contest. I don't have the money for it. There was a corporate event before the show and they tipped the coat check sixty bucks, which is basically unheard of, so we're all leaving with an extra twelve in our pockets, but it should really be going to my phone bill.

"Aww, is the princess not joining us?"

I look over. It's Rudy, one of the bartenders. He's already changed out of his black dress shirt and into a T-shirt with a little alien stitched over the pocket.

Rudy would be hot if he didn't have such a garbage personality. He's got a golf pencil tucked behind his ear and he's grinning at me, though I'm not sure why. I barely talk to him, though lately he's been bugging me if he sees me sitting in the lobby. Usually it's to ask if I want any of the leftover hot chocolate before he dumps it out, but the other day he asked what I was reading. When I showed him the real Maria von Trapp's memoir, he rolled his eyes so hard he nearly fell over.

"Princess has an audition tomorrow," I mutter, winding a scarf around my neck. Usually when I claim to have an audition, it's a lie, sure, but this time I'm telling the truth.

"Maybe if she spent some time relaxing and enjoying herself, she'd book more parts."

"Ah, yes, advice from a loser bartender, that's what my career's been missing."

"Be nice, you guys, come on. This is a really big deal for me," Sudi says. "One drink. Like, forty-five minutes. If I don't toast this with someone, I'm going to go home and stay up all night playing video games and shit-talking ten-year-old boys." She considers for a minute then smiles, which is rare for her. She's actually really pretty when she bothers to smile. "You know, I'll probably do that anyway. Way more fun to do it when you're drunk, though."

"Fine," I say, counting the twelve bucks in my pocket. I will have one glass of wine. To be nice.

"Yes!" Sudi says.

"Wow," Rudy says, stepping sideways to let us out of the coat check. "Was it something I said?"

"Absolutely not."

"Really?" He chases after me as I start toward the door. "Because it seems like you decided —"

"Listen," I say. "I'm not sure what's compelling you to spend all this time trying to make me like you, but I already have two boyfriends. I'm not interested in opening a spot up on the roster for a pathetic bartender."

Rudy laughs. "Two boyfriends, huh?"

"Yeah, and —"

"Two boyfriends. That's nothing. They're attention. You don't like either of them. I can tell. And don't flatter yourself, by the way, I'm just trying to cheer you up."

"I don't need cheering up, especially not from you."

"Well, you need it from someone."

I'm not sure what to say to this, because he's right. I reach up and flick the golf pencil stuck behind his ear, laugh when he turns, actually concerned about the little piece of wood bouncing on the pavement, chasing after it like a kid.

Sudi skips out, arm in arm with Kelsey, the other bartender. I grab her other arm and off we go.

...

My cheeks are hot. "To successing it up!" Sudi says, raising a bottle of beer over the middle of the table.

"Fuck. Yes," Rudy says. "Successing. That should be a word. I'm getting another round." He slides off the stool in the back of this shitty dive he dragged us to — because he knows the owner — and heads over to the bar.

"At least one of us is getting somewhere," I say. "To one of us!" Truly, I despise how nice I get when I've been drinking.

"Hooray!" Kelsey shouts. "One of us! One of us!"

Rudy's looking quite cozy over there, with the bartender. She's a tall girl, almost six feet, with incredible long, white-blonde mermaid hair she's got tied into two fat braids on either side of her head. A massive twig with a doll face.

34

She's barely got any makeup on, which makes her giant bulbous eyeballs seem like they're about to fall out of her skull. When she turns around, I see the back of her head is hosting a ratty old mat she isn't bothering to cover up. It's a mess back there. Nauseating.

Despite this, despite the disgusting, unkempt hair, she and Rudy are laughing together. He reaches forward and grabs the end of one of her braids, dips it in a tequila shot she's pouring. She swats at him, giggling.

I hate her.

Rudy keeps buying us drinks, which is really nice of him. Apparently, some rich guy tipped him a hundred bucks for making him the perfect martini at intermission. Or so he says.

"When do you find out about *The Sound of Music*?" Sudi asks.

"I don't know," I say. I haven't told them that Maria's already been decided, that some friend of the artistic director will be in the role. That once again, sucking up to those jerks wins the day. I supposed I could spend more time kissing ass, but that's not the way I want to be cast. No. I want to earn it on talent. I need them to see in me what I see in myself. And they should. They absolutely should.

So now I'm waiting to find out if they think I'm young enough for Liesl (not likely), or bitchy enough for Frau Schrader. I do have the Nazi-friendly look needed to sell that part. I'm very blonde and have big boobs and am tall enough to seem Austrian.

And if that happens, I'll have to decide whether or not I want to jeopardize my future by taking a supporting role and poorly branding myself for the rest of my career as someone who doesn't deserve to step into the spotlight because I was impatient. Become one of those old crones from the open call at the Franklin — riding a public bus to auditions, trying to get my relatives to buy my homemade jewelry. A pity case. A side character. A nobody.

Which, no. Never. Never, never, never.

Rudy puts a tray of shots down on the table, gold, the scent of tequila wafting up my nose.

"Oh no," I say. "No."

"Yes," Sudi says.

"I have an audition tomorrow."

"What's it for?" Kelsey asks.

"Laundry detergent," I say. "I'm going out for 'Mom Who Smells Her Kid's Hockey Equipment and Looks Like She's About to Barf.'"

"No, you are not," Rudy says, laughing. "That's not the part."

"It is. Look." I pull out my phone and flip to the sides my agent sent me that morning.

"Wait a minute." Rudy grabs the phone from me. "The guy part is 'Dad Who's Glad to Be Home Until He Smells the Smell?'"

"Yup."

"Wait, oh my God, please, please show us what you're going to do."

"I haven't had a chance to work it yet," I say.

"There aren't any lines," Rudy says. "It's just you sniffing the hockey equipment."

"And looking like I'm about to vomit — don't forget that part."

"Do it! Do it! Do it!"

It's impossible for me to turn down an adoring crowd. I look for a prop and spot Rudy's jean jacket on the chair next to me. "This'll be perfect." I make eye contact with him. "Extra stinky."

"Hey!" he says, but his smile is warm, and it's obvious he's enjoying the attention. He catches my eye and I'm so momentarily lost in the depths of his soul. Because he's just . . . he's really seeing me, I think. He's seeing my entire person. And there's something so intoxicating about it.

"Oh my God," Sudi cuts in, in her loud, obnoxious way. "Get a room." Everyone laughs.

I wink at Rudy then swivel around in my stool and clutch the jean jacket in my fists. I take a deep breath, inhaling slowly, exhaling slowly. They're all waiting for me. Anticipating me. They can't look away.

I think about "Mom Who Smells Her Kid's Hockey Equipment and Looks Like She's About to Barf." Really consider what her day was like. Laundry, laundry, and more laundry. Then organizing the hall closet again. The kids were off camping all summer, and they'd just chucked their stuff in there. I actually found a ball of tinfoil with a burnt marshmallow still inside, ants crawling all over it. By lunchtime, I simply didn't have the energy to make myself a sandwich, so I warmed up a Lean Cuisine in the microwave, ate half of it, then threw the rest out while watching the news. It got too depressing, so I switched over to a daytime talk show and half-listened while making a shopping list for the week. And when I checked my calendar, I realized that hockey was about to start, and little Andy's equipment had been sitting in the basement storage room, sealed up all summer, baking in the heat. And I've been avoiding this line on my calendar because I know, I really do know, that it's going to be disgusting.

I clench my fists and bury them in Rudy's jacket, spin around in my chair and smell it, then wretch one, two, three times before dropping it on the floor, back of my hand under my nose. Assaulted. This is cruel and unusual. My eyes start to water. How is this my life? My one precious life?

And then I break, smile, and everyone at the table erupts in applause.

"Inspired, truly," Sudi says.

"They'd be fools not to cast you," Kelsey agrees.

"I've never seen someone smell something so sexily." Of course, Rudy, leaning down to pick his jacket up off the floor. "First stop, detergent; next stop, Ibsen."

The shot of tequila goes down easy. I'm surprised it doesn't leak out the sides of my smile.

···

It's difficult to say when everyone slinks home, but suddenly it's two in the morning and only Rudy and I are left at the table.

"So why do you care so much about *The Sound of Music*? And at this company. It's such a joke."

"It's not a joke; it's a lead role in a musical. You should see those houses at Christmas. Packed."

"But musicals? They're just so . . ." Rudy trails off, staring down at the beer bottle between his hands. He scratches at the label, avoiding eye contact. I suppress the urge to kick him. "Ugh. Why?"

"Because when I'm watching a musical, it's the only time I'm sure, without a doubt, that I am alive."

His face is passive, though I see a twitch in his cheek, the suggestion of a mocking grin.

"And I don't mean it in some, like, teenage girl in-love-for-the-first-time-with-a-vampire kind of 'he makes me feel alive' BS. The first time I felt like I was a person. That I existed. I don't know. It's like when you see yourself reflected in someone else, you suddenly know where you belong in the world. What your life's purpose is. I saw this dinky little touring production of *The Phantom of the Opera* and knew I belonged. That was it. I had to get up there."

Rudy eyeballs me. I can't quite tell why he's so entertained. "*The Phantom of the Opera*?" he says. "That musical is so problematic."

"Who cares?" I say, and I mean it. Because the drama of it, the mystery, the absolute surrender. There's a reason it's a classic, that it's stood up to the modern morality tests people ascribe to art because they're afraid of what their own tastes reveal about them as people.

I'll never forget the feeling of seeing "Think of Me" performed live. The woman playing Christine standing center stage, arms flung wide, the crowd drinking in the beauty of her performance. How she transcended everyone in the room. How breathless we all were, there. The power of it. Watching her. Seeing her.

It's the only time I've seen my father struck dumb, his mouth hanging open. Pinned to the chair. My father isn't the type to relinquish himself to anything. He isn't lazy, no, far from it. He's run so many marathons, he works out every single day, he screams at his employees. But there he was, absolutely controlled by the power of the soprano.

He didn't move. He didn't look at his phone.

And she was flawless. She was perfect. There's a high note in that song that is utterly breathtaking. The note. That goddamn note. Anyone who has seen it has witnessed a feat of pure genius. The years it must've taken her to get to that place, where she could sweep us all away with the power of her voice. The dedication. The devotion. How could you not be moved?

My father leapt out of his seat at the curtain call, screaming for her. Losing himself completely. I'll never forget it. We saw that musical three times.

"I'm just saying, you can do better than *The Sound of Music* at the Franklin." Rudy's still on this, apparently. "C'mon, it's such a joke. A musical about the Second World War that doesn't even acknowledge the holocaust? Give me a break. Tell me you went out for some other Christmas shows. What about *The Family Ford* at the Young Electrics?"

I scoff and shake my head. What a moron. The Young Electrics? What's next, slam poetry?

"What?"

"Because . . . I don't want to be, like . . . *an actor*," I say. I feel my nose crinkling at the thought of it. "Like some tortured soul who walks around sad all the time. No thank you."

"You don't have to be sad to be an actor," he says.

"Right, but musicals. I mean, come on. Plays make people dwell on their own sad, pathetic lives. But musicals. A talented musical theater actor can pull someone out of their seat, allow them to forget their stupid little life for a few hours, they can erase any kind of horrible day, reach inside of them, and open up their soul."

"Great theater —"

"Can provoke and shock and blah, blah, who cares. But even an extremely mid musical is nine times more transportive than a play."

"But —"

"And in this age of social media, when we know everything, all of the time, we need an escape. A balm. And I am that balm. Look at Maria von Trapp. She's goodness, she's purity, she can pull off short hair without looking like a man. Everyone loves her."

"That role is fucked," he says. "C'mon, can you imagine living in a time when you're cast out of your home at the nunnery because you climbed a tree and scraped your knee? You ripped your dress? And those cloth-bound jerks sing a whole song about what a mess you are?"

"So you do know the lyrics."

"Everyone knows them," he says, but I can tell he's pretending to be cool. "Be serious, Jessamyn. That musical is bullshit."

"It's the perfect part. Maria von Trapp is the ideal woman."

"She isn't a human being," he says.

"That's the point."

"But . . . what?" He examines me like I'm a math equation that keeps stumping him. I shrug my shoulders and smile. Obviously, I'm known to be a great actress — this is something I'm complimented on all the time. Even Michelle has heard of me. And I guess I am good at it, in the sense that I can fake it. I can build characters and do my best to inhabit them. But that next-level commitment, that depth, I mean, it's just not what I'm interested in.

There's something too naked about the whole thing. And honestly, no one likes a drag. No one likes to be forced to consider their, like, humanity all the time. You need a break. Stars don't make people feel bad. They make them feel good. Has George Clooney ever made you feel bad? Of course not. He makes you feel like he's very hot and you just have to keep staring at him, and if you don't, you'll die.

"You should just —"

"You should stop giving me advice I didn't ask for," I say, interrupting him. But I do it all sing-songy so it doesn't become, like, a thing. Because what is worse than someone telling a performer what to do, especially someone who has never risked anything?

Who has never stood before an audience and opened their mouth to sing? Who has never given an audience every feeling pouring out of the depths of their soul repackaged into something beautiful? Who has never swallowed their ego, their pain, and smiled through it for someone else's happiness? Tucked away the agony and said, no, we will not dwell in the depths of sorrow, we will make it joyful, we will make it upbeat.

Like, how dare he even have an opinion. He's just a bartender. He knows nothing of the risk that comes from stepping onstage.

"I hate to see talent go to waste, is all."

"Julie Andrews was a great Maria because she was a great actress," I say, "but she was also a star."

"And you want to be Julie Andrews?"

"Well, obviously not, I have way better bone structure. I am Jessamyn St. Germain, and I will be beloved by everyone."

He laughs then gives me a look. One of those looks. Adoring. Horny. Breathless.

Silence falls between us, and I check my phone. I should really get going, but I want to, well, I just want to win.

We sit there in silence, Rudy now pulling the label off his beer bottle, the tiny slices of paper scattered on the table like a boundary between us. "Typical."

"What's typical?"

"Kiss the boots of Rodgers and Hammerstein, but God forbid you appreciate any theater that challenges the audience."

"I mean, I'm fine if it exists, I just don't want to do the challenging. Life is hard enough without me making it harder for what? My own ego?"

"It's important!"

"Why?"

"Because we need to talk about what it means to be alive."

"Uh, I'm confronted with that every day, I don't need to pay two hundred bucks to feel like shit. If that's the whole point of art, pardon me for misunderstanding the last twenty-six years of my life."

"You're twenty-six?"

Crap. Oh crap. I hate admitting it out loud. Even worse is the surprise in his reaction, like he didn't realize how far I was from where I need to be, how much more work I have to do, how opportunities are slipping away from me with each passing breath.

"Oh, don't rub it in." I sink down onto the table. Because twenty-six. What that means for my career is so pathetic.

He reaches across the table and squeezes my arm. "It doesn't matter." His face betrays exactly zero irony, which is crazy. And enraging. Maybe it doesn't matter to him. But it does matter.

"Don't give me that bullshit."

"What?"

"That bullshit. Of course, it matters. What sort of female performer builds a career in her late twenties? In her thirties? You know it's not true. As much as we all want to pretend it isn't, it is. I'm too old. And I'm not getting anywhere. So at least show me some respect and stop pretending like it doesn't matter when it does."

"I'm sorry."

"This is why I have to get Maria," I say.

"You will."

I lean into it, because it feels good to be sure about something, even if it's probably not going to happen.

"I am going to be Maria."

"Hell yeah!" We smile at each other. Rudy stares at me. A shiver runs down my legs and I shift in my seat.

"What?" I say.

"Nothing."

I'm as surprised as anyone when Vishal walks in the front door then, suit jacket damp from the rain, his tie balled up and shoved into a pocket, top button undone, his presence a bucket of cold water.

"There you are," he says.

"Hey!" I totally forgot I texted him. "Are you picking me up?"

"Yeah, I was late at the office. Hey, man." He nods at Rudy.

I introduce them. Vishal barely smiles. Even though it's weird that he just showed up here, this is honestly the best way to leave a night out. If only the girls were still here to witness it. It's not like either of them have even one boyfriend, meanwhile I have two. Better if I'd drunkenly texted them both at the same time and they showed up and had a fist fight over me or something.

"You want to get out of here?" he asks. "The Uber's outside."

"Oh my God," I say, jumping off the stool and into his arms. He smells like whiskey. It doesn't really matter though, because he's here to save me from Rudy, the asshole. "My hero."

Outside, Vishal glances back at Rudy, sitting alone, staring at the wall. "Who is that guy?"

Is that jealousy?

Vishal's craning his neck, still watching, trying to unpack the threat. Oh yeah. Definitely jealously.

"Just some bartender. A nobody."

Vishal doesn't have faith in me. "He likes you."

"And I like you," I say and wrap my arm through his, pull him toward the Prius idling in the middle of the street. "C'mon, let's get out of here."

But he glares back at Rudy and keeps glaring at him. He isn't looking at me at all.

V

Vishal always does this thing when he wants me to leave. Most mornings, he'll be getting ready, slapping on cologne to cover up whatever boozy smell is still hanging around him, or tying up his tie, or checking some fantasy sports thing on his phone. And then, while he's reading, he'll hop up on his bed and start jumping next to me, so I know it's time to go. The first time he did it, I thought it was an earthquake and woke up gasping.

My dream is that one day he'll forget, or he'll decide he's so in love with me that he lets me hang out in his swank apartment all day, eating all the man-food in his fridge and using the gym at his condo, which has a hot tub and a steam room and even a tanning bed. But he always makes me leave, which is . . . whatever.

Today, when the bed starts shaking, I have to sprint for the toilet. I make it just in time to hurl, then I roll off it and onto the floor and press my cheek to the tile, groaning. The entire world is spinning. I wish I was dead. This is why I don't have friends.

Vishal follows me, chuckling. His laugh echoes in this very tiled, cavernous bathroom. "What happened to you last night?"

"I don't know. I didn't get Maria. I think I'm depressed."

He crouches down next to me on the bathroom floor. "Do you want some water?"

"Yes, please," I croak, sort of surprised at how nice he's being. That's not usually the play. He once told me bullying is his love language. I hear the fridge open and close, and he returns a moment later with a square white carton that he opens and puts on the bathroom floor next to me.

"This is water?"

"Yeah, it's some new environmental thing, I don't know. They're a client."

I have no idea what Vishal does. I mean, there's real estate, but he also invests, I think, in lots of weird businesses. He usually has crates of junk all over his condo. For a while, every time I left, I got to take a case of these weird protein shakes with me. It was great, really helped me reduce my grocery bill. I got sick of them, though. There are only so many tasteless, gray blobby protein smoothies you can suck back before your poops start looking apocalyptic.

"What's Maria?" he asks.

"The lead in *The Sound of Music*."

"Oh," he says. "That sucks. Did you try out for any other parts?"

"It's kind of like a marketing thing. You don't want them to think you're worth less than a lead."

"Oh yeah, that's smart." He checks his phone. "I have to go. Listen —"

"I think —"

I lean over the toilet again, letting loose big time. The sound of the vomit splashing on the water is definitely the worst part. Eventually, I sit back and breathe. He looks at me with a mixture of pity and amusement and passes me a washcloth.

"I've got an audition at eleven."

45

"You going to make it?" he asks.

"Maybe. I don't know. It's just a commercial. Whatever."

"You can stay here and prepare if you want."

"What?" I lean against the wall, shocked.

"Yeah, it's fine. C'mon, I'd be a real asshole if I kicked you out now, wouldn't I?"

I laugh a little because I'm so confused. Usually as he's hustling me out the door, he asks me if I want to go get my nails done and then shoves fifty bucks in my fist.

"Just make sure you lock the door," he says, tossing me a keychain with a fob attached. "And leave those at the front desk."

"Thank you."

He pats me awkwardly on the shoulder. "I left some cash on the table by the door if you want to order soup or something." And there it is. It's like sleeping with someone's dad. His phone starts ringing and he gets up and walks out of the bathroom, his heels clicking on the tile. I hear the front door shut behind him.

I lie flat on my back and stare up at the pot lights on the ceiling and wonder about Vishal. He's tall and kind of skinny but has really gorgeous curly black hair that he wears a little long, and big dark soulful eyes.

We met at a bar when I was waitressing and he tipped everyone really well, even the men, which made me like him more. But it's sort of a weird thing — an exchange of money was at the heart of our relationship from the very beginning. And it's not like I have a price list for sex acts or anything. It's just assumed that if he was poor, I wouldn't want to hang out with him. And if I'm being brutally honest, that's probably true.

I think he likes things this way. It's simple. And I don't ever make him talk about his feelings. Probably because there aren't any. Just sports, cartons of water, and now, a house key.

I crawl into his shower and sit there for what feels like an hour, choke down some Pepto Bismol I find in the medicine cabinet. By the time I've finished my makeup, I can barely see any evidence of last night's dark deeds. There's some undereye bagginess, but it's just a commercial audition. It's not like I'm supposed to look like I normally do — brands are all about "real" people now.

My phone's charging next to the bed. When I grab it to call an Uber, I notice I've got a missed call.

From the Company.

I scream.

There's a voicemail. I frantically scramble for it, my fingers shaking so much I get the code wrong and have to type it in twice.

"Hey, Jessamyn, it's Michelle. I've been thinking about your audition and wanted to see if you'd come in for a chat. As soon as possible. I've got something I'd like to discuss with you. I'm in the office until noon today, if you're free. Swing by any time before then, otherwise we can set something up for early next week. Thanks!"

My heart pounds. I check the timing for the commercial audition. I might have time for both, but I know I've got to go talk to Michelle first. Because this is it. This is finally it. My life as I know it is about to change. Forever.

VI

In the Uber, I start to really think about it. Strange that I haven't heard from my agent, but I do think it's possible I'm about to receive some incredible news — maybe Samantha Nguyen turned them down! Could be money, or maybe the schedule. I could see her booking things in LA, what with that stupid channel of hers and all the schilling and husting she does. Total marketing ploy, sure, a great business maneuver — to walk this far down the road with Michelle, then just not be available, knowing full well that'll just make them want her more for the next role.

I'm going in to meet with Michelle about Maria.

I knew the audition went well. She's had second thoughts. It's a business, after all. People change their minds all the time.

My phone rings and my heart jumps. Maybe it's Michelle. Maybe it's my rep, prepping me for the meeting, the offer sheet on his desk. Everything I've been through now totally worth it, all of the groping and abuse, the late nights and early mornings. All the times I burned my cheek with a curling iron. All that time spent on my knees, begging the universe for a hint, for a win, for anything. All of it worth it, because finally, I'm getting my break.

I check the caller ID and groan. It's my father. I answer it on reflex, even though I know it's not going to be a pleasant conversation. It rarely is.

"Are we doing Christmas this year, or what?" he asks. I usually have to work. He lives in Montreal and doesn't like to travel in December, because he's this intense hypochondriac but also refuses to get a flu shot. He's the CEO of a big company, but I'm not supposed to tell anyone that — he's always paranoid I'm going to get kidnapped and ransomed, and then I'll have to pay him back. I mean, he says I would. Sometimes I wonder if I should try to get kidnapped, just to see what he would do. That idea drives me crazy. Would he actually make me pay back my own ransom? I don't know. Maybe.

"Hi, Dad, nice to hear from you. Wow, it's been a while." I always do this, to bait him. It makes him gruff. He cut me off years ago, which I understand. He grew up poor and resents how spoiled I am. He thinks I'm an idiot for pursuing this career despite all of the opportunities I've been afforded by the life he gifted me on a silver platter (his phrasing, of course). But I don't think he really knows what it's like to love something as much as I love musical theater. He certainly doesn't love me that much. "I miss you."

"I miss you too," he says, probably because his secretary is standing in the same room, listening to him talk on speakerphone. "I need an answer today. Sophie and her friends are doing Christmas in Aruba, and she wants to go."

Sophie. His girlfriend. A real talent. She's only ten years older than me and used to be a cheerleader for the Buffalo Bills' cheer squad, the Buffalo Jills, and apparently led a lawsuit about groping and poor treatment, which was settled for a lot of money. Now she's a newscaster for some local morning show.

"I might be getting cast in a musical," I say. "And the part's a lead, so I won't be available." The words come out before I can stop them. The news is just never good, but this morning . . . I'm positive that Michelle wouldn't bring me in just to discuss, well, I don't know why she'd be calling me in if not to offer me a part. It just doesn't make sense. She'd say so on the phone if she wasn't, I'm sure of it. No one is that depraved.

"Really? You might be?"

When I was cast in *Alien XXX* last summer, I made the mistake of telling him the title of the show, what the role was (Euphasia, hot alien wife), and of course, it sent him into a spiral of anger — he thought the XXX meant I would be showing my tits. "Pornography!" he shouted. "What's next? Prostitution! You give this up right now!"

I just hung up. I'm not sure we've spoken since.

"I'm heading to the meeting now." My voice is smug, which, you know, I can't help it.

"What's the contract?"

He always calls shows or roles "contracts," as if it's a business thing and not the song of my heart.

"*The Sound of Music.*"

"Maria von Trapp?"

"I think so," I say. "They called me in."

"That's a good show," he says, and it's hard for me not to drop the phone in surprise. A good show? A musical my father actually likes? A show he actually respects? "Send me the dates and we'll come and see you."

"Really?" I feel tears gathering in the corners of my eyes. He's never said anything like this. These conversations always veer toward some reason he's invented for me to quit, to go back to school, to get some boring degree like communications or medicine, to get an internship at his company.

But every time we'd fight, when I'd tell him what I was doing, he'd just shout the same thing at me, over and over: "It's just a song and dance! Jessie, it's a song and dance!"

But you know, *exactly*. And I'd try to remind him of *The Phantom of the Opera*, of our three-day musical bender and the power of Christine's voice, and he'd pretend like it didn't happen. Like we hadn't even gone to see it. But we did. I know we did.

He's had trouble trusting me for a while now. Trusting that I'm on the right path. See, when I was nineteen, I'd gotten into theater school. I spent a few months trying it out, but I realized quite quickly that if I spent another minute among those pretentious know-nothings, those professors who claimed greatness yet had never studied outside of Canada, had never worked with names, never really made it, then I, too, would emerge mediocre.

And so, I did what any reasonable person who believes in themselves would do. I dropped out. I got my tuition back and used it to take real acting classes, to study with people who were actually in the business. I found the light of my life, Renée, who had a Tony award. I really began to learn.

When my father realized I'd used his tuition money to fund my education in my own way, he cut me off. And so I was forced to do what millions of actresses have done before me: become a waitress.

But none of that matters now. Because it's finally happening.

And I get choked up a little because, you know, I finally get to be right. I finally get to show him what I can do. I get to prove myself in front of him and his little rat of a girlfriend. Oh, I can't wait to see the look on her face.

And before I'm really ready for my life to change, the Uber stops out in front of the molding old building that houses the Company's administrative offices and I say goodbye to my father and climb out. My smile is so wide. Why wouldn't it be? I'm about to be a star.

...

The phones in the office are ringing so much they're making me nervous. The receptionist has me seated under a poster of Scott Baio who inexplicably performed in a two-month-long production of

51

Glengarry Glen Ross here in the early aughts. "Michelle's swamped," the receptionist told me. "But I'll get you in before noon."

"Thanks."

My phone buzzes in my hand. It's my agent, probably pissed that I blew off the commercial audition this morning and what could have been a fat commission for him. I silence the call. There're always better agents circling at opening nights; I'm sure once I get Maria, I'll be able to upgrade my representation. I'll start getting flown out to New York for auditions. Real ones.

My phone rings again. I put it in my bag and zip it shut so I don't have to look at it. Sometimes Adam can be a real jerk, and it won't be helpful to be *in a mood* when Michelle and I have this chat. Despite the fact that I've worked at the Company forever, she doesn't know me well. Our old artistic director used to speak to everyone who worked at the Company, even us toilet scrubbers. But Michelle does things just a little bit differently.

I meditate on some lyrics, try to embody a personal glow, consider Julie Andrews and the innate sweetness of her personality. Certainly not something I have. I've always wondered if she was secretly a giant bitch. As if she saved all of her niceness for performance and the stage, and in real life she slapped coffee cups out of hands and never knew anyone's names and stomped around with a storm behind her eyes just waiting to be double-crossed or groped or glad-handed by some Hollywood douche so she could righteously unleash the beast.

"Jessamyn?"

I jump. I can tell the expression on my face is not what I wanted it to be — not serene or pleasant or kind, but desperate and unsure. My hands shake. Michelle stands at the front door to the offices, leaning out with a smile on her face. "Come on in."

...

"This place is a disaster, I'm so embarrassed," she says. "But I'm trying to embrace the chaos." Takeout containers are piled up behind her desk, an entire city of soy sauce–stained Styrofoam towers with chopsticks poking out the side. A stack of costumes from what is likely a Shakespeare play lie flopped on a chair in the corner, and everywhere else there's paper. Stacks of it, folders, files, notebooks, slim play volumes and printed-out scripts. A large maroon binder sits on her desk, flipped open to reveal *The Sound of Music* badly photocopied, scribbles, doodles, and Post-it notes all over it, so much so that only the title is visible.

Michelle reaches down and brushes crumbs off the seat across from her chair, and I sit down. "This is the biggest musical I've ever attempted and, well, what with the budget, and the size of the cast, the stakes are high."

"Of course," I say. She hurries back around her desk and sighs as she flops into her chair.

"Thanks so much for coming in. It's been a hectic few weeks. We got so behind on casting, like monstrously so, but we're close to getting it all settled. Agents and such. I'm sure you know what that's like."

She's babbling so much it makes her sound incoherent and sort of like a moron. "You should see the kids. They're so little. It's absolutely terrifying. Okay. Sorry. Vent over, that's not what this meeting is about."

"It's all right," I say. "You must be so busy."

Michelle's eyes fill up with tears. "Oh yeah. Thank you. I just didn't realize how full-on this job would be. I mean, directing is my passion, but curating plays for a company this size, with this kind of audience — I don't really know what to do. And everyone just expects me to be, well, anyway. Neither here nor there. Listen, sorry. Sorry."

It's fine. I get it. We aren't LA and we aren't New York, and we aren't Toronto. We are a regional theater in Vancouver, British Columbia, that was once known as a creative incubator but now can't draw an audience under the age of fifty-five. How do you push boundaries when you're playing to people with one foot in the grave?

Michelle stands up and paces to the window, knocking over one of her piles of takeout containers. "Shit. God, I am so all over the place today. Okay. Jessamyn." She rubs her hands on her face. "Do you like children?"

My stomach bottoms out. It's happening. Maria has to spend so much time with the children. She has to guide and carry them, party with them, teach them, laugh with them. It's the entire arc of her character. It's her boundless heart that leads her to the love of her life.

"I love children," I say. "One of my part-time jobs is babysitting." A lie. But a good one.

"That's perfect," Michelle says. "Okay, I had this stroke of genius last night. What this production really needs is a childminder."

The world shrinks around me. I am weak. I am dying. Small, in the room, gasping, suddenly. Reality splits in two — I see two Michelles in front of me. Close my eyes, blink quickly, and everything rights itself.

"A what?"

"Someone to help the kids get through the production."

My eyeballs bug out. Michelle is back to pacing around the office, her hands in her hair. "Let's face it, we cast the kids because they're cute, but none of them can act . . ." Her babbling is replaced with this very intense ringing in my ears. The humiliation of it. I should've taken that call from my agent in the Uber this morning. It was probably the entire context from this meeting. That dipstick could've at least sent me an email.

In a performance that would shock just about anyone, I somehow swallow an entire emotional meltdown, take a deep breath, stomp down my desire to throw this flimsy Ikea chair out the window, and listen.

"So basically, you'll be there day one, at rehearsals, making sure they're paying attention, being an extra set of eyes and ears, helping them to stay on track. Their schedule is a little all over the place, because we don't want to fully pull them from school. So, help with that, and then on show days, meet them at the front door, make sure they get their mics, get through a vocal warm-up, hair, makeup, costumes. And then throughout the show, make sure none of them run off and ruin everything. It's a big job, but you'll make more money than you would doing front of house, and it's good experience. You haven't worked on a professional production before, have you?"

"Just the Fringe Festival," I mutter, thinking back to how doing that musical, even though it was small, even though we were playing to a house of only fifteen or twenty, was the best ten days of my life. I don't mention my brief stint at Shakespeare on the Lake, and she doesn't bring it up.

"Good. Part of it is knowing their lines, helping them with cues, all that. I know it's thankless, but we can give you an assistant director credit, and it brings you into the fold a bit."

I gape at her. I was at least expecting this to be an offer for the chorus. A Baroness or a nun or something. Her right eye twitches. "Please say yes."

The silence throbs at me. How could this be happening?

Suddenly, the humiliation of having to tell my father overwhelms everything. Thinking about having to speak the words out loud. Oh my God. It's going to be so terrible.

I was so sure. I was so sure this was going to be an offer.

"Jessamyn! Just find a husband, for fuck's sake." He said that to me once. The husband thing. Which, I mean. C'mon, what is it, 1952?

Michelle sits again, making eye contact that's so intense. Her desperation is confusing. I don't know why she's so convinced I'll be good at this.

"Please."

"Yes." I say it only to escape her office. I don't remember much after that, just the booming humiliation pounding inside my ears, the rush of blood to my cheeks. Once I'm outside, I don't even want to lean against the building and cry for attention. I just start walking. The sun is annoyingly bright, and my hangover pulses behind my eyeball, and I walk and cry, and once I'm far enough away, I call the only person I know who truly understands me and of course she answers on the first ring.

VII

"**M**y darling," Renée says, throwing open her front door and pulling me in for a hug. I fall into her arms, bury my face in her chest, the intensity of the sandalwood oil she wears overwhelming everything. "What happened?"

The sobbing comes then, my entire body collapsing. I eventually wheeze out, "It was *so* humiliating," a bubble of snot popping and landing on the front of her caftan. She doesn't care and pulls me inside her house, and we stand in the entryway, rocking back and forth until I calm down.

She leaves me at the coatrack to ready the chambers, which is what she calls her music room. I always feel better when I'm at her house, my favorite house, my favorite place really. It's small, cramped, low to the ground and filled with trinkets, posters, scripts everywhere. Framed playbills from all the classics — *Cabaret, Miss Saigon, Les Misérables,* hang on her walls. A bust of the costume she wore as Cosette sits on a dummy in the corner, its shabbiness still somehow elevating the room around it, suggesting a grandeur most mortals will never get to experience. A tradition. It's powerful to see history like that.

When I'm here, the connection between me and every other artist who has pushed to become a star, who has tried and failed at the feet of the muse . . . it feels as if we're together in one room. We're the same. I am a part of them, and they are a part of me. When I really let myself feel it, it's powerful. I'm not alone in the universe; I am singing songs other women have been singing for thousands of years. We are one.

The house is foggy from all the humidifiers she constantly blasts to protect her vocal cords. I have to take off my sweater. "Come in!" she trills down the hallway. "Come in! Come in! Come in!" She always sings me in, because she knows I'll sing back, and I do: "I'm here!" My heart isn't in it, though; I feel wrung out and exhausted when I sit down on the bench next to her, my shoulders slumping forward, a posture that would usually cause Renée to rap on my back with her fan.

"What happened to you, my dear?" she asks. I lean forward and play a G, let the sound fill up the room and then fade away. Her Tony sits in a glass case on the wall across from the piano, glaring at me. She put it there for her students so we can imagine ourselves stepping onstage, accepting it, enveloped in applause. But today, it mocks me.

Renée seems to understand the brutality that has my soul in a headlock. "Shall we run some scales?"

I nod. And we do. For a bit. Until I choke up and have to stop, overcome by thoughts about herding little brats around. I've seen the kinds of kids they usually cast in these shows. Most of them are annoying and never do their notes. They try things onstage when they get bored, running around the theater pre-show while the professionals are trying to warm up. And there I'll be, on the sidelines, probably looking sweaty and gross, making sure their flies are zipped before they go onstage, to take their places in the world. To become who they're meant to be. While I stand on the sidelines and rot.

The story comes out in a tumble while Renée sits next to me, cooing and rubbing my back. "I hate children. I hate them," I say.

"Well, you can simply turn it down," Renée says. "There's no point in wasting your talent."

"You should've seen her. Michelle. She's so disorganized and behind. The production is going to suck. She practically begged me."

"She shouldn't have put you in this position," Renée says. "Your talent. Behind the scenes. Carrying around costumes. Babysitting brats. It's absolutely unseemly."

It's everything I want to hear, but I can't feel it. Instead, there is only emptiness chewing on my insides. The conversation with Rudy about my age, the number twenty-six flashing over my head like an omen, in time with the phrase *you're never going to work, you're never going to work, you're never going to work* over and over and over. I slam the piano lid shut. Renée jumps.

"Why don't we go have some tea?" she says, gesturing to the kitchen with a tip of her head, as if she wants to have this conversation away from her Tony, like it's about to bear witness to something and she can't trust it not to snitch.

I've never been in her kitchen. We step through the bead curtain, and I'm disappointed at just how bland it is, how boring. The cabinets are beige, the pulls rusty. I sit down at her table, something she probably inherited from her mother. It's chilling how different this room is from the music room, how bare. I blink in the harsh overhead light.

Renée busies herself with the kettle. She drops a teabag into a mug she then puts in front of me. It says, "Sopranos Sing It High."

"You know, there is another way to look at this." Renée is choosing her words carefully, gazing off into the distance and avoiding eye contact.

"What?" I ask.

"You can learn the part," Renée says, very gently. "You're going to be there. You'll know the part."

"What part?"

"Maria," she says. "The part you deserve."

"So?" Hopelessness overwhelms me. And then I think of the phone call, oh the phone call with my father where I will have to tell him it isn't going to happen, that he should flit off to Aruba with Sophie because there's nothing for him to see here.

"So, you'll know the part," Renée says again, very deliberately. The kettle starts to boil faster, the sound of it roiling. "You'll know the part, so if something should happen to Maria, you could step in to the role. The show must go on, after all."

"What?"

"They can't afford an understudy. You know that. They aren't budgeted for one. So, perhaps, Michelle offered you this role for a reason. Everything happens for a reason. Think about it. It really does mirror Maria's journey, keeps you close to the children, has you at the show every night. It's almost as if she's casting you as the understudy without casting you, you know?"

Renée picks up the kettle and pours the tea. An answer to a question. Possibility. A raw kind of hope blooms inside me. It does, in its own way, make sense. Theaters are always trying to find ways to save money. This way is risky for Michelle, and nefarious, but rumors about her poor budgeting are everywhere. They shut down the black box theater last year. The Company hasn't had a smash in years.

"The unions are so strict about this," Renée says. "And what better way to force you to embrace her, holistically — embrace Maria, embrace her journey — than to put you through the wringer? It's almost like a test. It's almost like she's pushing you into the method."

I consider this.

"The theater isn't, well, it isn't a place for the doe-eyed namby-pamby. You can't just sit there, waiting for someone to pick you. If you want it, Jessamyn, if you really, really want it, you have to take it."

Renée considers me as I digest this. I stay there for too long, much longer than I can afford to be there. When I leave, she pulls me into a hug, then hands me a folder and closes the door before I have a chance to look at what it is. It feels terrifying, this secret in my hands, even though it's just a plain black Duo-Tang. Still, I don't open it until I get home.

And when I arrive, it strikes me — right in the heart. She's handed me Maria's parts, the photocopied sheet music. She has thousands of these in her library, claims to pull them out all the time, can spend an afternoon doing any part she wants in the comfort of her own home. In my hands, it's an opportunity. But a dangerous one.

I sit down at my little keyboard and start practicing.

VIII

The morning of our first rehearsal arrives and I'm slumped outside the junky rehearsal studios attached to the Company's offices on Granville Island. I wish I smoked. Instead, I've got my peppermint roll-on stuffed up my nose. I'm breathing so deeply, desperate to relax. I'm about to burn my throat. The cast list was attached to the email telling me to come to this session, and of course, Samantha got Maria. Because she has a vlog. Because she was willing to go on the internet and beg. I didn't bother scanning the list after I saw that. I just slammed my laptop and had a glass of wine.

I hear giggling and see a tiny girl skipping toward the theater, her dad jogging next to her. She stops and hops into a puddle with both feet. "Julie, come on," her dad says, reaching down and swiping at the dirty, gray water splattered on his khakis. "We're going to be late."

He pulls her along as she laughs, and I want to throw up. She's tiny. And I'm going to be the one who makes sure she doesn't, like, choke on a grape or something. I hate this already.

"Jessamyn?"

Oh no. Rudy? He's locking up his bike at the rack across the alley, must've ridden up while I was spiraling about that child.

"What are you doing here?" I say it as mean as I can, hoping he'll take the hint. We're at the Company's second stage, a seaside black box that's now a rehearsal space — financial troubles pushed the smaller, weirder shows on which this company built its reputation to the wayside. Not that I mind, the artsy crowds are always a pain in the ass. They like to loiter and discuss after the show. Really take things in. And they always have something to complain about.

He ignores my slight. "Why are you skulking in the doorway?"

"I'm not skulking."

"What's that thing you're stuffing up your nose?" he asks, vaguely concerned. Like maybe I have a drug problem or something. I can tell he's been thinking about me, telling himself stories about who I am. Stories where I'm attainable, available. Attracted to snotty, pretentious bartenders.

"It's peppermint."

"Right."

"Can you just buzz off?" I wince at how pathetic it sounds. "Now is not the time."

"Okay." He turns toward the stage door.

"That's the stage door," I say.

"I know," he says, pulling it. And it might be some surprised rage, but I launch out of the alcove after him, not quite computing what he's saying.

"Why do you know where the stage door is?"

"I'm in the show. They were short on Nazis."

"You're in the show?" I repeat, slowly putting it together. "You went out for a musical? Wait, you're an actor?"

Rudy wiggles his eyebrows at me, and I realize I don't know much about him, other than his love of "real art" or whatever, and the fact that he just moved here a few months ago.

"I'm an actor," he says, and has the decency to sound at least a little bit ashamed.

"And you got cast. In this show."

"Yeah, I need the money."

My stomach sinks. "You're not the Captain."

He laughs. "No. Chorus. Nazi, dinner guest, I think they might even see how I look in a habit, though I do not want to shave."

"Oh, come on," I basically scream. To God or whoever it is that's spending all of their time chuckling while they twist the thumb screws on my dignity.

"Wait, are you in this?" he asks.

"No," I say, following him down the hall. "They hired me to be an acting coach for the kids."

Rudy dares to laugh at my humiliation. "I think you mean babysitter."

Dammit. I double down. "Acting coach."

"It's a babysitting job," he says. "Don't lie to yourself."

"I'm not lying, I had a meeting —"

He cuts me off. "We both know Michelle's too nice to say it. The kids need a babysitter to get them through hair and makeup, help them remember their lines. My ex did this for a run of *Billy Elliot*. It's a babysitting job."

I feel like an idiot, and I really regret going out for drinks the other night. Because once you let someone in on what's going on with you, you become attainable to them, become a part of their world, instead of your own little island where you get to make the rules. Control the narrative.

"I just think you should be honest with yourself about what you're in for."

"Oh, fuck off, why don't you," I say, then hear a gasp and spot another shrimpy kid, this one a boy, sitting on a bench, alone, a comic book on his lap.

"Get used to it." I roll my eyes at him and head inside. Rudy disappears and I'm grateful. I don't want to be seen walking in with a bartender anyway.

He's tall, I reason. That's probably why he got cast. Tall men are good in theater spaces — you can create great tableaus with them. Nice images. Levels. And if you're a man working in regional theater, you only have to be able to do one thing — sing, act, or dance. Usually it's sing. And then you just get to sway in the background while smiling women leap around you. Totally sexist. So disgusting. The world needs to change.

Inside, the rehearsal hall is bubbling over with conversation. It's packed. There're so many people. You can tell who the actors are though — they're prettier and shinier than everyone else. A group of greaseballs stand clumped together in the corner; I'm guessing they're the band. Some nerdy girls at the front hover next to a thick tree trunk of a woman wearing glasses who definitely has the posture of a stage manager — a gigantic binder tucked under her arm, a weariness to her that I can tell is only going to get worse. Michelle's talking to her rapidly and waving her hands over her head.

And then I spot the kids. They're clustered together, off to the side. Their parents are waiting for them, still wearing coats, clearly unsure as to what they should be doing. The boy with the comic book hurries in and sits down a few feet away from them and goes back to reading.

I suppose I should go over and introduce myself.

A girl from the Shakespeare festival, a reedy soprano with the purest horse girl energy, someone I cannot believe has been cast, waves me over, smiles at me through her big teeth.

"Jessamyn, hi. Can you believe it? I'm here."

"Sorry, do we know each other?" I ask, because it's always best to be the one who's forgotten the other person's name. A little trick I've developed over time that helps me maintain my edge.

"Oh my God, Jessamyn, I know, I lost like, twenty-seven pounds. It's me, Kathy! Remember? From Shakespeare on the Lake? Remember we did that hilarious movement class together? I used to not be able to hold my crab walk, but now I'm a part-time Pilates instructor."

"Oh, right. Hey." And now I'm not sure I remember who this is at all. It's the strange thing about that summer, everyone crowds together in my brain. I unfollowed all of them on social. It's not a good idea to be around other people constantly projecting their needs and successes on me. I just wanted to focus on me. On what I was doing. But sometimes I wish I had a better memory for this kind of thing.

"Isn't this, like, so exciting?" I can tell she thinks I'm going to be in the chorus alongside her. "I'm so glad I lost some weight, like, I get called in so much more often now. My life has totally changed." I smile and nod. "I saw you talking to that guy," she says, nodding at Rudy, who's sitting in the corner with a binder in his lap. "He's cute. Is that your boyfriend?"

Kathy starts to become clearer in my mind — a sort of strange fangirl, always off to the side, observing, her enthusiasm so palpable. I feel bad for her. Always excited about what's to come, endlessly optimistic about the future. That kind of energy isn't sustainable.

"No, I can't stand him," I say.

"Oh my God, what happened?"

"Nothing dramatic." I do remember her now. Such a sap. "He's just annoying. And maybe a little obsessed with me."

Kathy rolls her eyes a little as if to signal she understands what it's like to be constantly fending off men. "I'm so glad you're here," she says, putting a hand on my shoulder and tilting her head to one side. "It's really great to see you're still in theater. And so crazy to be reunited like this. We should go for drinks."

So she can brag about being in the chorus while I'm shunted off to the crew? No thanks.

I smile at her, give her a chirpy, "Yeah, totally!" then pretend to be looking for the kids. She'll find out I'm not in the show eventually. I don't want to be in her vicinity when she does.

···

"Are we going to do a get-to-know-you game?" one of the brats asks.

"No," I say.

"I have perfect pitch," another barks in my ear.

"Yeah right."

"I need to go to the bathroom."

"How is that my problem?"

We're only forty-five minutes into rehearsal and I'm tempted to walk up to the roof and throw myself into the sea. They've shunted me off to a side studio with streaky windows and now the kids are sitting on some aging gym mats, staring at me.

Half an hour after we were supposed to start, Michelle stepped into the middle of the room, frazzled as ever. Her glasses were fogged, sitting on the end of her nose. She waved her arms until everyone quieted down.

"Sorry, sorry," she said. "My teacher used to clap loudly, and I hated it. Hi, everyone, thanks so much for waiting." She then proceeded to introduce the creative team: music director/conductor, the stage management team, and the assistant directors. I was forced to raise my hand, smile graciously, and wave when she introduced me as "assistant director, kid's department." Vomit, vomit, all the vomit.

Captain von Trapp wasn't there, was coming in hot off a cruise ship contract at the end of the week. A cruise ship. And not even a good route — Alaska! What a hack.

That Kathy girl I allegedly know from Shakespeare on the Lake seemed impressed and excited that he was rolling in on a ship, was bowled over by the fact he'd been basically singing karaoke on the high seas for the last six months. Big whoop. As if I'd ever take a cruise ship contract. I only do the auditions for practice.

While the grown-ups worked on some blocking, we were shoved into this side room, so I could presumably help the kids warm up for choreography.

I count five, which is right, because the kids playing Liesl and Rolf are actually in their early twenties and I guess are considered professionals and don't need me. Usually there are seven children, but they merged the two youngest girls for budget, which makes sense. Seven is far too many.

"I thought they told us to warm up," says one of the tinier ones in glasses. I glare at her, and she shrinks immediately. Wimp.

"Run around the room," I say. "Ready, go."

None of them move.

"I hate running."

"Then jump around the room."

"This doesn't seem like an official warm-up."

"I have a hurt ankle."

"Fine, who knows how to stretch?"

One of the littler girls raises her hand, desperate for attention, any kind of attention, good or bad. "I do yoga," she says.

"You do?"

"I'm home schooled."

I eye her. She's wearing a top hat and a dressy vest over a Spider-Man T-shirt so, yeah, I believe her. It's high time we reconsider our negative stance on bullying. Has anyone ever considered it might, occasionally, be in the public good?

"Okay, everyone do what that one does." I point at her, then pull out my phone. Last night, my rep, after a long argument about my acceptance of this job, sent me sides for a commercial. The audition is tomorrow evening, and apparently, I'd best make it out for it.

"My name is Carla." She readjusts her top hat.

I squint, thinking back to my introduction to these kids' parents. There definitely wasn't a Carla.

"No, it isn't," I say.

"It's Francesca," she says, really emphasizing the "ca."

We have a little liar on our hands. Perfect.

"I thought you said you could do yoga."

"I can," she says.

"Well prove it then." I go back to my phone and open the sides. *Mom Opens Yet Another Bill She Cannot Pay Unless Her Husband Gets His Job Back*. I start reading.

Carla bends over and does a handstand. The littlest girl sits cross-legged and stares at the ground, her fists on her cheeks. I can tell she wants sympathetic attention, because I've definitely used that posture before and I'm not falling for it. The other one, the older one with perfect pitch, comes over and leans on my shoulder. I freeze up. I am being touched by a child.

And she doesn't seem to notice my ick. She's probably used to older performers enjoying her presence because she's cute, I guess.

Well, was cute. She seems to be just out of that phase, moving toward her teenage years. She'll spend some time in limbo, greasy and disgusting, waiting to see what puberty will do to her face.

A career-defining time for a child actor. Stressful. Yes. Unfair? Absolutely. But true.

"What's that?" she asks. "What are you reading?"

"Sides," I say.

"You're an actor?"

"Yes."

"Then why aren't you in the show?"

I feel that one in my stomach. She's got long, braided pigtails, this girl. I consider what it'd be like to grab one of those pigtails and stick it in a paper shredder, just watching it pull her face toward the blades while she begs me to *Turn it off, turn it off, oh please God turn it off.*

I grin and bare my teeth a little. "Because I was told you all needed a lot of help. A lot. So, they're paying me big money to teach you how to act. Bigger than I would've made in the chorus."

"What?" The girl jumps back, horrified and lets out a theatrical gasp.

"It's true."

She gasps again!

I can relate to her dramatic attitude. I too was twelve once. When I was her age, I fake-fainted in the middle of a McDonald's when the line was too long. My father kept looking at his watch, looking up and over the heads of the people in front of us, making these restless sounds as if it was the worst thing that had happened to him all day. But I was so terribly hungry, and the entire situation just felt so impossible, so I collapsed — closed my eyes and crumpled to the floor, let my body go limp. A woman actually screamed *Oh my goodness!* And my father, well . . . I don't know what he did, because my eyes were closed. He certainly didn't fall all over himself, desperate to save my life. There was no shocked gasping, no wailing, no fear.

Someone called an ambulance. I never revealed it was a performance, but I knew it was authentic because I was rushed to the hospital, the siren roaring overhead, an oxygen mask covering my mouth. At least three people were standing over me, so much care in the way they spoke to me, so much fear and determination in their eyes. They weren't going to let me flatline. Not on their watch. My father met us there. Didn't even ride with me.

Of course, I was fine. I was released the same day. But I'll never forget that feeling — sitting in the hospital bed, everyone gazing at me, giving me all the attention I knew I deserved and knowing that I'd just nailed that performance. I was flawless. I never felt more loved in my life.

"It'll be okay." I pat her on the shoulder. "You just have to do everything I say." She walks off, sick to her stomach. The two boys are now doing headstands, the littlest girl is crying, and the other girl, the one who was supposed to be leading the warm-up, is staring out the window at seagulls while hugging the bound pages of her script, like a little creep.

If anyone were to walk in, it wouldn't look so good. I clap my hands together.

"Okay, all of you, stand up and touch your toes."

They ignore me.

I clap my hands again, louder, but still they ignore me. They're all watching the eldest boy do a handstand.

And then it happens. The eldest girl, the one who wouldn't shut up about her perfect pitch, the one with all the questions, who I crushed with the truth about her lackluster acting, leans over and shoves him. I don't know how it happens, but the boy screams and flails, tumbling out of his handstand, and kicks the younger girl in the face.

A scream, and then blood everywhere.

Hell.

I am in hell.

IX

Anton rubs my feet as I tell him about rehearsal. He purchased an expensive lotion I asked for without questioning it, even though I know it's more than he can afford. He's some weird robot computer researcher up at the university and has been stuck in his Ph.D. for seven years. He spends most of his time trying to teach robots to read sheet music with the end goal of having a robot write a musical that I then perform. It sounds like a completely dumb idea, because the root of music is feeling and robots can't feel. But whenever we talk about it, Anton gets snappy, so I don't say anything. I'm not super interested anyway, if I'm being honest, but a part is a part. I'd sing his stupid robot songs if the contract was right.

He slides his fingers between my toes and squeezes, barely suppressing a moan. I don't think I've ever met someone as horny as Anton. And when I say horny, I don't mean he's always trying to throw me over his shoulder and take me to bed. It's this really intense energy he has, this strange, panting quality about him, like he doesn't really believe I'm here — he can't quite compute what I'm getting out of this relationship.

It's this horny energy that drives him to bike across town in the pouring rain to pick me up — because I refuse to pay for an Uber. Then he trucks us back to his basement apartment where he heats up some weird lentil dish he's made for dinner, and then he sits and listens to me talk about my day with such intensity he has to remind himself to blink.

And I tell him about it all — about the children and how miserable they are at their choreography, which I learned in five minutes flat, by the way, losers. How they never pay attention to anything, how they don't seem to be treating this opportunity with any kind of care or respect for how special it is. To finally have this vision of themselves confirmed by an objective power; to finally get to lean into themselves, truly. Yet these miscreants dance around the opportunity, like a flock of screeching banshees. They flout the gifts the muse hath given them. It is, in itself, the biggest insult I have ever personally borne witness to.

After dealing with the bloody nose, we spent most of the afternoon locked in the side room, running a very basic number over and over again. I played Maria, and when Michelle came in to observe, I made absolutely zero mistakes. I was radiant. I was surprised she didn't bring Samantha in to see me and say, "See, Sam? This is what I'm talking about."

No, instead when we took a break, the stupid kids swarmed her, and she put her hands on her knees and spoke down to them like they were morons. "Are we having fun with Jessamyn?"

Fun?

Is that really what we're meant to be doing in here?

Of course, I didn't say that. I just laughed, and thankfully, none of the brats sold me out. They've got survival instincts. I was worried for a minute, when the littlest one, the pouter, tugged on Michelle's wrist and pulled her down, whispered something in her ear. But Michelle gave her a big hug and said, "We're definitely going to rehearse on the big stage. Just not right now, there's another show using it. In three weeks, we'll move up there."

"In three weeks?" The little kid asked.

"Yes, we go off the island to the big theater." Michelle said. "That's where the big stage is."

And then Michelle left, without a word to me. Not a compliment or anything gracious. She didn't even give me any notes. So strange. She must be intimidated. Or regretful. Feeling badly that she cast Samantha instead of Jessamyn.

I put my left foot down and give Anton my right, which he gladly massages while I complain more about Samantha. He laps it up.

"You're absolutely going to take over for that Samantha girl. An opera singer? In a musical?" He lets out a *pshhh*. I have this urge to put him in his place whenever he tries to weigh in on anything theater related — he acts like he knows what he's talking about, but he doesn't. Not really.

Like one time he pronounced "mise-en-scène" as "m-eyes in seen," and I laughed and pronounced it correctly and he locked himself in the bathroom and wouldn't come out until I told him he was a genius. I know it sounds absolutely nuts, but he was in there for six hours. I think he cried. But then I cried too, and we sat on either side of the door, and I'd never felt so emotionally fulfilled in my life, trying to coach him out from the cage that was separating us.

I've had to read for a few roles since, and I always recall how I felt. How I was afraid and exhausted and broken up and a little bit horny, and all of those emotions collided there, in that moment. And when he came out, we had the wildest sex.

I booked at least two commercials based on memories of those orgasms. No question. You think a housewife picking tiny pieces out of her new lint ball isn't radiating with horny energy? Think again. That commercial got syndicated and paid for my Invisaligns.

"I've seen Samantha's work. Pedestrian. Simpering. Not even close to what you bring."

Later, when we're sitting at his little kitchen table, eating the weird lentil soup he made, which actually has gotten a lot better with my coaching, he puts his hand over mine and squeezes.

"I don't like to see you like this."

"Like what?" I ask.

"Depressed."

"I'm not. I'm thinking. I'm plotting. I'm not depressed."

"What are you plotting?"

"Renée thinks I could win the role in the rehearsal room. That they might want me to learn the part, that this is just some method exercise to get me there."

"Renée," he says, looking into my eyes intensely, "is a genius. I know you can do it. I know you can."

I stare down at my lentils, affecting a persona I know he wants from me: unsure, broken, exhausted. Because now he can save me. He can lift me up.

"Are you sure?"

"More than anything, I'm positive. You deserve that role. Not Samantha. You."

"But how do you know?"

I've asked him this before, and he never disappoints. He rattles off all of the highlights from my performances, which he so cannot forget. When I fell to my knees in *Alien XXX* and sobbed in the center of the stage for a solid five minutes. The entire room was suspended on a single breath, incapable of moving because my grief at losing my alien husband was felt so deeply. The Jeep commercial where I played an adventurous woman out on a daytrip who changes her own tire. Was ever the spirit of the open road so firmly supplanted in thirty seconds? And then the creepiest one, the thing that makes me wonder what is really going on with Anton. My Shakespeare on the Lake monologue. My audition, a scene from *Hamlet*.

He always says the same thing. "When I heard you whisper the words of the bard, I knew right then that I had to do anything I could to help you become the star you were meant to be."

The one thing he will not admit to me is how he heard that monologue. Where he was when I performed it. Because as far as I know, there were only two people in that room, sitting at a table. It was a black box theater with nothing to hide behind. He didn't work at the venue. It scares me a little bit. He scares me. Where was he? How does he know? How could he know?

I finish my lentil soup. He takes the bowl over to the sink, then makes us both mugs of tea. It's all very innocent and I shake off any lingering fear. I know him now. He's harmless.

"You know," he says in a tone that I don't recognize. "I think you should move in with me."

Silence. I bite down on a laugh. What?

"Move in. I could take care of you while you fight for Maria."

Oh my God. The silence expands between us.

"It's just an idea."

"I don't think I can do that," I say carefully. This is new. He's never asked me for anything, not really. Never asked me to be something or do anything publicly. I thought we had an understanding, that we both knew what this was. He turns and glares at me.

"Why not? You're here all the time."

Well, that's a gross exaggeration. I scramble for a reason that isn't "because you're sort of weird." Think of what he admires about me. Art. Right.

"Creatively, I just need space," I say. "But thank you."

His face contorts, and I can't tell if he's going to scream or cry. Or both. I look up at the light above, a white bulb hanging from a beaded steel rope that's so strong it makes the entire kitchen seem far too bright.

And then he upends the table. Dishes fly through the air, glass smashes on the ground. "I do everything for you!" he screams and storms out of the room.

His bedroom door slams behind him, the force of which shakes the house. Usually I would go with him, retreat into this imaginary universe where we're just two hot people enraged and horny, whose lives are glamorous and not *lentil soup* and not *let's move in together to save money.*

This kind of passion is exactly what I need to keep going, but I'm just not feeling it. I remind myself that nothing bad happened, not really. He didn't hurt me. My body is fine. And the idea that a man as pathetic as he could truly have an impact on my spirit? Laughable.

Even though my heart is pounding hard and fast. I feel hives creeping up my neck. Thick welts form that I'll have to cover with makeup tomorrow before rehearsal. Doesn't matter. I'll be fine.

Anton's sobbing in the other room. Good. He should feel horrible. I stand up, pick my way through the broken glass, the lentil slop on the floor, and leave. He'll text me soon to say that he's sorry, that he's nothing, that I am everything. Things will go back to normal. They always do.

X

Rudy's waiting outside before rehearsal, smoking a cigarette. My phone buzzes as I approach. It's my father, asking for hotel recommendations for when he comes to see me do Maria. I ignore it.

Rudy nods at me as I walk up. Sides for another audition are hanging out of the pocket of my leather jacket, just so everyone in this show knows that if I wanted, I could quit this job and take a part somewhere better, that it could happen for me at any moment.

"How're the brats?" he asks, smiling a little. I roll my eyes. Brats. He doesn't think they're brats — he knows all of their names. It's so sad when a guy pretends to be something he isn't just so I'll like him.

"The brats are brats."

"They seem to like you."

"How do you know?"

"I noticed. You're a natural."

"With kids?"

"Just like Maria." He grins. He's trying to flirt with me. It's not the worst feeling in the world. "Whatcha got there?"

"Oh, just another commercial." I take the sides out of my pocket and start fanning myself with them.

"Another mom who just can't keep it together?"

"You know it."

"Want help with it later? Go for a drink, maybe?"

"Help? From you?" I size him up; it makes him squirm. He sticks his chest out, just the littlest bit. I have him, I so have him. "You ever booked a commercial?"

"No, but I'd like to learn. You know, from the best."

"Maybe." I've got to keep him on the hook, so he'll think about me for the rest of rehearsal.

A car pulls up and one of the brats climbs out. I'm supposed to meet them out here, on the sidewalk, so no perverts can snatch them up between here and the doors to the theater. It's the weirdest girl, the liar.

"Jessamyn!" she shouts and runs up to me. "Is this your boyfriend?"

"Him?" I say, smiling. "No, I have a way cooler boyfriend."

"Not possible," Rudy says. The girl stares at him, her mouth open a little bit. "See you in there." He winks and walks off. She watches him, then reaches into her pocket, pulls out a handful of Cheerios, and starts eating them.

The oldest girl, Lily, runs at us from another vehicle. "Jessamyn, I learned all my lines."

"Don't you only have five?"

"Yeah," she says, just a little bit defensive. "So, I have to nail them." She clocks the stack of pages in my hand. "What's that?"

"Sides. I have an audition for a commercial later."

"Can I see?"

I hand over the sides, and she flips through them.

"You're not old enough to play a mom," she says. Now this one has quickly become my favorite.

"I have a costume and a wig," I say. She hands the sides back to me.

"My mom says I can't do commercials."

"Why not? The money's good."

"She says she doesn't want to stink up my resumé with hack material."

"You know, maybe you should get a different manager," I say. "Your mom might be messing up some opportunities for you. Something to think about."

"Yeah," Lily says. "Yeah, I guess."

"You get a national commercial, you get money and exposure for years." I don't know if it's true, but I like the way this kid is talking to me. Finally, some deference.

"You know," she says, "my vocal coach says I'm not supposed to tell people this because it makes them feel bad, but can I tell you something?" I eye her, feeling suddenly suspicious of her motives. "You know how we were singing yesterday in rehearsal? And how I have perfect pitch?"

"Vaguely."

"Well, sometimes . . . you're flat."

"Am not."

"I told you, I have perfect pitch," she says. I'm about to rip into her, to demand the credentials of whoever told her she has perfect pitch. Because there's no universe where I'm flat. I mean, I'm not perfect, sure. We all miss notes. But I'm not unknowingly flat. And I wasn't yesterday. But I hold back, because she's a kid. Because I'm supposed to love this child, despite her idiocy.

"And it's only sometimes," she says. "Sometimes you're good."

Sometimes? Good? Her words stab me. Good doesn't make it on Broadway. No. This can't be right. I've been to see Renée every night this week. I've been living off hardboiled eggs and discount shrimp rings to pay for it. There's no way I can possibly be "sometimes flat" or just "good." It's an impossibility. Because . . . what, Renée is just lying to me when she calls me transcendent? Absolutely not. She has a Tony.

"Don't get mad," Lily says. She reaches up and takes my hand. I can tell: she's had to learn to be kind like this, to answer for her wildly inhumane treatment of others. "Samantha's flat sometimes, too. But she's more often sharp. Though her tone is pretty incredible."

Disagree. Samantha's tone is not incredible! It's reedy and thin! How come no one is with me on this?

Whatever. I don't know why I'm listening to her. Lily's just some mush-brained child. Likely jealous of me.

I follow her gaze to where Samantha is set up near the door, her cellphone propped up on a tripod. "Oh my God, you guys," I see her mouthing. "I'm so excited."

"She's such a phony," I say without thinking. I realize too late I shouldn't be talking shit about Samantha in front of the children. Probably.

"I don't think she's ever booked anything outside of Canada," Lily says, relieved that we have a shared enemy.

"What a loser," I say. "You know, she told me she hates working with kids but lied to Michelle about it."

"Wow."

"How old are you, anyway?" I ask, suddenly curious about my new ally.

"Ten." She straightens up. "I'm almost eleven."

The final kid arrives, the younger boy, and just like that, the gang of us is complete, and only ten minutes late. We march toward the theater.

"Want to see me spit?" he asks.

"No."

"We're meeting the Captain today."

"Really," I say. "Interesting."

"I heard he's tall."

"I heard he's a boat captain."

"I heard he's a baritone," someone else says.

"Well, that has to be true," I say. "The part is for a baritone."

"Are you going to go out with him?" Lily asks. My little ally.

"Maybe," I say. "If he's hot." She giggles, and when I ask her to lead the other kids in warm-up, she does.

...

After a morning of the kids learning harmonies from the music director and fidgeting and asking me if they can go to the bathroom and getting "bored," I let them break for lunch early and take them outside to sit by the water.

Flocks of seagulls circle overhead, swooping down occasionally to try and steal our lunches. The kids take turns chasing the birds, throwing bits of food to them only for the seagulls to run and scream and fly away and then come back again moments later.

There are several texts waiting for me from my father, with links to Vancouver luxury hotels; questions I don't know the answer to. Surely his little girlfriend can handle a hotel booking. Can't she? Last I checked, she was so good at spending his money.

I pull out a baked sweet potato wrapped in tin foil and bite down on an edge of it. It's gone quite cold and mushy, and the entire experience of chewing and swallowing makes me feel an irrational kind of anger. The rage boils so hot I don't even really notice the hunk of aluminum foil I've bitten down on. Right as I spit it out, the adult performers pour outside — I'm hacking and coughing, and my eyes are watering as they walk past me. None of them notice, though. They're on union time.

I watch Samantha and the Captain (Steve), who we were briefly introduced to earlier, walk together along the boardwalk. I can't hear them, but she seems to be talking very quickly, gesticulating wildly. He nods, his hands clasped together behind his back. When they reach the end of the pier, she pulls out her cellphone and turns to take a selfie with him. He puts a hand on her shoulder, shakes his head. It's interesting, this dynamic. I can tell his denial pisses her off. It's all in her body.

It's why she's such a horrendous actress; she can't hide anything. You have to stomp it all down. You have to bury it. You have to bury all the messy parts and let your bright parts shine.

His phone seems to ring. He takes it out, pressing it to his ear and leaving her alone. It's hard not to . . . like it. Watching her be rejected. Even if that's not really what happened, it's the story that I prefer. Cracks forming between the two of them are only good for me. He ducks in to an alcove. I stand and wander over to a garbage can, wait, listen while keeping one ear open for any wailing from the kids. They are quiet, which is perfect. As they should be. This job is basically going to do itself.

"Yeah, it's me," the Captain says. "Can we get out of this?"

I bite down on a smile. Yes. Yes. Yes. Oh my gosh. I can't help but love this. He already wants to quit the show!

"Why? The cast is . . . It's just . . . budget."

Budget? I guess. But he is a Canadian theater performer. We're not exactly rolling in it.

"They're going to reflect badly on me," he says. "I can already tell. They've cut one of the child roles to save money. There are no understudies. Is that even legal?"

I laugh at how dumb he sounds. Legal? This is theater. Someone's spent too much time on the high seas. Steve leans against the corrugated metal of the building, squeezing his eyes shut.

"You're right. The relationship is important. I'll try my best."

"What are you doing?"

I jump. I turn and see Rudy hovering over my shoulder, his cheek inches from mine. Loser.

"Nothing," I say, though it's obvious I was eavesdropping. Whatever.

A sharp screech fills the air. I leap out of my skin and hurry back over to the kids. What is it now? The boys are standing near the edge of wharf, the younger one pointing out to sea.

"Dead body!" he screams.

Rudy and I race over. All of the kids gather round and peer down. Except it isn't a dead body, no, it's a man in a scuba suit, scraping something off one of the yachts bobbing at the dock.

"He's just cleaning the hull," Rudy says. The man can't hear us, clearly, his entire body encased in shining black foam. "He's not dead." The man dives down beneath the surface. The kids watch him curiously.

"Is that his job?" the younger boy asks. "That's so cool."

"Wicked," the older one says.

He might be older than Lily. It's hard to tell because his voice hasn't dropped yet. Michelle's clearly playing with fire here, as, judging by the acne scars on his face, it's going to happen any day now. I wonder if I'm short enough to take his place. I could strap my tits down, get a little Dutch boy haircut. Hunch a little. It could totally work.

The kids, bored now of watching the man scrape junk off the yachts, go back to their lunches and phones.

"Don't be salty I caught you eavesdropping," Rudy says.

I ignore his chide. "How's the morning?"

"Oh, boy," he says, shaking his head. "That guy is something else."

"The Captain?"

"Yup." Rudy smiles, and I can tell I'm about to eat up this gossip. He tells me how the Captain showed up with some ideas about his character, big ideas, that Michelle didn't share. How he had suggestions for every bit of blocking; how he reacted when playing scenes with Samantha. Every time she said a line, he'd fall out of the scene and grimace, saying, "Sorry, can we take it again?" And that after, Rudy heard him bitching to the stage manager that Samantha's delivery "just didn't feel honest."

Apparently, Michelle was near tears when they called lunch.

"Man, that guy is a real piece of work. Seemed annoyed with Samantha just for existing. Hey, you know how she keeps going around forcing people to be on her vlog? What's up with that?"

I shrug. "She's always lacked professional boundaries."

Rudy nods. "I get the social media thing. Everyone should be doing it. Seems like it's part of the job now. But it'd be nice if she asked first."

I'm lapping this up. Rudy seems relieved, like we've finally found common ground. "Do you want to split some noodles?" he asks. "My treat."

I think about the grease, but my stomach seems to have already absorbed the sweet potato, the sides of it sticking together. The thought of trying to make it through the afternoon without something else makes it twist. I tell him that I need to stay and watch the kids, make sure they don't murder a seagull. He laughs. I've got him in the palm of my hand, just like the others. He'll certainly be useful. It'll be good to have an ally in the rehearsal room.

A few minutes later, he returns with a gigantic serving of pad thai and offers me a fork, which I gladly accept. Lily's nearby, seems to be trying not to look at us.

"Hello, Lily," Rudy says.

"Hi." She's sizing up Rudy, maybe deciding if she has a crush on him, what kind of grown up he is. It's amazing to me that he's learned the names of these children already. Insane, really.

"How are you liking rehearsals so far?"

"Okay, I guess," she says. "I thought we'd have had more time with the director by now."

"She's a little disorganized," Rudy says. "But I think you'll get your shot this afternoon. We're going to block the party."

"With the dance?" I interrupt, my mouth full.

"I guess," Rudy says. "I didn't read the scene."

"What?" the girl asks.

"Listen, by the time you're my age, you'll be able to pick up on things like that," Rudy says, snapping his fingers.

Lily gives him an if-you-say so look. "What's your best credit?" she asks him. I choke on a bit of tofu, laughing. The kid really knows how to cut to the chase.

"Um, I was in the chorus on Broadway for *Hairspray*," he says.

Lily stands up and opens her mouth wide. "What."

"I was."

"You made your Broadway debut?"

"I guess, yeah," he says. "I've done some touring productions, too."

"What. The. Hell are you doing here?" she demands. "How old were you when you got your visa?"

Rudy shrugs. "I was nineteen. And, well, you know. Sometimes life gets in the way."

I know that desperate feeling. The cost of the visa, weighing when you should try to get it, questioning if you've done enough to earn it. And to imagine him just walking away.

"Do you have your green card?" Lily seems to be hovering on the edge of disbelief, and honestly, I don't blame her. It's batshit crazy that he's been to Broadway and is here, now, at his age. Back in Canada, where everything is so, so much smaller.

"You know, I made second round for *Matilda*," she says, desperate to impress him. "But I was too old."

"Bummer," he says.

"I got offered chorus, but my mom said it was a bad business decision."

"Yeah, well," Rudy says. "You're not paying rent now — you can afford to make those choices."

Lily grins. I can tell she loves being spoken to like she's one of the grown-ups. A professional. Man, this whole childcare thing is a piece of cake. So easy to deal with kids once you figure out what they want. People are so dramatic about raising children. What a load. Just figure out what they want and give it to them, and they'll leave you alone. I should write a parenting book.

One of the girls on the stage management team leans out the door, a half-eaten foil-wrapped burrito in one hand. "That's five!" she calls, her mouth thick with rice and beans.

Rudy dusts his hands off. "I should get back," he says and waits.

"Have a good rehearsal," I say. I can tell he was expecting more — for me to follow him — which is exactly why I don't give it to him.

I turn to Lily. She perks up. "Can you do me a favor?" She's the special one. The one I can rely on. "Can you go round them up?"

"Yes, I can!" She runs over to where the boys are still huddled around an iPhone, then to the other two girls. I should probably be paying more attention to the littlest one. She's so small. She's just been eating sushi, anyway, and singing to herself, having a great time. The other girl, the weirdo who can do yoga, is standing at the end of the pier, staring off into the distance, her arms wrapped across her belly.

Lily takes the littlest girl's hand and yells at the boys and the weirdo, and we all head back inside. A seagull starts screaming its head off. As I open the creaking door to the rehearsal hall, I see Samantha walking back toward the theater, wiping tears from her cheeks with the sleeve of her purple coat.

XI

It's early, too early. I've just woken up, am standing in my little bathroom, staring into the mirror. I'm about to start my daily affirmations, the first step in a complex morning routine I concocted to ferry me toward greatness: I gaze at my reflection, tell myself I'm the most beautiful woman in the world, the most talented. I will be on Broadway. I say it over and over again. Then Pilates, green tea, vocal warm-ups, rehearsal. All of this comes screeching to a halt when my agent texts and requests a quick chat.

A slave to the dollar, this man. If I did everything his way, he'd have me on my knees, shilling for big FroYo, food delivery services that break labor laws, hemorrhoid wipes.

We've been at odds for a while — he simply cannot understand my choice to accept this childminding position. He doesn't understand what it takes; he never has. Still, it's good to have a rep, especially when you're in conversation with others. There's no better feeling in the world than saying, "Actually, I have to take this" when your phone rings while out with friends.

Sorry, I can't make it; I'm hopping on a call.

Even when people say they haven't heard of your agent, you just get to smile, knowingly. *It's boutique. A very select client list. Of course YOU haven't heard of him.*

"I have a play for you," he texts me. "Call me back."

And I do, because this is new for him. I wonder how he even heard about a play. What is this? My agent actually trying for once? Shocking.

"I think it's a great part for you, Jessamyn, real juicy."

"What is it?"

"Still in workshop with Seventh Street in Toronto, but the buzz is Canada-wide."

"Really?" This is strange. "What's the part?"

"So, you're playing a nun. I figured because you were so stoked on *The Sound of Music* you might want —"

"I'm excited about my current role because it's a musical," I say. "Is this a musical?"

"No," he says. "But you're playing this totally badass nun who stood up to the church and stuff. Everyone is really excited about it. There are big names circling this part, but the producers are interested in newer faces."

"Wow," I say, trying to sound vaguely interested, because, you know, relationships are so important. Even if it is just a play. "What does she stand up to the church about?"

"HIV."

"Ugh."

"I know, real bummer. But it's a searing new work about how we must stand up to institutions when they do wrong." I don't laugh, but I want to. He must be reading this from the email.

"There have been so many plays about AIDS," I cut in. "Like, so many. We get it. It was bad. But c'mon, they couldn't have done tuberculosis or something?" I try to think of diseases. "What about smallpox? Think they'd be open to changing it?"

"No," he says. "But they're really excited to see you. They'll be in Vancouver next week."

I leave a little silence between us. Really let it fester. "Great," I say, but like how you'd say it when you'd rather suck on a hot curling iron. I didn't want him to think I was into it. Not at all. Because with men, you never want to seem, like, happy with them. You never want them to get comfortable.

"Would it interfere with *The Sound of Music?*"

He runs through the dates. I'd have to be in Toronto for all of December for rehearsals. It's not even a Christmas show. I tell him to pass.

"But you're not . . . really . . . in *The Sound of Music,*" he says. And while I could've made some snarky remark, I remain silent. And in that silence, he grows uncomfortable, starts babbling about direction and growth and how I should really consider chasing work outside of the musical theater space. This could be a breakout role for me. Get me to Toronto. Toronto! Ha! As if it is difficult to get to Toronto. I want New York. I want London. I want to be flown private to Dubai to perform for a sheikh for an exorbitant amount of money, then get canceled online and have to donate my fee to charity.

Which. Ugh. My agent thinks an AIDS play in Toronto is going to get me there? Really?

"Promise me you'll look at the sides," he says.

"Promise," I say back. He emails them to me and, of course, I don't bother opening it.

•••

For once, the children are quiet. They're paying attention to the choreographer in the middle of the room as she explains the blocking for the big dinner scene all over again. We tried to get through this yesterday, but the Captain kept stopping and restarting, so much that Michelle called rehearsal early to huddle with the stage management team. Now we're back at it.

It helps that the boy playing Kurt has been dragged up almost immediately to dance with Samantha. The other kids are clearly jealous — he's the first one, the one who gets to walk among the grown-ups. I can feel Lily, swathed in jealousy, so desperate to be seen — she wants applause before she's done the work.

The chorus has allegedly learned their choreography already. We're supposed to be working on the flow of the scene, the entrances and exits. I'm sitting with the children, in the crowd, as if I'm already Maria. I almost want to drag the littlest one onto my lap, but I figure that might be a bit much. And I'm not sure I trust her. Looks like a biter.

Our Captain sits alone on an old piano bench, watching with a bemused expression as the choreographer walks Samantha and Kurt through their paces. It's the scene where Maria dances with the kid — *one two three one two three one two three* — but he messes up so badly, it gives his father an excuse to take over. And then things get horny.

The dance itself is sort of a mix between a folk dance and a waltz. In the film version, it's the most romantic moment between Maria and the Captain, when the two of them realize their feelings for one another — feelings so intense that Maria runs off, terrified of how her life is about to change.

"And then Captain von Trapp steps up —" the choreographer says, glaring over her shoulder at the Captain, who stays seated with his legs crossed, a smug smile on his lips.

"Do you mind if I observe this round?" he asks after a long, awkward beat. "It's part of my process."

Samantha bristles, her eyes widening with rage. The Captain doesn't notice, or maybe he doesn't care. He's fresh off a cruise ship contract, after all. This must seem so pedestrian after so many nights singing ABBA under the neon lights of a dinner theater, following fake-tanned divorcées back to their staterooms.

"Of course," Michelle says, stepping in when it seems the choreographer is about to tell the little brat to get up here, right now. "Big respect to your process. Can we get a volunteer?"

"I don't see how it helps your process to not experience the movement," Samantha says. I almost applaud her moxie, but then I remember I hate her. "We're learning the steps. That's like learning lines."

"I want to see how it's supposed to look."

"Why will that help?"

The entire room is hovering on a pin.

Michelle steps between them. "Why don't we —"

"I don't want to take five," Samantha says, a sharpness to her voice, a strength that surprises me. "We already lost hours yesterday because of him."

"Okay, then consider this me . . . stepping in," Michelle says. "Let's all be respectful of how others learn."

Samantha's cheeks burn red. She bites down, her jaw tensing. If she keeps that up, she's going to start grinding her perfect white teeth. "Well," she says, smiling congenially, "I guess I should take a seat then, with my Captain, to learn from his process. If I'm such an amateur." She sits right next to him on the piano bench and crosses her arms. "You see, I haven't had the opportunity to do cruise ships. I'm still learning." The snide, clipped ending to the word "ships" makes a few of the chorus members giggle.

Samantha raises an eyebrow as if to say *so there*. The former chub with the red hair nods in approval. Michelle freezes and her shoulders begin to roll together as if she's about to start crying. I realize: this is my time. Right now. What she needs is a hero.

"Why don't I do it?" I say, leaping to my feet, remembering what Renée said about opportunity, about how I just need to be there. To be a better option. "I can show them. Happy to help." Total Maria move, being helpful. Being empathetic. I'm doing it. I'm totally doing it. How kind is this, right? So kind. So thoughtful. Full Maria.

"Me too," Rudy says, from his seat in the crowd.

He smiles at me, almost embarrassed, as we cross the room and meet in the middle. Maybe he, too, understands that this show doesn't have understudies. Maybe he also knows how to play the game. He's just come from Broadway, after all, where dreams are worth killing for. Him mirroring me, well, it gives me confidence that I'm doing the right thing.

"All right, great," Michelle says, rolling with it. "Thanks for stepping up."

I can tell the choreographer wants to mutiny, but instead she leads us through the steps. Rudy's hand is firm, warm on my waist. He expertly holds my arm aloft as we waltz. He seems so confident at first, but he keeps one eye on the ground and the other on the side of my face. I've never been so fully aware of how nervous I make him.

He accidentally steps on my foot and blushes. "Sorry."

"You should be." I squeeze our clammy hands together as we follow the choreographer and her assistant. It's a simplified version of the scene in the film, likely to accommodate both Samantha and the Captain's dancing prowess, which I'm sure is sorely lacking.

"Now spin," the choreographer says, "spin . . . spin . . . spin . . . yes!"

We travel across the room, weaving our hands together, stepping back and forth, tangling, stopping, a correction. But I'm perfect. I know it. This is it. This is the moment I've been waiting for, for years. Everyone is watching me. My heart fills so quickly I think it'll burst.

XII

I'm waiting at the pickup point with the youngest boy, who is running circles around a yellow concrete pylon, when Rudy pulls up next to me on his bike.

"So," he says, adjusting his cool boy messenger bag. "That was tense, eh?"

"Pretty unprofessional," I agree. Rudy and I ran the choreography over and over again, until Samantha stormed out of the room and the entire rehearsal ended early. Again.

I'm expecting him to give me a compliment, compare me to Samantha. To say that I dance professionally, that I'm clearly up to par and it won't be long before Samantha's out and Jessamyn is in. Instead, he takes out a pack of cigarettes and rolls one between his thumb and forefinger.

"Why don't you just get a vape?"

"This looks cooler." He puts it behind his ear.

"And no bike helmet."

"I like to live on the edge."

The kid finishes running around the pylon and starts stumbling, exaggerated movement. He slams into me.

"Hey, watch it," I say.

"Skylar," Rudy says. "You're going to fall over if you keep doing that."

"That's the idea," he says, spinning and bouncing into the wall of the building next to us.

"But if you get hurt, you won't get to be in the show."

"Yes I will, I signed a contract," he says.

Rudy laughs. "Kid's got a point." He then appears to check me out, gives me a furtive glance. I can tell he's about to follow up with an ask — a date, a drink, a lifetime together in love — precisely as Vishal's Audi pulls up and honks once.

Rudy sizes up Vishal's car. His face falls, for just an instant, and then the wry smugness returns.

"Now that is polite," Rudy says. I wave to Vishal, ignoring Rudy while gesturing to the kid who is now rolling against the side of the building. Vishal appears annoyed that I'm making him wait. He texted me to let me know he was coming, and I told him I had to wait for this kid's parents. It's rare for Vishal to pick me up himself, and this is the second time he's done so this week, which could mean only one thing.

He wants to do something weird in bed. It's possible I assume too much, but I speak from experience here. See, a while back, I had this much older boyfriend. We were together for about a year. He bought me clothes, took me out to eat. That part was fantastic. For a while, I thought it was a status thing — he liked to be seen with someone young and beautiful and vibrant and creative and talented. And I do think most people would expect an attractive woman like me to be seen in the company of an older man. To seek that kind of security. But they never really know what goes on in those sorts of relationships. What it's like.

For example, this guy took me on vacation with him, to this exclusive ski town in the mountains. I should've seen the red flags from a mile away. This asshole took me to this cabin way up in the middle of nowhere, got me drunk so I couldn't escape, and then tried to make me do anal. I pretended to have diarrhea, but I said I'd do it the next day to get him off me. Then in the middle of the night, I stole his car and drove back to his apartment. I left it there, gave the keys to his concierge, and I never heard from him again. After that, I stopped dating older men. Never again.

You have to learn from your mistakes. Because you get blamed, you know? When men like this turn on you, everyone tells you, you should've known. He paid for you, so you deserve what comes next.

I'm not putting myself in that kind of situation ever again.

The little boy's mom rolls up in a minivan. She slides open the door for him. He throws himself across the floor in front of the back seat and lies face down, his backpack, his water bottle all splayed out around him. She gets out, which is strange, and approaches me in her puffer jacket, arms crossed over her chest.

"How's he doing?" she asks.

"Fine," I say.

"Is he having fun?"

I furrow my brow. Fun? What does she think this is, camp? He's being paid. I'm about to launch into a diatribe about how this is a job, how it's not supposed to be fun. It is work. To transport audiences away from their wretched lives, we have to commit our bodies, our hearts, our selves.

Fun, no, and it probably won't be. It's never fun being perfect. But I'm cut off when Rudy sticks out his hand and introduces himself, smiles, and says, "We're all having a great time."

The mother is relieved, relaxes visibly. "Oh good. Good. That's good."

I'm able to swallow my rage. The nerve of this woman. As if this is just some after-school activity.

"Not causing too much trouble?"

"Nope," I say — I'd like this interaction to end as soon as possible. I'm basically the lead now, I shouldn't have to grease these citizens.

We chat for a few minutes. Eventually the boy yells at her, saying he's hungry and wants some hot salty nugs, whatever that is. She obediently gets back into the van and drives off.

See? The disrespect with men. It starts so young.

I'm about to tell Rudy what I really think when I realize he is pedaling away. He calls over his shoulder, "He's just a kid." And then, seemingly to satiate my curiosity at his totally abrupt departure, he adds, "Have fun with your boyfriend."

Right, right. I wave him off and turn around, remembering Vishal waiting for me in his stupid Audi. I see him inside, glaring.

When I get in the car, he doesn't greet me. "Why were you talking to that guy again?" No hello. No how was your day.

"I had to wait for the kid to get picked up," I say. "It's not my fault if Rudy wants to hang around. He's in the cast."

"I told you he likes you."

I shrug. "A lot of men like me." I don't say, *That's why you're interested, isn't it?* Because that's what I don't understand about jealousy, about men like him. Of course it's insecurity, but the reason he wants me is the same reason he hates me. Because I am so beautiful that everyone is interested in me. That everyone wants me. And he gets to feel something about himself for having me. And you know what? Good for him. But that comes with risk, from men like Rudy who circle on their bikes, pretending they aren't daydreaming about sleeping with me.

Vishal mutters something under his breath, slams the car in reverse, and pulls out too quickly. I have no idea where we're going, but it isn't his place.

XIII

The restaurant Vishal takes me to is far too cool for him to have found it himself. It's intimate, has a hominess to it — as if we're sitting inside the kitchen at some chef's house in the French countryside, watching a butter-colored sunset. It's definitely the sort of restaurant you need a reservation for too, which means this was planned, though he's trying to pretend it wasn't. Strange. We've never been to a restaurant like this.

He's in the bathroom now. I'm staring at the menu, which is very expensive, but he brought me here, so I'm thinking appetizer, entrée, and dessert. There will be no sharing. As I study the entrées, I'm suddenly concerned this isn't about doing something degrading in bed. No, I'm convinced I'm about to get dumped.

It's not like we have some deeply emotional connection, but it's also not the first time I've been fed before getting kicked to the curb. And Vishal seems like the kind of guy who would want to shell out before breaking up with me, to alleviate some of his guilt.

Because even though he is a douchebag, he is a douchebag with something of a conscience.

Not that I'd necessarily be heartbroken or anything. But still. It's nice to have options. What I've found, having all these boyfriends — two, now maybe three, if Rudy ever works up the courage to do something — is that it's way easier to keep from falling for any of them so long as I keep rotating between them. Sure, anyone can get caught up in a moment or two, but ultimately, if you're constantly shifting your focus from one thing to the next, it's easy to care about nothing.

The main thing is, you just never say their name, ever. Which is, honestly, really easy if you think about it. I think it's been six months since I've said any man's name out loud, and I don't intend to start anytime soon. I tell every woman I know to see how long they can go without saying their boyfriend's name.

The waitress comes over and asks if I want anything while I'm waiting. I order an eighteen-dollar cocktail, just to try it. It's got pineapple and rum and coconut essence, and some kind of a foam on top.

Vishal comes back from the bathroom. He sighs when he sits down.

"Everything okay?"

"Yeah, just work," he says, then sighs again, fiddles with his napkin. He seems so lost. Different from how he was in the car, swerving through traffic, clearly panicked at the idea that I'd cheat on him. And with Rudy of all people, with his bicycle and his cigarette behind his ear. Which is certainly absurd, because to dump Vishal, we'd actually have to have a conversation about our relationship, which last I checked wasn't exclusive.

"What happened?" I ask, hoping for some juicy gossip.

Instead, he reaches across the table and squeezes my hand, but he seems immediately embarrassed by the act — so much so that he gazes out the window instead of looking at me. I squeeze back. It's oddly cool and limp. Hand holding in public. Man, what's next?

The waitress returns with my cocktail, which is gigantic. I smile as she puts it down — everyone in the restaurant has turned to look at me. Inside the glass is a big skewer with these huge slices of pineapple interspersed with cherries. Vishal chuckles when he sees it. I think maybe this is it, he's about to say the words — "I think we should see other people" — but instead he nods at the waitress and says, "Can I have one of those too?"

The waitress is hot, very hot — she has one of those nose rings that goes through the middle of her nostrils and red lipstick on. She pats his shoulder and laughs at the order. This seems to annoy him and he turns to face me, takes my other hand across the table, ignoring her. Snubbing her, even. Score.

"It's good. Do you want to try it?"

"I can wait." He stares into my eyes with this strange simmering intimacy, this fear, this pain, this agony. I can barely look at him and dive back toward the cocktail instead, taking another gulp.

"So," he says when his equally obnoxious drink appears — I use its arrival as an excuse to drop his hands, to make room for it on the table. "I've been seeing someone."

I nod. Affect an impassive face. Here it comes. The breakup. The farewell.

"That came out wrong." He pauses and takes a sip from his cocktail, looking down at the tablecloth as he does. "Wow, this is hard." He's probably seeing someone he isn't afraid to introduce to his family. That's something I've noticed about him. He texts his parents and siblings a lot. Probably embarrassed to be dating an actress or a white girl or whatever.

I'm about to remind him that we never said we were exclusive, so there are no hard feelings. It's a speech I've used a few times before, at the end of one of these ceremonial meals. It gets it over with faster, gets me back out into the world, fishing for a new business boy to fill this spot on my roster.

We start to speak at the same time. "It's really okay —"

"It's a therapist. I've been seeing a therapist."

Twist. I lean forward and suck the cocktail dry. Definitely wasn't expecting this.

"I just . . . I'm not sure what I'm doing with my life, and it's been nice to just have someone to talk to, but I did figure out that there is something I do want. It was actually the other night, when I saw you with that guy —"

The waitress returns. "Another cocktail?" she asks.

"Still working on this one," I say, squeezing one of the maraschino cherries and watching the pink liquid fall to the tabletop, a small circle of sweet syrup spreading out on the polished wood.

"Can we have a minute?" he asks. It comes out angry. Vishal buries his face in his hands. The waitress nods, turns on her heel, and stalks back to her station where she starts folding napkins while peering at us over her POS machine.

"I like you," he says. "I know it's been . . . it hasn't always been like romantic or something . . . I mean . . ." He gets frustrated and clams up. It's difficult to watch.

"We were just hanging out," I say. "I get it, I understand."

"I know, but listen." He stops and picks up the water glass, downs it in a single gulp. I've never realized how large he is, but watching him sip from the cup . . . It's one of those uselessly small cups they give you in fancy restaurants, but still. It's interesting to see him in that light. I take a bite from a hunk of pineapple and study him. It's as if, all of a sudden, he's a person. A scared, weird person. "I think you should move in. With me."

I take a deep breath, forgetting about the pineapple. It gets lodged in my throat. I immediately start coughing, the inhale and exhale causing it to move up then back down my esophagus. My eyes swim. He stands up and reaches over, pounds me once, twice by the shoulder blades, and the offending hunk of fruit flies out of my mouth and hits him in the middle of his dress shirt before tumbling to the floor.

The waitress rushes over. Everyone is looking. My cheeks burn and I grab my water glass and take a long sip. "Thank you,"

I say through a hoarse gasp. I can feel my mascara running down my cheeks.

He's staring at me so lovingly and with so much care that I need a second. I get up and rush to the bathroom. Reeling. It seems insane. When Anton asked, it caught me off guard, but it made sense, at least. He's obsessed with me. But Vishal? Everything about our relationship, to this point, has been an after-hours transaction.

I wet a piece of toilet paper in the sink and sit down on the toilet and start blotting away my bleeding eye makeup. My breath returns to normal. This is totally a situation that I'd get myself in. Some guy accidentally falling in love with me because I'm so unavailable. I mean, it's easy, I guess, to seem busy and important when you have your own stuff going on. But seriously, move in? This is our first date in the daylight. Maybe even our first real conversation that goes beyond trading facts and information and making sex plans.

What the hell is going on? First Anton and now Vishal?

They're older than me. These men. Probably thirty, maybe even mid-thirties. Basically middle-aged. It's this man, realizing he wants his life to be different. Because he's ready. Because he wants what he wants, right now. He doesn't want some hipster bartender on a bicycle to take it from him. Because now that he's ready, he's just grabbing the first attractive woman he deems worthy of him and settling down. Because who I am doesn't really matter at all, as long as I am hot enough.

I feel violence revving inside of me, the way it always does. I think of Vishal, of what I would do to him if I could do something to him. I think it would have to do with his car — no. I stop myself. Maybe he's about to treat me to some soliloquy about all the things he adores about me. That he loves about me. My qualities — things that have nothing to do with him. I should give him that chance. Or at least eat the free food. And to do that, I need to be pleasant.

I stand up, check my reflection — perfection, honestly, save my eyebrows, which could use some attention — and walk back to the table. He's just sitting there, not even scrolling on his phone.

"Sorry." I slide into the booth.

"Are you okay?" Again, he reaches over and squeezes my hand. It's like he woke up this morning and decided he was in love.

But, you know, I'm nothing if not an incredible actress. I smile back.

We get another round of cocktails, we eat, he orders dessert and doesn't discuss his proposal. I try to pay more attention to what he talks about (work, boring) and why he's so upset (he had to fire people, boo hoo). He doesn't say a word about me. Doesn't ask me any questions.

I keep waiting for him to bring it up again, to ask for my response. Do I want to move in? Do I feel the same way about him? Do I like him? Am I even here at all?

Why me? Why is he choosing me?

But the crème brulée, which was so sweet it made me want to vomit, leaves the table and he still hasn't bothered.

He pays, seems to enjoy sliding his credit card into the machine and typing in a customized tip. The entire time, I'm trying to dig into the role presented to me, of a woman who might settle for this. I try to think about who she is. What her life is like.

She's not as smart as I am; she doesn't have my charisma, nor is she very interesting. She has a perfectly nice apartment and a slow-moving career in fundraising, or perhaps she works for a sexless non-profit like an arthritis foundation. She posts on Instagram every single day because it provides her with the illusion that she is indeed interesting, when the reality is that she is indeed the exact opposite. She thinks her spin instructor is her therapist and that street murals are real art, and coffee dates are great ways to meet people and build relationships. Once, she tried rock climbing because she saw it in a romantic comedy and desperately wishes she and Vishal had met there — maybe he caught her when she fell off the wall instead of on a dating app. She gets upset every time she's single on Valentine's Day. And now this guy that she's been hooking up with and has been calling her boyfriend — despite the fact that she's too chicken shit to force the conversation and —

I just can't do it. I'm not this woman. Because I don't want him. That's what separates us. Sure, I say boyfriend, but only because it's hilarious to call someone who treats me like this my boyfriend. Obviously I don't give a shit about him. It's only funny because he also doesn't give a shit about me.

Because, come on.

I'd rather shoot myself then move into his stupid apartment, made of steel and glass, filled with ugly brown furniture and mismatched plates he bought at a thrift store because it made him feel interesting for five seconds. I'd rather break one of those plates and jam a piece of it into my eye!

From his pocket, he pulls a set of keys and a fob. My head is spinning, like, *Wait a minute,* I want to say, *Hold on.* He might've asked me to move in, but I never said yes. I never said anything at all.

I take the keys and the fob, and he smiles. I guess that was an answer. Or at least he can interpret it that way. If he wants.

He looks at me, asks me if I'm ready to leave, to go back to *our* place, and I grab my jacket and gesture to the bathroom, hop past him and hurry back to my throne, the toilet. Taste the bitterness of the perfumed air and try not to lose my mind.

He's just so boring. I can't. I can't do it. I can't.

And then, my thoughts start to spin in circles, running faster, hotter. Because he didn't need me to say yes, apparently; he seems to have convinced himself that between the food and the coughing and dessert I had agreed to it. To all of it. To move in, to be his.

I look in the mirror. My eyes are shimmering.

The edge of the mirror is cracked, the tiny version of myself, divided up into hundreds of little pieces. I take off my shoe and tap it, just the corner of it. The crack spiders outward. I use the key he gave me to dig out a shard — a sizable one, as long as a finger — and hold it flat in my palm. The paper towels here are thick, expensive. I wrap the shard in it, put it in my jacket pocket.

I think about it. About him and how pleased he was to have claimed me. And in turn, how easy I made it for him. I put my hand in my pocket and squeeze the napkin-wrapped shard, feel its dulled edges, its potential. And as I do, my pounding heart slows to its usual thrum. The energy coursing through my body steadies. The rage is quiet. For now.

Deep breath, in and out. Smile. Back out to the car where he is waiting, a lifeless peck on the lips, my hands still squeezing the paper-wrapped shard.

Back at the apartment, he makes me use my fob to enter the lobby, and my new key to unlock his front door. He carries me across the threshold, smiling like he's never smiled before, as if we just got engaged.

Even when we have sex, he stares deeply into my eyes, thinking about loving me. And the entire time, I just have this frozen expression on my face, this portrait of a life I never agreed to, the words stalled in my throat. I think of my jacket, crumpled in the corner, sharp glass snuggled inside the cotton.

As he orgasms, I look at his stupid face, at the wide howl of his mouth, the twisted grimace. Then softness in his eyes as he kisses my cheek and flops over on his back. No, no, no. This won't do at all.

XIV

Renée remains the only person who could possibly understand me. I was able to slither away from Vishal this morning by reminding him of my session with her. He didn't want me to leave — he thought it romantic to hold me close in bed while I giggled, growing more and more panicked by the second. He wanted to order breakfast and then go for a walk. A walk! Outdoors! This man who I hadn't seen in daylight hours, who would kick me out of his apartment at eight in the morning, wanted to buy me a cappuccino and an egg sandwich and then sit on a bench near a dog park holding hands and talking about the future. What's next? Matching sweaters?

My soul is so shaken that I arrive at Renée's sweating. I practically fall through the door, am convinced I look like I've just outrun a tornado. She fetches me a glass of room-temperature water with lemon, and I start pacing around behind her while she sits at the piano bench.

"How's my understudy?" she trills.

"I'm not —"

"Visualize. Internalize. Manifest. Breathe." She turns to the keys and starts playing a ditty, the short, clipped beats of a swing tune, staccato and up tempo. *Dum, dum, dum. Da dum dum dum.* Very out of touch with the moment.

I take a long breath in, expand my diaphragm — and out and in and out. Hold it, let my cheeks bulge. Take another sip of this warm lemon water. They all flood toward me, storming my subconscious: Rudy, Vishal, the Captain, Michelle, Anton — over and over again, I can't seem to shake them. Then Lily, our conversation. *You're flat.* A kid who has no reason to lie, unless there is some strategic-mind-game-advanced-level-fuckery afoot.

"Am I flat?" I blurt out.

Renée stops playing and turns, peers over her glasses at me. The room is momentarily thrown into sharp relief. I see her now, washed up, alone, surrounded by remnants of a career that's now in the gutter, a career that maybe never was. I've never seen her perform. Her curly hair could be a wig; the red lipstick she hastily applied this morning is dripping outside the lines of her mouth, bleeding onto her cheeks. She's wearing a muumuu that zips up and her feet are bare, and I suddenly can't breathe, start looking around the room, all of it swimming in front of me, wondering if it was all a mirage, this dream of mine, if it's been propped up for so long I've lost sense of reality.

Renée claps once and I gasp, stand up straight, snap back to this room. I focus on the Tony in its little case across from the piano. Gleaming. What was I thinking? What is going on with me?

"Hi," she says. "Stop it. I see what you're doing. Stop it."

"But —"

"You are one of the most talented performers I've ever had the privilege to coach. It's all politics out there, but in here, you and I, here. This is real."

"There's just —"

"I asked you when you first came to me, do you trust me? Do you remember that?"

I nod. Remember it so well. I'd just dropped out of theater school when I realized the instructors, or whatever they called themselves, were a bunch of know-nothing hacks with embarrassing resumés. I knew if I wanted to release the power that was buried underneath this human flesh, I'd have to design my own educational program. Institutions are over, anyway. Degrees are useless.

And I knew, having been raised in a world of wealth and power, that the truly talented instructors, the coaches, they were never just available to the public. I'd have to go looking. And so, I dug around online. I sleuthed. And there, in the corners of the internet where private school moms hang out, I found a phone number. Just a phone number. No website. No advertising. Nothing.

It was fate.

After a three-hour audition, Renée invited me to come and join her exclusive practice. "But you have to trust me. I don't just take on any student. There must be total acceptance of one another, absolute trust. You have raw talent, but you're getting old, too old to be shaped like clay." I was nineteen. But I understood what she meant.

I had to focus. I was already behind all the child actors and nepobabies. I had to catch up.

And since then, it's been the two of us, just the two of us, speaking the same language.

I drain my glass of water. The lemon slice hits me in the nose.

"You're right, it's stupid. Those little jerks are getting in my head."

"And you cannot let them undermine the strength you bring to every single room you walk into. Who said this to you, about you being flat?"

"One of the kids in the show. Who claims to have perfect pitch."

"Pfft." Renée rolls her eyes. "Children." She starts to pound on the piano, moving from the up-tempo swing tune she had been playing to something slower, more somber, almost like a funeral

108

march. She's incapable of saying anything else; she seems stuck. "Children. Pfft. Pfft!"

I think I broke her.

"One of my students, letting a child undermine them. Do you think I spent three years in Moscow, sweeping out dance studios so I could afford operatic training to have one of my students, one of my prodigies second guess themselves when questioned. By. A. Child?" Her voice has reached a fever pitch. I put my glass of water down on a windowsill. The piano thunders under her fingers. And then suddenly, she stops.

"Back to fundamentals," she says, a triumphant finger in the air.

"What?"

"You heard me. Scales. Fundamentals. Until you remember who you are."

And for the next hour, we run scales. Complex, tricky scales, chromatic scales where I work to hit every note and also every space between the notes. When I miss one, we work backward. We sing it over and over again, until my voice mingles with the piano, gets lost in the accuracy. Until the right pitch is burned into my brain. We repeat this exercise until I can find the tiny tonal differences, until I land on top of each one without the help of a pitch. The music begins to flow through me. I find myself losing sense of everything but each individual note. I lose my ability to be, to breathe, to dream. It's just me and Renée and her fingers and the piano and her ragged inhale before she shouts, "Again!" It's a kind of devotion, like my soul and spirit have detached from my body and are hovering above us, and I'm trying to claw them back under my skin.

By the time the hour is finished, Renée is sweating. I collapse into an armchair, my entire body screaming, tense. Running the tiny exercise over and over again was akin to flicking something for an hour straight, in the exact same spot. I never want to sing again.

"Now. Match this pitch." She hits a note. I sing.

"Now this," she says, hitting another note. I sing again.

She glares at me with contempt. I should've never doubted myself, because when I doubt myself, I'm doubting Renée. And what greater insult is there? Than to doubt? To poison the sanctity of this space we have created together with weakness?

She slams the piano lid and stomps off.

I am dismissed.

XV

Rehearsal days begin to blur together. It's usually just the kids and I in the side room with moldy gym mats and flickering fluorescent lighting overhead. The mood in the room constantly shifts between various states of excitement and/or emotional turmoil. The youngest girl, who I now know is named Julie because she tells me, constantly, has learned the power of her tears and uses them all the time. Do I blame her? Of course not. She reminds me of myself. Before I didn't know her name and now, I have to say it every day. Outfoxed by a six-year-old. Good thing there's no one who matters here to witness it.

Attention is a drug, and whoever's managing Julie's career has had her hooked to the IV since she first appeared in a Huggies commercial. She is very adorable, has pudgy cheeks and pigtails and big glasses, and she knows how to walk up to an adult and twist her toe on the ground, capture their attention. Enrapture them with cuteness to get what she wants.

Lily told me about Julie's Huggies commercial. She's a good little gossip; she's realized how much I value information and has taken it upon herself to get it for me. She has a cellphone with an unlimited data plan, the names of everyone on the crew already memorized, and the curiosity of a beat reporter. It's incredible.

She's unearthed everyone in the cast's best credits, and it's frankly depressing how many of them have kissed the boards of Broadway only to make it back here, to hole up and ride out the rest of their boring lives at a regional theater that pays them so little most will likely retire in poverty. Just being around them, with that knowledge, is doing a number on my will to go on.

Rudy is the most interesting. Lily was able to dig up all kinds of dirt on him. He was in the cast of *Hairspray*, like he said, but he's also done almost every major tour of the last few years. *The Book of Mormon*, *Wicked*, *Newsies* — you name it, he did it. And now he's here. I can tell he's downplaying his dancing abilities so as not to show up the other members of the cast, guys whose kicks aren't as high, whose hips are closer to a replacement surgery than they are to the splits. I can't understand why, though. If he's trying to establish himself here, he should be showing everyone what he can do. Not hiding on the sidelines.

A stagehand leans in to let us know it's time for lunch. As we leave the rehearsal studio, the gang of us almost run right into Samantha. She's taking videos for her vlog, a manic smile on her face. "Hey, guys. Hi, guys. Hey, guys, what's up, guys," over and over again. "Hey, guys, I'm so excited."

After filming the same aggressively joyful video for what feels like most of the break, Samantha grabs her little tripod and walks over to the benches where the kids are sitting and eating their lunches. They're low energy and grouchy — it's tough to try to cheer them up, so most days I don't bother. My personal approach thus far has been to keep them quiet and on my side, and so far it's working.

Julie's eating slices of pear, slowly chewing them and ignoring Samantha as she approaches. "All right, little ones. Who wants to be on my vlog?!" She sounds like she's auditioning for a princess role at an off-brand theme park. It's surprising to me that none of the kids move.

The older boy is watching something on his phone while he eats dry ramen noodles out of the packet and doesn't bother taking out his air pods.

Lily says, "PR isn't written into my contract," which makes me laugh. Samantha is stricken by this remark, though. I can tell she expected the kids to rush to her, clamoring for a spot, desperate for her acceptance. She's doing the smile though, a big wide smile, with a kindergarten teacher's voice that makes Michelle's sound nihilistic. My kids, though, they're better than that.

Samantha sits down next to Julie, who is finishing off her pears. "Hey, Julie, do you want to be on my vlog? I'm interviewing every-one in the cast and you could be the first kid!"

Julie gazes contemplatively at the ocean while licking her finger. Six going on forty, this one.

"Do you have her parents' permission?" I ask.

Samantha is taken aback by this. "It's just a little video, we can shoot it now and I'll ask them at pickup."

"I'm not comfortable with that," I say.

Samantha rolls her eyes and grabs Julie's hand. "C'mon, let's go over there."

Julie gets up, but I can tell she's confused and doesn't want to, that the power of the lead actress, the one she's supposed to be sucking up to, is getting to her. "She hasn't even digested her lunch yet. Digestion is incredibly important."

Samantha keeps walking. "It'll just take five minutes."

"Julie, come here," I say, standing up. Julie stops walking, but she's still holding Samantha's hand, though I'm not sure if it's by choice. From here, it seems like Samantha is gripping hers too tight. This is part of my job. To protect the children. In two steps, I'm next to them. I grab Julie's other hand so she's stretched between us. "C'mon, let's get back to the others."

Samantha doesn't move, doesn't let her go. Her eyes narrow. "Just get over it," Samantha hisses at me. "You didn't get the part, I did. Get over it."

I see Lily bristle at this in my peripheral vision. My girl!

"This has nothing to do with you and me." I'm proud of how icy my voice is. The shift of it. I'm really conjuring up, like, an activist type, someone who feels called to protect something — a historically important building or a really, really old tree. "This is about the kids, who I am responsible for from the minute their parents drop them off to the minute they get back into the car at pickup. Me. And I'm not going to let you manipulate them into being in a, what did you call it, vlog?"

Samantha feels seen, I can tell, and a bit ashamed. It's hard not to feel a little bit bad for her. The Captain's attitude is toxic. His dismissals, his refusal to co-operate has driven Samantha to tears more than once. I see her after each rehearsal, after everyone else has gone home, slumped at the piano with her binder in her lap and Michelle standing next to her, whispering kindness while she cries.

It's getting hard to watch. Samantha seems so optimistic when she shows up to rehearsal, hopeful that each new day will be the one where, finally, everyone decides they're going to rally behind her. Except, like, come on, right? Sometimes you just have to admit something isn't working and move on. And this clearly isn't working.

The hope makes me hate her even more. I stand there, watch as the Captain treats her like garbage, watch as she dies a little inside. She stands up for herself, but only in response to his diva behavior. No one buys her strength when they hear the pain that leaches into the corners of her voice. I want to see her fight for it.

It's a tough pill to swallow, but the truth is, no one likes a fragile little bitch. People want to be led. They don't want to see weakness. They don't want to see defeat. They want power. They want influence. They want someone like me.

Samantha crumples a little and releases Julie's hand. I'm not sure if it's on purpose. Julie runs back to where we were sitting and plops down beside Lily on the bench. Lily puts a protective arm around her and stares down Samantha as if to say, *How could you. You're supposed to be Maria. You're supposed to be good.*

"You don't have to be so dramatic," Samantha says, shrugging, playing it off as if it isn't a big deal. "I'll ask her mom at pickup."

"Great," I say. Then I go in for the kill. "You do that."

Samantha sighs as if I'm the problem and wanders off. I return to the kids and sit next to them, separating them from that monster.

Julie pokes me with her finger. "I think we're going to pass," she says. And I laugh at that.

"Good," I say.

Julie nods, and I'm not really sure how much of it she understands, if she's just parroting words that her mother barks into her cellphone when negotiating her deals. Either way, the kid has solid instincts. You've got to respect that. Samantha is a sinking ship, and you don't tether yourself to a sinking ship. You simply don't. Even a six-year-old knows: Samantha's time is almost up.

XVI

"**I**'m not getting what I need here," the Captain says as he breaks away from Samantha, dropping her hand and abandoning her in the middle of the room. They had been standing there, staring into one another's eyes, the entire cast and crew surrounding them. He walks back to his piano bench and takes a swig from his thermos of tea. His abandonment is like a slap.

We're working the scene at the party once again, the one where the Captain realizes he's supposed to be in love with Maria and not his mean blonde girlfriend, Frau Schrader, with her tiny waist and movie star looks. But it's her Nazi-enabling politics that turn him off. Her cowardice.

Like if I'd been alive during World War II you wouldn't catch me selling out king and country. No. I'd have been one of those resistance fighters, the kind that spoke in code and had cyanide capsules imbedded in their teeth and pieces of radios in her saddle shoes or whatever. And my look would have been so helpful, because I am tall and blonde and beautiful. Total Nazi-bait. It's really surprising they didn't offer me Frau Schrader. Though I probably would've turned it down.

Instead, it went to this old Company hag whose been around for decades. She sings two songs, one in each act, that are so goddamn boring they were cut from the movie. They had her in for rehearsal the other day. She sounded like a pack-a-day smoker. Pathetic. At the end of it, I'm pretty sure she was wheezing. I'm surprised they didn't have an oxygen tank waiting in the wings. Everyone gave her a standing ovation, probably just glad she didn't keel over.

"Interesting. Steve's not getting what he needs? Well neither am I," Samantha says. I consider how I would handle this. Probably with grace and a smile. I would say, "Well, let me try something different this time," and just outclass him in front of the crew.

"So, let's just read the scene," Michelle says. "We can stay after and work the lines, the emotion, but we're here with the cast. We need to get this blocking down. Just read it this time."

The Captain pauses, firm, fingers pressed to his temples. "It'll water down my performance."

The room is dead silent.

"I'll use stand-ins if you want, but I need you two to stop wasting time," Michelle says. Her phrasing is practiced, firm. "I need everyone in their first positions. Now, let's go."

Neither of them moves. I'm excited; it's my time to step into the part. These jerks are going to storm off and fluff their egos, and here I am, ready and willing to be shaped by Michelle's directorial vision, because, as a true star, I have no sense of myself. I let others flow through me. Like really warm, sexy water. Undulating. Available. Open for business.

The reasonable hero is a perfect role for me. I'm already running through the lines in my head, ones I've memorized while working this scene with the kids. I put my shoulders back and step forward, about to volunteer when the Captain speaks. His quiet voice slices the silence wide open, penetrating my heart.

"I'm sorry." Is he actually ashamed? No way.

"Apology accepted," says Samantha. Her arms are wrapped around her body, hugging herself as if attempting to protect herself from violence. The Captain's apology wasn't even to her; it was to Michelle, and here Samantha is inserting herself between them.

"Let's try it through without stopping," Michelle says. I can hear the celebration disguised within. "First positions."

Rudy finds my eyes from across the room where he's standing with a chubby member of the chorus. He gestures some kind of relief, the way that siblings of fighting parents might look at one another. Except, of course, I'm reeling. Absolutely reeling. The emotional whiplash of it all. And now everyone has perked up, seems ready to play together, to play nicely. Even the kids seem more engaged than they have been all day as I shove them into place.

They run the scene, over and over again, and naturally, the Captain and Samantha move from just reading their lines to acting. The kids keep messing up, but Michelle doesn't bother to admonish them or call cut, just turns to me each time they miss a cue or a step as if it's my fault the brats can't keep their blocking straight. Eventually she starts painting the air with a pencil to indicate that I should be writing this stuff down.

Of course, I don't have one. Who carries a pencil? I type a few notes into my phone, but figure I can remember the rest. It's not like this is complicated stuff. And even if I tell the kids what they're doing wrong, they don't care.

Rehearsal goes late, and for the first time, the parents are waiting for us — peering through the glass and checking the time on their cellphones, glancing back at their illegally parked mini vans and SUVs. The chaotic rehearsal schedule must be getting to them.

One of the moms keeps trying to catch my eye, waving and pointing at her wrist. I keep her in my peripheral vision. I know she wants to sneak a kid out, probably has to go pick up another kid or take them to an appointment. Still, I don't work for her. I ignore the waving until she opens the door and calls for the older boy. "*Zeke*," she whisper-shouts. "*Zeke. Your brother.*" Zeke's eyes bulge out and he takes a deep, horrified breath in, and ignores her. "*Zeke*," she hisses again.

He stares at her, all bug-eyed with rage, and shakes his head. No, there's no way. She cannot be doing this. She cannot be humiliating him now.

"*Zeke*," she hisses again. "You get over here, right now."

Finally, Michelle gives me a pointed look, then turns to the door, smiling big and bright, and says, "Can I help?"

"We're a little late, and I have to go pick up his brother. Can I have Zeke?"

Michelle pauses, considering the request. Deep down, I bet she wishes she could flip a table. It's finally working, right now. Everything is falling into place. The show is starting to look like something people might pay money for, and here is a mom to ruin it.

"Sure," Michelle says.

"I can stay," Zeke says, terrified, turning to his mother. The preteen humiliation is so present, I feel bad for him. "Mom. I'll get an Uber."

"Not happening."

Zeke ignores her.

"Now, Zeke," the mother says. Her voice is loud, commanding, performing for the other parents, for the cast and the crew. Zeke crumples, then gives in. He's heard this tone before. He ducks his head and hurries off to our little side studio, to gather his things. There's a small gang of other parents outside, a mutinous quality to the way they're now poking their heads into the studio, jealous of this bossy woman getting her way. The magic is gone, anyway, the room sapped of it.

Michelle's shoulders slump. "Let's call it," she says, and turns to Samantha and the Captain and asks them to stay behind. "Oh, and Jessamyn, once you're through with pickup, if you could come back for a few minutes, that would be perfect."

119

Of course, she needs me. Finally, I can dish out some truths to the Captain and Samantha about their performances. Maybe she'll ask me to step in for Samantha. I bet she wants me to show her how it's done.

I am positively giddy as I herd the kids out of the room, get them into coats, hand them off to their parents. When I head back to the rehearsal room, the rest of the performers are hurrying away, some of them checking their watches, talking to partners at home or bosses at their second jobs, to let them know they're running late.

It's so obvious why Michelle wants to talk to me. She wants me to stay and observe the rehearsal. Make sure I have the blocking down. Very sneaky of her, skirting union rules this way. I am so proud of her.

Walking back to the studio, I check my phone. A text message from my father, asking for the ticket link. I tell him it isn't up yet, but I'll let him know when it is. What if he googles me and sees the cast list online? What then?

Paranoid, I check the Company's website. Tickets for *The Sound of Music* are live, but they haven't released the creative team yet, no further details. There's still time.

I calm myself knowing that this is likely just a momentary hyperfixation. He doesn't google things; he isn't curious. The girl-friend is probably just grumpy about her trip to Aruba, and he's probably trying to pick out tickets so they can get their hotel dates, make restaurant reservations, get her a trip to the spa. Anything to shut her up.

Another text from my father, this time asking for dates. I put my phone away. Now is not the time to panic. Now is the time to step inside, be the calm one, the joyful one, the one Michelle can rely on to perform.

•••

When I slip back in to the studio, the stage manager presses a finger to her lips. The Captain and Samantha are in the middle of the room, lost in each other, holding fast to one another's elbows. They say their lines about falling in love. It's not great. The expressions are overly emotional — they're treating it like a performance. They're just saying words with emphasis. Nothing is coming from inside. It's all surface.

Still, Michelle is delighted, sitting off to the side, one leg crossed over the other, her hand cupping her chin as she watches them speak the lines with their mouths.

If I were her, I'd be pacing back and forth, screaming, *No, No, No. That's not it. Do you feel nothing inside of you, when you say these lines? Has the burden of these characters' pasts not weighed on you all day? Do you not wake up thinking about how deep and meaningful and transformative love can be? That it's supposed to take hold of you and not let go? That within this scene, you're both giving up a particular version, a vision of your lives that was cemented in place simply because you cannot stop looking into one another's eyes? No. You are thinking of whatever sweaty idiot you lost it to when you were fifteen going on sixteen, the slow gasp of disappointment upon discovering that what life told you was meant to be special was instead small, meaningless. You aren't thinking of the audience. You are only thinking of yourself. What kind of performer —*

But no. I cut myself off. Now is not the time to spiral.

When they stop talking, Michelle stands up and crosses the room to hug them both. "That was perfect . . . Oh." She steps back and whips off her glasses, wiping at tears. Tears! What a show she's putting on for these amateurs, these hacks. There's no way they can be real. Can they?

"I am so excited about the future of this. About you two. Thank you."

They all exchange words, but a dull thrumming in my ears, a roar at this injustice fills the room. My cheeks are hot, burning. They speak with excitement, about the show's potential, about the future. They put on jackets. The Captain seems happier, more relaxed now, with Samantha. I think they might be *getting dinner.*

The derision is gone now, the walls have been broken. Probably just insecurity, I reason. Because he is terrible. At least he has the strength to see it himself. But now, Michelle's lies, her overblown reaction will protect him like a thin layer of fat all over his body, insulating him from his own mediocrity. It's sad, really. There's so much talent here, standing behind these two losers.

It lights a fire inside of me. I need to save this production from them.

Michelle waits for them to leave, then calls me over. She seems casual as she slings a bag over her shoulder and starts gathering up armloads of binders, papers, and notes to go dump in her office. The tears are gone; she's all business. Exhausted. Finally, she's going to tell someone the truth, how she really feels about their performance. And that someone is me.

"Thanks for staying, Jessamyn. Just a quick thing."

I honestly think she's going to ask for my notes, for my opinion. I am a great actor, after all, she said it herself. Could I help Samantha? Give her some coaching? They can bring someone else in to watch the kids because this situation we're in is serious. It is dire. But then I'll turn her down, of course. I'll turn her down and leave her with a singular option, and that is to hire me to replace Samantha.

"The kids are leaving too much trash in the side studio. We've had a complaint from the cleaners. They really only come in to wash the floors and dust and all that. Can you make sure the room is tidy at the end of every rehearsal? The stage management team does it in here, but we really need all hands on deck for this. Thanks."

"Uh . . ."

But Michelle is already out the door, walking away quickly. Couldn't even make eye contact with me while she laid this insult at my feet. And here I stand, like a moron.

I look around the room and there's the stage management team in their disheveled glory, picking granola bar wrappers and tissues and trash up off the ground. Picking up after the talent. Not one of them is wearing a pair of pants that fits properly. Most of them have their hair back in ponytails or buns. There's more than one ass crack peeking out. It's enough to make you want to vomit.

I watch as Michelle's long red ponytail bounces against her puffer jacket. It shines in the streetlights, and I wonder what she would do if I followed her to her car, parked in the dark corner of that parkade where no one is watching. What she would do if I grabbed that ponytail, dragged her into the shadows. Kicked her behind the knees so she fell to the ground, then straddled her.

I can't imagine she'd fight back. Her body is all legs and elbows, sharp joints with no muscle, no substance. The ponytail in my fist, yanked upward, before she could react. I'd cut it off and stuff the hair in her mouth. Duct tape her lips together, pinch her nostrils, and watch as she inhales, desperately, pulling the hair down her esophagus, that tickling feeling in the back of her throat the very last thing that happens before her hair enters her lungs. I remember in high school we learned about lungs and how they are made up of thousands of tiny tubes. I picture the needles of her straight hair entering those tubes, clogging, widening them, the sharp edges puncturing the thin membrane when she tries to breathe, to scream. But she won't be able to. And this — this is how she will die.

No, no, no. I laugh. *No.* Let it go, Jessamyn. It was a long day. Michelle must've forgotten why she hired me, in the confusion of it all. Right? Because why else would she be doing this? Just a lot on her plate, really. She's emotional. Exhausted.

Poor Michelle. She just works too damn hard.

XVII

When times are tough, and Anton isn't available (I've been avoiding him since he asked me to move in), I have a routine to help cope. It goes something like this: a cheap bottle of wine and a descent into imagination. I gulp the wine, sometimes cut with a Diet Coke or some orange juice, and lie back on my bed, stare at the ceiling and imagine.

Usually it's about getting cast as the lead in a new musical, something risky, something that catapults me out of this misery and to the front of the line. The previews run so hot I get offers to bail almost immediately, move on to bigger and better and greater shows where I can push the envelope. *Breathe new life. Transcend the material.* I'm so hot I'm getting phone calls from Hollywood — everyone wants a piece. Everyone.

Even the late-night talk shows want me. And I get to pick and choose between my Jimmies, Jerrys, and Johns.

Of course, I choose someone New York–based — I'm no traitor. When I sit down on the little sofa next to the desk, I'm wearing this really incredible outfit that makes me look like sex, but also like I have this really innate sense of what's coming next, like I'm cool and not afraid to take chances with fashion, but those chances aren't cheap, like showing a nipple or something, no, they're more like a very daring shoe or maybe a statement chapeau.

Usually in these fantasies, after answering a few questions with charm and poise and just a glint of playful flirtation, I turn the tables on the host, somehow. Ask them a question that makes the audience gasp or roar with laughter. Something the host's wife or kid or producer whispered to me backstage. *Well, that's not what I heard about you, Johnny. You're the one hiding something, Jimmy. Don't talk to me like that, Dave, I know what you got your wife for her birthday.* You get it.

Usually I can pass out doing this, but tonight my brain won't go quiet, the insults of the day weighing so heavily that a bottle of wine just isn't enough. My hands are still sticky from throwing away a juice box, a wrapper for a granola bar, and an apple core. Children are disgusting. I keep thinking I smell poop, but I checked the bottom of my shoes, the clothes I wore today, my hands, everything. It's nowhere to be seen. It's clear their essence follows me around like a curse.

Plus, my soul is all twisted into knots by having to be around such subpar creative expression. What if I become a hack by association? My soul is a sponge, after all. What if they infect me with their mediocrity? My career might never recover.

And, as if my day couldn't possibly be worse, after rehearsal, I had to go for my bi-monthly wax. Because it's important to be desirable at all times. When you look like me, you have to be ready. Olga, the Eastern European woman I usually go to, was training a scared little eighteen-year-old, and she tried to convince me to let the kid, who had braces by the way, wax me. As if I was going to let someone practice on me. Absolutely not. I've already learned this lesson.

You see, when I was cut off by my father, I went through a period of extreme poverty. During that time, I went to a discount wax place I found on a deal website. This was a giant mistake. The room was obviously dirty when I went in, but it was something crazy, like, seventy percent off. So I decided to close my eyes and use the pain for future roles.

It's important to keep it up. You can't miss a month. You can't. This is what my old lady, Oxana, said. And she was good, the wax was always hot and I could barely feel it. But this discount place. Well. I should've been more on my guard. But it had been a long day — I'd spent hours prepping for an audition for some kind of gingivitis gel and lost the part to a man. Disgusting.

When I lay back on the table, I was surprised to feel this hard wax I'd never encountered before.

"What is that?" I'd asked.

"You don't need strips," the sullen waxer woman said to me as she applied this thick layer of goo to my vagina. I felt some of it dripping onto the soft inner skin, into the folds. I should've said something but simply assumed she knew what she was doing.

And then, the pain. Tearing. Blood. I screamed and turned. I was so out of my mind I barely remember anything but this extreme flash of white, my mind incapable of comprehending what my body was experiencing. I rolled over and vomited on the floor next to me. I only vaguely remember the ambulance ride, the twelve stitches I needed in my labia.

Of course, I've never used a coupon for a wax job ever again. And I wrote a scathing review of the business online, telling the entire sordid tale and embellishing a bit about some rodents I may or may not have seen and well, the business shut down a few months later and now the location is one of those stores that sells gigantic tubs of protein powder. This is what happens when you mess with Jessamyn.

But, you know, I have to stick up for myself. Because no one else will.

This wax, today, went fine, though when I lay back on the table a sort of panic grasped me. Relying on other people is truly so terrifying.

Now, I lie back on my bed and stare at my ceiling, at the cracks in it. It's painted white, but just barely. I can spot the shadow of a void forming, a void that wants to swallow me whole. This apartment. I tried calling my landlord, Mikhail, about it, and he demanded to know if there was water coming out of the crack. I said no, mistakenly, and he said it didn't matter. That cracks happen. To just deal with it. As if I, Jessamyn St. Germain, deserved to live in squalor like this. Looking at cracks. Like, what's next? Vermin?

No, I deserve so much more. I should stop paying rent here, I really should.

Earlier, Vishal texted me to ask where I was. I told him I had to go back to my apartment, to sort some things out. Kept it vague. In response, he sent a heart emoji. A heart! This guy. There must be something wrong with him. Maybe he's dying. Maybe it wasn't a therapist he saw but a cancer doctor instead, and he wants to fall in love before he leaves this Earth. Maybe I can give him a kidney, save his life, get on the news.

Now that would be perfect. I should marry him and take all of his money. Though marriage is a terrible idea for me, career wise. You want prospective managers and agents and business partners and vodka reps to think they can sleep with you. It seems important, if I'm going to make it. I need to be available, but not. That's why it helps to have two boyfriends. To seem desirable, but also attainable. Like, I have two boyfriends, why not three? Six? Why not you?

After the insult from Michelle and then the wax — which was fine, but still harrowing; it reminded me of the Great Tear — I know what I need, and it's attention, but the kind that isn't freely given. Attention I have to fight for. I find his number on the crew list and dial.

"Where are you?" I ask when Rudy answers, confused as to why I'm calling him at this late hour. Maybe why I'm calling him at all. He tells me he's taking shifts at the bar at the theater for the war in Afghanistan show when he isn't booked for rehearsal. That they're just about done.

"I'm tipsy and wish to be drunk," I say, rolling back and forth on my bed, squeezing my knees together, trying to sound horny. I eye the crack in the ceiling and roll onto my stomach. The sight of it makes me want to vomit.

"Is that so?" he says. I can hear the smile that's broken across his stupid face. "Well get over here."

"To the theater? What about Marge?"

"She's already gone. I'm locking up tonight."

I squeal, then roll my eyes at myself. Too much.

"I know," he says. "I think she might have a girlfriend. Anyway, whatever, get down here. We can go backstage."

"I'll be there in ten minutes."

•••

Rudy's sitting on the bar when I get there, drinking a Heineken and scrolling on his phone.

"What about the cameras?" I ask after we've said hello and he's locked the door behind me.

"They don't turn on until we set the alarm. This place belongs to us." He hops back up onto the bar, spinning around and landing behind it.

"Evenin' miss!" he says in a thick cockney accent. "What's yo' poison?"

"Ooh." The liquor selection is strange here, and I'm not really sure what to choose. "Make me something that tastes like candy."

"You got it." He gets to work. It's clear he knows his way around, even though he's only been here for a few months. He makes us both pink cocktails and then grabs my hand and pulls me inside the theater. Tomorrow, the depressing play about Afghanistan is closing. Then they go into turnaround for *The Sound of Music*. It's embarrassing how excited I am to see the set.

I take a sip of my drink. "This is actually really good."

"Actually?" He sits down in the exact center of the house. "C'mon. How do you think I got by in New York?"

"You were equity," I say. "Weren't you?"

"Not for the first few years."

"Ah."

"I like to be busy."

We sit quietly. My head swims. First the wine, now this.

"So why the late-night phone call? None of the other guys picked up?"

"Oh, ha ha."

"What happened to the daddy in the suit?"

"He's . . . I don't know."

"Boring? Soulless? A slave to a preordained corporate identity?"

"Someone sounds jealous," I sing, taking a long sip.

"Confused, maybe." I see through it, though. He thinks he's so cool, with his rolled-up sleeves and his forearm tattoo. Calling himself a bartender, talking about New York, shaking his little cocktail shaker.

"He asked me to move in with him. He thinks it's happening."

"What do you mean, he *thinks* it's happening?"

I shrug. "It would be the easy choice. I wouldn't have to worry anymore. I wouldn't need a part-time job. I could just focus on this."

Rudy squints at me. I'm, I guess, hoping, he's about to fall to his knees and beg me not to accept Vishal's offer. We sit with this news. He doesn't say a thing.

"You're judging me. But I don't care. I really don't."

"You sound like you don't care."

"I don't." I drain the rest of my cocktail.

"Do you want a refill?" he asks.

"Bring the bottle." I'm feeling daring and sexy, and like I'm going to probably make out with him later. When he leaves, I check my phone. I have two text messages. One is from Vishal, wishing me goodnight with another heart emoji and the other is from Anton, another long and desperate screed. Still pining.

It has been a while, but I haven't really needed to see Anton, because I've honestly been feeling really good about myself. Ever since my last session with Renée, I'm just, like, really grounded.

I pull up one of Samantha's social accounts. She's been posting a lot more lately, probably three videos every single day, her cartoony makeup overemphasizing what I remember someone, very kindly, calling a striking face. I scroll and of course find one with Rudy. The traitor. He's smiling in the freeze frame. It seems genuine. I'm immediately annoyed by him, more so than usual.

The video starts off with a normal intro from Samantha "Hi, you guys. It's Wednesday lunch chat and I'm here with Rudy." He nods, all stoic. He's wearing sunglasses, which make him look pretty hot, if I'm being honest.

Samantha turns to Rudy. "You just moved here from New York, where you were on . . . Broadway!" She squeaks the final word, so over the top, as if she can't believe it. Which if I were Rudy, well, I'd be insulted.

"Yeah, six months ago. Feels like longer, honestly." He laughs — he's uncomfortable and takes a sip from his coffee to hide it.

"What was your favorite show you did?"

"On Broadway or off?"

"Whatever," she says.

"Well, I actually got to do this choreographed version of *Hamlet*, which I really loved. It was off-Broadway."

"O-M-G so cool. Did you play Hamlet?"

Rudy appears next to me holding two half-empty bottles of wine. "Red or white?" he asks.

"White," I say, grabbing it, uncorking it with a dull thump and taking a long swig from the bottle.

Rudy smiles slowly. "Jess isn't messing around."

"I was just watching your interview. Needed a palate cleanser."

Rudy whistles and takes a sip from his own.

"I think it's cool. She's really working, you know? What a hustler. It's really impressive."

"I thought you said her vlogging was annoying," I say. Then I consider Rudy's position. It's obvious he's in love me. Maybe all this talk of Vishal and I moving in together has pushed him over the edge and he's going to make a play for Samantha in an attempt to make me jealous.

Me? Jealous?

Not likely.

"Well, I've been thinking about Samantha. The dynamics at rehearsal . . . the way the Captain treats her. How Michelle isn't sticking up for her. Do you really think they'd treat a white person the same way?" Rudy says. And I roll my eyes so hard I fall back into my chair. "And it's crazy because Michelle had to threaten the board with her resignation to get Samantha cast."

"Oh, come on," I say. "She did not."

"It's because she's half-Asian," Rudy says. "The board doesn't think they can sell out the run if Maria isn't white."

"There's no way that's true."

Rudy shrugs. "That's what I heard."

"Well, it doesn't make Samantha any less annoying. I mean c'mon. If I see that vlog one more time, who knows what I'll do."

"You should be nice to her," Rudy says.

"She doesn't even know I exist."

Rudy stays quiet. I can tell he doesn't want to fight with me, that he's struggling with himself.

"Besides, the power structure is such that if I'm mean to her, it doesn't matter. She's the lead. I'm the help. Now tell me, why'd you leave New York?" I make eye contact with him and while I do, I think about straddling him and whipping my top off, and he just melts.

"I don't know." Rudy puts his feet up on the row in front of us. "How much time do you have?"

"I could go all night." I try to make it sound as sexy as possible.

"I bet you can."

It feels like we're about to make out, but he sighs instead and stares up at the stage.

We sit for a while, drinking our beers in the quiet. When it starts to feel awkward I pull out my phone. Eventually he says, "I don't know if I should tell you."

"Tell me what?"

He gazes at the stage, this dramatic, pretentious, contemplative expression on his face.

"That what you're doing right now is the best part," he says. "It's the best it's ever going to feel."

"What do you mean? My life is trash."

He sighs and takes another sip from his wine. If I knew this night would be such a downer, I would've stayed home.

"Have you ever seen *The Seagull*?"

"Like the bird? Yeah, of course."

"It's a Chekhov play."

"Oh, right, yeah, that's my favorite play of all time."

"Really?"

"Of course not." I laugh a little. Like, really. Really! Look at me! See me, here. I've never pretended to be some woman that swans around reading Chekhov before wilting into sadness and blowing my brains out — I don't know if that happens in the play, but I bet it does.

"Well, I think you should read it."

"Why would I do that?" I haven't read a play since my brief flirtation with higher education, and honestly, I don't intend to begin. Who even reads plays? Isn't that why they invented Wikipedia?

"I think you might respond to it." Rudy speaks slowly and firmly, as if me reading this play is some condition for continued engagement with him. As if we're teenagers and he's trying to make me listen to his favorite band or whatever. He wants me. It's like he's trying so hard to deny it, and I don't know why. Just admit to yourself, you want to sleep with the hot girl. It would make things so much simpler.

"What, he's, like, Russian, right? Chekhov?"

"Yes."

"They're so, like . . ."

"What?"

"You know, arty. Depressing. That's not me. I'm . . ." I smile at him, pose, glittering under the dim, romantic lighting. He doesn't react. "Oh, come on. I'm not *The Seagull*! I'm *The Sound of Music*."

"Jessamyn . . ." he trails off and lets his head fall back. "I think you're more than you think you are."

I almost blow a raspberry. Instead, I pat his thigh because I do like this attention, despite myself.

"You sound like my agent," I say. "He wants me to do an AIDS play."

"*Sister Gorgeous*?" Rudy sits up immediately. "You have an audition for *Sister Gorgeous*? Everyone is talking about it."

"Ugh." I'm disappointed. Rudy really is such a shill for the boring. "You too?"

"Pull up the sides," he says. "I'll read with you."

I laugh. "No."

"No?"

"Not interested. C'mon. You know this isn't me."

"They're already talking off-Broadway transfer," Rudy says. That grabs my attention, just the littlest bit. Off-Broadway. Almost on Broadway. Practically. But there are a million things that could happen. I probably won't get it. And then all the Toronto casting agents will see me as some pathetic, sexless nun. Not the stunning, bright shining star I am. I'll be stuck in sad sack roles for the rest of my life where I wail instead of delight.

"Well," I say. "I'm sure whatever pretentious intellectual takes the part will do a great job making everyone feel bad about their lives. In February. I'm passing." It feels so good to speak the words out loud. My destiny is in my own hands. And there's something very empowering about that.

"Jess —"

"Rudy." I grab his thigh again, this time higher up, so he knows I'm serious. I'm intentional. At the very least, I'm thinking about where my hand is. What it is close to. "Stop being such a downer. I used to think you were hot." Rudy laughs. He can't help it — I'm contagious. I sparkle. I'm the most charismatic woman on the planet. And these men want to slap a habit on me, have me hold a bowl while some gay man barfs into it? No thank you.

Rudy shrugs. "You know, Michelle wants to do a jukebox musical next year, about Jerry Lee Lewis?"

"Was he the blind piano player?" I ask. Rudy laughs.

"No. He's a rock-and-roll musician from the south. Guy had seven wives. One of them was thirteen — he knocked her up a year after marrying her. And Michelle wants me to dance around a piano every single night, singing 'Great Balls of Fire'!" He looks at me, expecting I'll say something fiery, or thank him for his feminism, for his allyship, but my mind is already churning.

"Great song, though," I say, wondering if Michelle would consider casting a woman. Maybe I could talk her into it. It would be a transgressive move. Subtle. Take the power back from our oppressors. My heart starts pounding just thinking about it.

"She cast you already?"

"We're talking about it," he says, waving it off as if it doesn't matter. "Who cares! I'm not going to be a slave to the rich donors this theater services. Whitewash history to keep them comfortable. Celebrate a rapist. No thank you."

The booze is making him dark. I put my glass down on the ground and grab both of his shoulders, shake him. His head flops back and forth, though I sense some happiness buried deep under all that angst. He perks up a little, and so I lean in and kiss him quickly, on the lips. Because, you know, who needs some cheering up now? It's a little sexless, but it's enough to make him sit up and stare at me, get out of this dark, dreary, ranting little headspace he's stuck in.

"Would you lighten up?" I say. "I came here for a good time. C'mon. I want to try it out." I stand up, the wine making me stumble.

"What?"

"The choreography," I say, falling over him and out the end of the aisle before walking up the steps to the stage. "C'mon, Captain." My voice is sultry, sexy. Irresistible.

"Jessamyn." He's still in his seat, staring up at me. "Why?"

I feel his eyes on me and I know he's watching so I throw my arms wide and spin around, staring up at invisible mountains, thinking of what it will be like when I become Maria, when I fully inhabit her role.

"Why are you doing this?"

"Because it's fun." The truth, well, I can't tell. He's far too cynical to dwell in dreams — he's been chewed up and spit out the other side. The glowing that possibility can bring totally extinguished. He doesn't understand. He wouldn't. Maybe he's right. Maybe this is the fun part of becoming a star, the part where you're still full of hope.

"Come back," he says, slumped down and staring at me. "Tell me."

"No. You come up here!"

But he doesn't, he just watches me and I'm not sure why it bothers me so much. I like to be watched. But no, he sits in the middle of the audience, just observing me. It hurts. I feel it in my stomach every time I look at him, a little pinch. Of course, it's going to feel better when the house is full, when there are thousands of eyes out there. Then his won't matter to me at all.

135

XVIII

I find my way to the *Sister Gorgeous* audition, though I'd never admit it to Rudy. It's not until I get to the waiting room that I read the sides. I show up an hour early, expecting it to be packed, but there's only three women here. Women I've never seen before. I'm the youngest, obviously, and the prettiest. Sorry but it is what it is.

I think one of them is . . . I recognize her from an HBO show most people didn't watch because it was too sad. But she's here. In Vancouver. In this strange, airy loft that I guess one of the producers borrowed from a famous actor, one of the financiers of this play. This was all told to me by the gossipy intern who brought me upstairs, offered me a bottle of water when I took a seat in the open kitchen they're using as a waiting room. So much for "new faces."

The square bottle he handed me is now clutched in my fist. I've never been to an audition like this before. Not a cattle call, not a self-tape. Tremendously strange.

And now I'm looking at the sides. It's just a monologue. The context is, this nun, who has been caring for gay men during the AIDS crisis, goes to the church for funding, goes to this bishop she has a close relationship with, and he turns her down. And so, she goes to pray, falls to her knees and has this confrontation with God about abandoning these gay men to die of AIDS. Which, you know, fair enough. Seems like a good-enough reason to be questioning the god you've devoted your life to.

Memorizing the monologue is simple. That's never been difficult for me, and I have the words down in only a few minutes. I have that kind of mind. Like a sponge.

As I consider the text, I think about this woman and her faith. In one line, she talks about how the world is constantly shifting under her feet, evolving, changing, but her faith is the thing that helps her maintain her balance. She can always orient herself toward God. But now that she is losing her faith, what is there to hold on to? How can she remain upright?

It's easy for me to find that connection, which, like, I don't know. This is why I don't like theater. It immediately causes my breath to quicken. My heart speeds up and I feel, like, this pain at the bottom of my throat. It feels like a cancer spreading through me, paralyzing me, if I let it. This nun has a point. What is there to hold on to?

Now, when I think of my future, nothing.

But still I go forth. I continue to act in service of God. God is alive in my actions, but He has abandoned me. And He abandoned His own son, sure, but it seems so cruel to leave. I feel nothing. No one here. It's just me in the dark. God. Why oh why have you abandoned me? Abandoned Aaron and Tariq and Charles and Timothy and Marcel. If I am your shepherd, if you act through me, who is here to catch me? To help me? I am alone. I am begging you please, to help me, I cannot go forward alone.

I cannot go on. I cannot go on in service of you.

What have you done to me?

And on and on. It's a bit much. Kind of repetitive, if I'm being honest, just really beating it to death. But I know I'll be able to deliver. Piece of cake. I can do tortured. It's so easy, it's basically my life.

One of the women goes in, gulping, her complexion gray and drawn. Sure, the material calls for it, but she looks afraid. And that's no attitude to take into a confrontation with God. No, she should be pissed off. That's how I'm going to do it. Angry. Because this lady is working so hard and no one recognizes her labor. Not even God. And this piece of shit bishop she tries to turn to tells her no. The church will not publicly help these homosexuals.

She's been abandoned by the one thing she always thought she could count on.

Sort of on board. I guess. I mean. I don't know. It's not "Climb Every Mountain." But I suppose I can relate to her devotion, to knowing that there's only one thing that is meant for you. And what happens when that one thing isn't working.

I wait, tossing the square bottle of water between my hands. Honestly, I was expecting more women to come through the door. But it remains the three of us. I'm embarrassed I came early, though no one seems to mind.

Eventually it whittles down to me, the final woman in the room. The HBO actress comes downstairs wiping tears from her eyes and hurries out. Minutes later, I hear more footsteps and the door to the upstairs opens. A bald man in his fifties wearing a denim shirt with the sleeves rolled up appears, reading glasses perched on top of his head.

"Jessamyn?" he says.

I follow him up a metal staircase. As we walk, he introduces himself as the director and welcomes me inside. So warm, so kind, so interested. This is such a weird process.

In the room, I find two others sitting in chairs. The clipped procedural feeling of cattle call auditions that I'm used to has been replaced by warm smiles and, it seems, expectation.

"So this is Michelle's prodigy," someone says, smiling at me. I perk up at this. Michelle's prodigy?

"I'm sorry?" I say.

"Michelle. At the Company. We're looking all over for our lead, but our hope is to find that special newcomer for this role. We want to make a big splash with *Sister Gorgeous*. It's a hyper-local play with international appeal that's going to really put Canadian theater on the map. It's exciting for us to imagine introducing an actor that audiences haven't seen before. So we called all our contacts to see who they're excited about, and Michelle put you forward."

That wily little worm. Who would've thought?

It's true, then. All of it. She wants me close to Maria for a reason. This confirms it. She sees me. She really sees me. She knows what I can do.

They rattle off some stuff about the play, but I don't really listen. I'm busy considering the implications of what Michelle has done. She's so in love with my talent that she's willing to stake her reputation on it.

They asked me to go ahead with the monologue. I close my eyes and begin. Of course I'm off book, and the rage really takes over. I pound my chest. I shout at the walls. I wail. I give myself over to the unfairness of the moment; of Samantha in my part, mine; of the faith I have to have in myself. I feel myself enraged at all I have given and how nothing has come back to me. Nothing!

And when I finish, I spit the last words on the floor between us, spit them out with so much desperation and rage that I'm panting. I'm sweating. I feel as though my energy has totally changed the room.

I breathe deeply and look up at the table in front of me. They're all staring blankly. We are silent. For a very, very long time.

Eventually David, the director, nods. "That was an interesting interpretation," he says. "Can you step out for a minute and let us huddle?"

"Sure," I say, still panting like I've just run a race. It feels good, though. I feel grounded in the part. I made a choice. That's what matters.

I leave the wooden door open a crack and sit on the landing at the top of the staircase while they talk. They're whispering, so I only catch a few things here and there — "no one else did it like that . . . misread the text . . . off book . . . conviction . . ."

And on and on. It feels like forever. I'm ready to leave, to pick up and go home, because really, like, here it is, just another giant waste of time, of my talent, the disrespect really piling all over me once more. Then David reappears.

"Sorry for the wait," he says. "We're all really passionate about this role, and we love how committed you were to your choice. We wanted to see if you'd be willing to do it again."

I consider and eventually nod. Why not? I'm already here.

"Can you try it with more vulnerability this time? Less rage. Less anger. We really want this woman to feel abandoned by her God. To really feel her loneliness and her brokenness. There's still strength in that, but in this moment, she's really meant to be undone. Do you think you can do it again?"

I nod.

"All right," he says gently. "Take as long as you need to prepare. Come in whenever you like."

Abandoned by her God. Abandoned.

You're not good enough.

I can hear him, hear his voice.

You'll simply never be good enough. Never. The sooner you accept that, the happier you'll be.

Not good enough.

Incapable of it.

My knees on the concrete. Thin fingers squeezing my throat. *Not good enough. Never be good enough.*

But you said you believed in me.

No, I didn't.

Naked, on my knees. Naked before him.

Rage then, but something else, too. Something I don't recognize, beneath it all. A bottomless feeling, the kind that makes me feel like I'll never be able to get up.

The question that rises, all the time, at night, when no else is there with me. No one except that voice. It's impossible, really, to describe the bottomless depths of wanting to someone who has never been there before. The feeling that I'm totally alone in this pursuit of something I cannot grasp.

Because who will I be if I cannot do it?

What if I'm not good enough?

I stand up and walk back in the room. No one is there, though. Sure, the specter of them exists, but it is just me and my God, my belief. And my belief has abandoned me.

I fall into this place, have to claw my way through the darkness. The text pours out of me, but with it, fear. Who am I without this belief? Without this faith? Who am I without my God?

I hug myself. I howl. I demand to know why. Why have I been left here, alone? Why is it me? Why am I meant to hold this suffering?

Where is it? Where is that faith that brought me here, to this place? Why has it left me now when I need it the most?

Where are you? I scream. *Where are you, God? You're supposed to be with me? And I can't — I can't.*

My mouth is frozen open. I have left the Earth and exist only in this place of complete surrender to pain. To this pain. I've opened something inside of my belly, sliced up the fatty sack full of agony, of truth, and am letting it leak out into the room. I hold my abdomen tightly, clutch it, try to keep it all inside but it pours out.

I don't remember the audition ending, just stumbling to my feet and out the door, to the stairs, to a miraculous shining sunny day, and I vomit behind a dumpster in an alley.

I stumble into a cab, the reverberation of the audition ringing through me. My entire body aches. My head throbs so much I have to shut my eyes.

"No puking in my cab," the driver screams at me. "You hear me? It's a two hundred–dollar cleaning fee for puking."

"Fine," I mutter. "Whatever." I give him my address.

"Fucking drug addicts. Get a job," he mutters. I have no capacity for rage. For anger. I can only flop over on the back seat, the enormity of the question hovering over me like a cloud: *What if I can't do it?*

At home, I crawl into bed. My phone rings. I get effusive text messages from my agent — *they loved you* and *we got an offer* and *call me back* — but I know, lying in bed, that I cannot do this. That I am a star. I am not an achy, sobbing woman; I am strong. I am not this weak funnel. I am happiness and I am joy, I am joy, but why can't I stop crying?

No. I text him back, barely able to lift my phone. My body hurts so. *No. We're passing.*

And then, I weep.

I don't sleep. I stay up the entire night, staring at the cracks in my ceiling. The next day, I stumble out for wine, come home, and swig from the bottle until I'm able to quiet the voices, to smile once more.

XIX

The kids are supposed to be stretching, but instead we're all lying on the floor, pretending to make snow angels. I tell them it's a warm-up I learned from my vocal coach, but really I need the feel of the cool floor against my aching, tired body to calm my pounding migraine and the strange, dizzying feeling I get when I close my eyes. I'm never drinking again. I'm an alcoholic. I'm a wastrel. I don't deserve to be alive. If a child trafficker burst into the room and asked me to swap these brats for a daybed, a cold washcloth, maybe some reality television, and no questions asked, I would gladly offload the lot of them into his hairy, tattooed, arms.

My phone has been blowing up all day, first with missed calls and texts and voice mails from my agent trying to get me to reconsider *Sister Gorgeous* (not happening) and then as if he's got some kind of tracker on me that lets him now when I'm at my lowest, my father called during drop-off and again during warm-up, both times leaving messages. He phoned me once last week and I never returned the call. Just wasn't spiritually ready to admit to him my failure, to backtrack and tell him that I'm not currently a lead, that no, rehearsals aren't going well because, though this situation is rapidly evolving, at present time I am an acting coach.

Even thinking about this conversation makes me nauseous. I can picture him yelling at me — "The help? The HELP? What are you doing there?" I know he'll tell me I'm a disappointment, but he'll love doing it because he gets to be right. He gets to be validated for cutting me off all those years ago, for making sure I knew he didn't believe my dreams could come true, and that if I wanted to pursue them, I had to do so without his support, emotional (ha!), financial, or otherwise.

Still, it's not like I was eating him out of house and home, far from it. But because he chose to go into some kind of business that probably has to do with destroying the Earth and climate change, I don't know, he gets to live a charmed life. Meanwhile me, in the business of fixing the soul of this rotten country, of telling stories that reach down your throat and show you the light — like *The Sound of Music*, for example — well, I get squat.

What better way to fight fascism than to inspire men to act, to stand up for what they believe in. Men don't do anything anymore. Like, look, give a big fuck-you to the Nazis and you might get to bang a former nun. Right? What's more compelling than that? This musical could change the world. I could change the world. Me.

Yet I'm the one who lunches on cold sweet potatoes and lentils and whatever slop I find in the gutter. It's why I hate talking to him. Always so smug in his misery. As if misery is the price you pay for comfort, which is totally an oxymoron, if you think about it.

Ugh, I really shouldn't drink. I shouldn't. I'm starting to sound like Rudy. Boring, not sparkling and not charismatic. An actor. A depressing, struggling actor instead of a beaming, bright-eyed star. Which is who I am, goddammit. It's in my guts. It's in my very soul. And I have to start acting like it.

I sit up. The kids are all just lying there, like me. "Lily, lead us in a stretch," I say, and wilt back onto the ground, knowing that she's always waiting to be called on and will be happy to do it.

"Do we have to?" she whines, not getting up.

"Yes," I say. "Or no, I don't know, whatever. The choreographer's coming in five minutes, aren't you afraid of her?"

There's a collective sigh. The last time the choreographer attempted to teach them the steps to what she'd cooked up for "The Lonely Goatherd," she yelled a few times. Clapping her hands loudly, she said, "No, no. No, no. Like this," and grabbed the little one's arm, to pull her forward. Only she did it too hard and the child started to cry.

As Michelle consoled the crying girl, the other kids couldn't make their combinations work. The choreographer then pulled the music director aside and said, "I'm going to have to rethink this entire song," and stormed out.

"I'm not scared," the crier says, defiantly. Ha! Yeah right.

My phone rings again. I check it and of course it's my father. Again. I silence it. Hopefully he's not, like, dying or anything. Though if he was, I don't think he'd admit it. Ever.

"I'm going to go see what's taking them so long."

I get up and cross the room. The grown-ups are working through some blocking in the main rehearsal hall. Most of them are sitting off to the side, bored, while the Captain stands in the middle of the room, listening to Michelle and nodding. Samantha's lower lip quivers and she stares at the floor.

"I just don't know why we have to go over this again," the Captain says. "She should have picked this up already. You can understand why this is frustrating, yes? It's been like this all week."

"It's a rehearsal," Michelle says. I can see her working through the machinations of it in her head. "I just want it right."

"Well one of us has it. I'm getting a coffee," he says as he strides out of the room, pulling his phone from his pocket. Surely to call and berate his agent.

"All right, let's take it from the top. Rudy, step up," Michelle says. "You all run it, we've got to spend some time with the kids."

She makes eye contact with me and nods. I head back into the other room while Michelle has a side conversation with the stage management crew, the choreographer. How to tame an out-of-control male ego. And here I was, worried that the Captain was starting to relax. Thank goodness.

When I return to the kids, my stomach drops. Lily has my cellphone pressed to her ear and appears to be talking to someone. No. No.

"She's right here," Lily says, then holds out the phone to me. "It's your dad."

"What?" I see red, I see fire. Did she tell him I'm a babysitter? That I'm not Maria? Do I have to have this conversation now? I'm still fighting — it's not over yet.

I was just enjoying Samantha's daily humiliation, and now, hell. I grab the phone. This isn't how it's supposed to go. I stare at it, contemplate just hanging up or throwing it out the window or smashing it on the ground. Instead —

"Hey, Dad."

"Jessie! You're a tough kid to get a hold of."

"I'm sorry, I'm in rehearsal. One of the child actors got hold of my phone. Can I call you later?" Silence falls. I try to read into it, to figure out what he knows. What she might've told him.

"Sure," he says. I can see him mentally raising his hands, like "yeesh," calm down. Like I'm the one who's freaking out. Like I'm the one who's been phoning him all morning instead of the other way around.

"I'll call you back." I hang up and turn to Lily. She shrinks under the look I give her and steps back. I lunge, grasp the sausage of her upper arm and drag her to the corner, away from the others.

"What the hell?" I whisper to Lily when I release her.

"What? It was ringing." Her eyes are trained on the ground. "My mom always tells me to answer when hers rings. It could be important. It could be an offer."

She is small in front of me, smaller than usual. I'm clenching and unclenching my fist at my side. Her eyes flit down, look at it, then back to me. Her little brain is putting it all together. What this means. Her home life might be . . . well, I guess I understand why she's such a perfectionist now. What might happen if little Lily makes a little mistake.

"Yeah, okay," I say. "But you shouldn't touch my stuff."

"Sorry. I'm so sorry." I believe her. The line is well delivered, like she really means it.

"I overreacted," I say. "I'm the one who's sorry." I need this one on my side. She's the only one whose name I can consistently remember. The room's swimming. My mouth still tastes like alcohol. Michelle and the stage management team trundle in, holding what looks like seventeen binders somehow bundled between them. Gigantic coffees, water bottles. Chaos. But it's a comfort to remember the director from my audition calling me Michelle's prodigy.

"Where are my kids?" Michelle says, plastering a smile on her face so wide that it seems like her whole head's about to crack open. "Where's my lonely goatherd?" The only one who falls for it is Julie. The biggest attention whore. She runs up to Michelle, who wraps her in a giant hug. The rest remain seated, unsure.

They're shy now, every time she comes in. At first, I thought they were too cool for it, but now I think this little room where we are, off to the side, is a deliberate play. They're kept apart from the grown-ups, so the children understand that being around adults is a privilege. Something they have to earn through hard work they refuse to do. Michelle really seems to have a handle on this production. She's really making it happen.

Of course, she asks me to stand in for Samantha, which I do. The stage management team assembles a platform in the middle of the room, a holdover for the bed for the lonely goatherd scene and I work through the scene with them.

The choreography has little moments for all the kids to show off, either by just being cute or doing a little cartwheel or a turn. It's sweet. There are puppets. It goes so well, I forget we're dancing to a backing track and singing along. I know I'm owning it. The kids love me. Every time we reach the end of the song, the big finish, huddled on the platform together like a little family, all of us panting and beaming, the stage management team breaks out in applause that's clearly tinged with so much relief. This show isn't doomed at all. We're going to make it. We are.

We run it over and over again, adding little tweaks. It's like this sort of magical alchemy has descended around us and we're moving in sublime synchronicity. It's perfect. Everyone's smiling and sweaty when we break for a fifteen. The kids have energy. There's promise here. All because of me.

I notice Michelle heading to the water jug in the corner. I have this genius idea I'm sure she'll be excited about, I just know it and I hurry over, smiling.

"Jessamyn," she says as I sidle up next to her. "Thanks for your help. Samantha has a costume fitting. She's just upstairs though, she should be down in a bit." Her voice is chipper.

"Of course," I say. "Anytime."

"I'm glad this worked out," she says, filling up her water bottle. "The kids seem to be responding to you."

"Yeah, great, listen, I just had a thought about the end of the scene, when Maria puts her arm up —"

Michelle closes her eyes while I'm speaking, almost like she's trying to meditate or something. I don't get it, so I stop talking and wait for her to finish. She opens her eyes, impatient. "What's the idea?"

"So, Maria puts her arm up, and I thought it might make more sense if she did something like this." I squeeze my hands together.

Michelle nods, but she isn't falling all over herself like I thought she would. My suggestion is specific to the moment, really captures Maria's joy and happiness and abandon and devotion. It's clearly the better move.

"I'll think on it. Ultimately, it's up to Sam, right?"

"Sure, but —"

"You're doing great with the kids. Keeping them quiet. And I didn't get any complaints from the cleaners." Michelle pats me on the shoulder and takes a long pull from her water bottle, then exhales in my face. "So, thanks for that. I so appreciate it. Every little bit helps!"

Her grin is so wide, I'm confused. She's going around town telling everyone I'm a prodigy. I've basically been doing this part more than Samantha. This is about a scene with the children too, so obviously what I think is most important. Why won't she listen to me?

Then I hear a titter. See Samantha across the room, leaning on a door jamb and laughing at me. She's in her costume. Not her habit, not the dress she wears when she's a nanny, no, in her dirndl. I'm disgusted to report that she looks great in it. Her waist is tiny and her breasts are full and spilling over the low neckline. And there she is, laughing at me. Laughing!

I move toward her, hands out as if I might strangle her. I imagine my fingers tightening around her little neck, finally, finally giving in to my . . . No. No. I must calm down. I'm able to stop walking and just stand there instead, watching her watching me. My chest is heaving.

"How's it going today, Jessamyn?" she asks. Her voice is perky. But she was laughing at me, just moments ago when Michelle insulted me. Laughing at my humiliation. Wasn't she?

Lily runs over. "What are you doing?" she asks. "We want to run it again. Steve came over!" Steve. The Captain. This should be interesting. Finally, I can show everyone my chemistry with Steve. I can have chemistry with anyone but —

"Oh, I'm back, Lily! I can run it." Samantha reaches out her hand. Lily, the little traitor, takes it.

I almost run and get the costumer, to sell out Samantha, because this is something that is not done. Right? She could tear it. She could get dust on it. One of the children could touch it with their sticky little hands. Or gum! What if there's gum?

Still, no one says anything as she steps into the scene in costume, like some weird mirage. Meanwhile everyone else is wearing their rehearsal clothes: jeans and athleisure, spandex and sneakers. Michelle doesn't admonish her. It's the exact opposite. She claps her hands as Samantha spins around in a circle. "Oh wow, oh my goodness. Look at you. It's perfect. You're perfect."

"Let's not dance," Michelle says as if reading my mind. Thank God. Even if she still has that dopey, thrilled, spewing-positive expression on her dumb face. "I know" — oh she is so pleased with herself, I hate it so much — "let's do the scene we were working before, but we'll run it with the kids."

And everyone is thrilled, for whatever reason, that our rehearsal has been derailed by this costume. None of it makes sense. They take first positions for the scene where Captain von Trapp and Maria argue — he's brought Frau Schrader back to meet the children, but Maria has them in playsuits made from curtains and they're all running around and enjoying their lives. He yells at Maria, he tells her, *No! This is not how my children are. They are obedient, they behave for me.* But of course, this isn't true; the children behave for him, but they chase away governess after governess because all they want is their father back in their lives. They want his love so desperately they behave terribly in hopes of getting his attention.

And here he is, and here Maria is, and they are facing off, screaming at one another, yelling and shouting about how best to love these children. In the movie, this scene always makes me cry, I have no idea why.

But of course, watching Samantha and the Captain butcher it, over and over again, Michelle clapping brightly at the end of every scene, is just grating. And of course, it keeps happening. We cycle through it, the kids resetting back to ones, back to ones, back to ones, Samantha and the Captain screaming at one another, going too big, pulling it back, back to ones, over and over, and my head starts to feel like it's about to burst, to pop open like a balloon, and there's a ringing in my ears, a dull quiet thrum — and then my phone! My stupid father calling me, over and over again, a missed call, I'm at work, Dad, come on, Jesus Christ, I'm at work. Leave me alone. My chin trembles a little and I swallow it. I swallow it all down, stomp on it. No. I am Jessamyn. I smile. I sparkle. I shine.

XX

After Michelle finally lets us go, I decide to call my dad, rip off the Band-Aid. Then I can have a good cry and get Anton to suck on my toes or whatever. He's back to texting me desperately, pretending he never asked me to move in, that the table-flip never happened — which honestly feels like it's for the best. Our relationship really only works when he's capable of worshipping me.

I go around to the back of the theater and crouch, staring at my phone, then give in to gravity and sit back on the pavement like a toddler who has had enough. I'm so tired and the dumpster is cold against my back. I look out through the fading light, at a couple crossing the road. They're in their thirties. The man is tall, has all of his hair still, is laughing at something the woman is saying. She's unexpectedly dumpy, has on oversized sweatpants and a sweatshirt. He's pulling her along by the hand. Laughing, laughing. So loud. Once they reach the sidewalk on the other side, he pulls her toward him and holds her face in his hands, gives her a kiss so tender, my heart screams. But seriously, I want to vomit. Look at her, in those clothes, with that hair. She's not even trying. The way his hands hold her greasy, chubby cheeks. Disgusting.

I dial my father's phone. It rings, once, twice, three times. I picture him checking the caller ID, deciding if he's going to answer or make me wait, the way I made him wait. Play the game I made him play all morning. On the fifth ring, he picks up. "I'm driving," he says by way of greeting.

"What's up?" I ask. "Is someone dead?"

"You thought someone was dead and waited until the end of the day to call?"

"It was a joke."

"Well, ha ha ha."

The line goes quiet. I hear a turn signal in the background. The steady rhythm of it, on and off and on and off. My heart pounds.

"So, we bought tickets."

"To what?"

"To your big debut." His voice catches a little as he says it, as if pride is welling up. I've never heard that tone of voice before. I stop breathing. He's sent me plane tickets, but he's never come to see one of my shows. He's never even come to visit. But now.

"To the first one, on the Wednesday, then Friday, and, uh . . . the matinée on Saturday."

"What?" It's a whisper. I don't recognize myself — who is this wavering woman? "That's three shows." I well up. I can barely breathe. Press my hand against my forehead just to feel something real. I whisper again, "What?" It comes out emotional, high pitched and embarrassing. My throat swells, burns, forces tears. Why am I crying?

I remember what he said to me, all those years ago, when I called him and had to ask for money (not that I liked doing it, it was completely humiliating). I remember every single one of his words. "That's it! That's it. We're done. Enough. It's clear this isn't what you're supposed to be doing, so do us all a favor and give it up. It's over, okay? If you were going to make something of yourself, you would've done it already. Just give it up."

I sobbed into the phone and hung up on him, feeling the residual shame of being a untalented brat not hungry enough to make it. It wasn't even my fault. I'd shot a commercial for this new kind of toaster danish, but the company folded and never paid me. It's not like I didn't try, it wasn't my fault. I even offered to pay him back and everything. Such a stupid prick. It's not like he would've even noticed. But no.

And now.

"Listen," he says. "The past is the past. I don't want things to be like this. And *The Sound of Music*. This is big. I mean, that's a show."

"It is." It's all I can get out without fully breaking down.

"And what I really want to say is, I should've — well, it's all over now. But even if it wasn't about the money, I wish I'd been more supportive. You know? Listened to you talk through it at least. Given you advice. Honestly, I didn't get it then. But Maria von Trapp . . . she's . . ."

He trails off then. His voice shakes on the other end of the line. Tears roll down my cheeks. I tilt the mouthpiece away from me so he doesn't hear me cry.

"I'm just so proud of you."

A seagull screams. I can barely breathe; my jaw is wobbling violently. My dad seems small now, fragile, not a guy in a suit who yells at his employees over the phone. He's softened into one of those old men who sits by a duck pond with a newspaper and a coffee and watches the world go by.

"We're coming for a week. It'll be great. We can really spend some time together."

He talks a bit more about regret, how he doesn't like that I'm so far away. He says he wants to get to know me again, that he's going to retire soon and he wants to take a trip somewhere, maybe Italy or Greece, and he wants me to come. I'm barely holding it together.

When we hang up, I bury my head in my knees and lose it. Shoulders shaking. Finally. Finally.

Except, a small voice whispers, bitter and angry, *the part isn't yours. Not yet.*

"But how?" I whisper. "How?"

When I hear her reedy voice on the other side of this marine shed, it all boils up so quickly. Her camera must be on because I hear her unmistakable yowl, clearer than ever.

"What's up guys."

Picturing her standing there, so unfocused on the task at hand, this important moment in her career, her one shot. All she has to do is be Maria. Just be Maria.

"You've heard me talk about rehearsal dos, but today I'm going to focus on don'ts. In particular, don'ts for other members of the crew who think they're part of the show, but they're, like, really not."

But instead it's all vlog this and promotion that and the Captain doesn't like me, no one is worshipping me.

"For example, if you're standing in for a lead while they're in the bathroom or taking some personal time, DO NOT go to the director of the show and pitch ideas. It's just embarrassing. You're there to be seen and not heard. If you were going to be cast, you would have been cast. But you weren't. So, shut up and learn from those who are, let's face it, better than you. Because this sort of behavior, like, it's standing in the way of you being cast in the future . . ."

If it were me, I'd be cradling this opportunity like a baby bird, holding it close. Working. Working hard. I'd be off book. I'd know every note. I'd do it all. But no. And now she babbles on and on and on. "You just shouldn't say anything" — different iterations of it over and over again, and I can't move. I'm glued to the spot, the snot and the tears dried to my face. Wrung out. Deflated. Used. Lied to.

I keep telling myself that she doesn't deserve it. She's not owning it. She's not grateful for the part, she's not taking advantage of it. If the Captain was treating me the way he is treating her, I would do something about it. I would sharpen the knife. I would reel him in. I would do something. I wouldn't stand there, like a wimp. I would work for it. I would make him love me. I would do anything to make him love me.

Instead, she just talks, talks, talks, won't stop talking about this, won't stop circling the process and the notions, and at the end of the day what she really needs to do is just learn her fucking blocking and her lines and stop talking so much about what other people need to do. Because if she doesn't focus on what she's doing, she's going to ruin this production for those kids.

And those kids! I think of the kids, so innocent, so noble, so adorable. I think of my love for them.

What's best for them.

What they need.

Someone has to look after them. Someone has to look after the children!

"And another thing," she says, her voice so annoying. "Just a little piece of career advice. If you're twenty-six, you're basically pushing thirty. Just some used-up wrinkled old crone. A rotting sack of flesh. If you're pushing thirty and you haven't been cast in a professional role yet, perhaps it's time to give up and try something else. It's clear you're not wanted. It's clear you're not talented. It's clear you can't do this. Musical theater performers are specialists. They are the best of the best of the best. They are truly special. It's not for everyone. And if you're that old and you've never been paid to sing? That's information. And the fact that you can't see that? Well, I'm not sure there's anything more pathetic. It's over for you. So why won't you simply just —"

A scream tears out of my throat and I stand up and run at her, to where she stands on the edge of the wharf. It's not difficult, not really, to push her over, she's just a little thing. She doesn't see me coming. I don't think she does. Two hands on her back, a shove and a stumble. There's a scream, a loud, pained scream. I can't be seen — while her body is in the air, I turn and sprint down a nearby alley, away from anyone who might've been there, and I run, and run.

XXI

"Help! Help! Oh my God, help!" Samantha screams, splashes, coughs. I imagine that coat she was wearing getting heavy in the water. Really dragging her down. I'm panting, hidden around the corner, crouching by the dumpster with my face in my hands, listening to her struggle.

Oh no, oh no, oh no, oh no.

What if someone saw me? What if they saw me push her?

"Someone please, help me!"

My head throbs. I need to help her, I know I should. What if she can't swim? This isn't what I meant to do. It just happened.

I should go. I really should.

But this fear, this terror is keeping me from moving. No one can know I pushed her. And if I'm the first one there, they'll know. They'll know what I did. And then my career will be over. I'll never make it onstage. Not here. Not anywhere.

It's totally possible she didn't see me. "Right?" I say it out loud, as if there's someone nearby who can give me advice. And we are out behind the theater, around a corner where no one really wanders, away from the tourists, away from the Market.

"Help me!" More splashing. "Please! I can't get out! Help! Help!"

It's not like she's going to die. She must know how to swim, right? Everyone knows how to swim, don't they? The human body knows how to react as long as you don't panic. That's why people just toss their babies into pools and let them bob up to the surface. Because of instincts. Samantha should be fine, so long as she doesn't panic.

"Help me! Someone help!"

Oh God, she's panicking. She's totally panicking.

I sit back and look around. The alley is deserted, so I focus on the stairs above me. They are green and rusty. I count them. Breathe in, breathe out. I don't exist. I am just breath in and breath out. Everything slows down. Calm melts through me.

My body has stopped shaking and the tears are gone. I rub my face, pull out my phone, check my reflection. My eyes aren't that red or puffy. Not really. I just need to relax. *Deep breath in, hold, one, two, three, four, five —*

"Help me!"

— six, seven, exhale, one, two, three, four, five, six, seven —

"Help me!"

There's a bit of dried snot on my top lip, which I swipe away with my sleeve. I take another look, another inhale, another seven count, check myself again — this needs to be perfect. And I see nothing. Just myself, staring back, except I seem perhaps a bit more forlorn, and therefore more gorgeous than usual. I look normal. Totally chill. Not at all like someone who just snapped and pushed her friend, someone she truly admires, into the ocean.

It wasn't me. I didn't do it. I was talking to my father on the phone while waiting for a ride from my boyfriend, Vishal. See? I am a boring woman with a boring corporate boyfriend. He drives an Audi. He wears suits. We're moving in together and getting a dog. A rescue, most likely. I couldn't have pushed her. I was way over here.

"Someone call 911!"

It's Michelle. That's my cue.

I run down the alley and round the front of the building, so I look like I'm coming from the wrong direction, cellphone clutched in my hand. A hero, dashing to the rescue. Confusion on my face. What's going on? What's happening?

Michelle's crouched on the edge of the wharf, two of the production assistants running for one of those orange ring buoys hanging near the edge of a pier. "What happened?" I shout while running up to Michelle. My performance is totally selling it — the wonder, the innocence, the panic.

"I don't know," Michelle says. "Call an ambulance."

It seems like overkill to me, but I dial 9-1-1 as I peer over the edge where Samantha is splashing around. She's treading water. It's clear she can swim. Her purple wooly coat is floating out on either side of her. Her hair looks like wet garbage.

The 911 operator asks me rapid-fire questions. I answer each with the intensity of someone who wants to be helpful.

"Please," I say, "please, we need help. Right now. On Granville Island."

I must really be selling it because the 911 operator tells me to slow down. That everything is going to be all right. She asks what happened. I look down. "The lead of our show fell into the ocean!" I screech this loud, to put this idea into everyone's heads. She fell. She wasn't pushed. She fell. If I say it enough times, we'll all believe it.

Is she drowning? "No, I don't think so."

Is anyone helping her? "Yes, some of the stagehands are attempting to help her, but it isn't going well."

Who am I? "I work for the theater company."

Michelle paces back and forth, trying to discern some way to help and coming up short. The stagehands toss Samantha the ring buoy and tell her to climb into it. She splashes toward it.

I tell Michelle that help is on the way. She has a phone out and is looking at it, seems unable to figure out what she should do. I wonder why she didn't call 911, why I had to arrive and do it for her, as if the position of director has stripped her of her agency, her ability to do anything that isn't delegating. Giving commands. Looking outward.

Eventually, she snaps out of it, gets down on her knees at the edge of the pier and starts calling down kind comments to Samantha: *we're going to get you out of here, just hold on, help is on the way.*

Samantha splashes into the ring buoy and pokes her arms through it. She falls back against it, panting, as if this is, like, difficult for her? I mean, it can't be that cold in there; she's being a little dramatic. It's November. Right? Like, November is chilly, sure, but it's no January.

The stagehands shout down to her, tell her they're going to start pulling her up.

"Okay!" she shouts. She sounds fragile, exhausted. Really laying it on thick.

"Jessamyn," Michelle says, suddenly remembering me. Her voice is snappy. "Go and help." I don't like to play the "I'm just a woman" card, but really, what is she expecting me to do? I'm obviously skinnier than Samantha. When I was a child, my gym teacher said if I didn't gain some muscle, the wind would blow me away. That kind of compliment stays with you for life.

Still, it's important for me to play my part. I nod and hurry over to the stagehands, affecting a kind of dazed, useless fear, as if this is all too much for me. I hold the end of the rope behind two guys whose names escape me.

"On three, take a step back," one of them says to me, over his shoulder. "One, two," and they both step back. I thought we were going on three, but I don't say anything, just stumble away from them. We keep going at this rhythm. It's tough to just drag her up. Michelle's still shouting encouraging remarks. "Hold on, Sam! You're doing great, Sam!"

I picture her just lying there, flopped in the ring, her long hair draped over the edge like a dead body. The stupid pier isn't even that high. I'm sure she's totally fine, just a little cold. People in Scandinavia go swimming in cold water all the time. Over there, it's considered healthy.

"Oh my God!" Michelle shouts. "Hang on, stop! Stop! What is that, Sam?"

"We can't hold it!" one of the stagehands shouts. He's got an Australian accent and is actually pretty hot, now that I'm looking at him.

"She's slipping." Michelle's pacing back and forth. "Lower her back down."

The guys in front of me are struggling to hold the rope. The Aussie takes a step forward and suddenly we lose all momentum, the rope whipping through our hands.

Samantha screams and the weight disappears in an instant. Another splash. "No!" Michelle shouts, then knits her fingers through her hair. "No!"

The stagehands and I rush to the edge to see Samantha still splashing in the water. "My . . . my ankle," she shouts. "I landed on something in the water, I think it's broken." I lean over and look. There's nothing there. Just water. God, she's really so dramatic. "It really hurts."

Michelle turns to the three of us. "I think one of you should go down there."

No one moves. I assume one of the guys will step forward, but neither does. It is November, after all. Pretty chilly.

"How is that going to help?" one of them mutters.

"It's broken, it's definitely broken," Samantha calls up. Michelle shakes her head at the three of us, disgusted. But c'mon, it's not like she's taking her jacket off. It's not like she wants to be the hero. And I spot a ladder, way down the pier, wrought iron bars hammered into the concrete for this exact situation. But Samantha would have to swim around a few parked yachts, and now it seems like she's can't climb out herself.

"The ambulance should be here any minute," Michelle calls down. "Just hold on."

Inside, I'm celebrating. I manage to keep my cool, though. Michelle closes her eyes and I hear her quietly murmuring, "This can't be happening."

The four of us loiter on the dock while Michelle continues to shout platitudes at Samantha. Eventually a fire engine trundles up going about four kilometers an hour, lights flashing, and some very disappointingly average firemen lower a ladder into the water. They manage to haul Samantha out, her body flopped over one of their backs. She's conscious when they place her on the gurney and two waiting paramedics cover her with a blanket. Her dark hair is glued to her pale face with salt water. As this all goes down, I look around discretely for security cameras and see nothing. Perfect.

I stand with Michelle, channeling extreme stress and concern. So she sees me, remembers that I'm here, that she wanted me close to the production for a reason, for exactly something like this. An accident. In case they need a professional to step in.

Samantha sits on the gurney while the paramedics discuss something with the firefighters. She's searching the crowd, her eyes stopping when she sees me.

"You," she screams at me. "You!" The second "you" tears out of her throat loudly, viscerally, like a seagull's yelp. A little *much*, if you ask me.

"What?" I am calm. I am reasonable.

"You did this!"

I am water. I am light.

Michelle's eyes bug out. "What?"

"No, I didn't," I say.

"You pushed me," Samantha says.

"Oh my God." Michelle turns to me, disgusted.

162

I rip out my heart and throw it on the ground between us. My body shakes, my expression limp-lipped and quivering. "What? Sam, we're friends. I'd never do that." The injustice rolls through me. I'm Norma Rae. I'm Rosa Parks. I'm a suffragette screaming, "Votes for women." The agony of being misunderstood steadily grows inside me. Every heartbeat pumps pain, anger, all of it colliding in my voice when I say, "How could you say that?"

The stagehands appear on either side of me, clearly eavesdropping. "How'd you see someone push you?" one of the stagehands says.

"I was taking a video," Samantha says. "One of my vlogs. I saw her come up behind me."

"Where's your phone?" the stagehand says. He's accusatory. Angry, even. Nothing like some good old-fashioned workplace solidarity.

"I . . ." Samantha feels around for it and comes up empty. "I must've dropped it."

"This is so . . ." I play up the sputtering, really lean into it. "I can't even . . ." I must be putting on a good show because the other stagehand looks at me with pity. They probably saw me picking up trash and decided we were the same. I appreciate the backup. "I can't believe this, I really need this job, why would I push you? We're friends."

"Listen," Michelle says. "We're not going to solve anything now. Let's get you to the hospital." She takes Samantha's hand. The paramedics load her into the ambulance, and Michelle climbs in after her.

The stagehands stand with me, shoulder to shoulder. I hug myself. This is concerning, after all. This deceit could cost me my job. I could become homeless because of this. Because of Samantha. It's, like, almost Christmas, too. What, does she want me out on the street or something? Where I could freeze to death?

"We're not going to let her get away with it."

"I bet she tripped while taking one of her videos and is embarrassed about it. Actors, man."

I nod along with them, because we all must agree: Samantha sucks. She's exactly the kind of person who would lie to save her reputation. Protect her career at any cost, even if it means a crew member could become homeless.

I know where her phone is, too. There's no question about it. It makes me smile, considering the only real evidence against me has now sunk to the bottom of the ocean.

The stagehands eventually wander off. I sit down near the edge, where Samantha fell in. I sit for a long time, staring down at the water, struggling against, and eventually giving in to the impossibly wide grin that hurts my cheeks. The soundtrack of the last hours playing over and over in my head.

Her ankle, her ankle.

Oh no.

Her ankle.

XXII

Night falls, the moon hanging low over the ocean like it's about to be swallowed up, and I'm still sitting, gazing out at the water where Samantha fell. Waves quietly lap at the pier's poles. I picture her wet hair, the way her body flopped over as they pulled her out, as if she were trying to pretend to be dead. It's almost like she wants to be dead. Maybe she doesn't even want to *do* the musical anymore, what with the Captain and all the pressure and everything. Like instead she wants to be memorialized. I get it. Legacy and all that. I don't know. Something to keep in mind!

Crazy that she tripped on the pier, that she stumbled over a rock or a seagull and fell. So nuts that she was walking while filming another one of her silly little internet videos, lost sense of her surroundings and stumbled into the drink. Hilarious even, that it was her own ego that took her down. The irony! The irony is just so precious. This is the best version of events, the best.

I just have all this energy and don't know what to do with it. I could go home, sure, but it feels like a waste, to surrender all this feeling to an attempt at sleep. I'd just lie down on my bed and stare at the ceiling, and what good is that? What is useful about it? What's going to push me forward? I need to focus, I need to focus on what's important — what's going to get me on that stage. Not going home. Not going to see Vishal who is texting me about Thai food. Really? Thai food! Takeout! No. I'm not going over there; it's like quicksand, a swirling quagmire of love sludge from whence I will never escape. No. He cannot take me! He cannot!

Once I dated this man who kept me on a couch for three months. Three. I suddenly saw the calendar one day and realized I was being swallowed up by pleather. His arms trying to stuff me into the cracks and crevices of his crumby existence. Like, what's next? Pop-Tarts for breakfast? It still terrifies me to know I fell for it.

I just walked out of the room one day and never spoke to him again. Stars don't let themselves get eaten by the couch. Stars don't give in to the aimlessness of life. No, stars have plans. Stars take action. They execute! Stars aren't afraid! Stars don't lose themselves in the goopiness of being a human being. Stars transcend the mess!

I cannot go home now. Tonight is the night I abandon my sluggish humanity and become a star. And I need the one who understands. The one who sees me for my greatness. The one who has always known and isn't afraid to admit it.

I buy tequila, ignore my phone, and for once decide to walk to Anton's house. That is the right kind of gesture, to bridge the gap between where we were before and where I am now. That's right, I am going to find my own way there. I am going to do it. And he will love me for it.

As I think about him, the energy that's been coursing through me swirls, throbs, beats at my bones. I am weightless. If I sneezed, I might just float away.

I wander through Point Grey and south into Dunbar, toward Anton's little basement suite. I leave a busy street and turn onto a residential one, quiet and dark, trees and bushes hiding me from eyes who might see me with the tequila and interpret it poorly. Still, I unscrew the cap and take a swig.

Some children have drawn a hopscotch court on the ground, and I hop toward Anton's basement. Hop, hop, hop.

There's a white poufy dog sitting on someone's front porch up ahead, his head on his paws. I stop and call, "Here, doggie doggie," but he just sits there, tilts his head at me. I stick my hand out. "Here, doggie doggie." Instead of running down to greet me, he stands, turns in a slow circle, then disappears through a dog door. I've never been a dog person, but I feel spiritually connected to them in the sense that they're beloved by everyone. Their presence lights up any room, changes the energy in a space. Lifts people away from their darkness.

From the sidewalk, Anton's basement suite seems quiet. As I creep up to the house, the light from the TV flashes bright blue. I can tell he's up and watching something. Waiting for me, probably, even though he doesn't know I'm coming. "Anton!" I scream. Wild abandon. The most romantic thing. "My heart!"

It takes a few moments, as if he's trying to decide whether or not he should do it. Eventually, he opens his door and steps up onto the little pathway that leads to his apartment. His arms are crossed, conflicted joy on his face. I can see the fight in him, the desire to punish me for my absence, my silence. And the roaring inside of him that wants me, that loves the drama, loves me showing up at his house by surprise, holding a bottle of tequila, looking gorgeous, calling for him with my very soul. Anton! Light of my life. Anton! Your star has arrived.

I run to him and leap into his arms. "I missed you," I say, as I wrap my legs around his waist. He surrenders in an instant, shedding his anger, and carries me inside. Our lips tangle together. We breathe into one another and fall to the floor, clothes discarded, nails scraping at skin, the tequila bottle rolling under his couch. His hands pinch my sides too hard and I cry out, and I can tell he likes it because he squeezes tighter.

I shove him and try to roll away, but he climbs atop my back, lies flat over me. I love it, I hate it. His rug scratches against my chest as he pins me to the floor. "You're never leaving me again," he whispers into my ear, then bites my earlobe so hard I scream.

"Never," I say. I've fallen off a cliff. All that he does to my body — the tightness, the stinging pain, the shock — is undeniable and terrifying and exhilarating and awful and beautiful.

"Tell me you'll never leave me," he says. "Promise."

"I'll never leave you."

"I don't believe you."

I say please, please, please, please, Anton, please. Let me. Let me show you. Let me show you.

He does.

Later, when he falls asleep, I stare at him, my heart still pounding, the adrenaline fighting through my veins. The rage, twisted up with love, with revulsion. The pleasure. The agony.

I pad across the carpet, naked, raw, and pull the tequila bottle out from under the couch. I take a long swig. It doesn't slow the pounding of my heart the way I want it to.

I stare at him on the kitchen floor. Asleep. So peaceful. Probably dreaming about me.

My leg stings. I look down, spot a section of red where I have been rubbed raw by the carpet. Shining skin dotted with bloody prick marks.

More tequila. The bathroom, next. He has only alcohol and cartoon bandages — no cream to make this clean, nothing painless in this apartment. I bite down on a towel and splash the alcohol on the wound and scream into the cotton.

I go sleep in his bed. He wakes in the middle of the night and finds me, holds me from behind and cries, terrified of where we went. What I made him become. The monster I pulled out of his chest.

"I hate it," he says. "I hate myself." He monologues for hours about my virtues, about how beautiful I am, about how I'm going to do incredible things. How every inch of my body is flawless. Perfect.

I'm the king of this universe. His only choice is to worship me, so I let it fester. I am the only thing that matters; I am everything he wants, and he wants me so badly it makes him grotesque. And he's forced to see it. See what he's capable of. See the truth. That I am a bright light, and he is a little worm beneath my boot.

I play up my anger now. My power. The power he's giving me.

"I'm not sure I'll ever forgive you," I say. Oh, it feels so good. In shame at who I turned him into, so animalistic in his wanting that he loses his humanity. I do that to him. Me. That is how incredible I am. "I don't know if I can come over ever again."

"No." He sobs into my armpit. "Please, no." He holds me against him tightly, my body shuddering with his sobs.

"I'll do anything," he says. "I need you. I need you so badly. You are everything."

"I don't think we should see each other anymore." The sun is up. It's early. I need to get dressed, to shower. Today is a new day where anything can happen.

Anton's gone deadly silent. He crumples then. "No. No. Please. I'll do anything. This will never happen again. Never."

"I'll think about it. Don't text me."

"Can I at least take you home?" His voice is getting higher and higher, and he begins to cry. Oh, it feels so good to say it. Here, I am God.

"No."

XXIII

The sun is bright, happy, positively lighting up everything around me. I'm bathed in gold as I lean against a stop sign sipping on a coffee, content. All is right with the world. The children are about to be dropped off, then I'm sure I'll have to face Michelle's questions about Samantha tripping and falling into the ocean. Good thing the truth is on my side. Because, man, what a klutz Samantha is. Making her video. Walking off the pier like that while talking about herself, to herself. It's really upsetting, but maybe, also, a little funny. Right? Maybe?

Oh, why did she accuse me, you ask? Me?

Great question.

The truth is, Samantha was probably embarrassed she tripped while filming a vlog and had to blame it on someone, to make herself feel better. Everyone hates that vlog, and I know that deep down, Samantha has noticed. She knew the schadenfreude among the cast and crew would be too overwhelming if she was honest about how she went into the water, so instead, she's pulled me into her drama. My God. She is just totally out of touch with reality. And she and I, well, we have a bit of history.

See, we both got cast in this summer Shakespeare festival the year they decided to do musical adaptations of a bunch of tragedies, to try to lighten them up. Samantha might have had a bigger part than me, but I was Barnes, the director's, favorite. He'd co-created a series of indie musicals on Broadway when he was in his thirties, then gone on to teach at NYU. Had a real career. And he loved me. And no, nothing happened between us. I wasn't involved in the scandal. But he saw something in me. Even though, once again, she was the lead, she couldn't enjoy it because he loved me. Me. And Samantha knew it. She couldn't handle it. She never let it go, even after everything that came out about him.

I've never really said it out loud before but, she's sort of . . . obsessed with me. Which is weird, because she's had a bit more luck with her career, recently, than I have. And c'mon. She already has the lead role. Why should she care about little old me?

So, you see, there's history here. It's personal. You're right, she's not being very professional.

Oh, you want to fire me? Me? I may be a nobody, but surely my presence looms large enough among the cast and crew that people would notice, would be angry at the injustice. We don't want to upset everyone. And the children. This is the kind of thing that could stay with them for life.

I grin just thinking about it. These scurrilous and unfounded accusations will not stand!

The Australian stagehand sidles up next to me on the sidewalk where I'm waiting for the kids. He's drinking a coffee and has a cigarette between his dirty fingers. Nods. "Morning."

We chat a bit. His name is Jack. Tells me a bit about himself. Things I promptly forget. "Really messed up that Samantha accused you," he says, and I nod. It is messed up. "What's going to happen, do you think?" Oh yeah. He's invested.

I shrug, try to smile, just a helpless, innocent little girl. Powerless within this grand system, which could swallow me whole at any moment. Australian men are notoriously sexist, so he's going to want to protect me because he thinks I can't protect myself. "I really like the kids," I say. "I just really want to see it through with them."

"They seem to like you," he says.

"I hope so."

As if on cue, Lily practically leaps out of a vehicle. "Jessamyn!" she shouts as she runs up to us, all excited. I notice that she's done her hair like mine, a long braid over one shoulder, except hers is thin and wet and has a bauble at the end of it. "Oh, hey Jack," she says.

"What up?" he says and high fives her. I'm surprised she knows his name. Then I remember Lily's pedigree. I bet her parents coached her to walk around the room and shake everyone's hand. I once worked with a kid from the Disney Channel who did that and it is a great move, if you can pull it off. You never know where you'll get your next job.

"I don't know," Lily says, smiling. "Did you hear about the meeting?"

"No," I say. "What meeting?"

"Michelle called a meeting this morning. She wants everyone inside ten minutes before call."

"Is that so." Jack says it in a big voice that he clearly puts on for the kids. Lily doesn't seem to mind though, which annoys me. The kid could do with just a touch more cynicism. "Probably to tell everyone what a great job they're doing!"

"I bet that's it," Lily says. "I was thinking about it last night and . . . I think this show is going to be really great." She throws herself at me and wraps her arms around my torso, letting out a delighted howl as she does. I pat her on the head a few times and she seems to like it, twirls away from me and starts skipping in circles around a lamppost.

"Aren't you nervous?" Jack asks.

172

"Yes," I say, sighing. "I really want to keep my job." He reaches out and squeezes my shoulder, as if to say, *Over my dead body. They're not going to get away with this.* And then, as if he's been conjured, Rudy peels up on his bike. Clearly he's been pulled over here by jealousy, this other man fondling my body. Jack nods hello at him, then walks back over to the stage where another of his grubby coworkers is holding open a door.

"Hey, Rudy!" Lily says as he climbs off his bike. He's panting, his chest rising and falling.

"Morning, ladies," he says, out of breath. I roll my eyes. Why is he always here? Lily blabbers at him as he locks up his bicycle. I gaze down the road, as if I'm annoyed that the rest of the children aren't here yet. I don't want to get into it with Rudy. Especially if he caught wind of what happened last night. I know his reaction will be aggravating. But he keeps standing there, reacting to Lily's yammering and looking over at me, hoping I'll join in. Lily picks up on this and grabs my arm, swings it a little so I'll pay attention to her.

"You know, Jessamyn, I was telling my mom about you last night, and she said my agent sends out open calls sometimes and she saw someone auditioning backup singers for their '80s cover band," Lily says. "Maybe you could go out for that."

I bite down. Hard. Feel the pressure of my teeth pushing against each other, like they're about to crack. "Oh really?" I say.

"Yeah. I think you'd be great at it."

"What makes you say that?" I could strangle her. I really could. I want to.

Lily looks back and forth at Rudy, then at me, as if it's all obvious. "I think you could get that part. If you wanted it."

"Wow," I say, still struggling to keep it together.

"Hey, now," Rudy says, cutting between us. "I think what Lily means is, we'd all just love to see you onstage. Right, Lily?"

"Of course!" Lily says. Thankfully the weird girl arrives, and Lily sprints over to her. In an instant they're both barking like dogs.

"See? She's just a kid," Rudy says. And I nod, take a deep breath in and a deep breath out. Count backward from ten. He's right. She's just a dumb kid. Rudy also rubs my shoulder, like the stupid Australian, as if to say, *It's going to be okay. I'm also on your side.* And then he heads into the theater, leaving me behind with the children.

The rest of the kids are on time, for once. It's a real shock to the system. We all trek inside together. They find spots on the ground while the rest of the crew hurries in behind them clutching coffee cups and water bottles, scripts and binders, bags, shoes, and croissants in loud pastry bags. I settle in next to Lily, who beams up at Michelle, perched on a stool in the middle of the room with the entire cast and crew assembling around her like she's Mother Goose and it's story time at the library.

"Hello, everyone," she says. "Thanks for coming in early. I think we're all here."

My heart pounds and I don't know why. Because I'm innocent.

Michelle looks around the room, as if she's counting and can name everyone on the cast, everyone on the crew. Doubt it. "Great. So, I just want to inform you all that Samantha took a tumble last night and she's sprained her ankle."

My face is impassive.

Fuck.

A sprain?

She was howling that much over a sprain?

Why couldn't she have broken it? I mean, it's awful. Obviously. But a sprain is muddy. A break is cleaner. A break means it's time to find a replacement.

A distressed murmur rises up through the crowd. "The doctor thinks two weeks should do it, but obviously that cuts into our rehearsal time here. She's taking the next few days off, to rest up, and will be back observing rehearsals on Monday, when we move off island to the Franklin. The set should be ready for us then, or at least the pieces we need to start really nailing that blocking."

Lily reaches over and clutches my hand, obviously distressed. She truly has a *but what does this mean for me* expression on her face. What a natural. This kid is going to outlast us all.

"We're still talking through next steps, but the circumstances around Samantha's tumble are a bit foggy for us right now, so if anyone was hanging around the stage late last night, about an hour after rehearsal, we'd like to speak to you. Thanks, everyone . . ."

The stage management team immediately starts shouting, and the original schedule resumes. I try to make eye contact with Michelle. I know the position she's in. I'm the accused but also the only person here who can do the part. It's me. It's me and only me. It's efficient that I step into place. I already spend all my time with the children. I know the choreography. Why not, right? Why not me?

It's not about recognition or the applause. No. It's about the work. It's about helping make this the best production it can be. Michelle calls out the schedule. We're on vocals, the kids and I, in our side room. I round them up, even the little one, Julie, who's hanging around Michelle, trying to appear adorable, hands behind her back and toeing the ground as if she has a question. And I realize then — she's acting out some blocking from act two, plastering it on her face as if it's hers. The sneak. I grab her hand.

"But I have a question," she says as I drag her off. "It's important."

I pull her toward the side room, maybe a little too hard. Lucky no one here is watching me; they're all too into themselves, huddled about, probably trying to crack the code of what really happened to Samantha.

"What's your question?" I ask as we cross the room.

"Is Samantha okay?"

"I think so. Why?"

"I don't know," the girl says. "I think she's pretty."

Oh, come on! The words reverberate in my head like a gong. Of course, the children love a victim. Love some conflict. Love to be a part of the drama. Clearly, I have work to do.

XXIV

All morning, I sing along with the children, the music director standing in front of us, waving his arms, conducting. *One two three one two three.* I help the kids find the pitch. "I'm up here," I sing, holding it, listening to the piano, listening the way Renée taught me to listen. Occasionally I look at Lily, and she jams her thumb in the air, either up or down, and I scrunch up my nose to get it right. The tweaks are small, but these tiny differences, the ability to hit a note exactly right, is what differentiates the professional from the hobbyist. And I know because I'm a professional.

By lunch, the kids don't sound so terrible. Even the music director is nodding and smiling. He's stopped looking out the window and sighing, which seems like a good sign.

It's a very vocals-forward show, this one. You know, because of the subject matter. You can't be doing jazz hands when the Nazis are afoot. It's got to be at least a bit serious. They accomplish this by singing with some dancing thrown in, marching in squares and circles and in lines. Which, thank God, because the kids . . . they just don't have it.

You have to want it. I'll be surprised if any of them build careers off of what I'm seeing here. Singular threats, all of them.

We break for lunch, and I spot Michelle at the door. She's leaning on the frame, watching us, her forehead crinkled. She calls the musical director over and whispers something to him. They go back and forth, and it becomes clear they're talking about me.

"That was great," Lily says, sidling up next to me. "You're not so tone deaf after all."

"I'm not tone deaf." I'm annoyed at the little runt, so much so that I'm not even going to have some of her lunch, not even if she offers it.

"Sorry, you're right. You aren't!" She says it like it's a mystery she's just solved. Like isn't that great — we figured out you're not tone deaf. Like a doctor telling me I don't have cancer or that I didn't actually eat my twin in the womb.

Michelle appears next to me as I'm opening a bag of fruit snacks for one of the brats. I take one piece as tribute. It's blue, and I realize as I'm chewing it, the gushing, oozing between my teeth, that it's going to dye my tongue. Evidence I've been pilfering food from the children.

"Jessamyn, can we talk? Over there?" She gestures with her head. I swallow the candy, hopefully before it gives me away, and follow her to the corner of the room. Whenever I'm waiting for life-changing news, my body always seems to become weightless, like all the marrow in my bones has been sucked out by some sort of God-like vacuum. I'm on edge, anticipating the question I know is coming. For her to say she was *listening*, that it was *gorgeous*, that *my tones mingle so well with the kids', that they all obviously adore me, can I please save the day and stand in for Samantha until she is better? My voice is just as strong, my acting skills surpass hers. This is obvious to everyone, and my knowledge of the choreography, really is just a bow on top of the gift that I am, that I've given them by taking this job that is so, so beneath me.*

I actively try to keep my imagination from spinning off to opening night, where Samantha, after watching me perform at dress because of some other freak accident to come, just admits that I'm better in the role and offers to step aside for the rest of the run. Because it's the truth. For art's sake. It's not so far-fetched. I could see her doing it. The power and depth I bring to the role, my loving relationship with the kids, the undeniable chemistry I have with the Captain that I can build when given the chance. "We owe it to this show," she'll say to me. "We owe it to beauty."

Michelle folds her arms and eyeballs me, whispers, "What are you doing?" in this voice that instantly pulls me out of my daydream.

"What do you mean?"

"Why are you singing?"

Excuse me?

"This is a tricky show, for vocals, I thought helping the children was part of my job."

Michelle purses her lips, sighs out of her nose. Because she knows I'm right. It's part of my job. She said it was in our meeting. Again, she seems to be counting in her head before she speaks.

"We're in a tough spot now, with Samantha out. I just need everyone to stay in their lane."

I pause. My heart pounds. This can't just be about the singing; it must be about what happened yesterday. "I didn't push her," I spit out. It's angrier than I want it to be. I can barely keep myself from spiraling, thinking what might happen if I lose this job, if I lose my shot at Maria. I've come so far and I'm so, so close. And the phone call I'll have to make to my father, to admit failure. It's not an option. It simply is not an option.

Michelle's eyebrows shoot up. "That's not what this is about," she says. "And I think it's best we all move past yesterday. Samantha's in a difficult place, and we all need to support her."

"You don't believe me?" The tears come easy. This is a true injustice. I reach up and wipe them with the backs of my knuckles. "I've been working so hard —"

She cuts me off. "It's not that I don't believe you. It's that I need to be on Samantha's side. I need to be on her team. This show is . . . well, there's a lot riding on it. We all need to work together, every single one of us, from the assistant directors" — she looks to me wide-eyed, as if I give two shits about that credit — "to the stars. And I mean that. Everyone is playing a part here. And I need you to play yours."

She leaves me there. So, she doesn't want me to sing in order to save Samantha's ego? Oh, come on. She's not even here. So outrageous. Ridiculous. Play my part? My allegiance is to the show, to the children. I have to do what's best for them.

...

In the afternoon, I'm supposed to be coaching the kids through some choreography, running it over and over again. Instead, Lily runs in after an alleged trip to the bathroom and says, in front of everyone, "I heard what happened to Samantha. In the bathroom. Some of the dancers were talking."

Everyone rushes over to her, tries not to salivate too much while we wait for her to unleash the gossip, which I know is just as important as what might've actually happened.

"She fell into the ocean while filming a vlog and was so embarrassed, she lied and told everyone Jessamyn pushed her."

The kids all react in different ways.

The boys laugh. The littlest girl's eyes bug out. She's afraid. Confused. She's too young to understand. "Jessamyn pushed her? Why'd you push her?"

For some reason, I was expecting this to be a rallying cry, for them to become outraged and start talking about how they were going to protect me. That they'd know, implicitly, in their hearts, that this was out of character. That there's no way I could ever do something that heinous because I'm pure of heart. I'm their friend among this wild pack of adults who speak to them like idiots.

Instead, I'm about to be burned at the stake. A witch hunt. Coming for me. Every last one of them. They're all coming for me.

"I did not push her," I say. "She's lying. I was waiting for my ride and talking to my dad on the phone — you know he called me yesterday." I gesture to Lily, bring her in, make her feel important. Lily sits up at being noticed, nods. "I heard a scream and ran around to help pull her out and she accused me, in front of everyone. She lied."

Oh, they all perk up now. They're invested. Kids hate liars, probably because they're the biggest liars of all. Lily is beside herself, throws her hands in the air and buries them in her hair. She starts pacing back and forth. "What are you going to do?"

"I don't know," I say. And then I start to cry. I sit down on the ground. I expect them to arrange themselves around me, like they do to Maria in one of their tableaus, instead they just stand there and blink at me, patently uncomfortable that an adult, the person who's supposed to be caring for them, is showing weakness.

"I'm just worried for you kids. I want this to go well for you. Your professional debuts."

"Well, it's not actually," the oldest boy interrupts. "I did *Les Mis*."

"So did I," says another one, the jaded one who seems like he'd rather be anywhere else.

"I was in *Annie*," says Lily. "Just a West Coast tour, but still."

The realization that they all have more professional credits than I do just makes me cry that much harder.

"I just don't want to get fired because Samantha made up a story about me. You get that, right? How would you feel if I made up stories about you? You wouldn't like that, would you?"

The pack of them shake their heads. The littlest one seems upset about everything all at once but isn't yet smart enough to comprehend injustice.

"They can't fire you!" Lily says. The others don't seem to care. "They can't. I . . . I won't go on."

"Really?"

"Yes," she says, nodding. I wipe my tears away. Lily doubles down. "There's no way I will. Ever." Her cheeks are flushed. She's telling the truth.

"Thanks, Lily, that means a lot." I open up my arms and give her a chaste hug. The creepy girl throws herself on us, too. "Me neither. I'm not going on without you." So fickle, these kids. I love it. I'm obsessed. The little one arrives next, leaps into our puddle, buries her face in my armpit.

"It would be really unfair if you got fired," the oldest boy says. He's hugging his elbows, seemingly terrified to join the love-in. He keeps glancing at the Tupperware container across the room where I've stored their phones, as if he's desperate for something to help him escape his emotions.

"It's really unfair," the younger boy says.

I shrug, doing my best to summon the far-away stare of a woman who has seen some things. Who has *lived*. I am a warning to them. About showbiz. About growing up. About life. "Life just isn't fair."

This seems to spark something in him. That brief, pre-adolescent fire, the slow unfolding of how the world treats *people like us*.

"I hate her," the younger boy says. "I hate Samantha."

Finally. They're committing. They're committing to me.

"I love you . . . kids," I say, conjuring up the emotions I've felt during the hundreds of hours I've spent doing detergent commercials. "I want nothing more than to be there for you, every day until this show is over."

"You will," Lily says. "There's no way." She holds my hand.

"Thank you," I say, then stand up. "We should probably go through the choreography."

The kids groan in a good-natured way, the kind of groan that acknowledges me, loving them, having their best interests at heart, knowing at the very least a few of their names.

At the door, I spot Rudy watching, arms crossed, brow furrowed. I smile at him over the heads of the children, as if to say, *See? Look. I am doing my job.*

XXV

"**H**ow are you doing?"

Rudy asked me to have a drink after rehearsal, and we wound up on a dumpy patio near where the fishermen park their boats. The bar has a real nautical theme, and like most places I go with Rudy, he seems to know someone who works there. This time it's a man with a fuzzy beard and two plate-sized plugs extending his earlobes, perched on a stool near the register, cleaning his fingernails with a knife.

"Who cares, I want to hear about Broadway," I say. He chuckles.

"I don't know," he says. "What's there to tell? It's a job."

"But you're here."

"Yes."

"Instead of working my dream job."

"It's not a dream when you're doing it. It's just the same thing, over and over again, every night for different busloads of tourists. Too much smiling, too many assholes. It starts to drive you nuts."

Impossible. "I would love that," I say, because I know I would. All of those faces, staring up at me every night. The applause. The laughter. The energy. The support of my cast. Knowing I was on the right path. That I was building something. A career. My chest hurts thinking about it, picturing it. It feels so close, being here. I am so close, and also so far away.

I vaguely remember him saying something about his parents and having to come back, but honestly, I don't like to keep track of that kind of thing. He abandoned Broadway, his dream, to come home and care for his parents? I guess some people would call that nice and cute and devoted and like he has his priorities in the right place. And other people, like me, would call it lunacy. Just become rich and then you can pay someone to do it for you.

"I also, man, I don't know," Rudy says. "It was the wanting that killed it for me."

"Wanting? What do you mean?"

"Like when I was fighting for these parts on Broadway, it all began to feel as if I just became my desire. I was just this person who wanted something, and that's the only way I could define myself. It felt really gross. That's not real. Just wanting all the time. And it's not worth it. I promise, it isn't. One day you'll wake up and you'll have no friends . . . no one will like you. You'll have a few lines on a resumé, but it won't really mean anything. Because the thing that made you love it in the first place has been destroyed by all that wanting."

I blink at him. It's the dumbest thing I've ever heard. I'm not in this to make friends. I'm in this to be great.

"Every morning I woke up and every choice I made was about getting onstage. And that is just not sustainable. You don't make good art that way. And I wasn't." He gives me a pointed look as if to say, *And you won't either.* Then he stares off into the distance, doing this haunted-man bit. Haunted by his past. Lost to himself. Gross.

A seagull lands next to us, outside this strange bar. I glare at it through the muck on the window, the fug. It ignores me and starts to scream, its entire body undulating as if it's trying to excise a demon from the pits of its very soul.

"It's all just so . . . hollow," he says. "You know?"

I shake my head, no. No, I don't know at all.

"You're so stubborn," he says, smiling. "I think you get it, even if you won't admit it."

I shrug and grin, just a hint of mystery added to it, as if to wink at him, as if to say, *Whatever you say*. Because he's made up his mind already. About what I think. Why bother fighting with him?

I think back to our night in the Franklin after closing, when he watched me sing onstage. The way he watched me. His eyes sliding over me. Conflicted. Pained. For once, torn between this vision of me in his mind, this intellectual art freak who doesn't shave her pits and what he saw in front of him. A vision. A star. A beautiful bright light he couldn't touch if he wanted to because she's too hot. She's moving too fast. She cannot be contained. And I was onstage, and he was in the audience, so he had to watch. He had to see me. He couldn't look away. And he hated it.

"So, you know what I heard," Rudy says, desperate to escape the awkward silence. "And you can't tell anyone. It's gossip from one of the guys in the box office."

"Ooh, tell me, tell me, tell me."

"What have you heard about the Company's financial situation?" he asks.

"That it's not great."

"Yeah, they're in big trouble," he says. "And it just got worse. There was a hack, because of course this company doesn't have any kind of cybersecurity. Anyway, the hackers stole all the subscriber information and held it ransom."

"No way." Even though I want to take the lead in this musical — and I will — the thought of the Company being embarrassed publicly for having poor judgment is deeply satisfying to me.

"Yeah, and get this, they just paid the ransom. It was a hundred grand, and they just forked it over because they're afraid some news outlet would find out and all their old subscribers would panic. Apparently, they're deep in debt, about to go under. So if this musical sucks . . . that might be it."

My mouth flies open like I'm some bumpkin. "What?" I don't know why I thought this institution was bulletproof; the signs have been around for a while. We're down to two stages from three. And this whole "no understudies" thing. The picture of it is much clearer now than it was before.

"Yeah," Rudy says. "I know. Michelle might sink the ship, and in less than two years."

For some reason, I feel slightly panicked and cover for it by taking a drink. Most people might see this as bad news. Yet, me? This just makes it all the more exciting. When I step into the lead role, which is going to happen any day now, my performance is going to save this company. A hero. I'll be a hero.

Rudy's expression turns concerned. "Are you all right? Why are you smiling?"

I shake my head. Take a long drink from my pint. "Sorry," I say, swallowing my beer, grimacing a little — he ordered me an IPA. Me. He said he thought I'd like it. "That's terrible, I don't know what came over me." Still, the smile twitches at the corners of my mouth. "Wasn't rehearsal nice today?" I think of the kids, how they rallied around me. "So nice to have a break from Samantha."

"Really? Why?" Rudy studies me, confused.

"I don't know, the energy just felt so . . . relieved."

"What are you talking about?"

I can't believe he dares to try to gaslight me like this. "Well, everyone hates Samantha."

"No, they don't," he says.

"Yes, they do. She's a burden."

"No, she isn't. We were all talking about how awful it was without her. She's the lead. You support your lead. Didn't you sign the card?"

I suppose I remember someone passing around a get-well card, but I just scribbled something illegible in it. You know, for appearances.

Rudy is such a child. He's such a baby. "Well, the crew hates her."

"No, they don't. They just like to bitch." Rudy sips from his beer, contemplating me over the foam. "Just like we complain about the patrons. But it doesn't mean anything. C'mon, you know that."

Inside, I am rage. I am boiling. I picture Rudy falling into a roaring fire over a bed of hot needles. He screams in pain as hundreds of tiny pins puncture his skin, and I raise my foot over him and stomp down.

On the outside, I try to look happy. So. This is information. Rudy doesn't hate Samantha. He believes in her. I sigh. "You're right. I just love to get caught up in the gossip."

Rudy leans toward me with a conspiratorial gleam in his eye. "Speaking of Samantha," he says. "I heard the rumor. Did you do it?"

I laugh. "Yeah, I did. And I'd do it again." I mime shoving Samantha off the pier. What a hilarious joke. He pauses, clearly unsure how to react. Like he thinks I'm being serious! Where is his sense of humor? "Rudy, I'm kidding."

He blinks. Uncomfortable. Takes a drink.

"Oh my God, you're being so dramatic. My theory is, she was filming one of her videos and wasn't paying attention, and she just walked right off into the ocean."

Rudy nods. "Yeah. One of the props guys said the same thing."

"It's just so stupid. This whole thing. They should recast her. She can't rehearse!" Rudy stares at me again, as if he's trying to solve a puzzle. "Why are you looking at me like that?"

"You need to stay positive," he says, putting a hand over mine. "Remember, I said this job would be difficult."

"It's not about me," I protest, shifting, always shifting. "I'm just thinking of the children. You know? They deserve a functional Maria."

"I guess." He's hovering on something but decides to ignore it, which, honestly, great, because the last thing I need is Rudy being suspicious.

"And . . ." I start, though it makes me want to scoop out my eyeballs, "maybe you're right. About Broadway. Maybe."

The satisfied smile that breaks across his face is enough to make me throw myself off the pier, give myself to the waters. A real testament to my acting ability that I'm able to sell it enough for him to believe me.

"I only opened up to you because I care about you," he says.

Though he really does make it so easy.

He pays, of course, and we walk out of the bar to his bike locked to a nearby parking meter. I hug him goodbye. Linger with my arms around him. He smells like stale cigarettes and dirty laundry.

"I always feel so much better after talking to you," he says, which is hilarious because I'm not sure *talking to you* is the correct way to phrase it. *Talking at me*, maybe. He didn't care what I had to say. I make an excuse and leave. There's something about him that's just so content. Like he's diagnosed me as troubled, but then he put me on the right path and now gets to feel good about himself. Whatever. In his dreams, maybe. No, definitely. When he closes his eyes at night, I know I'm there.

I check my watch. I know she'll be awake. She's always awake. The Company's in trouble. This isn't just about me anymore. I need to phone Renée.

•••

"Well," Renée says. "I think I can clear my schedule, if it's an emergency."

"It is," I say. "I need you. Samantha walked off the pier and sprained her ankle."

"Really." Renée lets out a tinkling laugh. "Oh, my dear! The muse is smiling on you. What did I say? What did I say about you, knowing that it was right? Committing yourself fully. Giving your-self over. And now —"

"It's happening," I whisper. "I mean, it's going to happen. But I need to be ready."

"Of course, of course. My goodness. I am so proud of you." I hear noise in the background, the shuffling of papers. "I'll just get my calculator, hold on."

I wait, as she rummages around. "All right, so here's what we need, I think. Emergency all-day session on Sunday." Tapping, tapping. "Plus the last-minute booking fee. Then every night next week, let's see here, hmm. And I'll make you an early morning training plan, something to work on, on your own. Independent study fee. Yes, yes." Tapping, tapping. My heart pounds. I know it's going to be a lot, but it's worth it. It's always worth it. Because it's an investment, right? An investment in myself. "Should we say three thousand?"

I breathe. What is three thousand, really, when you think about it? It's nothing in the grand scheme of things. "Okay," I say, taking a deep breath, exhaling. Excited, even. Because it's going to be transformative, I know it. We're going to dig in together.

"You know what? Because you're so loyal, we can make it twenty-five hundred."

"Really?" I whisper. Oh, she loves me so much. What a beau-tiful soul.

"You're my finest student, Jessamyn. Yes, let's say twenty-five hundred, but it'll need to be cash."

"Deal," I say. "Thank you. Oh, thank you so much."

We hang up. I don't have it, now, the cash, and I don't know how to get it. Still, I promise to call her back to confirm when I have the funds, any day now. It's a lie, of course, but one I'm committed to, because I'm not going to let something as meaningless as money stand in my way.

XXVI

"**W**here have you been all my life?" Vishal asks as I snuggle deeper into the couch, wedged under his armpit. He's drinking and watching hockey and boy oh boy, he's very invested in it, I can hear his heart pound under my ear. I don't know how to answer this question, so I just smile up at him, give him a quick peck on the lips.

At the little intermission, Vishal gets up to get another one of those canned vodka sodas. I'm not really drinking mine because I drank with Rudy and need to be one hundred percent on next week when we move into the theater, so that when Michelle turns to me, I'm ready to shine. Alcohol just muddies my light.

Because, against all odds, Samantha hasn't given up. I checked out her channel yesterday, and her ankle is in one of those big boot walking casts and she's pretending like nothing happened. "Just a sprain," she trilled. She didn't tell the story. "It's no big deal. I'm going to be back on my feet in no time."

It has to happen, any day now. I think about how it will go. Michelle will call or text and ask me to meet her at the stage before rehearsal. She'll give me the news, give me time to celebrate, to react, to call whoever and tell them, but then we'll have to keep it quiet. We'll have to announce it that day, but somber, because it's sad when a lead hurts themselves and someone has to step in to save the show.

"I want every night to be like this," Vishal says as he sits back down. He lifts up his armpit, and I slide back under it, press my head against him just like before, gaze up at him and bat my eyelashes like a cartoon.

"Me too," I say into the fleece of his sweater, even though I want the exact opposite.

"We should go look at dogs this weekend," he says.

"I would love that."

"When are you moving your stuff in?"

And I realize this is the perfect moment. "I think I might need to delay a bit," I say. I thought this through. I know I can get Vishal there, it's all just a matter of the performance.

"Why?"

"I need to start working nights again. At the theater." This is a lie, of course.

"But I thought you were working days?"

"I'll have to do both."

"Oh." He seems to be considering if he wants to keep digging. But if he really wants to be in a relationship with me, if he's really in love with me, as he claims, he'll keep digging. He'll express some kind of curiosity. "Why?"

"I need to pay for an intensive with my vocal coach."

"That's too bad," he says. "Why do you need the coaching? I'm sure you're incredible."

I give him a look that is so loving, so deep, so meaningful. We're really connecting.

"Yeah, it's kind of exciting, though, I mean, you can't tell anyone."

I'm letting him in. I'm pulling him toward the goal. The dream. Trying to intoxicate him. "But if it happens, it's huge. I might be getting cast."

"What?" he perks up. He's excited. Everyone loves news. Everyone loves a dream come true. Everyone wants to be there, wants their name in the credits. Wants Special Thanks. It's like he can smell the Oscar and wants his name in the speech. Well, if that's the case, he'll need to get on board now. On the ground floor. He'll have to invest.

"It's complicated. The lead sprained her ankle."

"In rehearsal?"

"No." I tilt my head toward him. "Get this: she walked off the pier while filming a vlog."

He raises his eyebrows. I expected him to laugh, but instead he seems concerned. "That's horrible."

"I know," I say, changing my tone of voice, mirroring his emotional state.

"So, wait, you're going to work nights —"

"Well, I'm going to give my vocal coach all my money, for now, and then once I get through the intensive, I'll start working nights to pay it off." Which is a lie. But what I'm really giving him is an opportunity here, to step up. To love me, just like he claims. If he does he'll invest in my dream. Instead, he just nods.

"But wait, how will you work nights if you're in the show?"

I take a deep breath, which hopefully makes him feel a little embarrassed that I have to explain things to him.

"Well, if I get cast, I won't have to work nights. But if I —"

"Wait, but aren't you working nights anyway? As the babysitter?"

"You're right," I say, playing dumb. "I didn't think through this plan. Shoot. Gosh." I sit back. He's caught me. He's poked a hole in my fake plan. Deflated it. Ruined it. Now is the time to step up and save the day.

"There's no understudy?" he asks.

"I'm the understudy," I say, impatient. Any minute now.

"You are?" he says. "Then why do you need coaching? Sorry, I'm just trying to understand."

I am patient. I am loving. I love him, in fact. So much.

"I think the director secretly hired me to be the understudy, to skirt the union, but I really need to be ready, you know. For when she asks me to step up." I totally thought he was going to offer to pay for my vocal coach. He knows how much this means to me. And he gives me money all the time.

He's about to say something, then stops himself.

"What?"

"I don't know anything about it," he says.

"No, you don't."

"It just seems like —"

"What?"

"You book so many commercials."

"And?" I say.

"Why don't you just do what you're good at?"

Silence. I let it drop like a stone between us. I stand up, walk to the kitchen and open the fridge, not because I want anything, but because I need him to feel this anger between us. Feel my anger. I ground myself, the way Renée taught me. Breathing in and out. Feeling the energy in the deepest part of my body, coursing from my toes to my chest, the tips of my fingers.

I slam the fridge. A bit too hard. The condiments on the door rattle. How did I find myself here? With this rube? This life?

"What is a commercial?" I ask. My entire body is shaking. Hot acid rising in my throat.

"Huh?"

"It's a sales tool. You want me to sell myself? I may as well become a prostitute. Do you know what happens if your commercial goes viral these days? Do you think anyone takes you seriously once they've seen you selling fabric softener? I only do it when I have to. Do you want me to make desperate decisions? If you don't support my dreams, then you don't support me. Period."

My chest is rising and falling quickly, as if I've just been sprinting. He is so ignorant to how delicate these choices are. I weigh every commercial that comes in, consider the potential for internet ridicule, whether it could go national and cement me as a laughingstock. Like that woman in that commercial for back medicine that a bunch of teenagers became obsessed with. Reacting and acting her out, over, and over again. She wanted to be an actress and last I heard she ended up an accountant.

In Oklahoma.

Vishal doesn't say anything. His face is blank.

"I'm not giving you the money."

That feeling, shame, surprises me, takes control. "I wasn't asking you for the money," I say. "I was sharing my life with you. The life you seem to want to share. Or was that all bullshit?"

He rolls his eyes, so I do him one better and turn and walk out the door. Seriously.

The nerve of this asshole. Hockey. The couch. A dog?

Who does he think I am?

...

Outside, I spot a man virtually identical to Vishal holding the leash of a dog. They're about the same age. I don't know kinds of dogs, but he's a normal sort of dog, kind of medium-sized, nothing super specific about it. The guy is wandering down the street, thumbing his phone while the dog smells rocks. I'm sure that Vishal is copying this guy, or maybe this guy is copying Vishal. Vishal is such a bland person. He doesn't understand what it means to dream, he only knows to want what other people have. Not an original thought. Not ever. I'd respect him more if he wanted a fish or an iguana. Not a dog. Not a rock-sniffing, slobbery dog.

He needs me. That's what it is. He needs me to make his life interesting, to make it entertaining. To give him something to think about that isn't a dog! Sports! I can't. I cannot.

Of course, as I start walking toward my apartment, which is too far away to walk, he phones me. Some conflict will do us good. The night was too boring. I decline and he calls me again.

I know how this will go. He'll apologize and ask me to come back. We'll make up and maybe have sex, or he'll cry and I'll hold him while he falls asleep and confesses something wild to me, like how he had an affair with his teacher when he was a teenager. It was supposed to be hot, he'll say, but it makes him unable to trust women. Now he hates them. He's been unpacking it with a therapist. This commitment is supposed to be a big step for him, but he forgot about me. He forgot to see me. He forgot to think about what I might need, what I want. And that's the essence of a partnership, is it not? He'll fork over the money for my vocal coach, he'll believe in me. He'll invite me to meet his family. He's got, like, seven sisters — they're all taped up on his fridge, smiling. Sisters who are married, with children, with families. My phone rings again. I answer.

"Jessamyn, come back," he says.

"No."

"We can figure it out. We can talk. I can help you get a loan, maybe."

A loan!

I hang up. What does he think this is? As if he can just suddenly change the entire dynamic of our relationship based on the whims he's calling love. As if the money that he so freely used to reel me in is no longer a factor in our relationship. Like I don't get to have what I want because I have him. Like he should be enough.

And when I really consider the money, well, it's always been about the money. Always. The biggest joke is that he thinks this rock-sniffing dog-on-a-couch life is enough for me. No! Absolutely not. And it never will be.

He wants his little girlfriend who acts in commercials now, who is hot enough to be a star, but she'll give it all up to have his children. Is that what he wants? I bet it is. Well I'm not falling for it.

I walk and walk, back to my apartment. If I'm going to commit to this workshop with Renée, then I need to focus. He stops calling. It doesn't matter. Renée loves me, she wants me to succeed. I'll figure out the money thing later. I think of my father, briefly, attempt to concoct a lie, but the thought of asking him makes me want to shrivel up and die. No, I can't ask him. He has to think I've made it. That I've finally made it. He has to believe in me.

I'll have to find another way. And I will. I always do.

XXVII

The kids are wide-eyed, excited about the set. "Wow!" Even the oldest boy can't stop staring at it. He takes out his phone and starts videoing, and I grab it from him. Delete the footage.

"Hey!"

"You can't take a video. Don't you know anything?"

"I just want to show my friends," he says.

"Then make them buy tickets." His face falls. I guess for a kid like him, there might be some social capital in getting cast in a professional production, to get to brag a little online, but also I understand him not wanting people to come see him in his nerdy lederhosen.

"Can I have my phone back?" he asks.

"No, they're going in the bin."

The rest of the cast is seated in chairs in the audience, feet up, eating snacks, unimpressed. It's a fine set. Perfectly fine. But it's two dimensional, the paint job just a little . . . I guess the kind word would be "impressionist." It's certainly not of the level I'd expect for the ticket price.

I spot Michelle and the Captain at the back of the house. He's standing there with his arms crossed, nodding. They're discussing something serious. He's listening, taking it all in. His ego has cooled a bit now that we've entered the meaty phase of rehearsal. The working phase. Maybe he got his agent to get him more money.

I edge closer, pretending to search for something on the ground.

"I could really use your help," Michelle says. "Just keeping the energy in here upbeat. You're a leader. Everyone looks up to you because of all of your credits and experience. We're so lucky to have you. I don't want anyone to start snarking about Samantha's injury, which she should recover from handily in time for the show."

"So, she's all right?" Steve says.

"She should be. And I need us to be a team. Can you do that for me?" Michelle reaches up and squeezes his shoulder. Stares into his eyes. I feel the energy crackle in the air between them. Damn, Michelle. Doing what needs to be done. If I wasn't so desperately annoyed by the fact that she's clinging to Samantha as the lead, I'd be impressed by her commitment.

"Yes," Steve says, a little breathless.

"Thank you," Michelle says. The relief in her voice is palpable. It's almost like she's telling the truth. "It means . . . so much."

I have to choke on a laugh at the breathiness of her delivery, but the Captain is eating it up.

"She's here!" one of the assistant directors shouts from the lobby.

She's here. I crane my neck around the door. It's Samantha, of course. Good Lord. She's here. Roll out the red carpet.

I go stand with the kids and notice a La-Z-Boy on the stage, ratty, patched with duct tape. It's strange, and it takes a beat for me to put two and two together. Then I see Michelle with Samantha behind her, crutching into the room. The cast starts to applaud and cheer, clearly happy to see her, which is just bananas to me.

And now, here she is, swinging down the aisle, the black boot on her foot like a pendulum. It's called a walking cast, though, doesn't she know? Doesn't she get it? She's allowed to walk on it. The crutches are such a theatrical move. As if she's Tiny Tim.

The applause gets louder, reaches a kind of wallop. Disgusting.

"Oh, stop it," she says, grinning widely. Even the kids, who were so recently supposed to be on my side, are just clapping along with everyone else. Where is the loyalty? I've been training them, haven't I? Helping to shape them? And now here they are, rotten turncoats, applauding the enemy.

When she reaches the stairs to the stage, the Captain steps up next to Samantha, so she's between him and Michelle. She holds their shoulders and hops up the steps, takes them one at a time. It's obvious she's moving slowly, really basking in the attention, the momentary bliss of all eyes watching her, of the applause.

Michelle takes the stage. "Let's get going, everyone. Samantha's going to be here, watching."

At least she's going to ask me to stand in for Samantha. At least I'll get —

"And I'll be standing in for her today, so please, be kind." A warm chuckle rises up from the crowd.

I am rage. I am fire. Michelle? Michelle standing in for Samantha?

What? What? It's all I can do not to rush the stage and shove Michelle into the wings.

No one is looking at me, so I slip away, stumble out the door to the alley. I shove my fist in my mouth and scream. A muffled, frustrated, howl. Beastly, almost. I don't recognize it.

It's never enough. All I've done and still, it's never enough. Whatever happened to working hard, committing, and achieving your dreams? Whatever happened to that? Instead, it's just insult after insult after insult. The shame of failure hovers around me. The sound of my father's voice telling me to quit. Of Barnes telling me, as I lay naked in his bed, that I couldn't do it. Vishal unwilling to pay for my coaching.

I'm panting. All of my cells are vibrating, rushing all over. My vision grows narrower, like I'm unable to see the edges of my own mind. Spinning. Nausea. I lean against the disgusting concrete wall outside, brick that smells like rotten, sun-baked piss.

There's a dumpster next to me, green, rusty metal. I start to picture shoving Michelle down into the gap between it and the brick wall but stop myself. No. I need to behave. I need to be helpful. Because Maria is helpful. I need to be good because Maria is good.

I catch my breath. Inhale, count to seven, exhale, count to seven. Smile. Picture myself onstage.

It's impossible to know how long I am in the alley. You'd think they'd miss me. But no one comes to check on me, to make sure I'm okay. No. Out here, I am alone. Eventually, a white truck pulls up. A bunch of the stagehands hop out. "Can you get the door?" they ask. I ignore them and go back inside, let it slam behind me.

...

It's a big scene we're running after lunch, and I take a seat in the audience. If Michelle doesn't want me to step in, I may as well let her deal with the kids. After all, that's Maria's job. If she's standing in for Maria, she should do it. I open my email and read a few opportunities passed along by my agent. A voice over audition for a Ziploc bag commercial, an ad for a digital home assistant where I'm the nerdy life of the party, more TV commercials, mothers in various states of shock and awe at the disgusting shit their families put them through, others I don't bother looking at. The smells. The stains. The chaos. One of the auditions is at three today and frankly, I don't think they'll miss me here. My agent texts me, *Did you see the sides?* I leave my ringer on but quiet, so I don't miss anything.

It was so stupid to take this job. I should be out there. I should be away from this cesspool, finding a way to make it happen.

I watch Michelle onstage as she places everyone where they're supposed to be. She has a strange way of walking about the stage, as if she's almost stumbling, like she's on a rocking ship in the middle of an angry sea and can't quite get her bearings. It's the dinner scene. The so long, farewell dinner scene, and the entire cast is involved. We've run this so many times, but transferring from the rehearsal room to the set seems to have made everyone act like they're blind.

Samantha's sitting in her La-Z-Boy, with her leg propped up, her chin slumped in her fist, her other hand on her phone. From one angle, it seems like she's videoing the rehearsal, taking B-roll for her stupid vlogs, maybe, but I'm not sure that's the case.

To me, she looks bored. I don't blame her. This is tedious. Watching Michelle flail about, unable to keep her attention on any one given moment, seemingly obsessed with this perfect tableau. She's pulling the kids this way and that, and I can tell the littlest ones don't actually know what's happening, where they're supposed to stand. Lily is biting her lip. She seems troubled by the chaos. I know these kids now, I know them. We nailed this blocking during rehearsal, we've been running this over and over again, and now that we're onstage, Michelle wants to change it.

I stand up and wander to the other corner of the theater, sit down. Almost gasp out loud, almost laugh as if to say, "Ha! I knew it!" From here, I can see Samantha's screen. I can see her scrolling through Instagram, stopping on different blobby photographs. I watch her subtly flick her thumb, the entire operation so careful and underhanded and phony. Exactly what I'd expect from her. She's not committed. She's just here to be here. For the performance of it. To make sure that no one is taking her place.

And it's then that I know: Samantha will never make it. She doesn't have it. She doesn't want it enough. Some people say talent is this unknowable thing, that it's transcendent of developed skill, that it exists inside of you, and as long as you nurture it and care for it and treat it delicately, there's no reason you won't find some way to share it with the world. But she isn't here to share anything. It's vile to watch her thumb that screen so delicately, pretending to be focused on the work, when really all she wants to do is share

201

and brag and promote, become a commodity. Capitalism's final conquest, her human body. And she's putting a cute little bow on it, leaning in.

"Okay, let's run it," Michelle says. "First positions."

Everyone scrambles. The kids, I can tell, are not in the right spot. Michelle grabs their hands and pulls them to wings.

"I have a question," the littlest one, Julie, says.

"Can we just run this one quickly?" Michelle says. "Then I'll answer your question."

"But I don't know what to do."

"Just do your best," Michelle says. "We'll have to practice, practice, practice to get it right. Okay?" Michelle turns and leaves little Julie there at stage left and she immediately falls back onto the floor in that way only tiny kids can.

Michelle gestures to the music director. He counts everyone in and the soundtrack blares from the speakers.

The adults do fine walking through the choreography, until Michelle herself turns in the wrong direction and hits Rudy right in the chest, causing him to step back and onto Lily's foot. She screams and falls down, rolling around on the floor with all the drama of someone who's just been struck by a vehicle. My girl!

The actors all stop and Michelle hurries over to Lily, looking around the room for me. "Where is Jessamyn?" she snaps and peers out into the audience, to where I'm sitting, trying not to laugh at this clown show.

"You asked me to stay offstage, Michelle," I say. She didn't specifically say those words, but it's what she meant. "I'm doing what was asked."

"I'd also like you to do your job."

"It's not her fault," Lily says from the center of the stage. I could kiss her. The stage manager is hovering over her with an ice pack, trying to decide if she needs to pop it or not. "I'm okay. But Michelle, you don't know the steps. You're not a dancer. Jessamyn knows the steps. Why can't she stand in?"

A murmur goes through the cast. Oh, Lily. Brilliant, beautiful Lily.

"I think it could be helpful," the Captain agrees. Always loved this guy.

"We like Jessamyn," the littlest one says, stomping her foot. A roaring flushes through my body, a smug pleasure radiating all over. Michelle's face is near purple. I want to hang on to this feeling forever. I've done it. I've won.

"You're right," Michelle says. "All right. Back to ones." The adults in the cast move back to their first positions for this number, most of them in the wings, a few at the back of the auditorium.

I slump to the stage. I can't look too happy. Can't seem too eager. But inside, I am bursting. I am exploding. As I walk past Samantha, on her stupid overstuffed chair, I laugh quietly, so only she can hear. And she does. Her eyes narrow. She sits up. Puts her phone away.

The afternoon positively flies by. Everything gels after this. The children laugh, have fun, even the Captain seems engaged. There's so much joy on the stage. The kids run around in circles during lunch. They're amped up, playing a weird combination of hide-and-seek and tag that Rudy and a few of the other chorus members join in on. It's almost as if we're a family.

After lunch, we run it over again and again, the choreographer screaming, "Yes! Exactly! Beautiful! This is exactly what I'm talking about! Hit it! Hit it! Hit it!" And by the end of the day, the kids and adults are all exhausted, sweaty, cheerful, elated; even Michelle seems relaxed.

"Excellent work, everyone," she says.

I'm doing it. I'm really doing it.

I loiter in the lobby after the kids have gone home, make myself available in case Michelle or the stage management team wants to speak to me, give me notes, maybe check my availability to step in as, at the very least, the official understudy. Instead, I hear the crutches coming up the aisle on the other side of the door, two voices speaking low.

I slip into the coat check, crouch down against the door where they can't see me, and pray that no mice will come running out of the corners.

"It just doesn't seem appropriate to me," Samantha says.

"I know. You must so badly want to get out there."

"Exactly," Samantha says. "Maybe we should get me a wheelchair, so I can be rolled through the motions at least. Maybe Jessamyn can push me through the choreography since she knows it so well."

I picture doing it, grasping the handles of the chair, tripping and accidentally dumping her in the orchestra pit. I bite down on a chuckle at the thought of her going headfirst into the timpani.

"That's an idea," Michelle says quietly. "Listen, though. You have nothing to worry about. There's no universe where it isn't you on that stage opening night."

"I know. It's just . . . That's my part."

"And you said the doctor gave you a week or two to heal, right? And then you're back on your feet?" The desperation in Michelle's voice is so obvious. It's very interesting to me that she thinks Samantha is lying.

"My follow-up is on Monday," Samantha says. "Just to clear me, so there's no long-term damage. That's the only thing delaying. I could probably hobble through it tomorrow, if you really need me on my feet."

I nearly laugh at the desperation in both of them. So much riding on it. So much. And the loss of confidence in her voice seems to awaken something in Michelle. A reminder of sorts.

"The part is still yours. It's yours!" Michelle says, seeming to accept Samantha's dodgy diagnosis. She's speaking with a fire and a fierceness that makes my eyes fall open, wide, angry. "There's no replacement for you. Absolutely not. Patti LuPone could walk through those doors and demand it, and I'd still say sorry, that part is for Samantha."

This makes Samantha laugh. Soon they're both laughing, and Michelle is slopping on the compliments. Their laughter is so high pitched, it makes my eye twitch. I mean, of course Michelle has to keep Samantha happy. They wouldn't even be having this conversation if I wasn't luminescent onstage today, right? If I wasn't perfect? Samantha's threatened by me. And she should be. The part is as good as mine. It's about to be mine.

My phone buzzes in my pocket. It's Adam, my rep. Maybe Michelle's called him. Maybe I'm getting some paperwork on this stand-in thing. Putting me on hold for Christmas, just in case.

I answer. "Where the fuck are you?" Adam hisses at me.

"What? What do you mean?"

"The commercial — you replied to the email yesterday. And now they're waiting for you. You'd better get there right the fuck now. I've had enough of your shit, Jessamyn."

"All right," I say, trying to remember replying to an email. But I don't. I don't remember. "All right. I'm going." I really shouldn't even bother, though. Judging by the fear, the intimidation in Samantha's voice, I should just be focusing on Maria, should be loitering around, waiting for Michelle to pull me aside. To tell me she was just talking up Samantha so she wouldn't be upset. But I'm the one she really believes in. I'm her prodigy. Can I make sure I have the choreography down? Can I start running the songs? Am I off book?

Of course I am. And what's infuriating is we're opening in three weeks and Samantha isn't. I know she isn't. I saw her reading off the page today at lunch with the Captain. Reading. She hasn't even bothered to memorize her lines.

I hover in the lobby, near the doors, but Michelle hurries off without even thanking me for today. Confusing.

Still, Adam is useful enough that I shouldn't piss him off completely. Pretty soon I'm going to need him to negotiate a new, much bigger contract.

XXVIII

"**Y**ou didn't read the sides?"

The room is of the normal, depressing, office park variety with a stained drop ceiling and a gray folding table. Three bored people slouch behind it, and a laptop with a large woman videoing in on screen sits between them. They introduce her as a representative from the Turkey Farmers of Ontario.

The entire set-up is absolutely normal, except this audition has an extra folding table full of giant turkey legs sitting on paper plates, at least a dozen of them, all in a row. A fly lands on the cold, congealed flesh. I wrinkle my nose.

"There was a mix-up," I say. Mostly because I don't want this. It can't happen. There's no way a digital ad with me taking a giant bite out of a turkey leg and saying, "That's turkey-licking good," is going to be put out into the world for everyone to see. I will not become known for turkey. I cannot be associated with turkey.

"We waited for you," the casting director says. I know him, have been in front of him a few times and he's always pissed about something.

I can't help myself. The way Adam spoke to me is still bothering me. As if he doesn't have to care about my emotional state. He treated me like a child. So unprofessional. I've made him thousands of dollars. And what has he gotten me? A meat commercial? What does turkey-licking good even mean? I ask the question, though I phrase it as if I'm curious and not thinking this is the stupidest shit I've ever heard.

"We want people to think about fried chicken when they think turkey," the woman on the screen says. "Because there's really nothing better than turkey."

I nod. "Right." I take a beat to process what is happening to me. To be sure of it. I give them my most accommodating smile. "I just need to step out. Just one second."

The casting director throws his arms up. I walk past the turkey legs, several still sitting there with a bite taken out of them. So unsafe. I could catch a disease. I could get herpes from accidentally eating a used turkey leg. Herpes on my face! Do you think Idina Menzel has face herpes? No. No, she doesn't. Because she would never subject herself to these conditions. Do I really want to be encouraging people to lick turkeys? I could be sued.

My cellphone in hand, I scroll through to find Adam's contact information. He answers on the fifth ring. I wedge myself into a doorway so they can't see me.

"Jessamyn, what's up?" he asks, though his tone is clipped. It's only six-thirty. It's not like he was asleep. Maybe he regrets the way he spoke to me.

"I can't do the turkey thing."

He sighs, long on the line. "Why not?"

"It's humiliating."

"You haven't worked in months."

Has it been that long? I could've sworn I did a life insurance commercial. No matter. I'm doing something. I'm really doing something now, for myself. "I'm an assistant director at the theater," I say. "It's a passion project. It's important. We spoke about this."

"That might be important, but so are your relationships in this industry. Carlos waited forty-five minutes for you because I begged him to. You said you were going. And now you're just going to walk out of this audition? Think about this, Jessamyn."

I am thinking about it. What I want my future to look like. It can't just be a dream. I have to make choices. I have to commit. And it sounds like Adam doesn't believe in me enough to really see what I'm trying to accomplish. What my heart dares me to try to do.

"If you think I'm going to take a bite out of a turkey leg and say wow, that's turkey-licking —"

"Okay, Jessamyn," he says. "First you pass on *Sister Gorgeous* and now you're just going to blow this off. I think it's time for us to part ways. Our priorities are clearly different." And he hangs up on me. He hangs up on me.

Me.

His best client.

His most talented client.

My cheeks burn. I don't bother popping my head into the audition again. I don't want to face that turkey farmer. Why should I be speaking to a turkey farmer?

I stride past the door at least, so they can hear me leave. So Carlos can hear me leave. I won't be working for him again, but I don't care. I can't. I am a star. I have to commit. That's the only way I will get respect; the only way I can respect myself.

As I walk out the door and into the night, I feel incredibly light and wild. As if my life has suddenly been unburdened by this thing I do not need. Something that has been holding me back from being truly great.

When Adam emails me, confirming that he's terminating our relationship because of my behavior, I tilt my head back and laugh to the night. Who cares? Who cares about money? Who cares about turkeys and commercials? There are only better things in front of me. Great things. And I know exactly who can help me. Really, the only person.

XXIX

The night is dark and quiet as I make my way to the ATM machine near my apartment. It's in a vestibule. I slide my card in and see that I have exactly seven hundred dollars in my account. I withdraw all of it and begin the long walk to Renée's. She isn't expecting me, but it doesn't mean she won't see me. She is my light, after all. And I am hers.

Especially when I explain about the turkey commercial, about Adam discarding me against his better judgment, all because of his ego. She'll have to take me in when she hears the story. She'll have to help me. Right? I bet she knows people. Bigger, better people. I bet she is just waiting to introduce me.

Besides, it's not like Adam saw me, *really* saw me. Saw my star power. No, he saw a commodity, a body to hold up a box of Tide. But that isn't me. He never even got me a musical audition! Not once over the course of my career. Because he doesn't understand that world. He doesn't have any cultural capital. He's just a businessman, holding his little briefcase. I don't need him. I don't need more businessmen in my life. I need creatives.

The path up to Renée's house is long and winding, built over old train tracks. It's so quiet and beautiful, and I feel so peaceful as I trudge up the gentle curve. Sure, my feet ache, but it's easy to forget about the discomfort, because me? I'm ready for Renée to push me toward transformation. I know I don't have enough money, but I also know that she appreciates me, how hard I work, how much I want this, how much I need it, how much I deserve it. Because I do. Deserve it. I've worked for it. It's supposed to work out. This has to work out. Because if it doesn't, then everything I've done up until this point is meaningless. All of the groping, the harassment, fucking all these losers for attention and money and self-esteem. And for what? For what? What am I supposed to do now? Quit? Leave it all behind and try something else?

Who am I without it?

It has to mean something. Everything happens for a reason, and so much has happened to me that there must be a reason for it. It can't be random. It can't just be this. So many moments of being made to feel small, like I don't exist, like I'm an idiot for wanting this, for wanting to be more than I am. I mean something. I mean something. I matter. I have to matter. If I don't matter, then what else is there? What's the point of being alive?

This fist of energy gathers in my chest, between my collarbones. Tiny pinpricks of it. I can't escape it. Put my hands on my knees, head down at the ground. The man, I remember him now, the man, his greedy fingers reaching out to pinch my breast in front of six hundred people in the audience. All of them just sat there, eyes forward, waiting for the show to start. They weren't looking at me because I wasn't onstage. I was nothing. I was alone. But if I'd been onstage when that happened to me? Well, I wouldn't have been so alone, then, would I? Wouldn't have been so vulnerable to this perversion. I would be someone worthy.

Of course, Renée is going to let me in. Of course, she'll help me, even though I don't have all the money. I've given so much to Renée, she should give something back to me. She should because I deserve it. I deserve something good to happen. I'm a good person. I am so nice to those children.

There's an odd lightness surrounding me, a buzzing energy inside of my head, like I've had six or seven or eight cups of coffee. I feel incapable of focusing on anything at all. My phone has missed text messages from everyone.

Vishal wants to talk, of course. Boring. A series of long monologues from Anton about how he's going crazy and needs me and wants to see me now, right now, because if he doesn't, he doesn't know what he'll do, what he's capable of. The small blue bubbles get larger, expand, threatening to burst, just like my heart.

Even Rudy has slid in there. "What are you up to?"

Everyone wants me. Everyone.

Now it's just about choices. About what I choose to do.

Renée's house is quiet, dark. No sign of movement. The gnome that usually stands smiling by the door has fallen over, his demented grin half-buried in dirty leaves. Still, in the quiet, I take a deep breath and realize it's started to snow. Maybe it was snowing the entire time and I didn't notice. I breathe in and out, and take in a moment of peace, watching the flakes as they drift through the darkness. My heart hammers in my chest. Dizzying, really, to feel so breathless, weightless. It's almost like I'm about to die. I need to convince her. I need her to help me. She will. I know she will.

I don't know why I'm nervous.

I step up to the door and ring the bell. Wait. No lights come on. She must be home, though. I ring the bell again. And again. A light flicks on upstairs. It feels like hours, but eventually she comes down to the door, opens it.

"I'm here!" I say, and walk through the door. "I'm here. I have an installment." I hand her the cash. She was clearly asleep, but it doesn't matter. She can help me.

"Are you all right?"

"Fine," I say and push past her into the living room. "Don't we have a session?"

Renée looks at her cuckoo clock in the corner of the room. "It's late, Jessamyn. And you're so sweaty. Did you walk here from the theater?"

"No, an audition. I didn't book it."

"Oh," Renée says. "You should sit down. I wasn't expecting you."

I take off my jacket and my shoes and duck into the music room, sit down in my usual seat, next to the piano, hoping that she'll follow, that she won't ask questions, that we can just practice. Instead, she stays in the front room. Why isn't she coming?

Eventually she shuffles out through the kitchen, the bead curtains rattling behind her, a glass of water in hand. She's wearing slippers and a robe. I look around the room and see boxes, half opened, stacks of music books and playbills, lush scraps of fabric, masks and costumes all half in and half out. The light behind her Tony is off.

"Drink," she says, hovering over me. I accept the glass of water and take a sip. "What's going on?"

"I need help," I say. My voice cracks.

"What's going on?" Renée says again, with more intensity. "Jessamyn. Tell me."

"I thought we were doing a boot camp. I'm ready to start. There's more where that came from. Can we start at the beginning? It's a very good place to start."

"This isn't the price we agreed on," Renée says, staring at the damp money in her hand. "Why is it wet?"

The injustice builds and builds inside of me. I've given her so much money. She takes everything from me. I subsist on food from dumpsters, root vegetables, bananas, and for what? So that when I really need her, when the moment has arrived and it's time for me to step up, she can just turn me away?

I snap then. "I've given you so much. You can't help me now? Just once?"

"Drink," Renée says, and I obey her, drain the glass and hand it back to her.

She turns and leaves the room. I contemplate following her back into her disappointing kitchen, the human side of her that I cannot stand. She was once a star. And now it's like she's quitting. She's giving in to life, to aging — no! You have to fight! She should be fighting, and she isn't. Why isn't she fighting?

She returns holding another glass of water, hands it to me. It's lukewarm. At least she's abiding by the tenets of vocal care. The thing is, if she really cared about me, she would make me warm tea with lemon, or put lemon in the glass. She would squeeze the lemon and the juice would come out and she would fish out the stray seeds with her fingers because she doesn't want me to choke. If she really believed in me, that is what she would do, she would always have lemon juice on hand. If she was a good coach, if we were really crouched in the dirt, together, inside of this, that is what she would do. But she isn't doing any of it.

This is just water. Just water! I take a sip. Then another. My heart is still beating fast, like my body is chasing something, like I've been running, trying to catch a bus or a train, but it's long gone, in the distance, and I just haven't quit yet. I don't know why. It's so far away. The lights are fading. Renée here, staring down at me, her skin, her jowls descending like a curtain. I'm afraid. My heart. I rub my face. Everything shrinks away from me. I can't stop from swaying in my chair.

"What's going on?"

"I think I really have a shot —" I say, but then I begin to weep. My shoulders shake. Sounds come out of my throat. There's burning everywhere, all over. I howl for what feels like a decade. Snot bubbles and sweat all mingling, wiped and swiped away into the palms of my hands. Rubbed off on my jeans. The anguish just pouring out.

Usually, she wraps me in a hug. But right now, she isn't moving. She's simply standing in the middle of the room, frozen.

214

"This is what it takes," I say, my voice caught on a ragged inhale as I attempt to calm down. "This is why you never made it. Not really. Because you didn't want it. But I'm here! I'm here! I'm going to be Maria! And I need to be ready. I need . . ."

And then rage. Why isn't she saying anything? Was it all just made up? Just a part she played, a fake and phony thing? Why isn't she fighting back?

Renée keeps standing there, watching. And her standing there, staring at me, watching me suffer, it makes me so angry that I stand up and shove her backward.

"Hey." Renée steps back with one foot, but her gigantic form stays upright. "Hey."

"Why aren't you saying anything?"

Renée steadies herself. Takes a moment. "I'll call you a cab. Sit down."

Her voice is commanding enough that I listen to her. Do what I'm told. I will. For now. My knee jiggles. My stomach, it's all butterflies. No, we don't call them butterflies. No.

This is love.

This is passion.

This is pure commitment.

This is the hard work that I need to do to succeed. I need to surrender everything, give everything to this. Who will I be if I don't?

Her voice murmurs in the other room — she's on the phone, giving her address. The boxes I noticed before seem to loom now, more prominently in the space of this small, low-ceilinged room. It's all very British, as if Renée is attempting to connect herself to the bard, to the lifeblood of theater, to the mothership. But now, it's all been dismantled, like watching a set come down. Who she is, right here: a half-empty box, a discarded playbill. There are the people in the audience, and there are the people on the stage. Never have I been so sure of which one she is. I need to get away from her. It's going to rub off on me. The stench. The stench of her failure.

She sees me taking it all in and sits down across from me, takes my hands in her hands. Looks me in the eyes.

"What is all this?" I ask.

"The fates have decided it's time for me to move on."

"Move on?" I don't understand. "What are you talking about?"

"It's time for a change."

"What do you mean?"

Renée shrugs. So powerless. But we aren't powerless. We fight. "Yes. Well, it just hasn't been working out. I need to find somewhere else to live."

"Are you leaving?"

"Just looking for a new place. I need to take a break from training."

"What about your other clients?"

Her head tilts to the side, her smile crooked. "You're my only client," she says. "You know that."

"What?" I jump up from my seat. "But you're always so busy."

"Yes," she says. "I have a full-time job. I just do this on the side."

The horror of this roars at me. Not Renée. She's supposed to be my rock. She believes in me. It's her belief in me that's been holding me up these last few years. She can't have a day job.

"Wait —"

"This old house is too expensive. But I can't teach out of an apartment unless I find the right set-up. So, I'm going to do that and then we can keep going."

I'm still stuck where I was before. "I'm your only client?"

"For now. I'd love some referrals if you know anyone."

"I'm your only client?" The question lands between us like spit.

Renée steps back, a hand to her heart. Shock curled on her lips. As if she'd been assaulted. And in a way, I guess, she had.

"You knew this, Jessamyn."

"No, I didn't. You made me audition for you! You told me I was special."

Renée just stares at me. I stare back.

"Well, I have a standard," she says.

My fist clenches. Renée eyes it.

"I think you should go," Renée says. "We'll talk when you . . . when you feel better."

"I feel fine!" I say.

She hands me back the money. "My dear," she says. "I think you need to consider some options. Call a family member or maybe —"

"Why should I listen to you?" I say. It's all breaking open in front of me. Renée cracking like an egg. I see it then, glinting in the moonlight, across the room. The Tony in its little house across from the piano. I lunge for it, throwing open the case, grabbing the little statue. I expect it to be heavy. But it's not. Of course it's not. It's cheap, plastic. An imitation.

I scream, "Liar!" and throw it at her, hard.

"It's inspiration!" Renée says, confused. Why is she acting so confused instead of caught? I've caught her lying to me.

My knees buckle. I slump down onto the piano bench, sobs coming out dry, my whole body shaking. No. No. This can't be. No.

She reaches out for me, as if she's going to hug me. Her arms come toward me, her face droops, so haggard in the moonlight. No makeup. Hair flat. I hate her. I hate that she's showing this side of herself to me. I stand up and shove her backward again. This time, she stumbles away, shocked, lets out an operatic scream that shakes me to my core.

Coat on, shoes on, and I run. Outside, I slam the wooden oval slab behind me, over and over again until she yells at me to stop. A small, terrified voice to match a small, terrified woman. A yellow cab turns up the road and I wave it down. I do have all my money in the world in an envelope in my hand, after all. I get in and give him Anton's address and sob.

XXX

Renée who, right? Who cares, she's over. Old news. Just a bitter old hag who's jealous of the promising career I have laid out in front of me. Renée, well. I mean. It's not like she couldn't sing. I heard her voice with my own ears. Even if she was a poor business-person who had trouble cultivating clients, well, that's just because she spent so much time working on her art. Artists are notoriously bad with money.

The cab slows in front of Anton's and the cabbie flips on the overhead light, and I shove some of the cash I was supposed to give to Renée into his fist and get out.

I scramble across the wet lawn, the slick patio stones, and throw myself toward Anton's door, tumbling forward, down the steps. It's unlocked, thank God. It's always unlocked.

Anton's on the couch in sweatpants, watching an old episode of *Jeopardy!* One hand down his pants, the other inside a bag of chips.

He looks up at me, shocked at the mess of me. I start to cry. He immediately moves toward me. The psychic link he claims we share must be on the fritz, because his place is disgusting. Full of old takeout containers and empty cans and bottles, scraps of paper torn as if he was constantly coming up with ideas and throwing them over his shoulder. The room has a dank, damp, musty smell I've never noticed before, like a dirty bathroom.

He puts his arm around my shoulder, and the hand that was previously fondling his balls is now on my cheek, pulling me close.

"What happened?" he whispers into my ear, ragged, like some kind of hero. "If anyone hurt you, I'll destroy them."

I consider telling him about Renée, but then he'll have questions. He'll want to know details. And I don't want to get into it now, no. Now is not the time.

This feels inevitable, this moment where I have to make a choice. How far am I willing to go? How much do I believe in myself? How much do I want it?

Prove it. Prove it. Prove it.

I'm reminded, as I sob into Anton's disgusting armpit, about all the others who came before me, who didn't just wait in the shadows to be discovered. How they didn't shy away from the spotlight. They saw what they wanted and took it. They took what they were owed.

I need him on my side. I need him. "I'll move in," I whisper. "I'll be yours. If you help me."

His eyes bug out of his head, even more than usual. Pure ecstasy at the thought of our lives finally intertwining. What that means for the vision he has of his own life, of himself. Confirmation for him that he actually deserves me. What an idiot.

But the happiness distorts his features, his face melting together. I look away, confused.

It's never going to get easier, I realize as I sob, rub my eyes until he looks somewhat normal again. It's never going to get easier unless I do something big, something important.

Stop waiting for the universe and prove myself to the muse, prove myself to God, to whoever is watching and forcing me to suffer, that the suffering is over now, that it's my time. That I believe in myself so deeply that I won't let anyone stand in my way. I won't take no for an answer.

My time. Mine. Me. Mine.

XXXI

It's the night before dress rehearsal, the night I'm going to save the show. It's important work that I'm doing here. If you think about it, really, I'm saving Samantha. If she does this show on that ankle, if she is forced to perform eight shows a week on that bum ankle, my God, well, some damage is just irreparable. Some damage will stick with her forever. Her career could be ruined, her future flushed down the toilet.

We're in the theater until the last possible moment. Samantha's ankle is not great. It's really, really terrible. She keeps saying it's fine, that it's workable, that she isn't feeling any pain, but no one believes her. I watched her closely as she attempted to make her way through the choreography during "The Lonely Goatherd" and she couldn't skip, not really, couldn't throw her knees up to her chest like I know she wants to. They're talking about adjusting some of the choreography, to help conceal her hobbling.

Me, on the other hand, well I'm off book. I'm sitting in the audience, watching the kids. They're all equally terrified and exhausted, which is just the perfect mood for a pack of children. The tiniest one, Julie — I know her name — it's Julie — has little bags under her eyes. Actual dark circles. Ridiculous, because I get the sense that her mother probably has about nine hundred kinds of cream to fight that. And she's not sharing.

Life really is a dog fight. And it's the wiliest dog, the smartest dog, the dog that's willing to fight for it that wins. Julie's mother is teaching her daughter that nothing, especially not expensive eye cream, is just handed over. If you want to compete, you've got to earn it with hard work and discipline. And that hard work and discipline pays off.

It has to.

Right now, Michelle is working out some performance notes onstage and has banished the kids to the front row of the audience, where they're supposed to be sitting and observing but are either running around in circles, lying on the floor, or pretending to sleep. I'm keeping my back straight, watching, making sure nothing happens to them. Because I am Maria, and Maria is gentle and good and, when the children are around, she always smiles. So, I am smiling. Very serenely. Very, very serenely.

Rudy finds me in the middle of the room and slouches down next to me. I smell cigarettes. When I don't immediately say hello, he pulls out his phone.

I have a mission now, a plan, and it all comes together tonight. I don't need distractions.

"That's a lot of unread text messages," he says, gesturing to my phone after a long stretch of the two of us ignoring one another and scrolling.

"I'm really popular," I say. The fewer words the better. What I don't tell him is that about twenty of them are from Vishal, sent over the course of one night, slowly evolving from asking me why I wasn't talking to him, to calling me a *whore* who just *used him* for his *money*. The insults were so boring, so stock, that I think he might've googled them. So out of touch with his own personhood that he had to turn to the internet to teach him how to be angry.

And then, of course, the obligatory apology, sent this morning. Saying he was drunk. Asking if he could take me out to apologize. Of course, I ignore them all.

A few are from Renée, checking in. One is from my dad, trying to make dinner plans, seeing if I'm available before my big debut. And two are from my landlord, telling me eviction is on the way if I don't pay my rent. But like, why bother? My landlord is totally useless anyway, there's no way he'd actually go through with it. He's the laziest man alive. But I need to avoid this kind of thinking. I am grace. I am poise. I am kindness. I am Maria.

"I think they need you." Rudy says.

"Who?"

"The kids. They look tired."

"Hmm." I need to at least appear eager and helpful, even if what I really am is a woman with a mission. The kids aren't doing anything particularly noticeable, though the littlest one could start crying at any moment.

"All right, all right," he says, clearly uncomfortable with my silence. "They just look sad."

"I'm trying to pay attention," I say. Michelle is changing one of Maria's entrances. I need to make a note of it.

"You sure about that?" Rudy asks. He leans into me. Presses his shoulder to mine, an awkward catch and release. He's tiptoeing around the edge of whatever strange relationship he's decided we have, built up over hours and hours of bored time, bar rag slung over his shoulder, thinking about what I'd look like naked, what he'd do to me if he wasn't such a little bitch. No! Stop it. God. I love God. Jesus is great. And all that. Mountains and hills and Vienna. Love and light.

The little one crumples to the ground in the middle of the aisle. None of the adults, the kneecaps around her, bend to check on her.

Oh right. It's me. Maria! A sad child — I must go to her!

I slink over and talk to her quietly. She needs a juice box and the toilet and a snack and a leopard, which of course, I cannot provide, but luckily her mother packed extra juice boxes and packets of dried seaweed. I leave her sitting on a chair, on her cellphone, punching the keys on some game about a cat that knits.

Rudy's smiling when I return. "She's fine."

"Good," he says, satisfied I obeyed him. I go back to listening to Michelle's direction. But Rudy is still here, so I guess I can ask him. It's time to save the show. It's time for the ask. The first step in the plan.

"Hey," I say, trying not to sound too obvious about it. "You know how it's Samantha's birthday on Friday?"

"I didn't know that," he says. "We've got a show."

"Yeah, it's right in the middle of previews," I say. My head is buzzing. This has to work. It has to. "I was thinking, we should get everyone out tonight for a quick celebratory drink. Make her feel better about how rocky this whole thing has been."

"That's really nice. She might not want to, though. A drink the night before dress?"

"Well, we can get her a club soda or something. Can you invite her? I feel like there's bad beef between us still, you know?"

"I've never heard the expression bad beef."

"Well, now you have." I wait for him to say he'll do it. He stays quiet. "So?" I ask, suddenly worried he can see through me, as if my performance isn't winning him over. That he doesn't believe I want to celebrate her. And I do! Because I am kindness, I am love. I am God's child or whatever.

But Rudy is confused. He's pausing. Come to think of it, he's been distant the last few weeks, avoiding me, until today, and I have no idea why. "Will you ask her?"

"Sure," he says. "Absolutely."

"Thanks, Rudy." I break my rule about men and their names and say his. Out loud. He smiles. I even go so far as to kiss him on the cheek, and he blushes.

"Of course." Rudy reaches out and touches my shoulder, holds my gaze. A move he probably saw in one of those cheap movies they make for teenagers. "I . . ." He trails off. I dig in, stare into his eyes, think about sleeping with him, so he feels it. Cheeks red. He shakes his head. "Never mind. I'll tell you later."

"Okay." I turn and walk back to the kids. The game is afoot. I stomp down on my anxiety, on the buzzing that surrounds me. I am kindness. I am grace. I am Maria.

...

It isn't until after rehearsal that I get the news. Somewhat predictable but annoying all the same — Samantha doesn't want to go to the bar. "She says she's on vocal rest," Rudy reports back, his delivery so entirely smug I want to slap him.

Oh, come on. She is not. Why would she be on vocal rest? She's only really been rehearsing for ten days.

"Did you specifically tell her the party is for her?" It comes out like a snap and Rudy raises his eyebrows at my intensity. I cover it up with a smile. Breathe deeply.

"Yeah, she said everyone would understand. 'Me making this sacrifice is for all of us,' is what she said."

I have to physically stop myself from knotting my hands through my hair, screaming. I shove my fists under my legs and bite down. Count to three. Remind myself to blink. I need her to go to the bar tonight. I need it. Other nights would be fine, but tonight is the best, the cleanest version of it all. The timing is perfect. Anton is in position. It's a flawless plan.

"But it's her birthday," I say.

"Yes," he says. "Well. You know. Dress is tomorrow. She doesn't care about her birthday. You get it. She's a pro. You'd be the same."

My insides curl at this compliment. Rudy, come on. She's not a pro, she's not even doing an impression of a pro. I heard her speak to herself in the mirror this morning, in a baby voice.

"I think someone needs a widdle more bronzer," she said. And she keeps flubbing lines. What was she doing the entire time she was laid up, resting, sitting with her foot in a cast? Because it certainly wasn't getting herself off book. And Michelle doesn't even care. It's like she just decided the entire production was resting on Samantha's back and made no plan B! What kind of leadership is this?

"You're right. I guess a birthday drink was a stupid idea."

Relax. Breathe. In and out. My feet are on the floor. It's okay. This is why I have a backup plan. This is why there's a backup plan.

Rudy hovers, still panting for my attention. "If you want to go for a drink so badly, why don't you ask me?"

I ignore him and eventually he wanders off, pouting.

I send a text to Anton with the code word, telling him that the bar is off. He'll have to come to the theater instead. This is going to be more difficult than I thought.

Eventually Michelle calls it. Rehearsal is over. It's time. It's time!

The kids run up to me — a chorus of needs and questions and nervous energy. *Can I have my phone? Is it time to go home? I want some water. This water tastes weird. Will you run lines with me while we wait for my mom?*

It's Lily, in front of me, who wants to run lines. "You barely have any," I say.

"Which is why I have to nail it. It's so easy to get complacent," she says.

"Complacent," I say. "What have you been reading?"

She ignores me. "If I'm going to speak lines, I want to know what they mean. Vocabulary is important."

I nod as we gather their things and head outside, to wait for their parents to pick them up. The kids all collapse on the ground outside the theater, exhausted, even though it's December in Vancouver. They don't care. And Lily won't leave me alone (shocker). She keeps delivering her lines to me, then waiting for my reply, saying, "Well, what do you think?"

"I'm wondering about your intention," I say, distracted. Anton's down the street, waiting, staring at the theater doors. He's supposed to follow Samantha to her car. But, I realize, bug-eyed, she isn't parked around the corner on one of the side streets like the rest of the cast and crew who can afford to drive. She's printed out what can only be called a DIY wheelchair sign that she's placed in her windshield and has parked in the loading zone, right out front. Which means if Anton tries to intercept her, it's going to be in front of everyone. There will be witnesses.

"You're right," Lily says. "It's just not there. How would you say it?"

She says the line again, but I'm distracted by trying to look casual, to not notice Anton on the street, pacing back and forth, really inhabiting his own chaos in a way that's so natural to him. Trying to act like I don't know who he is, or how everything I've been planning is about to go so terribly wrong.

"What about this," Lily says. She's about to open her yap again when Samantha hobbles out. These days, she uses a cane when she's not onstage. A cane. Like a pimp. It's not even, like, a medical cane, with the four feet. No, it's a decorative cane with a rabbit head and a silver cap on the end.

Anton rushes up to her. He doesn't seem to have showered or changed his clothing in a long time. His hair is sticking up on top of his head; his eyes are wide and terrified. A manic energy hovers around him. If I saw him on the street, I would look away, pretend he wasn't there.

Is he always like this? No, right?

"Samantha," he says. "Samantha, I love your videos. Why haven't you written back to me?"

Samantha flinches as the entire sidewalk stops to stare. Anton's got a black-and-white headshot of hers in his fist. "Will you sign this for me? Will you sign it?" The way he's standing, way too close to her, feels so violent, crazed energy radiating off his body. No one steps up to help Samantha. We all gape at Anton, frozen.

"Uh, sure," she says, "do you have a pen?" He holds out a Sharpie.

"I'm your biggest fan," he says. "I've seen all of your videos and I already bought tickets for *The Sound of Music*. I'm going to come to every matinée."

"Wow, thank you," she says, as she finishes her signature.

"I wish I could come to more. My boss said I couldn't pick up extra shifts though. Still. I need to see you."

"Oh," Samantha says, gently. And then unsure. "Wow." She isn't afraid. She's supposed to be afraid. Instead, she seems to be enjoying the attention. She passes back the headshot and smiles warmly. "Always great to meet a fan."

"Can I just say, thank you." He gazes at the headshot, the signature. Feels it with his thumb. "I'll treasure this forever. Can I walk you to your car?"

"Um, that's okay," Samantha says. "It's right here." Adults are leaving the theater now, pouring out in groups of twos and threes. It's Rudy, of course, who zeros in on the situation, reads it quickly and strides over to Samantha, wrapping an arm around her shoulders. Rudy the hero. Rudy the nice guy.

No.

Not now!

Get out of here, Rudy!

"Thanks for waiting for me," Rudy says. So kind, lifting her out of it. The jackass. He wasn't supposed to do this. "Sweetheart." Oh, come on. This move is straight out of a romantic comedy. Seriously?

Samantha's shoulders drop from her ears. She understands the scene Rudy is laying out. The fake boyfriend play. He gets to be the hero. She gets to be rescued.

People see her. They care about her. She's important. I remember how it felt, walking down the street, Anton throwing lit cigarettes at me. I was alone. No one gave even the tiniest shit if I lived or died. But I saved myself. I did it. Me.

I avoid Anton's eyeline, though he keeps glancing at me, as if I'll step up and provide some direction. I ignore his gaze, but I feel his frantic energy, the bend in the plan. The twist. It isn't working. He's not a great improviser. The number one rule though is that I can't be involved. I can't be linked to him. He has to do this on his own. No one can know this was me. It could ruin everything.

"I'll walk you to your car," Rudy says pointedly, over Samantha's shoulders. Diffusing the tension. Managing the escalation. Signaling to Anton that he can leave now. The car is only a few yards away, anyway, but they're all still on the pavement.

"No, I will," Anton says, his voice too loud. He steps forward, looping his elbow through Samantha's arm on the other side, holding her close. "Sweetheart." She freezes, straightens up. Holds the cane in her fist like she's about to bop Anton on the head with it.

Rudy glares at me, as if saying, *Do something.* I pull out my phone, act confused. *What?* I mouth.

"I'm really fine," Samantha mutters, her cheeks turning red.

"No, you aren't," Anton says. "Your foot. I've been following you. I know you. You're in pain. It's not okay. Let me help you."

"Really," says Samantha. "My car is right there."

Rudy glares me again, wide-eyed as if I can read his mind, as if we're so deeply connected that I know what he wants me to do. I fumble for my cellphone. The cops seem like an overreaction, if I'm being totally honest. Anton isn't threatening. He isn't at all. Even if he is now yanking on Samantha's arm.

Rudy turns on Anton, rips his arm off of Samantha's and shoves him to the pavement. Anton lands, an embarrassing yelp of pain escaping his mouth and I gasp, probably too dramatically. But it is very exciting to watch them fight. Even if it isn't over me.

I can't be enjoying this, though, I remind myself. I need to be grace, kindness, poise.

"What are you doing? Someone . . . hey, Jessamyn!" Rudy shouts over his shoulder as Anton rolls out from under him, then skitters backward like a crab. "Call the cops."

I realize I'm standing there with my phone out, watching them. But in my defense, so is everyone else.

"Sorry!" I say and dial. It rings. Rings. I wait. Anton leaps to his feet and I see something flash in his eyes, something crazed. He bares his teeth, lets out a growl I've never heard before and faces off with Rudy.

"Get out of here!" Rudy shouts at Anton, whose hunched-over posture is, well, it makes him look like a werewolf. I ask for the police and the 911 operator asks for more information.

"It's a strange man!" I say. "He's grabbing my friend." Hand over all the necessary details while Anton hovers, trying to decide what to do next. This wasn't supposed to go this way. He was supposed to charm Samantha, he was supposed to charm her the way he charmed me, walk her to her car and then —

"Go!" Rudy shouts again, stomping forward. But the words don't seem to be reaching Anton, seem to slide off him like grease.

Instead, a wide smile spreads across Anton's lips. He grins, yellow teeth beneath a vacant stare.

Even I'm disturbed. I haven't seen this before, from him. Have I?

"I'll see you again soon," he says directly to Samantha. It's an incredible delivery. So foreboding. As he walks away, sirens ring out in the distance, and he's about to disappear down an alleyway when Rudy runs after him and tackles him to the pavement.

"Oh my God!" Samantha screams, her legs giving out under her. She sinks to the ground shaking, terrified.

Anton flails underneath Rudy, almost humping the air, grunting, as Rudy simply lays all of his weight over him, flat like a pancake.

"Hey, c'mon, man," Anton says, trying to wrestle out from under Rudy as the sirens get louder, closer. I don't know what to do, so I crouch down next to Samantha and summon all of the patience I have in the world, put a hand on her shoulder and affix a concerned expression.

"Are you all right?"

She's shaking, her bottom lip trembling, eyes on the pavement, not looking at me. I resent this, having to help her.

Rudy sits on Anton's back, pressing Anton's shoulders to the sidewalk, Anton is faced away from me, which is good because if he could see me now, I'm sure this entire scheme would be shot. Everyone would know.

Red and blue lights flash. I don't know what to do, so I sit next to Samantha and hold her hand. A few of the chorus members do the same, seemingly embarrassed at how this sensitive pack of performers reacted so uselessly in a time of violence.

This wasn't how it was supposed to go.

...

After the cops arrive and cart Anton off and we get Samantha into her car, I go for a drink with Rudy. He's shaky, and I need to pretend I'm also shaky. This is a good role for me. Disturbed by the unhinged man, spiritually crumpled by violence. I follow him to a cozy bar around the corner. Quiet, a little booth where we sit together with our knees touching underneath the table. His hands are quivering, actually moving in the air. His skin is pale. I take his palm and squeeze it, and he dips his head, makes a noise like a laugh.

"I haven't done that in a long time," he says.

"Wrestle a homeless guy?"

"Wrestle at all. I used to with my little brother. It's been a few years."

"Well, you did a good job."

We talk about the incident. I let Rudy feel like he saved the day, like this unhinged man would have killed us all if not for Rudy. "Have you heard from Samantha?" I ask.

"She texted. Home safe," he says. "Poor Samantha. It seems like this production is cursed."

"Yes," I say, taking a sip of my cocktail. "Poor Samantha."

My tone of voice isn't exactly earnest. I expect a lecture from Rudy, about how we all have to get behind the lead, blah, blah, blah. Instead, Rudy leans toward me, tilts his forehead down. At first, I think he might be leaning in for a kiss and I draw back from him, confused.

"I don't know how to bring this up," he says. "But I want you to know . . . that I know."

He gazes into my eyes with what only can be described as compassion. As pity. Directed at me.

"Know what?" I ask.

"Samantha told me." He reaches under the table and grabs my knee, squeezes it between the V of his thumb and forefinger. My stomach drops. Samantha told him. Told him what? I resist grabbing him by the shirt and shaking him. Told him what? Is she still lying about me pushing her? I thought we were past that.

"What did she tell you?"

"You know, about that summer."

No. No.

She didn't. She's not. She can't be talking about Shakespeare on the Lake. Not to the cast. Even she wouldn't stoop that low.

"It's not your fault," Rudy whispers. He leans over and says it in my ear. I feel his moist breath enter the curve of it, the hole into my brain. "What he did to you."

I picture it now, with Samantha. I see us now, feel a prickling I haven't felt in so long. I see how it will end. Her body lifted up over my head, slammed down on my knee, spine snapped in half. A vacant stare as she floats away. Forgotten forever.

Because how could she? Go around, talking about what happened when she doesn't know. Not everything.

I can just picture it now: Samantha, basking in the attention, smiling and gesturing to me. "She was one of Barnes's . . . you know. Victims."

The bitch deserves to rot.

"Where did you go?" he whispers, hot, into my ear, and I jump, recoil. Swallow down on my gag reflex. "Just now."

"Sorry," I say. "Just . . . thinking."

"He won't hurt you ever again." Rudy's hand is sneaking up my thigh. "I won't let him." His fingers absently stroke the inside of my thigh, nails scratching at the seam of my jeans.

"What did she tell you?"

"That you're a survivor," he says. "I mean, everyone heard about that predator at Shakespeare on the Lake. Fuck him. But Samantha told me the year before he got busted — you were one of his favorites, and you just disappeared one day. Didn't tell anyone where you were going. It's obvious now, why."

Pity drips off of him. I suppose he thinks I ran off afraid.

As if.

I slept with Barnes. He put me in the chorus in the first place. Close to the part that I wanted. So, so close.

And when it became clear he wasn't going to promote me to lead, I walked.

Simple.

Barnes wanted something from me, I wanted something from him. I didn't get what I wanted that time, but he did. That time, he won. People went on and on in articles about the power dynamic and how he lied to all these women and whatever, but at the end of the day it was me. I put myself in that situation. I made choices. I got duped. Sometimes you lose. At least I'm strong enough to admit that. And I'm fine now. I'm totally fine. There's nothing wrong with me. I'm not a victim.

I'm not.

But that's what makes this win all the more important. Because I was able, despite everything he said to me, everything he did to me, to rise. I'm here. And I'm about to be Maria.

I don't bother to correct Rudy. He keeps talking about looking out for me, keeps slamming this man as pathetic. It's clear he loves to pretend to be this hero who says all the right things, who listens when women speak, who is perfect. Who is willing to put his body on the line.

But his hand is still heavy on my leg. "If he was here right now," Rudy says. "If he was here right now, I'd beat him to a pulp." Have his fingers moved up? "I'll kill him for you."

And then I'm back there, in bed with Barnes, his fingers around my neck. Squeezing. Pushing. His breath in my ear. Whispering.

Jessamyn. Oh my God. Jessamyn. The feeling like I'd never breathe again, black clouds bursting in my vision, the sharp pain of his elbow digging in my sternum.

The bar swims in front of me. Eventually I tear myself away from Rudy, leave him there. He thinks I'm upset about what happened, but of course not. I'm not upset. I'm not upset Rudy thinks I'm some victim. That I'd willingly put myself in a situation like that, where some old man has power over me. That could never happen.

I leave because this isn't going to help me move forward. I need Anton. He's just what I need, his devotion, his confidence that I am a bright shining star. That I'm untouchable. I need Anton.

XXXII

"**G**ot off with a warning," Anton says. He leans back on his couch, fingers knit behind his head. "Those guys know me anyway. Fucking pigs."

"They know you?"

"Oh yeah," he says.

"How do they know you?"

"If you're like me," Anton says, "you court controversy." He's proud of it. He isn't afraid. And even though I was the one who put us on this path, I'm frightened by how comfortable he is with all this, when in reality, he screwed the plan up so hugely that I'm not sure I can save it. How I can move forward.

But what's worse is how he's speaking to me. Like I'm a familiar.

"I think we should call it off," I say, even though I don't mean it. I wait for him expectantly, wait for him to fall to his knees, to beg me not to give up. That's usually what he does. Grab my hands and squeeze. Stare into my eyes. Tell me that it's me, that it has to be me, that I've been working too hard for too long to give up now. That we have to commit. We have to. That he's willing to do anything for me. For my dreams.

He just shrugs. "If that's what you want."

What?

A cold sweat breaks out on my forehead. The world falls in and out of focus. I need to lie down.

"Honestly," Anton says, with a kind of dull simplicity. "I'm kind of looking forward to seeing how Sam handles the role."

"What?"

"There's just something about her," Anton says.

"Samantha?"

"Yeah . . ." he trails off, staring up at his popcorn ceiling, smiling. Obsessing. "I watched all her YouTube videos."

I see Anton more clearly now. The jogging pants he wears that I once thought were trendy, in a European way, are frayed and dirty, the white line down the side gone a dull shade of brown. His curly brown hair isn't cute and rumpled, no, it's simply a result of him not bothering to take care of himself. His rotting apartment isn't messy, those are dirt streaks on the walls, clusters of dust and grime in the corners. His couch is a futon mattress on the floor. His shoes are barely held together, a strip of duct tape down the edge.

The distant look in his eyes. I never noticed it until he trained them on Samantha. Now I don't know how I failed to see it. Unsettling. Almost terrifying.

I want to scream, but the last thing I need is a neighbor coming to my aid, a witness to Anton and me together, to tie me to this place of decay. How could I not have seen it? How could I have let myself come back here, time and time again? How did I miss this?

"Do you still get comps?" Anton asks. "For the show? Can I have them? I'm not sure I'll be able to afford more than a few tickets."

"I don't —"

"And do the rehearsals end that late? When's the dress again?"

"I don't know —"

"Maybe you could text me? You'd do that for me, right?"

"I don't —"

"Jessamyn, come on. You have to."

Have to? He's telling me what to do now?

"I've got to go."

"No, you don't," he says, and he grabs my wrist, pulls me to him. The smell. Oh, the smell of him makes me wretch. His teeth are sharp and so close to me now. "You'll do this for me." A command. He reaches up and slaps me across the face. Sharp. Hard. I gasp. "You will!" The sting of it arrives and makes my eyes water.

"Okay," I say. "Okay, I will." I turn and hurry away before he can do it again, thoughts roiling in my mind.

Anton. Anton slapped me. He slapped me.

I throw the hood of my jacket over my head, ducking into darkness. It's raining and the sound of the fat drops on my hood is disorienting. I point myself toward home, constantly turning around as I walk, feeling like he is behind me, sure that I hear footsteps. Orange streetlights reflect back at me, blink in the puddles. The roar of cars whizzing past, sending curtains of rainwater up and onto the sidewalk, splashing my ankles, is all so loud I want to scream.

Deep down, I'm expecting Anton to follow, to throw himself onto the ground and beg forgiveness, to take it all back, to tell me it's always been me. But he never appears.

I duck into an alcove. The rain is too much. I don't want to walk in the rain. I could get sick. I take out my phone and dial and he answers on the first ring. "Hello?"

"Can you come pick me up?"

"Jess . . ."

Silence on the other end. A sigh. I probably should've read some of those text messages, but they were so long. And really, I've been focused. That's what he loves about me, right? That I'm a passionate, focused woman.

Right now, I just need a ride. I'll let him do anything to me for a ride.

"Please?" My voice must be vulnerable enough that he agrees, that he trusts it. I tell him where I am and he says he'll be here in fifteen minutes.

...

It takes me a long minute to realize Vishal's driving me back to my apartment. Mine, not his. "Where are we going?" I ask, the confusion in my voice very clear and very present. When I got into the car, he seemed curious, and then something like pity crossed his face. It must be the rain, making my hair hang down on either side of my face like a curtain, the makeup running in black streaks down my neck. No matter. The worse I look, the better he gets to feel. Like, look at how horrible my life is without him, right?

"I'm taking you to your apartment."

I don't even remember telling him where I live, but I guess he must've figured out my address from his Uber account, from all the mornings after when he sent me away.

"You don't want to go to your place?"

"No."

I think of the angry text messages he sent. Clearly he's been thinking about me.

"Why not?"

"Because we haven't spoken in weeks. After you said you would move in, then bailed when I wouldn't give you money. I thought you were different."

Do I finally do it? Do I talk about the money? All the tips? The morning after I gave him a blowjob, when he gave me extra cash? It's basically prostitution, what we were doing, just without rates, a pimp, job protection. Wasn't it?

I don't understand him at all. So convenient for him to just decide one day that he wants something different, to ask me for it, for me

238

to provide it for him, but when I want something, something that is actually meaningful, he denies me. How is this fair? How is that a relationship?

"I had to go get the money," I say. "You didn't want to help. I don't know why you're being so emotional."

"Why didn't you move in with me?"

"In case you haven't noticed, the show is about to open. What do you think I do all day? I have a passion. Maybe that's such a foreign concept to you, but it's all-consuming. I can't just get lost in life with you, abandon who I am. You didn't want to help. That was your choice. But now I have to go and do this on my own."

"Jessamyn, you make me seem like this monster."

"You make choices, I make choices. That's all it is. Choices." Rain splatters the windshield. He turns down the street and parks, turns on his flashers. I may as well have been sitting in the back seat.

It appears this is what he wanted to hear, because he sighs, turns toward me. Exhales. Is he wanting me to get out? I can't tell. He reaches across the console and takes my hand. "I miss you."

A roar of triumph in my chest. Of course he does. Of course he misses me. How could he not? I am luminescent. And yet he wouldn't pay for my vocal lessons, no he wants to trap me inside a glass box, drinking canned vodka sodas, getting slobbered on by a dog until all of my beauty, all of my potential, is dried up and he can't look at me anymore because the rot he sees on my lined face is just a reminder of his own age. A reminder of his own fragility. So afraid, men.

Here he sits, ready to take my dreams and extinguish them underneath the weight of his desire. When you really think about it like that, really consider it, his desire, his panting wanting for me is nothing better than hatred. What he wants, he can only destroy.

Because if he really loved me, he'd help me become the best version of myself, the bright shining star, to step into my destiny. But he won't, because that would mean I'd become too good for him. I'd be my own woman and I wouldn't need him anymore. His money would mean nothing and what is left then?

And he knows it. He told me with the ping of a text message in the middle of the night.

Whore.

I gaze into his eyes. Let the sound of the rain hammering on the roof eat up the silence between us.

"Say something," he says in a voice so deep and harsh and commanding that suddenly I'm afraid. We're insulated from the world. Passersby can't see us, no one can see us, and no one will hear us over the pounding of the water. He's said how he feels, and here I am, forcing him to wait in suspended silence. His hand twists on the steering wheel, squeezes the leather like skin. It could so easily be my throat. I think of Anton, of the sharpness of the slap. The sting. It could've been so much worse.

So I smile. Conjure up the boring woman, a boring woman who could love him back, a woman who doesn't care this man called her a whore. "I miss you too." Lean over and kiss him deeply, slide my tongue between his lips, then tear myself away, open the car door and run.

...

I dig my keys out of my pocket, drenched, my hair hanging down in slimy wet tendrils that stick to my cheeks. My hands are shaking. I'm far too preoccupied to notice the woman in the lobby leaning on the wall next to the fake potted ficus with Christmas lights left up on it all year. Dusty leaves and Christmas cheer. Depressing on so many levels. This woman feels me brush past her and lashes out, grabs my arm as I attempt to walk up the stairs.

"Jessamyn, 404?" she says, stepping up.

"Uh, yes," I say. "Who are you?"

"You've ignored our eviction notices and now we have no choice but to take serious action. You've got to get out now."

"What are you talking about?"

"No bullshit, Jessamyn."

"I paid my rent," I say. "Take it up with Mikhail."

"You did not," she says. "Now get your stuff and get out."

"I paid," I say. It sounds so real but even I'm not sure anymore. The last few weeks are so hazy. Time has a mushiness to it that makes everything feel smashed together. I paid. I had to have paid. I always pay.

She shoves me, and my lower back hits the dull gray railing. "Ow," I say. "What the hell? You can't just kick me out."

"Give me your keys."

"What? No. I'm not giving you my keys."

"Hand them over."

"No."

"Hand them over," she says.

"No."

She stands between me and my apartment, hands on her hips. She has a good fifty pounds on me.

"I'm calling Mikhail."

"Go ahead," I say.

When she reaches for her phone, I dive at her, shoving her as hard as I can. She screams and stumbles back into the ficus, and I sprint for the stairs. My feet pound against the hollow wood. It feels like I'm shaking the entire building. Up and up and up. In the distance, I hear her voice, but I'm so tired. My entire body is burning, aching.

There's an eviction notice printed on my door, which I rip down, peeling off some brown paint in the process. How long has this been here? She claims they've tried to serve it to me, but this is the first time I'm noticing it.

I slam and bolt the door behind me, slide the chain across, then grab my rickety, wooden kitchen table chair and wedge it under the handle, just in case she decides she wants to come and try to drag me out by the ankle. Asshole. This isn't even legal.

Inside, I collapse on my bed, the mattress on the floor in the middle of the room. I'm so exhausted, so hungry, my head and heart pounding in tandem. My entire body flushed and freezing. The water from my clothes leaks onto the comforter and when the tears come, I let them turn into sobs, and I let those sobs turn into wails until some neighbor of mine pounds on the wall or maybe it was the ceiling or maybe it was the floor and so instead of wailing, I bury my face in my pillow and scream.

XXXIII

The sun wakes me up, streaming through my window with a cheer that's out of place with the state of my life, my soul.

Wanting is so exhausting. Taking is impossible.

It's because you aren't willing to do what's necessary. The voice, the voice. I stuff my head under my pillow. I cannot die a nobody. I simply cannot.

I get up, out of bed. That's the first step. The first step toward greatness. Toward my destiny. That's all it takes, right? One tiny step? Changing my reality?

My clothes didn't dry overnight. There's a damp outline of a woman I don't recognize on my pink blanket. A quitter. That, I am not.

I struggle out of my wet jeans, the moisture adhering the denim to my legs. That's when I hear my phone from where it sits, battery nearly dead, in the middle of my bed.

Probably Vishal again. Or my landlord. Nothing I want to deal with right now.

I ignore it and step into the shower. I hear another *ping* from the living room as I'm scrubbing the rainwater out of my hair, trying to decide if I should just no-show on today. Let my absence speak for me. *Ping.* Because it will be loud. When Samantha is hobbling around the stage on that ankle, I won't be there for Michelle to seek out in the crowd, *ping* for Michelle to rely on. That's why she asked me to be there, after all, to make her feel better. Knowing there was an option out there, just in case things went south. Knowing someone was there to catch her when she fell. It's always been me. Always.

Ping.

I soap my body. I'm not going to rush for the phone. I'm going to finish my shower and drink a cup of tea, and once I've made up my mind about how to proceed — *ping.* Fuck it.

I have to check.

I rinse off quickly and wrap myself in a towel before taking a deep breath and picking up my phone. It's a series of texts — I don't recognize the number. But they're signed.

I scream and throw my phone on the bed, tears welling up in my eyes.

No.

It can't be.

I read again. Scream. Fall to my knees in shock. My mouth is wrenched open, curling in a kind of awe.

It's happening. I'm down on my disgusting carpet, next to my disgusting bed, slamming my face into the comforter over and over and over again. Me.

It's me.

It's finally me.

Michelle. The texts are from Michelle, asking for a meeting at the old rehearsal space, down by the pier. Michelle telling me not to tell anyone, to come as soon as I can. Michelle saying it's really important. It's about the dress rehearsal. Tonight. Don't tell anyone. Come as soon as I can. Just between us. As soon as you can, Michelle.

•••

I walk a block before I think to call an Uber. I have no idea how I'll pay for it. My card is maxed out. But the car arrives swiftly, and I get in, slumping down in the backseat, raking fingers through my wet hair. I don't want Michelle to think I'm crazy. I need to look stable, serene, capable when she offers me the part. I need to look surer of myself than Samantha. I know I am. I know I can hit all of the notes. I know I can do the choreography. I've been off book for months. The kids are obsessed with me. The relationship is strong. It's me. It's finally time.

It's all about to happen.

"Pull it together," I whisper to myself, pressing the heels of my hands into my eyes. "Pull it together."

I settle into an acting exercise, starting with a breath. A deep one. In and out. Abandoning fear. Abandoning doubt. Abandoning the parts of my brain attempting to sabotage my success.

The car slows and stops outside of the theater, the original rehearsal space — the smaller one. Seagulls scream as I get out, wiping my sweaty palms on my pants.

The building seems so quiet and empty. I love that she brought me down here. That she called me to this place. The spot in which I first stepped up for Maria now will be the moment I become her. A perfect ending to a perfect story.

I think about the curtain call. How it will feel to walk out when everyone is on their feet, the audience so much happier, their lives improved. My father smiling — no, beaming at me from the crowd. I won't know where he's sitting, but it won't matter. We'll find each other's eyes, and everything will be fine. We'll be fine. He'll finally see me, perfect, beautiful, untouchable. Everyone will be looking at me. Everyone.

I walk toward the doors, but there's a thick chain across them. The lights inside are off. I pull out my phone and check the text messages. There's nothing from Michelle about how to get in. I press my hands together and peer inside the theater lobby. Dull gray tile that reeks of abandon. Emptiness. I knock on the door with my knuckles. Maybe she went in the back. I check my phone again, start to type in a text message, when I see her.

Standing next to the yachts, the dock next to the theater, at the very place where she walked off into the water, then emerged, broken, incapable, whining.

Samantha. Wearing her purple coat. Holding something in her hand and looking out at the water.

Here she is. Is Michelle going to fire her right in front of me?

She looks up, sees me, and a wicked smile cracks her face open. A wide, satisfied grin.

"You came."

XXXIV

"What are you doing here?" My brain strains against the logic: Samantha standing here, at the edge of the dock in her long purple coat, smiling. It doesn't make sense. Something is wrong. "Where's Michelle?"

"You." Samantha smiles again. "I always wondered what the hell was going through your head," she says. "I thought maybe you were just dumb. But the craziest thing I've realized, watching you through this entire rehearsal period, is just how goddamn deluded you are."

"What are you talking about? Where's Michelle? We're supposed to have a meeting."

"Michelle's not coming. I texted you." Samantha emphasizes the words as if she's talking down to an idiot child. "It was me."

A seagull lands on a nearby trashcan and glares at me with a beady eye.

Of course it wasn't real. Of course it isn't going to happen. Not like this.

"I wanted to talk to you after last night. I know you had something to do with that . . . God, I don't know who that was. Where did you find him? The smell alone. Ugh. I hope you got him a hot meal afterwards."

I picture Anton, his wild eyes, his body flailing on the ground. "I don't know what you're talking about," I say, then turn to leave. This is cruel, this trick she's played on me. If she's going to gloat, I don't want to be around for it. I want to go home and crawl back into the puddle I slept in, the damp outline of my own body, and pull my knees up to my chest. "I've got to go."

I pull my phone out of my pocket, momentarily consider texting Anton for backup when I remember he's moved on already. Cast me aside. A vicious betrayal, the turncoat. Samantha snatches it away. Her pink shining nail polish glints in the sun. It's ridiculous. Tonight's the dress rehearsal and she's going to play Maria von Trapp wearing pink nail polish. It's a fresh manicure, too. It's not like this is some mistake she made a week ago and forgot to remove. No. It was a choice. A recent one.

This is the level of commitment she has.

"Give me back my phone."

"No," she replies. "I'm here to do you a favor. All right? Listen to me. You can't sing. The sound you make when you open your mouth is absolutely fucking horrible. Everyone in this community feels bad for you because they knew about Barnes. They knew he was a creep, that he was using that Shakespeare festival to lure in women like you. And you know what? Respect to you for walking. But this whole thing? The reason you're here? It's guilt. It's a bunch of people tiptoeing around you because you got sexually assaulted, and they knew what he was doing and said nothing."

She spits all of this out, so hateful. Like she knows everything. Like she's been waiting to gloat about this or something. Firstly, as if I could ever get sexually assaulted. As if I'd ever put myself in that position. To be pitied. She doesn't know me at all.

And even if it was true, the fact that she's throwing it in my face? That it's the only reason she's been nice to me all this time? What is wrong with her?

I hear a confidence in her voice when she spits those words to the ground, but I hear jealousy, too. I was the favorite. I loved being the favorite. It was this incredible boost when Barnes called me, cast me, pulled me aside after all of our rehearsals. Worked with me on the songs. Helped me run them over and over again until I got it right. Until I blended into the chorus. Biding my time.

He set me on the path. Made sure I could get what I wanted if I just committed to it. If I gave it everything I had. All of my time. All of my focus. All of my attention. To get better. To become great. Even if I was in the chorus. It didn't mean anything. Barnes assured me of that. It was politics. It was Samantha's close relationships with company directors. If it had been solely up to him, he would've made me a lead. But the chorus was a fine place to start. And the onstage experience was supposed to be worth it.

Until it was brutally uprooted.

You can't do it.

He can't be right about me. Not that disgusting bald freak with a thumbtack goatee and tiny little eyeglasses, whose nose hairs peeked out of their little caves. Not him. A man who paired a beret with that get-up could never be right about me.

No.

I have to be Maria.

Now Samantha.

With her pink nail polish.

Her fragile ego. Is she really going to make it out there? I'm supposed to step aside for her?

I keep staring at the nail polish. It proves what I always suspected about her to be true.

"I know I'm a better singer than you. At this point, it's fact. It's objective."

249

Samantha's trying to shake me. Trying to scare me away. It's bluster.

"I know what you've been doing, always waiting in the wings for your moment. But you are not capable of it. It's over."

I don't respond. I just watch her. Grasping. Trying to scare me. To intimidate me. I see her. I see the pink nail polish. I know that it's just fame she seeks, that she isn't committed to the work. She doesn't want to do the work, she simply wants to stand onstage and hear applause, she wants her face all over the internet.

Look at everything I've done for this part. I've worked so hard. And she just shows up, whines that she isn't adored when she's done nothing to earn our adoration.

"I'm twenty-six," she says. "Just like you. But I've actually gotten somewhere. This is a big step forward for me. Can't you see that? And you're going to try to stop me? You? With your nothing resumé? Jessamyn, come on."

My silence is unnerving her. She searches the world around us, suddenly frantic. She knows now that this meeting is a mistake. Luring me down here, early, in the quiet of morning when no one is around. The big yachts bob next to us quiet and empty. Not a soul is here to witness.

"How?"

"What? What do you mean?"

"How do you know?"

"I'm trying to do you a favor," she says, dodging the question. "You're a decent-enough actor, I'll give you that. But you're going to quit this company. You're going to do it today."

"But how?" I say. "You're so confident. How do you *know*?"

"Because I've achieved more than you. I've performed more than you have. Because I'm the lead and you're not."

She's scrambling now. She doesn't believe in herself at all.

"If you're so sure I'm this terrible singer, why are we down here?"

"Because you're a violent fucking psycho!" she explodes. "You pushed me off the pier!"

"Did I? I heard you were filming a video and tripped. Walked right off."

Samantha lets out a frustrated scream.

"And sure," I say. "It must feel good. You're the lead. For now. But this isn't big. This is regional theater. Why do you trust that Michelle knows what she's doing? If her taste was so exquisite, wouldn't she be working in New York? London? Anywhere else?"

It's clear Samantha has never considered this. But me? I think about it all the time. If you really think about it, Vancouver is just some small, podunk city. Are there real artists here? Swishing around in athleisure, sipping expensive coffee. What do any of these spandex-swaddled jocks know about art?

And they've anointed Samantha as their queen? Ha!

"I —" Samantha stops herself, redirects. "This is ridiculous."

"No, it isn't. You're so sure of something. But from where I'm sitting, I don't understand why."

"Because I do this for a living."

"You still work at your father's real estate office. Everyone knows that."

"A few months here and there to help him out —" She shrinks now. Her confidence shakes. Her wet hair. She can't intimidate me. I can tell she was up all night. That she thought through this, over and over again, this plan to scare me away. Drafted and redrafted the text message. To me. The person looming behind her.

"And the Captain was going to walk because you can't deliver lines. You're barely off book!"

"We worked it out." Her voice is wavering. She doesn't know. She simply hopes for something to break open in her favor, a sign from the heavens, from the gods. It's as foolish as anything, but at least I understand how empty it all is. No one is going to help you. The only thing other people do is hold you back.

She thinks everything she's gotten means something. That she's supposed to take that information as confidence and use it to propel herself forward. She's the fool. She's the deluded one.

"You don't know," I say. "You wish. You hope. But you don't know. You can't know. You can never know."

I study her standing there, shivering in the wind. Her lips are turning blue. Her hair is still damp from her morning shower, lies thick and ropey, over her shoulders. She's more striking now, here, than she ever has been. Beautiful. Gone is the makeup, gone is the bright light she attaches to her cellphone. Here, she is just a person who is as afraid as I am.

"I want you to quit. Tell me you're quitting." She's begging now. Broken. Regretful. Afraid.

I smile. "Why would I quit?"

"Because I found this," she says, and holds out her hand. In it is her old cellphone. The one with her recording the video of her going off the pier.

"It's been in the ocean for weeks," I say.

"This case is waterproof. Waterproof."

No.

No.

No.

"There's a guy, you've probably seen him diving around down there, who cleans the hulls of these yachts." She gestures to the boats bobbing in the waves behind us. "He found it. Plugged it in. And me? I check. Oh, I checked every night, to see if my phone showed up. And yesterday, can you imagine the timing? Yesterday it did."

She's so happy with herself, she's beaming so bright she could light up the sky.

I think of her, every night looking at the app. To prove that someone as supposedly inconsequential as me had pushed her. And for what? When she could be practicing her lines? Reading Maria von Trapp's autobiography? Running her vocals? But no.

If our positions were reversed, I know I wouldn't even speak to someone as low on the pole as me. I'd be focused. Devoted. If I were Maria, I wouldn't even know the childminder's name.

"All you have to do is quit," Samantha says. "That's it. So simple. Just quit. Leave. I never want to see you again. If I'm going to perform, I don't want you waiting in the wings. Hovering like a creep, trying to intimidate me. I don't feel safe, and if I don't feel safe, I can't perform."

Here she is, talking about performing when she's not even off book. When she could be learning her lines she's instead lying in bed, staring at her software, trying to prove that I'm out to get her. That I'm a liar. Me. A sexual assault victim. All because she thinks I pushed her off the pier. Well, newsflash, Samantha, friends push friends into bodies of water all the time.

She stands her ground. Seems taller than she was before. She thinks she has me.

"This show is important," Samantha says. "For more reasons than you know. And I'm not going to let you ruin it. Now tell me you quit. Tell me. Say it. Say 'I quit.'"

I take a step toward her. Staring out there, I can hear her voice, her pestering. Samantha. But my ears can only hear the sound, the lapping. The water, rushing, churning.

A sudden stinging on my cheek — momentum throws me sideways and I cry out. Samantha's slapped me. Her expression is desperate. She's panting. Red faced. How is she going to become a great if she can't control her emotions?

"Listen to what I'm saying. What are you doing? Listen. It's all over. Just say it. Say 'I quit.'"

Her pink nail polish flashes in the bright sunlight. I know she isn't going to be able to do it. The part. She's going to sink the show. She's going to ruin it. I think of the children. Of all the hours they put into rehearsal. I bet she doesn't even show up to opening night on time. Makes them hold the curtain for her. Amateur.

"I quit."

Words, on my lips. A voice I don't recognize. Dull. A trance maybe, or just dead inside. Wrung dry.

There's a disturbed expression on her face as she gathers up her belongings. She gives me my phone back.

"Good," she says. I slide the phone into my pocket as she turns to leave.

Wet hair, a thick rope down her back. I reach out, squeeze, feel the water leaching out between my knuckles. Slick. I pull. Hard.

XXXV

The stagehands lean against the door in the lobby, droopy head-phones around their necks, radios periodically squawking. They're whispering, but they don't notice me here, sitting on the bench a few minutes before drop-off.

"She never showed for her fitting this afternoon. Costumes is pissed."

"Honestly, doesn't surprise me."

My fingers ache. I can't remember why. It's a dull pain. I flex them, check them each in turn, try to identify the source. One of my nails, my middle finger on my right hand, has a dull purple tinge to it, as if I caught it in a drawer or in a car door, maybe. There's a black patch in my mind. A patch with fuzzy edges.

I squeeze the nail between my knuckles. It hurts.

And then I remember her hair in my fist.

The kids arrive. Anxiety hovers over them, making them quiet as we head into the theater. They sit with me in the audience, house right, and take turns being led off by assistants from the costume department for final tweaks, returning only to slump back into their seats, stare at the ceiling, kick the seats in front of them to try and piss one another off.

"Quit it," Lily says to the younger boy who decides in that very moment that his bones are made of Jell-O. He slides off the seat and onto the floor.

"It's just a dress rehearsal," I say. "There'll barely be any audience. There's no reason to be nervous."

The boy is under Lily's seat now. He reaches out and grabs at her ankle.

"Stop!" she says, and kicks back with her foot. She connects with his nose, the force of it causing the boy to cry out, blood to spurt across the floor. He screams and grabs his face.

"Oh hell." I jump to my feet and drag him up by the shoulder. "Keep your head forward, not on the costume." He's wearing his dull gray uniform, the first outfit we'll see him in when Captain von Trapp whistles them all to attention. And now there are little red speckles all over the collar. Thankfully, most of the blood seems to be getting on the ground.

I find the stagehand responsible for first aid. She fusses over him, sends me to the bathroom for paper towel, to protect the costume. I hurry in and stop short when I see her, there, leaning over the sink.

Michelle.

Her eyes are bright red. She's sniffling, swiping at her nostrils with paper towel. I don't know what to do, but I pause long enough, frozen in the entrance, for Michelle to look up.

"I just need a minute."

She thinks I want something.

"Sorry," I say, and grab some paper towel. "There's a nosebleed."

"Oh." She tries to smile but the tensing of her cheeks causes tears to run down them. "Right."

"We saved the costume."

Michelle laughs. It seems, almost, as if a costume is the last thing she could care about. "Great."

"See you out there," I say, and hurry back out to the children.

Lily's waiting for me inside the theater doors, looking pale. "Is he okay? Is he going to be able to go on?"

"He's fine."

"It was an accident." Her voice is high and shrill and terrified. She's shaking. There's a large splotch of blood on the floor the size of my palm.

"It's just a nose," I say. "It's going to be fine."

"He was kicking me," she says.

"I know. It's fine."

She sits down, leans back in her chair, eyes wide open, horrified.

"It's fine," I say again.

I leave her be. She doesn't move until the little boy runs back down the aisle, a tampon stuffed up his nose. One of the stage managers got to him. He has to be lying about being thirteen, because a thirteen-year-old would be embarrassed. Instead, he's delighted.

"This usually goes in a vagina!" he says, pointing at his face, clearly excited he got to say the word.

"I'm so sorry," Lily says. The performance of her apology is over the top. She grabs his hand and holds it. "I can't believe I did that."

"Who cares, this goes in a vagina!" The little boy is high on something, fear maybe, combined with this thrashing energy that kids have.

The stage manager steps up to the lip of the stage, the edge of the orchestra pit, and cups her hands around her mouth. "Hey!" she shouts over the din. "Has anyone seen Samantha?"

My insides feel cold. Sickly. I wait for someone to say, "I have! She's right here!" No one does. Silence. Then a muttering among the cast, half-costumed, most of them waiting for dress to begin, eating bananas and slugging water.

The stage manager looks around the room expectantly. But nothing. No Samantha. No Maria. Dress is in forty-five. She technically doesn't have to show up until the half-hour call. That's the rule. Fourteen minutes to go.

The stage manager and Michelle stand offstage left, are having a whispered conversation behind their hands. Michelle's eyes are red. She's not even trying to be happy; she's not pretending to be brave. She's falling apart in front of all of us. Maybe she has been the entire time. Watching her attempt to direct this production has been like watching someone swimming through a churning ocean, her body getting tossed around on the waves.

The stage manager whispers into the radio. I see her talk into the mic clipped to her T-shirt.

"Can I get everyone in the first few rows," Michelle calls out to the stage. The stretching dancers look up from their splits. "It'll just take a few minutes. I know we aren't going to start on time."

This has to be the moment. This has to be it. She's going to tell everyone Samantha isn't coming. It's going to be me. They need me. And I know the part. I'll be confident but humble. Satiate all their fears. It's important not to celebrate. No one will be happy Samantha decided not to show up, no, they'll be terrified, probably, for their careers, the risk of sharing the stage with an unknown talent. If the reviews are bad, what that will mean. It's understandable. But I know I can do it. And they'll soon know it, too.

Michelle sits down on the lip of the stage, her feet dangling into the orchestra pit.

Everyone's here. The sound guys and the stagehands and the costume assistants. The band and the choreographer and even some of the set builders. The cast slumps in the audience, while the crew mostly stands at the back of the room, arms crossed, black T-shirts and black jeans, barely hiding expressions of impatience.

Michelle looks around the room, laying her eyes on each member of the cast before moving on, almost as if she's counting. When she's done, she re-centers herself, throws back her shoulders, and speaks to the ceiling.

"And no one has seen Samantha yet, okay," Michelle mutters to herself, then remembers we're all watching. "I'm sure she's got an excellent reason. But I wanted to talk to you all before things get hectic tonight. There's something about the moment before a dress rehearsal that . . . well it feels . . . just like the right time. And first off, I wanted to say thank you. This musical means so much to me. It's the first production I saw as a girl, and the passion and excitement that I felt watching it has brought me to where I am today."

The Captain, now sucked into it, feeling his own importance as a leader, starts a round of applause that clearly embarrasses Michelle, even though it's obvious this is what she was after. She ducks her head. She's blushing. The kids clap lazily. The boy with the tampon up his nose pulls it out and examines it, smells it, then sticks it back up there.

"Now I do have some . . . some news." Michelle ducks her head. More tears. "Some of you already know this, but I wanted us all to be on the same page. You probably noticed that I have had to duck out of a few rehearsals early, here and there. Well. I've been seeing doctors, and I'm sorry to tell you this. I'm sick. Really, really sick."

A shocked hush rises from the cast, dramatic reactions from all of us who likely didn't notice Michelle's comings and goings. I certainly didn't. But now, seeing her in the light, there are sharper angles to her cheeks, fighting against a strange, bloated quality that makes it difficult to make out her features. She's barely into her forties.

"This is probably going to be the last show I direct." She breaks down suddenly, in front of us all. Shoulders shaking, staring at her knees, tears rolling down her cheeks. "For now. But . . . it's not looking good. My prognosis is . . . well. I'm glad I got to make some art with all of you. It's been a wild and wonderful dream."

The shocked silence in the audience slowly morphs into sniffles and tears. Lily is staring up at the stage, the bottom of her chin quivering uncontrollably. It feels almost authentic.

"I'm not telling you this for pity, I just wanted to thank you. This has been a magical experience. And I treasure you all." The effort it takes for her to get this out, to speak the words — my God, it takes forever. Gasping between each word. Kind of milking it, honestly.

The Captain is the first to leap out of his seat in standing ovation. I follow him. It's shocking, sure, but no one wants to be the last one sitting, incapable of showering upon Michelle the very thing that we're looking to audiences to do for us.

I want to ask, though, to raise my hand and say, *Where is Samantha?* I think about doing it, for the kids, saying it's for them. *The kids need to warm up with Samantha.*

Everyone is lost in this moment, though. They aren't asking the questions that need answering. Samantha isn't here. Where is she? Who's going to step in for her now that she hasn't shown up to her call time? Her equity-ruled, strictly enforced call time?

Instead, they're all running at Michelle, distracted. The cast throw themselves onstage and bury Michelle in hugs. I follow them — with the kids, of course. It's a dog pile, a sloppy one. I want to scream, *Have none of you noticed? Samantha isn't here! She isn't coming! There's no Maria!*

No one seems to be considering that we won't have a show, that we aren't going to be able to deliver anything for Michelle's final run as a director, that we won't be able to honor her work without a Maria.

Instead, the feelings take us to seven-thirty, everyone together onstage, teary-eyed, holding hands and embracing a collective swell of emotion, of heaving sadness and release. This is the happiest I've seen Michelle, perhaps ever. She wants this. She doesn't care about the show, clearly, otherwise she'd be asking the question. Her feelings, her revelation should've been pushed aside for the show. It must go on. It has to. And this means only one thing.

Michelle is no longer in control of this musical. I have to take things into my own hands.

With no one looking, I grab my bag and slip away to the bathroom, fishing out a comb as I go. The stalls are empty, though I half expect to see Samantha's ankles there, skin blue and white, waiting for me. I comb my hair furiously. It's full of matts and tangles. This won't do. I can't believe I let it get like this.

I need to be ready. I need to show them that I'm ready. I yank and pull, threading my fingers through the tight knots, grabbing two curtains of hair that are melded together and prying them apart. There's a stubborn knot close to my skull that doesn't want to come loose. I try and pick at it with the comb, but when it won't come, I simply yank the hair out of my head.

I scream. It hurts, but it'll be worth it. Blood blooms from the place I pulled, and I look at the hank of it in my hand, tendrils of pink skin, and blood attached to it. My hands are shaking. It'll all be worth it.

Pain throbs. I drop the skin and grab paper towel, press it to my head. I feel blood dripping down the back of my skull. I dunk my head under the tap, strain to jam it under the flow of water, and watch as blood swirls down the drain.

Wring my hair out. The hunk of wet hair between my hands makes me gasp. Somehow familiar. My hands get hot. Like an allergic reaction pumping between my fingers, all the blood in my body rushing for an exit. A head wound. That's all. I have a head wound.

I grow dizzy and have to lean, press my hips into the sink. I don't remember the last time I ate. I don't know what day it is. Deep breath in, deep breath out. There. It's fine.

I twist my hair up in two braids, cross them over my head. Maria's hair under her habit, for the entrance, for the big moment, her hair for the rest of the first act. See? I can do it. I'm ready. You can barely see the blood.

XXXVI

"**I**'m going to wring her neck," one of the stagehands spits out. I overhear her as I make my entrance. "Oh, there you are." She looks at my hair, confused. The kids are all upset and half dressed. The littlest boy still has a tampon in his nose, is batting the string with his hands. Lily stares at the wall.

"Can you help me with my lines?" The little one instantly starts tugging on my shirt sleeve. The tugs turn to yanks.

Michelle is by the stage with the stage manager, who checks her phone for the time and shakes her head. Another assistant is next to her, leaving a message. "Please call us." She enunciates loudly, but I can't hear anything else they're saying. I need to be in Michelle's eyeline. I need her to remember that I'm here, ready to go. I can be warmed up in ten minutes. Someone else will have to take care of the children, but that's not the most important thing. The most important thing is that we see this through, tonight.

There's already a small audience in the balcony, besides the techs and heads of department. They're waiting for a show.

I herd the kids to the other side of the room and try to look as loving and gentle as possible — patting their heads, fixing their costumes, smoothing out the wrinkles. I give Lily a long hug. She sighs into my armpit then steps away. I get them all to stretch their bodies, arms way up above their heads and down to the floor, get them to take deep breaths, in and out, while I eavesdrop on the conversation.

"Should we call the police?"

"Were you able to get a hold of her parents?"

"Yes, they haven't heard from her and are very concerned."

"Maybe they should do it, I don't want to overstep —"

"I think we need to make a decision about what we do tonight. Now." The stage manager with her calm, clear voice.

Lily is frightened, I can tell. She picks up on things, is listening the same as I am. What will they do about Samantha? What if the show gets canceled?

"Maybe we should get Jessamyn to do it." It's not Michelle who suggests this but the stage manager whose name I don't care to remember. I could kiss her chapped, bloody lips.

"I know she can't cover, but the kids are freaked out. I think it could help."

"Well, we should ask her not to sing."

"Who's going to have that conversation with her?" A dull silence. I feel my cheeks heating up. They don't know the work I've put in. They don't understand all the time I've spent at the side of a piano. I know more about the sound of notes, the shape of them, their expression from my diaphragm, the delivery. They don't know how ready I am. They've never even really seen me do it, right? It's all been about protecting Samantha's ego. But a shot to prove them wrong and here they are, the cowards. Still protecting her.

"Maybe we can get Kathy to sing in the background."

"Kathy?"

I'm going to vomit. Kathy? Not the horse girl.

"Yes. I think she'd be great, it's just everything else . . ."

"But who's going to talk to Jessamyn?"

Michelle says she will. "I created this situation. I'll deal with it." God, the lengths they will go to save Samantha's ego. So worried about how she'll feel if she walks in and sees me. So fragile.

I sit up, stand, hands in the air, fake stretching so Michelle can see me. The kids follow suit, silently, dully doing what they're told. Their nerves are keeping them quiet. Michelle pokes her head over the seats and asks me for a quick chat.

I follow her to a corner of the room.

"We're behind schedule," Michelle says. "We're all concerned about Samantha's well-being. You haven't heard from her, have you?"

My eyes are wide. I shake my head, furrow my brow slightly. "I'm sorry, no. Gosh that's not like her."

"I know," Michelle says. "But when she shows up, we don't want her to feel like she's been replaced, so we were hoping you'd stand in for her during the dress rehearsal tonight. You can wear your own clothing, and we'd prefer if you just did the lines, choreography, and the blocking. We'll get Kathy to cover the songs from the wings."

I listen. I smile. I nod. I say, "Of course," performing the humility necessary to get me one step closer to that part, to the role of a lifetime.

"I just think the kids would feel so much better with you up there," she says. "If it can't be Samantha, of course."

"Of course," I say again, nodding, agreeing, biting my lip. "Anything for the show."

"I appreciate you." Michelle reaches out, squeezes my hand, and nods gratefully.

My heart skips a beat. I nod back at Michelle, but fury blooms inside of me. Why can't they just let Samantha go? She's not here and that is so unprofessional. But guess who is here? Me. When do they give up on her and start protecting me?

Michelle's now talking to the dumpy stage manager, and here I sit, seething. I bend over, exhale rage, steam, hot filthy anger. Maria isn't anger. She is grace. She is calm.

Breathe in. Breathe out. Calm. Grace. Serenity. Calm, grace, serenity. I am one with Maria. I am good. I am kind. The stage manager is calling for places. The chorus members are taking their candles and heading to the corners of the house, beginners. A stagehand comes to find me.

"Jessamyn?" she says. I nod. Humming. My entire body vibrating. "You can follow me."

After that, I nearly black out. The entire night proceeds in a blur. The dancing, the singing. I'm not mic'd, so I do sing along with the kids, pick them up, swing them around, laugh, let Maria's joy run through me. When the Captain and I do the laendler, our arms float up and over our heads. I'm soaring on this vibrant energy, this assured notion that I'm finally where I belong. He stares into my eyes, with comfort and gratitude, my own grace reflected back at me. It's difficult to contain my joy, and instead of trying to bury it, I let it pour out of my body. Let it extend my wrists through the choreography, my fingers angled just so.

When the Captain cups my cheeks with his hands, I know he's feeling it, too, this energy pulsating between us. A shared dream, just for the two of us. Together. Forever.

And then . . . the curtain call. The applause. After so many years of abuse and time — so much time! — spent next to a piano, the universe has finally decided that it's my turn. Mine! And I'm not about to waste it. Bright lights flash and the sound of the band is so, so loud and we're all clapping. Our shared joy fills the space.

When I finally walk out and bow, I press one hand to my heart and smile, attempt to affect a silly grin, to acknowledge this funny situation, but I can't help but think that I deserve this. That I gave them all a gift just now, the gift of myself, suspended in time, my heart and soul, all of my human energy and experience, all of my memories, everything I've suffered to get to this point. I did it for them. I took my human agony and swallowed it down, made it beautiful. And now they're finally thanking me for it.

Eventually the applause dies down and the cast walks offstage, the costumers herding them to dressing rooms where the men will stand to one side and the women to the other, and everyone will do their best to keep their uniforms and dresses, their outfits off the floor. I'm not in a costume, so I find my water bottle offstage and take a sip, sucking the dregs out of the bottom, and it's then that I notice them. They slip in the back of the house, almost embarrassed in their stature, as if they know they're out of place.

Two police officers, road cops, hats on, radios strapped to their chests. Bulletproof vests. Looking straight at me.

XXXVII

But why are they staring at me? I have no idea where Samantha is. I woke up and went for a run, then showered and came to work. That's all. That's everything. I had an English muffin with butter and some coffee. I had some cheese. Ate an orange. No, an apple. A granny smith apple. Weird, I know. I like them. Most people use them for baking, but I like how sour they are.

Did anyone see me? Can anyone confirm my whereabouts? No, sorry, I live alone. No, there are no cameras in my apartment building. I'm not wealthy. I'm an artist. A struggling artist.

I look at them with curiosity. What are they doing here? Police? At a dress rehearsal? So bizarre.

I really hope it doesn't have to do with Samantha. But I can't see why else they'd be here. Unless they're bored? Or maybe the mics were up too loud and someone complained? We're downtown, though, a jewelry store on one side and a shoe store on the other.

There's absolutely no reason this should be a new problem. We've been blasting music in here for weeks.

Maybe someone hates us, though, has hated the noise, the joy, the voices of dreams coming true. And tonight, well, tonight the energy coming out of the theater was just so luminescent they had no choice but to call in a noise complaint. Noise complaint? More like a joy complaint. Because that's what happens when Jessamyn takes the wheel. Everyone around me is uplifted. Made greater. Because stars shine, not just on themselves, no, their light is cast upon everyone around them.

The police approach the sound guy, who approaches a stagehand, who taps the dumpy stage manager on the shoulder, who turns around, eyebrows up.

Rudy appears beside me.

"Do you think it's about Samantha?" he asks.

"I hope not," I say. "That's dark."

"Yeah," he says. "But it's really weird that she didn't show up."

"Mm," I say, as if I'm attempting to think it through. "Could just be car trouble? Or maybe a sick parent?"

"Car trouble makes you late," Rudy says. "It doesn't make you absent. And Michelle said they spoke to her parents. Weren't you listening?"

"Maybe she had a panic attack," I say. "I think I've heard rumors about that." Because really. Maybe she just isn't up for it. Maybe she found out the Company's financial future is riding on her performance and did the noble thing and slunk off into the night.

"I hope it's just nerves," Rudy says.

"Me too."

A stagehand hurries over to us. "We need everyone in the audience."

"Right," Rudy says. "For notes or for the cops?"

"Both," the stagehand says. I turn to go, and Rudy grabs my hand and I shout with pain.

"Jessamyn, what happened to your fingers?" He holds my hand flat in his. My knuckles are purple. The pointer finger has turned bright blue. I flash to a feeling — sea water and metal, my hand caught in the link of a chain.

"Jessamyn, what happened?"

"I don't know," I say and then regret it. "No, ha ha ha. What am I saying. I fell getting off the bus," I say quickly, my heart thudding. "Sorry, I'm so out of it. The bus. I fell getting off the bus. I should go get the kids." I walk away before his probing distracts me away from the absolute truth, which is floating away from me, into the air; the absolute truth, which is that Samantha didn't show up tonight and I have no idea why.

...

Michelle sits on the stage as the cast finishes shrugging into sweatshirts and cardigans, pulling on sweatpants over leggings, slugging water with lemon from crinkling reusable bottles as they settle in for notes. Even the crew take seats, a vague curiosity about the police in the room. The dumpy stage manager, oh how I hate the stage manager, walks down with her gigantic binder, a creased forehead, and sits in the front row, suckling the life out of a giant Starbucks drink.

The two cops hover on the edges. One whispers to the other. They're garden variety, barrel-chested white men. I corral the kids, keep them seated and quiet, and make sure they all have water in their water bottles and are eating the snacks their parents packed for them, because I am, if anything, a professional.

"Incredible work, everyone," Michelle says. The room breaks into applause, led by the Captain, his large hands cupped and making so much noise that I flinch. "There's some areas and notes to focus on. And thank you to Jessamyn, of course, for helping us with the blocking."

Blocking? What about my performance? I left my soul on that stage. I left my *self* on that stage.

More applause, quieter than I expected, honestly. Don't these people know the show would be dead without me?

"Of course, you see we have some visitors and some news, and then we'll get to notes. I know everyone is tired."

What if Samantha's dead? What if they found a body? They shouldn't be announcing that in front of the kids. Right? Kids don't know about death. Kids need to be protected from death. Just like on the *Titanic*. The women and children get lifeboats. I'm a woman, I shouldn't even be here.

The house left door creaks open again and there's shuffling as more figures enter: a mousy-haired woman with tired eyes, wearing an expensive coat; a balding man in his fifties with his arm out, supporting an ancient grandfather who looks like he's about to keel over. The grandfather takes tiny steps, his back the shape of a crescent moon. He's clutching what I think is his son's arm on one side and holding a bundle of papers in his other hand.

My chest tightens. It's Samantha's family. They walk down the aisle and stand next to the stage. It begins.

The police stride to the middle of the stage and stand next to Michelle. The taller of the two steps up, his hands on his belt. I focus on his ruddy red cheeks as he speaks. He says normally they don't investigate missing persons cases involving adults until they've been missing for twenty-four hours — unless, that is, something suspicious is unearthed. Samantha's parents were able to track her car somehow. They found it abandoned down by our other stage, near the water, parked illegally as if she'd just stopped to drop something off.

They ask if anyone saw anything. Rudy immediately raises his hand. "There was a man," he says. "There was a man outside last night who seemed to be obsessed with her. We had to wrestle him down. He appeared to be . . . well . . . unhoused."

The police tell Rudy to come speak with them privately.

Lily raises her hand, too, the little attention whore, and so I have to also. They look at Lily but go to me first. "We were all there last night," I say, gesturing to the kids. "Waiting for parents to pick up."

"Well, we should all have a chat," he says. "Even the smallest details can help." His partner passes out a stack of business cards with his name and badge number on it. Everyone takes one, passes it on.

"Anything you can remember from the last few days," they say. "Details big or small. If you remember anything, call me. Or if you're nervous, talk to your team here and have someone reach out."

The room is very quiet. Worry in the air.

"Do you mind if I speak to the people who witnessed last night's incident?" the cop asks. Michelle agrees, seems surprised that something happened of that magnitude, and she didn't know about it.

"Wait," Samantha's mother says when the feeling starts to shift in the room. "Wait just one second." They walk up and onto stage, Samantha's mother, father, and grandfather, who can barely move, who looks like his bones are about to disintegrate.

They stand together in a line. There's desperation in the mother's posture. Brokenness. The grandfather reaches under his arm and holds out a flyer. On it is a picture of Samantha smiling, laughing. The word MISSING booms over a phone number in bright red letters.

"She's our only child," the mother says, her voice trembling. Exhaustion in how she speaks, as if she hasn't slept. "She's so talented. So beautiful. If —" Her voice breaks and she begins to sob into her husband's shoulder. He hugs his wife, wraps her in his arms, and guides her offstage, leaving the grandfather standing there alone.

He starts to speak at us in what I guess is Vietnamese? He holds up the flyer, shows it to everyone. We all just sit in the audience while he talks. Eventually Kathy, the goody-goody, goes up on the stage and takes the flyers from him and starts handing them out. The old man points at us all, over and over again, as if he's accusing us of something. He jabs at us repeatedly, shouting in words that no one here understands until his voice breaks and he starts to cry, too.

The littlest girl comes over to me and climbs onto my lap, hides her face in my chest. I hug her to me, feel her heartbeat. "Why is he upset?" she asks in a too-loud voice. I look away from the stage. His face, the pure agony on it, it makes me feel embarrassed for him. Embarrassed that he's showing us all of himself.

I smile big at the girl, make a face. "Don't worry about him," I say. She bites her lip. I bounce my knees a little to distract her. This is my job, after all. Instead, she looks back up at the stage. At him.

"He looks like my gung gung," she says, and keeps watching him.

Samantha's dad walks up onstage and wraps an arm around the grandfather's waist, but the man continues to shout through his tears, keeps turning back to us with his accusing finger until his voice dissolves into wailing, the sound coming out of his chest is unnatural, like he's some kind of ghost.

At almost the exact same time, everyone in the room seems to feel like it's time to go, that we're intruding on something very private. We stand to leave, even though we haven't done notes yet. The kids follow me out.

The lobby is chaos. The cops shout out that any witnesses to last night's altercation should meet them in the corner, where they're standing. I don't think the kids should have to speak on this. They're so exhausted, and that was harrowing in there. I'm nauseous. My heart is pounding and I consider leaving.

But Rudy finds me and grabs my shoulder. "Don't forget about the cops," he says. "C'mon, kids," to the group of them standing beside me like a pack of lost little ducks.

"We're going to do notes upstairs!" the stage manager says. She's sitting up on the bar, has her hands cupped around her mouth. "No one leave. Notes up in the band's rehearsal room."

"We can't miss notes," Lily says as the rest of the cast trudges upstairs, leaving the kids, me, Rudy, and two chorus members with the police. I'm surprised to see this little people-pleasing suck-up torn between two authority figures and choosing the theater over the cops. What a kid. She's really going to make it in this business, I'm sure of it.

"We'll get them after."

One of the cops bites down on a huge yawn as we gather around them. I direct the kids to sit down on the chaises. They're tired, but they gaze up at the officers, their mouths in the shape of circles, eyes wide. The younger boy eyeballs one officer's gun. A few of the parents loiter nearby. The police notice them and explain that there was an incident last night, that the kids were witness to it. They need statements.

The mother of the eldest boy steps forward, her iPad in its pink silicone case tucked underneath her armpit. She says it's late and these kids need to get home.

"A young woman is missing. We need information."

The mom glances at me, surprised.

I nod sadly, and the mom steps off, hands up, as if to say, *Sorry, sorry, my bad, sorry.*

"Time is of the essence here," the first cop says, his voice sounding so incredibly bored.

"Who's missing?"

"Samantha Nguyen," he says. The mother gasps sharply. The other parents step forward as if they have questions of their own. The officer waves them off. "We just need to ask these kids a few questions and then you can do . . ." he trails off, gestures back toward the theater, "whatever it is you need to do."

He doesn't understand theater. It's fine. I wouldn't expect him to.

"Okay, kids," the officer continues, turning toward them now. "What happened yesterday at pickup?"

Lily's hand flies into the air. The officer points at her. "There was a man. Samantha was leaving, and he ran up to her and asked for her autograph. And then he got, like, really creepy."

"Did you all see this man?"

The kids nod.

"What did he look like?"

"Rudy tackled him, it was cool!" the littlest boy says. "He was, like, punching him and stuff."

"And Rudy is . . ." The cop looks at us. Rudy puts his hand up. The cop nods.

"How about a description of the —"

"He was, like, pow pow pa pow pow —"

"Hey," I say, putting a hand on the littlest boy's shoulder. "Let's just get through this and then we can go home, okay?"

Lily's hand goes up again. "He was homeless, kind of. He had brown hair, and I think it was curly."

The cop nods, focused on the kids, hands still on his belt. "How tall was he? Was he as tall as me?"

"No," Lily says. "He was shorter. But taller than Rudy."

"Anything else you noticed? Did he have a tattoo? Or a nose ring?"

"No," Lily says. The other kids are bored. The tiniest one stands up and runs over to her dad, who picks her up. Her head falls onto his shoulder. He squeezes her, tightly. "He looked like he smelled bad," Lily says. "Like, really bad."

"Did you smell him?" the cop asks.

"No, but you could tell. And he asked for Samantha's autograph. She was nice to him, but it was weird."

"Right, okay." The cop gestures to the parents and they all rush toward their children and gather them up, as if every night they clasp their hands and lead them off with love and care. Usually, they can barely look up from their cellphones.

I turn to leave, to head off to my notes session when the cop calls out, "Not so fast." The cloying, delighted tone he used with the children is gone. My stomach drops.

"Yes?"

"Did you witness the takedown?"

"Yeah," I say. "It was a homeless guy that we see around here pretty often."

"Got a name?"

"No," I say, feeling impatient. "It happened like the kids said, the homeless guy wanted an autograph from Samantha. He got violent, Rudy tackled him. I called the police and they carted him off. I'm surprised you guys don't know that already? Like, there's no record or anything?"

"Different unit." The cop checks his notebook. "And this homeless guy had her headshot. Where do you think he got it?"

I shrug. "Maybe he printed it out himself."

"A homeless guy?" the cops say.

"I mean, he just looked homeless," I say. "Like he didn't take care of himself."

"Right. And he wouldn't leave Samantha alone."

"He seemed kind of obsessed." I pause and think. "He did say something about coming to every matinée."

"And how would he afford that if he's homeless?"

I sigh. "Listen, I'm here sixteen hours a day, previews start tomorrow . . . I told you what I saw. I don't know anything about the guy."

The cops trade eye contact.

"What do you do here?"

"I'm the kids' acting coach," I say.

"But you were onstage," the cop says. "You were performing."

"Just helping with the blocking until Samantha's back," I say. "I know the show because of the kids. I run it with them all the time."

The cops trade eye contact again. The one taking notes flips out a card and hands it to me. "If you think of anything else."

I take the card. Walk past Rudy, to head upstairs. I try to meet his eyes, but he ignores me, smiles, and steps up for his interrogation. I realize, as I enter the room where the cast has gathered for notes, that I'm sweating.

XXXVIII

I have to wait until the very end of the session, but Michelle gives me notes. On my performance as Maria. She tells me not to sleep on an entrance, to give a bit more energy here, to be just a touch gentler with my wrists. She gives me *notes*. Me.

Because notes, if you don't know, are suggestions for improvement. Notes are for tomorrow night, when I'm to do the part again. Because there's no other option. There's no backup. Kathy, well, I guess she did lose some weight, but she still has a very ample bosom, well . . . and I don't want to sound like a bitch, but it's not like she's fitting into Maria's costume. And that's not cruel, that's just reality. Bones are different sizes. Some girls just have bigger ones.

It's going to be me. It has to be me.

As I leave, the stage manager asks me to wait in the lobby. Everyone else grabs their stuff and limps out in small groups, twos and threes. Who knew there was this much camaraderie between the cast? Once the lobby is quiet, I go to the door and spy through the crack, into the house.

"But what if she's fine?"

"Aren't you listening? You need to face facts, Michelle. The police were here. The police!"

My heart pounds.

"I just . . . I need her to be okay." Michelle's shoulders curl over and she starts to cry. "Not just because I care about her, but this show . . ." She trails off, and I can tell she's holding in tears.

"There's a lot riding on it," the stage manager says, shifting her gigantic binder from one arm to the other. "I know. I've heard the rumors."

"This is it," Michelle says. "If the house isn't at ninety percent for the entire run, we're done."

My jaw drops. Ninety percent is a lot.

"The way I see it, we've got two options. Kathy does the whole show with a script in hand, though she doesn't know the choreography or the blocking, nor will the costume fit her. Or we do it like dress, with Jessamyn onstage and Kathy piped in. Now, I think it worked tonight," the stage manager says. "With Kathy singing in the background and Jessamyn mouthing along."

"And Kathy's fine?" Michelle asks.

"Oh, she's a team player," the stage manager says. "Truly."

Michelle nods and then throws her head back, whipping off her big glasses. "Oh, hell," she says suddenly, then she begins to sob into the crook of her arm, quietly, her breath coming in short, uncontrolled gasps. "I can't believe it's come to this."

"Do you want me to talk to Jessamyn for you?"

"Who loses their lead actress the day of the dress rehearsal?"

Michelle's spirit seems crushed. That cancer thing must be really causing her a lot of pain.

"I just can't catch a break," she says. The stage manager pats her on the shoulder.

"Well, you know I hate platitudes as much as the next person . . ." the stage manager says.

"If you say the show must go on, I'll scream," Michelle says to the floor, and with a searing intensity that makes the stage manager step back, like she's been slapped.

"I'll go talk to Jessamyn," the stage manager says. I hurry away from the double doors, rush over to the coat check and pretend to be loitering there.

...

I am air. I am bliss. The stage manager spoke to me. Of course, there's the issue of them having someone sing over me, but who cares. I'll still have a mic for dialogue. It is happening. I am going on as Maria. For the entire run or until they figure out what happened to Samantha. It is official. They are going to reach out to my agent. There will be paper. Of course, he isn't technically my agent anymore, but still. He'll certainly reverse his opinion of me once this lands on his desk. Collect his ten percent. All of the choices, all of the money, all of the harassment and pain and agony and cold nights . . . it was all worth it. I made it.

"Jessamyn!"

It's Rudy, smoking, leaning against the door of the closed jewelry store next to the theater. I let out a little shriek and dive at him, throw my arms around his neck. "Did you overhear? I'm going to be Maria! Tomorrow night. It's official!"

"We need to talk."

His voice is flat. Not overjoyed. Not helpful. Not hopeful. Not the kind of celebratory energy he should be feeding me. Because I did it! I'm going to be the lead in a musical.

"About me finally getting cast?"

"No," he says. He takes a long drag from his cigarette, exhales up and away from me, then pitches the butt into a nearby puddle. "About this. About Samantha."

He takes my hand, my left hand and places it flat on his again, very gently strokes my knuckles. "Jess, what happened?"

"I told you. I fell getting off the bus."

He's staring at me, hard, fierce. "You don't take the bus."

"I had an appointment. Rudy." Suddenly, it all makes sense: what he's trying to get out of me, the sum of all these looks, the way he's been avoiding me. I realize what it means. "I'm going to go," I say and turn away from him. Because really. Really, Rudy? No. He's not taking it from me. Not now. Not him. He grabs my arms.

"Jess, I just lied to the police."

"Why?"

"They asked me about you. What I thought of you. If you were a performer. I lied!"

"Why? Rudy, what's going on?"

"I know you know that guy. He was looking at you. When I was fighting him, I could tell he was looking at you."

"What guy?"

"The unhoused guy who attacked Samantha. And now. I just . . . it all makes sense. You pushed Samantha off the pier. You're obsessed with this. And I know you are, because I was you! I would've killed to get onstage. I tried to tell you. I tried to make you understand—"

"Rudy." I cut him off; I'm starting to panic. "I think you need to talk to someone. Because this isn't making sense. I'm leaving."

I look down at him, holding me there, the intensity between us electric. I try to step back, but he won't let me. "Let go of my arms."

"I think you should come with me. Turn yourself in."

"What?"

"Confess. What you did to Samantha."

"What are you talking about?"

A bus roars past us. It starts to rain. No. No. Not tonight. Not now. It's about to happen. And I just can't . . . I just.

No.

He is not taking this from me. But he isn't letting go of me, either. Why isn't he letting go of me?

"Rudy. You don't understand."

"Yes, I do. I understand you." He reaches toward me with a knuckle and raises my chin so we're staring into each other's eyes. "Probably better than you understand yourself."

"I promise. I'll tell you everything and I just . . . I'm . . ."

He's hesitating. I know he's hesitating. But I just need a minute. A minute to figure out what to do. How can I delay him?

"I will tell you everything," I say, remembering what he wants. More than anything. "But you have to know, I have feelings for you. And I just, I want to put it all on the table before anything changes."

Hope seems to burst inside of him. Of course it does. I take his hand in mine and squeeze. This is how I can get him on my side. This is how I can get him to trust me.

"I knew it," he whispers. I step forward and kiss him. At first, he doesn't respond, but as I press into him with more urgency, he pulls my body in tight, gives into everything he's been telling himself he'll never have. I pull away, bite his earlobe. Revulsion churns inside of me. He smells like old cigarettes. His fingernails scrape me. Long, too long. And no reason other than laziness for them to be so fucking long. There's probably dirt under them.

His breath is ragged. He presses his forehead to mine. What will he do now? Now that I'm offering him the thing he wants more than anything. Will he take it?

I let him lead me to the rear stage door. It's been left open with a rock. His hands are greedy, moving around my waist, and he presses himself against me as we descend the stairs to the green room. He could shove me at any minute. End my career. The power of him in this moment, to hurt me. It seems to thrill him. His heart pounds against my back.

The basement is now cleared out — everyone has gone home. The green room is tiny, cramped. A kitchenette with a microwave, some cooking utensils, a knife block, an ancient bottle of olive oil. Someone has left a puzzle spread out on the table, for us to work on as a cast. We're going to be a family. A real family.

He closes the door behind us and pulls me down on top of him. His eyes are wide open, staring at me as I straddle him, some combination of shock, awe, disbelief that he's getting exactly what he wanted, exactly how he wanted it. The number of times I'd caught him staring at me from across the room. It's not like he was hiding it. His hands are all over me, under my shirt, nails scraping against my skin.

"Wait, wait, wait." Rudy stops, pulls his hands out from under my shirt. Takes hold of mine, remembering himself, remembering who he thinks he is. "What happened? Tell me."

I summon some angst, a wobbling chin. It comes immediately. Of course it does — I am exquisite. This is the role I was born to play. Tears track down my cheeks. He squeezes my hands, holds them to his chest. Presses his forehead to mine.

"Please. I have to know."

"Samantha texted me this morning. Lured me down to the wharf. And then she attacked me."

"What?"

I nod. Watch as my tears fall on my jeans.

"She sent me this." I show him the texts from "Michelle," from the number with no contact information. He studies it. Eyebrows knit together. "And then she attacked me."

"She attacked you? Why?"

"Because she thought I was trying to sabotage her. But I'm not. Obviously, I just want what's best for the kids."

"Why did you call the police? The other night? When that homeless guy was creeping on her?"

"I was terrified! The reason I know him is because he used to do the same thing to me. Hang around outside shows I was in, try to get me to sign autographs. He's totally deluded. Thinks I'm in a relationship with him. I panicked."

"Samantha texted you."

Rudy sits and digests this. Clearly struggling against the story of how this confrontation went, what he thought I did to

Samantha. A clear cut right-and-wrong story now is messy in his head. He thought he'd get to be a hero. Everyone would applaud, he'd get to do the talk show circuit. The fantasy version of himself where he's a real, true artist who turned away from Broadway because it was the right thing to do will flood the world. Ha! Yeah right.

Instead, he brought me down here. Because there's something he wants more than all of that. And he's convinced himself I'm going to just give it to him. Give in to him. Give in to this version of me he has constructed in his mind. He thinks he's so different, Rudy. Different than Vishal, leaving money on the nightstand. Different than Anton writhing on the ground.

He kisses me again deeply. I respond, but barely. But he's pushing here, pushing, tongue parting my lips, shoving down my throat, hands greedy, squeezing my body against his. I can barely breathe. I can barely think.

He made the choice. He brought me down here. One last night before he turns me in. Gets to be a hero. But he's no better than me. He's all desire. He wants something so badly, and he'll do anything to get it. Even if it means turning away from this vision he has of himself. Of who he thinks he is. Who he wishes he is.

"Wait," I say. "Hold on."

But he doesn't. He lifts me up and carries me across the room to the kitchen counter. When I put my hand down to steady myself, I feel crumbs, something sticky.

He buries himself in my neck, lips and teeth pulling at flesh. He's pushing. He's taking.

"Just a minute —"

"I'm in love with you," he says, pushing forward, ignoring me. He pulls open my shirt, his tongue moving down my stomach, toward the button on my pants. "Jessamyn," he whispers into my belly.

And his tongue feels like a slug. I think of what he's doing. What he's become.

My hand feels behind me on the counter. They're all the same, these men. Each and every one of them.

And now his tongue is in my ear. A fat worm darting in and out. He's got my jeans open and somehow his fingers are already inside. Rough. His nails bite at the most delicate part of me. It hurts. And not in the good way.

They're all the same.

Blind to themselves. Desperate to be seen a certain way. Desperate. But deep down, at their cores, they are all desire. Slaves to the thing they want more than anything else. Just like me.

You have to take it.

You have to take it now. Before he does.

The handle of a knife in my fist. My hand moves quickly.

It slides into his neck so easily. He makes a glottal sound and gasps. Blood sprays out in an arc, splatters on the ground.

He meets my eyes, shocked and betrayed. I am determined.

A voice whispers. Or maybe it's me speaking. If it is, I don't recognize it.

I see you.

The knife clatters on the ground. His eyes widen in realization. Seeing me, now. Seeing me. Seeing himself, down here. He's just as bad as the men he hates. And he hates them because he hates himself. He looks at them and sees his own reflection.

The light fades so quickly from his eyes. His fingers are still inside of me. I feel them go limp.

Then I grab a tea towel hanging from a cabinet and press it to his neck to help catch the blood.

...

You have to get rid of distractions. You have to stomp them out.

I clean up after myself, roll the body up in one of the rugs left over from the Afghanistan play and lug it out to a dumpster a few blocks over. Outside it's raining, hard. Anything I leave behind will be washed away. Inside, I get down on my knees and bleach the green room, the stairs, anything he might've touched. And while I scrub, scrub, scrub, I run the show in my mind.

Enter from house left. Sing up the aisle. Love the children. Fear the Captain. The emotional arc here is so simple. Maria. How do you solve a problem like Maria? How do you solve the problem of a woman who just won't behave?

I'll sleep in the dressing room, maybe I'll run the show first thing in the morning. I know every bit of blocking, I know all the lines, I know the songs — the notes are basically plastered to my heart at this point. They are gouged into my soul.

And despite everything, I'm able to smile. Tomorrow, I'm going to make my debut.

My father is coming. He told me he was coming opening night, which I thought meant opening night — the first night after previews, after the show has been on its legs for a few weeks, has had a chance to breathe — but no. He thinks opening night is the first night tickets are available, because he never listens when I speak.

We're having a late lunch tomorrow, around two, so we can celebrate.

He seems excited. And he should be. He finally sees me. Sees how talented I am, how wrong he was. He's finally going to get it. To understand that all the work I put in meant something. That it means something, this commitment. That all of the things I've done, good and bad, were worth it, because the performance, well, the performance is going to be exquisite.

I take out my cellphone and email my entire address book, every single contact, tell them I'm going to be making my debut tomorrow, that there are still a few tickets available, that I would love to see them in the crowd, supporting me. I really lean into the sweetness. Tell everyone they have been so important to me on this journey, they each played a small part. That I could never have gotten to where I am without my community.

XXXIX

The restaurant my father picked has white tablecloths and a maître d' who looks me up and down when I come in. I want to say, "Come on, it's not that bad," because there's a specific kind of energy that's pushing me through the world, hooked behind my belly button and yanking me forward. Making me smile. Making me smile really big.

There was nowhere for me to shower, because there's no shower in the theater. The best I could manage was a sponge bath in the sink in the green room this morning, and some dry shampoo I stole from someone's bag. But it's fine, I look fine. The maître d's eyes briefly linger on my shirt before he sighs, picks up a menu, and leads me into the restaurant. I know what he's looking at. I know.

A dot of red on my shirt that won't come out. I stood by the sink for what felt like hours until I thought it had disappeared. I thought I was perfect. But on my walk over here, it seemed to appear again. I'm not sure I'll ever be able to wash it off.

My father's sitting with Sophie at a table in the middle of an empty dining room in this hotel I've never even heard of. They're both dressed like daytime talk show hosts. She's on her phone, her dark, dramatic hair impeccably done, tossed over one shoulder. He's looking out the window, pinching his chin, lost in thought. So lost that I make it tableside before he notices me. Jumps up then back, and takes me in. Eyes widen slightly. Enough that I notice.

"Jessie!" he says, then throws his arms out to the side. I step into them and give him a hug. It's been years. He doesn't smell like anything I recognize. His round head seems to have gotten rounder and there's white hair sticking out of his ears.

Our hug breaks. He sits down. I do too. I notice how his jowls have multiped, the lines on his face deepened. I half expect him to pop out his dentures and put them in a glass.

Sophie puts her phone down and smiles at me with all eighty-seven of her big white teeth. "Hi, Jessamyn."

She reaches out and grasps my hand. I squeeze back. I always forget how unnervingly gigantic her nostrils are. How big her teeth. Her face is huge, which makes sense for her career as a newscaster, I guess. On screen she appears somewhat normal, they probably just have to zoom in a bit less. But in person, it's like talking to a human bobblehead. I wonder if that's why my father likes her. He's never had very good eyesight, but he refuses to get his eyes checked, as if doing so means he's accepting some kind of weakness. So, you know, he needs to be with a woman he can see.

My father stares at me, unblinking. Confused. It takes him a minute before he snaps out of it.

"So," he says, still jumpy. "Have you eaten?"

I shake my head and open the menu. My stomach grumbles. I want it all. The descriptions of everything in threes, each line a delicious little poem. Scallops Butter Caviar. Avocado Romaine Bacon. Prawn Lime Sourdough. Over and over again. The little descriptions run through me, flow like a drumbeat. Pear Gooseberry Crème Fraiche.

My future. Soon, this will be my day to day. I'll be able to live in a hotel just like this.

The waiter arrives tableside, a shining silver pitcher in hand, to fill our glasses. I hear the ice clinking and put a hand over my own. *Lukewarm. No ice. Squeeze of lemon. Large glass. Thank you.* He nods and leaves.

"For your vocal cords," Sophie says. And I nod. Yes. Exactly. My father is still silent, still staring at me as if I have a second head growing out of my neck.

"Of course, of course," he says, again a beat too late. Eventually he puts a hand on my back, rubs it, seems to be feeling the bones.

"Feeling limber? Feeling loose?" he asks.

"Absolutely." I smile at them both. Silence falls. I review the menu again. I could eat. I could eat a whole lot. But I should stick to light foods — salad, soup, vegetables. I wonder if I should get some chicken, plain grilled. A professional order for a professional artist.

"So, how are you?" my father asks, taking a short sip of his beer. It's got a skunky smell to it and is served in a tall glass.

"A little nervous," I say. "But ready. How are you?"

"Good, good." He takes another drink and his eyeline strays to the window.

Sophie picks up where he leaves off, asking me an array of questions — about the production, the other actors, the director, if I've had to do any early morning media calls, what's next for me.

"It's still regional theater," I say, smiling a little. "But you've got to start somewhere."

"Exactly, exactly," says my father. Sophie grins. We order. I get a salad with plain grilled chicken added. *Very little salt please.*

"So how was the dress rehearsal?"

I suddenly feel quite shaken. Things appear to me in flashes: a knife, a choking sound, an accusing finger punching the air. I inhale and something catches in my throat and I start hacking. My father rubs my back as I cough, take a ragged breath in. His hand seems to linger on my spine. Perhaps I've gotten thinner. But it's all in the pursuit of the work. My eyes water and I gulp down water. He should be looking at me as if he's considering a beautiful painting, a genius. And I want to glory in it, I do, but I can't quite shake this horrible feeling that everything is wrong. So, so, wrong.

"Jessamyn, are you okay?" Sophie asks and her voice is warm and concerned. I nod and move to use my napkin, pick up the roll and it unfolds, the cutlery clattering to the ground. I jump at the sound. Sophie flags down the waiter and gets me another set, then changes the subject.

She carries the conversation while we eat lunch, talking about her job, her interview for a national network, their trip to Aruba, about the place they're staying at and how Aruba is really safe, did I know that? She wishes I could come, you see, but the timing obviously doesn't work, but next time, though, definitely. The focus shifts to me and I tell them a few anecdotes about the child actors in the show, about the rehearsals and how much work we put in.

When the bill comes, I consider how painless this was, how I could do it again, in the future, eat a salad while listening to my father's much younger girlfriend talk.

He clears his throat, after downing his little cup of espresso, and says, his voice wavering just a little, "Jessie, you've really impressed me. Your work ethic. Your stubbornness. Well done." His eyes are watery as he reaches over and takes my hand. It's warm and dry. He squeezes and I try to squeeze back but my hand hurts. It hurts so much that I pull back quickly.

"Thanks." I feel tightness again, panic. As if I'm about to drown. I shouldn't have come here. My heart pounds. I have this totally embarrassing urge to crawl into his lap and wind my arms around his neck and start weeping. Bury my face in his chest. Surely, he'd push me to the ground.

Even though his words were proud, he isn't looking at me like he's proud. He seems nervous.

Sophie's phone rings and she excuses herself, strides through the dining room, her hair streaming behind her. Silence falls between us.

"I always knew you could do it," he says, staring off, out the window at the rain. I try to smile. To radiate calm. Take a deep breath in and out. "I always knew."

"No." The word explodes out of me. I feel like a small child. But this isn't how it happened, he never once said anything even remotely encouraging. All he's ever wanted is for me to quit. "No, you didn't."

His fist twists in his napkin and his gaze hardens.

"Don't tell me what I know," he says.

My chin starts to tremble. I won't take this, I can't swallow it. Not this version of events, not this story. Not after everything he said. How he abandoned me. I stare down at my lap, clenching my teeth together. "That's not how it went. Not at all."

He was supposed to apologize. To admit he was wrong about me.

"Jessamyn," he says in a voice that enrages me. Calm. Judgmental. "What happened to my good girl?"

My shoulders are hunched forward. I can barely breathe. I shouldn't have come here. Not today.

Out in the lobby, Sophie paces back and forth. I wonder what he told her. About me. About our relationship. About how he abandoned me in my time of need. Cut me out of his life. And now he's here to take credit. To be smug. And I'm supposed to thank him? For what?

I snort and stand up and drop my napkin. I don't need this. Not this insane fantasy version of events, the story where he is recast as the doting father who fought alongside me. Not now, the night of my debut.

I shouldn't have come.

I need to focus.

"Sit down," he commands.

I obey.

Sophie arrives back at the table. She apologizes, tells us about her producer, about how hard it was for her to get time off. She sits and puts her phone face down, clasps her hands together as if she's about to ask some hard-hitting questions. Then she notices the tension.

"Jessamyn seems to think I haven't been supportive," he says.

"What?" Sophie says. "Oh my gosh. Jessamyn. He never stops talking about you." And then she goes on and on and on, keeps talking about my father and his bottomless support for me, and a feeling like a boulder rolling downhill fills me, and I imagine both of them getting on their plane to Aruba, pretending that they helped me through my suffering, through the work that has made me perfect, through the work that has made me great.

And she just won't stop talking. Won't stop at all. She reaches out and puts her hand on my knee and I slap it away.

"Jessamyn!" my father shouts, sharp.

It's disgusting, you know, if you really think about it. She's young enough to be my sister.

Eyes are on us. They're crawling all over me. I stand to leave, say nothing as I walk away.

My father sent me a photo of their tickets earlier that day, texted it to me. *Can't wait!* The seats are front row center and now I'm not even sure they're going to bother showing up.

All night I will have to look down at the empty space where he was supposed to be.

But no matter. The show must go on. I must go on. And the show can't go on without me.

XL

"Jessamyn, is this on right?"

I've got my hair and makeup done, but my own costume is sagging in the front. The costumers are all huddled off to the side, trying to figure out what to do. Lily is next to me, staring at her reflection in the mirror. I'm not sure who let her put her own costume on, but they should be fired.

"No, you've got it backward," I say, pointing to the zipper at the top, along her neckline. "Who dressed you?"

"He did." She gestures to a young guy, probably twenty, pale, eyes so bloodshot he seems like he's about to puke.

I help her out of her costume and she steps around in a circle, putting it on correctly this time, so the neckline is in the right spot. I swipe my fingers along the top of it, clearing any dust, and smile at her in the mirror, hands on her shoulders.

"I'm so glad it's you," Lily says sweetly, staring up at me.

"Me too," I say.

"Are you nervous?" she asks.

I shrug, trying not to think of it. "A little. But I know the show. And I know you kids."

"Exactly. It's going to be so fun." She isn't sure of herself, but I know she's going to crush it. If she doesn't, it'll haunt her forever. That's what makes her so good. That's what makes me so good, too.

The lead costumer, Adele something or other, comes over and asks me to raise my hands as she pulls the saggy material tighter.

"We really should've done this classically, with real strings," she says, mumbling through the pins stuck in her teeth. The strings they did put in are just for decoration. "I'm just going to put in a stitch."

She quickly sews the sides together, then asks me to move my arms around. "Okay," she says. "This should be fine. We can reinforce it before tomorrow. Try to get something more permanent in there."

I nod at her, and I must seem nervous because she pats me on the shoulder kindly. "No one could've seen this coming," she says. "You'll be great. And the kids are cute. Everyone will be looking at them, anyway."

Excuse me? "What do you mean?" I ask, my voice quiet, delicate. Does she think I'm nervous? That I'm not ready? That I haven't lived and died for this a hundred times over?

"Oh," the costumer says. "I don't know, I guess I just — never mind. Break a leg."

I beam at myself in the mirror. I look incredible.

...

Michelle gathers us to the stage at the half-hour call and asks us to stand around her in a circle, holding hands. She slowly spins around while addressing us.

"You've all worked so hard," she says. "I'm so proud of you."

She starts naming everyone on the crew — the stage management, the costumers, the designers, the choreographer, the band.

Everyone in this room coming together to support me. The lead. The one who has to deliver. Finally, my name crosses her lips. "And thank you to Jessamyn, who needs our support tonight as she steps into the role." Applause, but it isn't loud enough. It isn't enough. I nod, smile. Why aren't they all behind me? You're supposed to get behind your lead. I look around at their faces, and they all seem to be hesitating, not fully understanding what is happening. Why this is going on.

But this is meant to be the moment we all band together. The show must go on, after all. The show must go on! I think about making some kind of speech, to make them feel more comfortable, to make them feel safe about what's about to happen, but Michelle jumps in before I can begin speaking.

"And of course, last but not least, to Kathy for doing the vocals!"

Everyone shouts their applause. There's a scream. There's loud whistling. Kathy seems to sigh a little, but then shies away from it, batting the air as if to say, *Oh stop*, as if to say, *We're all a team*.

Deep breaths. Whatever. These miscreants are pathetic anyway. Not a triple threat among them. Besides, I glow. I am charisma. I am beauty. I am relaxed. This is it. It's finally here. Tears well up inside of me. Finally. Finally, it's my turn. Mine.

"We're going to make something beautiful," I say, reaching out to my kids, my children. They rush to me and hug me. Already in character, ready to heap joy on everyone in my presence.

Now it's all on faith. Faith in the work I have done that has brought me here. The hours and hours I've spent working. Grinding. Obsessing. Learning. Growing.

I'm ready. I've done what I had to do, I've done what anyone would do, really, to get what they deserve. To serve the muse. I'm here and I'm ready.

Backstage, text messages flood my phone. So many of them. News travels quickly. All of them acknowledging the work. The sacrifices I've made. The person I've become. Of course. I read through each and every one of them.

There's even one from Renée. "I'm at the stage door," she says. "For good wishes."

I go to her, outside in the alley. Flashes from weeks prior try to penetrate my consciousness, but I block them with love, with the force of my heart, which is guiding me tonight.

I find Renée standing next to the dumpster, a bundle of cheap pink carnations in her arms. When she sees me in costume, she claps her hands, delighted but all I can see is the cheap, cherry red nail polish she's applied to her fingers so sloppily there's even a little splash of it on her knuckle.

"My dear, oh, you look fantastic."

I eye her, wary, arms crossed. Our last meeting was unfortunate. Both of us clearly regret our behavior. But now, it doesn't matter. Nothing else matters because I'm here. And I need to embody grace. I need to let it in. Let the goodness take over. Become Maria. But it isn't working. My chin starts to wobble, something roaring inside me. Something like fear, maybe? No, that can't be it.

But then Renée is holding me. She's wrapped me in her arms, which seems unlike her, because I'm wearing a costume. If she knew anything about theater, she'd know you can't just rumple a costume minutes from opening. I don't want to hug her back, but my arms seem to move of their own volition. They grasp at her, and I bury my face in her shoulder. I can't help it. I feel safe, suddenly, for the first time in years.

We stand there, locked for far too long, and are interrupted by a stagehand who opens the door with a bang, making us leap apart.

"That's fifteen," he says.

"I should get to my seat," Renée says, then wipes the tears away from her eyes. "Break a leg. You're going to be wonderful. You have this. Take it. Remember? You take it. Eat it up."

A sob hovers in my chest. But I quash it. I cannot disrupt this makeup. I need to be ready. I dab at it with my knuckle, careful not to disturb the makeup. I can't disturb the makeup.

···

The sound guy finds me backstage and fixes my microphone, then moves on to Kathy and fits hers. Kathy. My voice. I think about Kathy. About how she'll be in the wings, and that means no one will hear me. And that won't do. It has to be me. It's my time. I'm supposed to eat it up, but how can I eat a meal that isn't really mine?

This hasn't felt right, these last few days. It hasn't felt like I always dreamed it would, and I think it's because I haven't really been singing. No one has heard me. How am I supposed to take it if it isn't entirely mine? Samantha isn't coming, but no one seems to have accepted it. Not fully, otherwise they'd just give me the part. They wouldn't be protecting her anymore.

But we don't have to protect her! I realize this with a smile. It means we don't need Kathy. No one knows, but I know. I know!

"How are you feeling?" Kathy asks me after the sound guy leaves. She's wearing sweats tucked into Ugg boots. Without stage makeup on, I see her, these three cystic zits on her chin, throbbing at me. Gigantic. Didn't even bother to cover them up.

I need her microphone, so that when the time comes, everyone can hear me. So my father can hear me. He'll know what my voice sounds like. He'll know he was wrong.

"Would you come with me for a minute? I have an idea." Kathy nods, because Kathy is a good, sweet person who trusts people. Out the stage door and into the alley we go.

There's an old, abandoned storefront, its windows covered in brown paper, a few steps from the theater. I think it used to be a dry cleaner. Kathy follows me inside, grinning like a dope, like we're about to share some exciting secret.

The back door is unlocked, which can really only mean one thing. That the universe is on my side. And if the universe wants me to do it, that can only mean one thing. This is meant to be.

XLI

I'm back at the rear stage door at the five. The stagehand is waiting for me. He's got a coat for me to wear as we walk out of the alley, down around to the front doors, so no one we see on the street is going to know who I am, that I'm about to provide three hours of escape from the banality of the audience's lives. That I'm about to defeat the Nazis, but this time for good.

If anyone can do it, I can.

There are a few stragglers at the front door. A daughter with her mother, leaning on a walker, both of them yelling at Sudi as she scans their tickets. But behind them, chewing on his lip, a brand new, black wool coat stretched across his wide shoulders, holding a fat bouquet of red roses, stands Vishal.

"Jess," he says, then grins at me. "Wow. You look incredible." So much love wrapped up in his watery smile.

I don't say anything. I'm trying to become Maria.

"I got your email," he says. "Thank you."

Right. The email. And then I remember the stupid fucking dog pissing on that dumb tree. The fear, sitting next to him in the car. Kissing him, then sprinting off into the night. I can't deal with this right now. He must still think we're dating.

"Good luck," he says, goofy, joyful. "No wait, break a leg."

"I'll see you after," I say and brush past him because I need to prepare. To get in character, to conjure up all the questions. I need to love God, to bring him into my soul, to allow his light to flood through my body and out of my skin. His glow, his love, surrender to it all.

In the lobby, I stand in the corner, away from the other nuns who are preparing to make their entrance first, with the stupid Gregorian chant–style hymn.

I bet they're all gossiping about me. About how I made this happen. They're all still in the chorus, in the background, but me? I did this. I am taking it. It's mine. Any critique that comes from them is simply jealousy.

Applause from inside the theater. The nuns all disappear into the light lock, to their positions all over the house.

I bounce on my heels.

Something about this doesn't feel right. Which is stupid. It must just be butterflies. Fuck. They're not butterflies. Have I forgotten everything Renée taught me? No. They're not butterflies. They're never butterflies. This is love. That's what it is. This is love. This is commitment. This is ten thousand hours beside a piano; this is the inside of my soul gifted to six hundred strangers. This is all the work I've done to bring me here.

This is devotion.

The stagehand takes the coat from me. I swing my arms back and forth.

"Psst." It's Sudi from across the room, staring at me. "Fuck yeah, Jessamyn! You so deserve this."

I nod and swing my arms some more. Sudi gets performance. She gets it. She knows what it means to be *on*. I don't have to say anything to her. She knows.

All of my old coworkers are going to be so inspired when they see me up there. Not only am I giving them the gift of my performance today, I'm giving these plebs a real sense of progress. That they won't be stuck in this stupid job forever, that one day, they too can achieve their dreams. And that's such an important thing. All of the years they've spent in the trenches, worth it. All of the harassment, worth it. All of the abuse, worth it. Because one day they too can shine.

Vaguely I remember the taste of tequila, sitting around that bar top, laughing with all of them. Laughing. Locking my arms with Sudi and Kelsey, skipping away, and I feel some emotion swelling inside me but I stamp it down. Now is not the time.

The stagehand taps me gently on the shoulder, pulling me out of it. I want to slap him. He shoves the habit into my hand. Right. Of course. I need it for my opening number.

I step into the light lock. I am grace. I am calm. I am poise. I am a problem that only Captain von Trapp can solve. The house is still murmuring. Marge hasn't stepped up yet, hasn't done the house speech, so I can peek. I open the door, just the littlest bit and it's a punch to my solar plexus. My heart is in a vice — the seats in the front row, where my father and his little girlfriend were supposed to be sitting, are empty.

He didn't come.

I let the door click shut. Marge's voice booms through the loudspeaker as she starts the show. Asks everyone to turn their phones off. The nuns will begin to sing soon and then it'll be me. It'll be my time.

And as I picture the empty seats terror descends over me. I feel like all of my edges are falling away. Eroding. That there is a large chunk of myself that has disappeared.

And I am terrified. I can't do this. I can't.

I turn and press my forehead to the wall. Close my eyes. Breathe in, out. Puff out my diaphragm. Try to access that joy, that comfort, that feeling of sitting next to Renée at her piano, in her little room. The freedom, the wild abandon. But I can't find that Jessamyn. She's gone.

I'm going to run. Just go. Go to the airport, hop on a plane and leave, never look back. Go to some tropical location and learn how to scuba. Drown this soul-blistering phase of my life where I attempted to become who I am meant to be, to be seen for who I am, to exist as the best version of myself and be validated. Drown her. Kill her. Leave her for dead.

The habit is limp in my hand. The stupid habit that I'm supposed to put on my stupid head when the stupid church bell starts to ring and I'm called back to town. There's no way I'm going in there. To this small theater packed with nobodies, full of empty artists who have never really risked anything. I'm leaving. I'm gone.

I close my eyes, take a deep breath in and out. The nuns have begun. I hear them singing their Latin. It's cold here, in the light lock. Too cold. And when I open my eyes, I gasp, because standing there, in the dark, staring at me, is Rudy. But it isn't Rudy, no, he's pale and gray. He's wearing the outfit he usually wears as a bartender, and he glares at me, forehead angled down. So much anger, so much hate in his eyes. Panting. Seeing me. His entire face so tense it appears to be vibrating. Blood escapes his eyelids, tracking down his gray-white cheeks, beads of deep purple rolling toward the ground.

Panting. He's panting, his chest in and out and in and out, like he's been running. He reaches toward me with two fingers, but they aren't really fingers. I can see through them. They reach toward me, to pinch my chest.

I turn and run out of the light lock and into the bright lobby, gasping, almost falling over as the door clicks shut behind me. The world is shifting beneath my feet. I'll have to make my entrance on the other side. House right. It'll be fine. The spotlight will find me. It's me! I shine!

I cross the lobby and slip into the other light lock and pause. Breathe. In and out. Hands on my knees. It's fine. Everything is fine. I can make the entrance. I can do it.

But then I exhale and see the cloud of my breath. A shiver. I hear someone behind me. Shuffling. Groaning. And then a hand on my shoulder. Wet. Water seeping through my costume. And I turn to see pink nail polish and — no! No! She's not going to wrench this out of my hands. She's not going to take it from me, no!

I fall backward into the lobby, the world tilting back and forth, and rush to the water fountain across the room. The stagehand waiting with me, who's supposed to be cueing my entrance, is leaning on the bar and staring at his phone. I drink cold water and take a deep breath in and out. In and out. No. No. It's just my mind. It's just stress. The last few days have been difficult. It is just my mind.

But I can't go on. I can't because I'll have to go past them, past them again in the light lock and —

I have to make my entrance through that door and— No. I'm leaving. I have to go. Now.

XLII

Outside, I take a deep breath. The edges of my vision are blurry. This is the end, it really is. I don't know how I can do this. A bus pulls up next to me, wheezes and I watch an old man get off carefully, then turn to help his wife. She's got a rain bonnet on her head, steps down so slowly I get angry watching her. Holding everyone up.

Oh, I realize then, looking up at the sky. It's raining. I think about getting on the bus. It would be so easy. To just go.

And then, Anton sprints around the corner, feet pounding on the pavement. He runs up to me, panting. "Jessamyn!" he shouts, grabbing me by the arm, gasping for air. "Jessamyn!"

He's sweating, eyes crazed, but there's determination there, too. Warmth. This is the man I recognize. The one who adores me. He grabs my shoulders and shakes them.

"The police are coming!" he whispers. "Something about a body. They came to my house and spoke to me, and I overheard one of them say they knew you'd be here! I only just got away."

"What?" The police. No. They can't be coming. They can't be.

This is my night. I have to go on. I have to try. They won't stop it in production, will they? No. No. That would be crass. Tasteless. To rob the ticket holders of the show they deserve? No, I'm sure they just want to speak to me about something. To interview me. That can happen after curtain. They can't know anything because there is nothing to know. I am Maria. I'm goodness, I am light.

"I'll distract them. I will. Your email. That was such a beautiful email. What was I thinking? Samantha? Of course, it's always been you, Jessamyn. You and me against everything."

In the distance, sirens. Sirens? For what? It can't be the police. Not now.

"It's time." The stagehand appears next to me, looking from me to Anton, confused.

"You have to go on, Jessamyn. You have to!" Anton grabs me by the shoulders and shakes me. "I was such an idiot. I'll tell them it was me. You have to perform."

"We have to go now," the stagehand says.

I could run. I could make it to the airport. I have enough of a head start. But no. Anton is right. I have to share my gift.

I lean forward and kiss Anton and then turn, rush to the house left door.

"It's time," the stagehand says, holding the door to the light lock, focused on me. Focused on getting me in the theater. I'm about to step into the dark when someone yanks on the front doors now locked, causing a rattling sound. Whoever it is bangs on the glass, yanks on the handles. I peek at them out of the corner of my eyes. It's not . . . no. It's not Kathy. It can't be. She screams outside but her voice is muffled behind the glass.

The stagehand taps me on the shoulder. "Hey, focus. It's time. In three, two, one. And go . . ."

XLIII

A single spotlight flashes on the door, on me, and I can barely see anything. Just the brightness of it, fear rushing all over my body, sweat. I can barely hear the band. The music vamps. My heart thuds. I should've started already. I should've begun to sing. The musicians know though, they can hear me. They take the bars again.

I take a deep breath and begin. Smile. Breathe in. Deep. My body full. The follow spot finds me.

And I sing.

But the sound that comes out, that booms all over the room, it isn't me. It can't be me. I stumble through the first few lines, but I need to relax into my training. I need to remember what it felt like, next to Renée at the piano. I take another deep breath. It's coming. The high point. The moment that will make or break this for me. I throw my arms open, in the middle of the aisle.

My voice, though. Someone must be playing a trick. Someone must be trying to ruin this for me. That can't be me. It isn't me. The sound reverberating around the room as I soar — it's not mine. It can't be mine.

Someone laughs. Loud and high in the room.

I keep singing. I feel hot. Too hot. The thudding of my heart is loud.

It's okay, I think. *There's still time to recover.*

Muttering in the crowd. Shifting in seats. The flapping of programs.

I need to focus. Not a great start. Definitely off. Definitely not my best. But I can do better, I know I can do better. I can win them over. That's what I do.

My breath isn't there, I just don't have my — my phrasing stutters out. And the mic gets cut. Why is the mic cut? I'm not going to stop. I have to keep going. These people are here for a show, they deserve a show.

My feet move for me and I'm up on the stage now. My mic isn't on, but the show, the show can't stop. The show has to keep moving forward, no matter what. It never stops. We have to do this. I spin around, focusing. Focusing in on myself, my heart, the feeling of the glory of God and the beautiful world he built and gave to me, I have to remember what it felt like, next to Renée at the piano, listening, pushing, pushing the sound out.

The climax of the song. I face the crowd and throw my arms wide, but the note is garbled. It's rotten. I'm rotten.

"More like the sound of bullshit!" someone shouts from the crowd. A few people get up and I almost fall to my knees, beg them to stay, want to shout out, no wait, let me do it again. Let me take it again. I can do this. I was born to do this. Instead, I watch as they stand up, gather their coats, turn their backs to the stage. No. They're leaving.

I keep singing. I know I can do better. I scrunch up my cheeks, like Renée taught me. Focus the sound, squint, send it out through my eyeballs.

I forget the choreography and spin around onstage, smiling, grinning, my mouth so wide, but inside I feel panic, tears, fear lapping at my fingers, the ghosts of my enemies trying to pull me under. This can't be right. Someone is trying to sabotage me. Someone must've hijacked my microphone — they're trying to ruin my career in the worst way. They want me to quit! It's simply insane. How could someone do this?

As the song comes to an end, I hold the final note as gracefully as I can. Half of the audience is on their feet, grumbling, shuffling out of the room. Maybe it isn't me, though. It could be something else. Maybe the ceiling is dripping. Maybe the nuns were off. Maybe some alarm is blaring and I was just too committed, too professional, to notice. That must be it. The tiny differences in pitch that I hear sound giant to me, a professional, but are simply less than nothing to the ignorant public, secondary to the blare of an alarm that I cannot hear because I am too focused on delivering beauty.

"You suck!"

I'm about to turn, to rush off the stage, get ready for the next set-up when a loud *BANG* echoes through the room and I hear the sound of rushing feet. A high, terrified scream. The house doors fly open.

"Police!" a man shouts, and a gang of men in black, guns drawn, rush into the theater, crouched, as if this is a film. "Everyone on the ground!"

XLIV

Everyone in the crowd stops. The music stops. The room falls silent. People lower themselves to their seats, to the floor, some huddling together. Too many officers march down the aisles. A deep male voice rings out across the room: "Jessamyn St. Germain?"

There's no way I'm going to let them take me. I have a show to finish. I have to finish this show.

I see the littlest one at stage right, just a few feet from me, just out of sight of the audience, standing next to a costumer, the one with purple hair. The costumer is wearing her utility smock, a pair of sharp scissors sticking out from one of its pockets.

I rush over and grab little Julie by her little sausage arm, pull her to me, simultaneously picking the scissors out of the costumer's smock. I press them to the little girl's neck. She lets out a loud, terrified scream that slices through the room. Twists against me. But why would she? Why? It's me, Jessamyn.

"Stay away from me!" I shout, walking backward. I'll just get outside, get into the alley. And then I can run. Run. Run away to New York. I bet I could make it in New York.

The littlest girl tries to squirm away from me, and I hold her tighter. She screams out again then starts to sob, loudly.

I hear a woman's voice, high pitched, from up in the balcony: *"My baby! Get your hands off my baby!"*

"Nobody come near me!" I shout again. My voice is high and loud and desperate. It doesn't feel like me, doesn't sound like me at all.

The mother screams in the background, appears to be running down the stairs from the balcony where a police officer grabs and holds her. She's making such a big fuss over such a small thing. I wouldn't hurt this kid. She's one of mine. She's Maria's.

"I'll gut her."

Whose voice is that?

It can't be me.

The girl starts to sob in my arms. "You're hurting me," she cries. It's all a performance, though. There's no reason she should be afraid of me. I haven't given her any reason to be afraid. She knows me. She knows I wouldn't hurt her, not ever. We've been through so much together.

"Jessamyn."

A voice, a calming voice washes over me like warm rain. The voice of someone who believes in me. Has always believed in me. Renée.

I find her in the middle of the theater, standing in the aisle staring up at me, wide-eyed, two hands out like she's trying to calm a vicious animal.

"My darling," she says. "My darling girl." My heart explodes. I forgot she was in here, Renée. Forgot she came to support me.

The room is silent. There are so many eyes on me, as they should be, but it's only Renée I see.

"We both know you can do better than that."

We do! I want to scream and laugh. We do know that. A thought pries its way through the swarms in my mind, takes me back to the time next to her piano. The beautiful world we created.

Why wasn't it enough?

My time next to her at the piano, relaxed, free, joyful in the universe of our own making. Why wasn't it enough?

Distracted, my hands go limp and I let the girl go. She runs off crying and a policeman picks her up on his hip and takes her to the back of the room.

The scissors are still clutched in my fist and I point them at the audience now, wavering in the air. The lights overhead catch in the metal, a quick shot of bright pain in my eyes. Someone is trying to get me.

"Put down the scissors, my dear," Renée says, a mountain of fabric in the middle of the room. "Let's go rehearse."

"I can't," I say. "I can't."

Hot sweat pours down my forehead. The seams the costumer fixed on this thing, they're coming loose. The front of it sags. This isn't how it was supposed to go. I was supposed to shine.

Renée stares so intently. "Yes you can." She believes in me. She really does. But all I can think is it's too late. It's all too late. If only she'd focused on me. Gotten behind me. I could've practiced more. I wouldn't have had to suffer.

This is all her fault. Hers. Here. If she'd only given me more, if only she'd sacrificed more, I would've been Maria, instead of this person, this mess, here on the stage.

A scream rips out of my throat. I hate her. I hate her so much. I raise the scissors up over my head. She's so far away but somehow I think I can reach out, stab her in the eye.

A gentle *thwip* whispers through the air and then a stinging, a stinging erupts in my leg and I stumble, the scissors soaring, cartwheeling, spinning in the bright lights overhead. I hear screaming. The scissors land between us with a clatter.

A man rushes the stage, head to toe in black, shoves me down, then puts a knee in the middle of my back. The stinging in my knee intensifies, turns to a burn.

"Calm down, calm down." His voice is harsh, ragged. He smells like the most rancid body odor.

"Calm down. It's over."

"This isn't me." I say it over and over again, my jaw struggling to form words.

My cheek is pressed to the stage. I stare into the audience. Hundreds of people gaping at me, slack-jawed, terrified. They aren't being transported away from the messy humanity of their lives, no. Their expressions are twisted, lips and eyes muddied by disgust and fear and pain. My own mess reflected back at them.

This isn't me. This isn't how they're supposed to feel, looking at me. This isn't how it was supposed to go at all. I'm supposed to be a balm. A soothing escape from the chaos. I'm supposed to be good. If I'm good, they'll take care of me, if I'm good they'll love me.

And then I blink and he appears in the wall of eyes.

It's him.

My father.

He's sitting in the audience, in the middle of the room. It's not the seat he booked, no, it's a better seat. One of the most expensive in the house. He must have showed up, saw how terrible his view was from the front row and upgraded so he could see me. His jacket is off. He's holding a program in his hand.

He saw everything.

We make eye contact, and I'm filled with a very real kind of shame, now that I know he's been here the entire time, is seeing this mess, this disaster.

The cop looks up and shouts something out at the audience, at the people, at one of his friends maybe, and I think he's forgotten about me. His weight shifts onto my spine and the pressure, the pain, he's weighing so heavy on my vertebrae I think it's about to pop.

I can feel all of it as I make eye contact with my father again, silently pleading with him to move, to say something. Help me. To help me, please. This man is hurting me. But my father doesn't, no. He stays seated, turns away, disgusted, his face buried in his hands.

Like I don't exist to him. Like I am not here at all.

And at first I didn't notice her next to him. His child bride, Sophie. She rises, her hair over her shoulder, eyes cutting through the theater, pointing at the stage, her long fingernail sharp like a scalpel. "Hey!" she shouts, her voice loud and strong and sure. She shoves past my father as if he is nothing, leaps into the aisle. "Hey! You're hurting her!" she shouts again, throwing herself toward us.

"Get off her! Hey!"

Her delivery is enraged, the full force of it pushing her forward. But as she moves, the room starts to churn, the crowd, the police, so many people shouting, crying, as I watch her loom closer, fighting against a crowd of men, all of them together forming a dark wall between us, but she is fighting, I can see her, pushing, and clawing and crying out. "You're hurting her. Stop it!"

I spot her in glimpses, in the fray and then suddenly the spotlight finds her, bathes her in gold, and I witness her now in all of her power, raw and wild and beautiful. As the crowd surges, I believe. Finally, I believe. Here she is, a God, finally come to save me.

Acknowledgements

I'm deeply grateful to my parents who have always supported me as I pursued this career. They never wavered, though occasionally, very gently, wished I would chill out. I think some incremental progress has been made. Thank you for everything.

This novel is hard on actors and I'd like to state here that nearly all actors I've met and worked with are entirely lovely, talented, and gracious people. I'll also note that the characters in this book are wholly original and are not based on any actors I've met or seen perform.

I want to credit the "Las Culturistas" podcast which introduced me to (and potentially invented) the dichotomy of actor/star. It really informed Jessamyn's view of showbiz and herself.

I'm very grateful to my incredible agent Abby Saul whose notes really helped me crack this book. Thank you so much for everything you do. (It's a lot!)

Thank you to Pia Singhal who edited this manuscript and helped make sense of it. Working on this book with you made me a better writer. Thank you to A.G.A Wilmot and Jennifer Albert for the additional edits and everyone at ECW for all the love and care you've shown my work.

Many thanks to the Saskatoon Public Library's Writer in Residence Program and to Joe who shepherds it along. And many thanks to all the writers I met during my tenure there. I'm so grateful you shared your work with me.

Elle Grawl and Michelle Kaeser read early drafts of this novel and gave me invaluable notes. Thank you for your eyeballs. I'm also so grateful for my Lark Group pals. You make the hard parts fun.

I have too many family and friends to name but I'd like to say thank you specifically to anyone who helped me through the last few years. You really do make my life so much better and I promise, I know how lucky I am.

Entertainment. Writing. Culture. ───────────

ECW is a proudly independent, Canadian-owned book publisher. We know great writing can improve people's lives, and we're passionate about sharing original, exciting, and insightful writing across genres.

─────────────────────── **Thanks for reading along!**

We want our books not just to sustain our imaginations, but to help construct a healthier, more just world, and so we've become a certified B Corporation, meaning we meet a high standard of social and environmental responsibility — and we're going to keep aiming higher. We believe books can drive change, but the way we make them can too.

Certified
Corporation

Being a B Corp means that the act of publishing this book should be a force for good — for the planet, for our communities, and for the people that worked to make this book. For example, everyone who worked on this book was paid at least a living wage. You can learn more at the Ontario Living Wage Network.

This book is also available as a Global Certified Accessible™ (GCA) ebook. ECW Press's ebooks are screen reader friendly and are built to meet the needs of those who are unable to read standard print due to blindness, low vision, dyslexia, or a physical disability.

This book is printed on FSC®-certified paper. It contains recycled materials, and other controlled sources, is processed chlorine free, and is manufactured using biogas energy.

FSC
www.fsc.org
MIX
Paper | Supporting
responsible forestry
FSC® C103567

ECW's office is situated on land that was the traditional territory of many nations, including the Wendat, the Anishnaabeg, Haudenosaunee, Chippewa, Métis, and current treaty holders the Mississaugas of the Credit. In the 1880s, the land was developed as part of a growing community around St. Matthew's Anglican and other churches. Starting in the 1950s, our neighbourhood was transformed by immigrants fleeing the Vietnam War and Chinese Canadians dispossessed by the building of Nathan Phillips Square and the subsequent rise in real estate value in other Chinatowns. We are grateful to those who cared for the land before us and are proud to be working amidst this mix of cultures.

ecwpress.com